THE
DEATH MASK

Also by Iris Johansen
(in order of publication)

KENDRA MICHAELS SERIES
(written with Roy Johansen)
"With Open Eyes" (short story)
Close Your Eyes
Sight Unseen
The Naked Eye
Night Watch
Look Behind You
Double Blind
Hindsight
Blink of an Eye
Killer View★
More Than Meets the Eye
Flashback
★Starring Jessie Mercado

EVE DUNCAN SERIES
(Iris Johansen)
The Face of Deception
The Killing Game★
The Search
Body of Lies
Blind Alley★
Countdown★
Stalemate
Quicksand
Blood Game★
Eight Days to Live★
Chasing the Night
Eve
Quinn
Bonnie
Sleep No More
Taking Eve+
Hunting Eve+
Silencing Eve★+
Shadow Play+
Hide Away+
Night and Day
Mind Game★
Shattered Mirror
Dark Tribute

Smokescreen
The Persuasion★
The Bullet
A Face to Die For★★
Captive★
The Survivor★★
★Starring Jane MacGuire
+Featuring Margaret Douglas
★★Featuring Riley Smith

CATHERINE LING SERIES
(Iris Johansen)
Chasing the Night
What Doesn't Kill You
Live to See Tomorrow
Your Next Breath

IRIS JOHANSEN
STANDALONES
The Ugly Duckling
Long After Midnight
And Then You Die
Final Target
No One to Trust
Dead Aim
Fatal Tide
Firestorm
On the Run
Killer Dreams
Pandora's Daughter
Silent Thunder (Iris & Roy Johansen)
Dark Summer
Deadlock
Storm Cycle (Iris & Roy Johansen)
Shadow Zone (Iris & Roy Johansen)
The Perfect Witness
No Easy Target (featuring Margaret Douglas)
Vendetta
Chaos
High Stakes
On the Hunt

THE
DEATH
MASK

IRIS JOHANSEN

GRAND
CENTRAL

New York Boston

Grand Central Publishing
Hachette Book Group
1290 Avenue of the Americas, New York, NY 10104
grandcentralpublishing.com
@grandcentralpub

First Edition: June 2025

Grand Central Publishing is a division of Hachette Book Group, Inc. The Grand Central Publishing name and logo is a registered trademark of Hachette Book Group, Inc.

The publisher is not responsible for websites (or their content) that are not owned by the publisher.

The Hachette Speakers Bureau provides a wide range of authors for speaking events. To find out more, go to hachettespeakersbureau.com or email HachetteSpeakers@hbgusa.com.

Grand Central Publishing books may be purchased in bulk for business, educational, or promotional use. For information, please contact your local bookseller or the Hachette Book Group Special Markets Department at special.markets@hbgusa.com.

Library of Congress Cataloging-in-Publication has been applied for

ISBNs: 978-1-5387-2633-4 (hardcover), 978-1-5387-7453-3 (large type), 978-1-5387-2635-8 (Canadian trade paperback), 978-1-5387-2636-5 (ebook)

Printed in the United States of America

LSC-C

Printing 1, 2025

THE
DEATH MASK

CHAPTER

1

Unbelievable. Just unbelievable.

Alex Dominic lowered the binoculars and shook his head. He had traveled hundreds of miles to visit the African village of Karimu, but there was almost nothing left to see. A few smoldering huts, burned-out wells, and dismembered corpses of men and women.

Sam Rashid, who had accompanied Dominic on this hellishly long journey to the village, raised his camera and snapped a series of pictures. "No children yet. Do you think they were spared?"

"Doubtful. I found several infants who had been butchered and left to die in the chief's hut. My guess is that any older children were probably taken and sold to local traffickers." Dominic's jaw clenched. "The attack was just in the past few hours. We still might be able to catch up to the monsters who did this."

"Where we'll probably find an entire army of other monsters waiting for us," Rashid said. "Maybe hundreds of them."

"I don't care." Dominic's gaze went back to the bloody carnage he'd just discovered. "We'll find a way to take 'em on anyway."

"Shit." Rashid sighed. "I knew you would say that."

"Am I that predictable?"

"In cases like this, yes. We've been through too much together. Besides, I could tell by the look on your face. You're getting madder by the second."

"Aren't you?"

"Of course." Rashid adjusted his camera lens and snapped another series of photos. "Did you find any other evidence about who did this in any of those huts?"

Dominic nodded. "I found the main weapons cache in that third hut across the way. It came complete with a box of ammo that had very familiar ID marking the bullets. I'll have to dig a little deeper, but I'll be able to pin down the arms dealer very soon." Dominic pulled the blue kerchief from around his neck and tied it over his nose and mouth. The odor of burning flesh was overpowering. Shit, he'd hoped to prevent this.

Damn those bastards.

There was a sound behind them!

Dominic drew his Glock automatic from his shoulder holster and spun around.

Nothing but a burning hut and a few smoldering piles that had been living, breathing human beings just hours before.

Dominic cocked his head. It was that sound again.

"What is it?" Rashid whispered.

Dominic nodded toward a sheet of corrugated tin lying on the ground. It moved slightly.

Rashid lowered his camera and drew his own handgun.

Dominic tried to affect a casual stroll as he moved back in the general direction of the rusted tin sheet. "I've seen enough. Let's make our way back toward the river. Maybe someone there can tell us where—" Dominic kicked the edge of the sheet, flipping it over. He raised his gun and pointed it toward two figures crouching underneath.

Two children, a boy and a girl. They couldn't have been more than eight or nine. Their dirty faces were streaked with tears. They both raised their hands in surrender.

Dominic lowered his gun as he inspected the children for any sign either of them might be carrying a weapon.

There was none.

"Don't worry," Dominic said quietly, speaking Swahili. He wasn't a native speaker like Rashid, but he knew enough to navigate most social situations. "We're not going to hurt you."

The boy looked relieved, but the girl seemed distinctly doubtful.

"We're here to help," Rashid said. He pulled two water bottles from his pack and handed them over. "What are your names?"

"I'm Zola," the boy said after gulping down some of the water. "This is Alora. She's my sister."

"What happened here?" Dominic asked gently. "Do you know? We need your help."

"We were staying with our auntie today," Zola said. "Our mother went to another village to sell quilts that she makes. We heard screaming outside and saw the men and their trucks. They came at us with their guns and machetes."

Alora was crying. "Our auntie told us to hide outside. We crawled under here and heard her and our cousin screaming. There was blood...Those men were killing everyone for no reason."

Zola looked around dazedly. "Is anyone else still alive?"

Dominic glanced at a smoldering pile that he knew could be the children's aunt and cousin. "We haven't seen anyone else yet. I'm sorry."

Alora sobbed uncontrollably. "I want my mom!"

"It's a good thing she wasn't here," Dominic said. "We'll get you to her, don't worry. But we need to find out everything we can about the people who did this. We're not going to let them get away with it, I promise you."

The children were silent for a moment, until Zola finally spoke up. "They all had yellow scarves."

Dominic and Rashid exchanged a look before turning back to the boy. "Are you sure?" Dominic asked.

Zola nodded. "And they had yellow flags on their trucks."

"That's helpful," Dominic said. "Very helpful, Zola. Have you ever seen these people before? Any of them?"

He shook his head no.

"Did it seem like they were looking for something?"

"No. They just came here and started hacking away with their knives. People were screaming and offering them money and food, but those men didn't care about that. They just wanted to kill everyone."

Dominic turned toward Rashid and whispered, "Sounds like Zakira's followers."

Rashid nodded. "I'd bet on it. All it would take is for the village elders here to turn down Zakira's invitation to join his flock. He'd wipe them out without thinking twice."

"I'm familiar with their tactics," Dominic said. "But it's strange...Zakira's armies usually leave at least a few warriors behind for a few hours to eliminate residents who might have been away."

As if on cue, a truck engine sounded in the distance.

"You were saying?" Rashid turned toward the sound.

"Get down!" Dominic crouched next to the two children and grabbed the large sheet of tin. "Come on, get back under. All of us. Now!"

Dominic and Rashid slid underneath the tin sheet with the children and listened as the truck roared closer. They peered through openings in the panel and saw a beat-up old pickup truck with a machine gun mounted in the bed. Two men rode in the cab, and another manned the gun. A yellow flag flew from the car's antenna, and each of the men wore a yellow bandanna around his head.

"Zakira's crew, all right," Dominic said.

"We were lucky to get here," Rashid said. "They're probably patrolling the village and the surrounding areas."

"They were lucky we didn't see them earlier," Dominic said grimly. "But their luck has just run out."

"What's your plan?" Rashid glanced at Dominic's set expression and then watched as he grabbed his knapsack and unzipped it.

"Just a little welcome party. I don't like the idea of them having all the fun. You stay here and keep an eye on those kids."

"Maybe we should both stay here with them," Rashid suggested tentatively. "After the patrol passes, we can probably slide down the ridge without being seen."

"If my plan doesn't work, feel free to do that," Dominic said absently as his gaze narrowed on the patrol.

Rashid shook his head resignedly. "Dominic..."

But Dominic climbed out from under the tin sheet and ran toward the muddy road. He reached into his pack and tossed half a dozen black disks to the ground. They were each about the diameter of a hockey puck, but half the thickness. He'd been assured these latest models would work, but the field tests showed mixed results.

He was about to find out for himself.

The truck was already a quarter mile down the road, but the gunner had clearly spotted him and told the driver. The vehicle spun around and raced back.

It skidded to a stop just ten yards away. The truck's occupants stared as if trying to size him up.

Dominic smiled and spoke English to the men. "What happened to this place? I was just here last week, and it didn't look anything like this!"

The three men didn't smile. It appeared that the driver was the only one who spoke English, as the other two immediately looked to him for a translation.

"Who are you?" the driver said in heavily accented English.

"Just passing through." Dominic was still smiling. "Didn't know I was passing through a war zone. Think you fellas could give me a ride?"

The driver translated for the other two, and all three men burst out laughing. Dominic laughed with them.

The passenger climbed out of the truck and pulled a large handgun from his shoulder holster.

"Whoa whoa whoa!" Dominic raised his hands in surrender. "Okay, don't give me a ride. No problem."

The man leveled his gun at Dominic.

Dominic spoke a command under his breath, just loud enough to be picked up by his wristwatch: "Initiate."

BOOM! An explosion blew the man apart. Pieces of him splattered across the truck's windshield.

The driver and gunner screamed at each other as they reached for their own weapons.

"Initiate," Dominic repeated softly.

BOOM-BOOM-BOOM! A series of explosions destroyed the pickup truck and its occupants, triggered by the command and motion sensors embedded in the ordnance pucks Dominic had littered on the road.

Uh-oh.

The gunner had survived the blast, perhaps partially shielded by the truck. Blood covered his head and face, but he still had enough strength to raise an automatic rifle and fire it.

Dominic dove behind the flaming wreckage of the pickup truck, where he found a handgun that had been pointed at him just moments earlier. When he picked up the gun, he realized a hand was still gripping it, completely detached from the rest of the assailant's body. He tried to pry the fingers free, but they were locked in a death grip.

The man with the rifle jumped from around the burning wreckage and fired wildly. Dominic raised the detached hand and pressed the dead man's finger over the trigger.

BLAM! BLAM!

Two bullets went into the man's chest. The attacker fell to the ground, dead.

Dominic threw down the hand and glanced around. He didn't see any other patrols, but that didn't mean there weren't more out there somewhere. He turned to see Rashid and the two children running toward him.

Dominic kicked the hand away so the kids wouldn't see it and joined them at the roadside.

Rashid shook his head. "Interesting. I took a few pictures of that move of yours. It gives new meaning to the term *hand job*."

"I'm glad you were entertained. Now let's get these kids out of here. I need to get to my casino in Morocco right away."

"Still feeling lucky, are we?"

"Really?" Dominic gave him a sardonic glance. "It's not that. I need to talk to Hastings and get some information about this damn massacre." He was already heading across the road. "Come on, let's get moving down that ridge you were talking about..."

———————

BOSTON SCHOOL OF THE ARTS
8:55 P.M.

"Celine!"

Sighing, Celine Kelly stopped as she reached the back entrance of the studio. It had to be Jean Paul running after her down the hall, dammit.

Gary Barnaby, the uniformed security guard, chuckled as he got to his feet at the door. "Sorry, Celine. I think he's zeroed in on you. Better luck next time. Unless you want me to try to distract him while you slip out?"

Celine was tempted but shook her head. "That would lack dignity. I'll handle it. Thanks anyway, Gary." She turned to face Jean Paul as he came running around the corner. His expression was just as eager and intense as she'd known it would be. No one had more passion for his work than him. Except maybe herself when she was working at the hospital. But there was no way she'd go to the lengths Jean Paul did to get his own way. She ignored his pleading expression and firmly shook her head. "No, Jean Paul. You know I have another part-time job I have to do tonight. I can't give you any more time today. I'll be here at the same time tomorrow afternoon, and that will have to be good enough."

"Just call in sick to that stupid hospital for one more hour." His tone was wheedling. "I feel really good about where my painting is going today. But I need that wonderful face of yours to inspire me."

"Too bad," Celine said. "I need enough money to pay my share of the rent for my apartment and my lessons here at the studio."

Jean Paul frowned. "You could probably make much more if you posed for nudes here at the studio. I've already offered you twice as much as I'm giving you for that portrait I'm doing now. You can't be making much interning as a resident. Besides, why would you want to take care of a bunch of boring patients when you're an artist yourself?"

Celine shook her head in exasperation. "I'm only an artist because I'd be bored silly if I had to just sit there mindlessly while I was posing for you. And those patients aren't as boring as you're implying. Everyone has a story, and I can help them. Not to mention that at least I'm actually learning something worthwhile." She made a face. "And I appreciate that I'm inspiring your genius, Jean Paul, but I prefer to do it with my clothes on."

Barnaby suddenly chuckled. "You tell him, Celine."

Jean Paul gave him a dirty look before he smiled at Celine. "But it's such a terrible waste. Give me a chance and I'll make a goddess of you."

"I'll pass." She headed for the door. "There's not much call for goddesses in today's workplace."

"There would be for you," Jean Paul said. "Well, if you change your mind, be sure to let me know, and I'll make arrangements with studio personnel." He was turning and heading back toward his studio.

"Don't hold your breath." She glanced again at the security guard, who was still chuckling. "Stop grinning, Barnaby. He actually means it. It's quite a compliment to have an artist want to make you into a goddess."

"Yeah, sure," Barnaby said. "I was only thinking what a great pickup line it was."

"But it only works if the artist is as good as Jean Paul," Celine said. "There has to be a certain substance connected to it. Good night, Jean Paul."

He nodded gloomily as he wandered back toward his studio. "Tomorrow, Celine. Don't be late."

She grimaced as she headed for the rear door. "That takes a good deal of nerve," she murmured. "Considering he's probably made me late for my shift at the hospital tonight."

Barnaby was frowning. "Do you want me to call you a cab, Celine?"

She shook her head as he held the door open. "Nope, I don't believe you understood that I'd have a problem with that. Cabs persist in requiring me to pay them. I'm strictly a subway girl."

"You sure?" he asked. "Want me to walk you to the subway?"

"No, don't be silly. I'll be fine. By the way, how are your wife and kids doing?"

"Great. Judy said to tell you hi and thanks for the books for the kids."

"You're welcome. Books are important. They can change our lives. They were my best friends while I was growing up." She hurried out the door and said over her shoulder, "See you tomorrow, Barnaby."

She was already walking quickly down the street toward the subway a few blocks away.

It was a cold night, and the streets were deserted now that most of the shops were closed and the rush hour was over.

Not quite deserted—she could hear footsteps on the street behind her. Strange. She hadn't seen anyone when she'd come out of the studio a few minutes ago. But now she definitely could hear the rhythm of those steps on the sidewalk several paces back.

Was it her imagination that their rhythm seemed to be keeping pace with her own stride?

Was someone following her? She increased her speed.

The footsteps on the street behind her did the same.

Okay, someone might be following her. *Nothing to get in a panic about,* Celine thought impatiently. It wasn't the first time. It probably wouldn't be the last. Boston was a big city, and it had its own share of stalkers like any town. It wasn't as if she couldn't take care of herself. She just wished this particular creep would leave her alone. She took a quick look behind her. The only person on the street behind her was male, tall with dark hair, and wearing a brown jacket. There was something vaguely familiar about him...Maybe this wasn't the first time this asshole had decided to follow her to or from the subway? It was possible she might not have noticed him if he'd blended in with a crowd.

Which also meant she could have a decision to make. Should she take off at a run and try to make it to the subway, where she knew there would probably be a crowd? Or would it be better to go back to the studio where she knew Barnaby, the security guard, would be at the door as usual. That might be best. Even though Barnaby was only a security guard, the sight of a man in uniform could sometimes intimidate people who mistook them for regular police. She took another quick glance behind her. Now the man's demeanor had suddenly changed. He was walking steadily, purposefully, almost stalking her.

She didn't like it.

And he was speeding up now, and his gaze appeared to be focused on her. She was beginning to feel threatened. Had the creep finally made his decision? It appeared so, she thought impatiently.

Well, so had she. She whirled to face him.

He continued to come toward her. "Don't run away from me, pretty lady," he called out mockingly. "I just want to talk to you."

"And I don't want to talk to you," she said curtly. "Get lost."

"I can't do that. I have my orders." His hand fell on her shoulder. "Now just calm down and we'll get along fine."

She stiffened. "Don't touch me."

His hand pressed down on her shoulder. "I'm trying not to hurt you. I just need you to come with me and—"

She lowered her head and threw all of her weight into a rolling clinch, a move she'd mastered long ago. She'd started Muay Thai classes as a way to relieve stress in her undergrad days, but she'd never used it in self-defense.

Until now.

Her attacker staggered back, then hurtled toward her. She stood her ground and swung her right leg in a high round-house kick, hitting him squarely in the throat. He wheezed as he tried to pull oxygen past his crushed windpipe. He fell to his knees.

It couldn't be that easy, she thought.

It wasn't.

Another man stepped from the shadows. He was taller and more imposing than the first guy, and his bearing suggested a steely confidence. "Impressive," he said as he gestured toward the man writhing on the sidewalk. "But I'm afraid you'll still have to come with me, Celine. I don't want to hurt you, but I'll do it, missy."

"Missy?" Celine moved her feet apart in the classic Muay Thai fighting stance. "Are you trying to piss me off?"

The man smiled. "Far be it from me."

Celine nodded down to the first attacker, who was still gasping for air. "I'm pretty sure that your buddy here will survive, but he's in bad shape unless he gets help. Why don't we end this right here? I'm a physician. I can help him."

The man shook his head as he uncapped a syringe. "A generous offer, but he's on his own now. You're the only one I care about."

She lightly bounced back on her heels. "Wow. With friends like these..."

13

The man rushed toward her and jabbed at her with the syringe.

Oh, hell no…

Celine performed a series of matrix dodges to avoid each jab, anticipating his thrusts and countering with perfect ducks and weaves. But she had to do more than just avoid his attacks; she had to parry.

She ax-kicked his forearm and sent the syringe flying. She jumped forward.

What was it that her old master used to say?

Oh, yeah. *Unleash hell.*

She cut loose with a series of elbow strikes to his kidneys and midsection in a targeted barrage that made her realize that her medical training was as important as her exercise routine right now.

The man doubled over and grunted in pain. Before he could recover, Celine grabbed his wrist and flipped him over to the ground. She pressed her knee onto his throat and bore down with her entire weight.

She leaned down and stuck her fingers in his eyes and he screamed with pain, reaching out with his fist to strike blindly at her midsection. Time to get away before he fully recovered and decided to go after her again.

She jumped to her feet and ran back toward the art studio.

She heard him screaming and cursing behind her as she flew down the street.

Then she reached the back entrance and threw open the door. "Celine?" Barnaby was suddenly beside her. "Are you okay?"

She nodded. "I just ran into a little trouble with some

jerks out there. I guarantee they got a hell of a lot worse than I did."

"Where is she? I'm going to kill her." The door was flung open again and Celine saw the man who had been chasing her burst through the doorway. "You bitch! You could have blinded me." He was wiping the blood away from his eyes and nose. "And I think you broke my nose."

"You attacked me," Celine said coldly. "I think we're even." She gestured to Barnaby. "My friend here doesn't like to have women threatened by strangers when his job is to keep the clients of the art institute safe while they're creating their work."

"You'll pay for this." He was still almost screeching as he wiped the blood from his face.

Barnaby shook his head and stepped between the attacker and Celine. "Not one step more."

"Or what?" the man snarled.

"You don't want to know. The police are already on their way, but trust me, I'm your biggest problem right now." Barnaby's fingers closed around the nightstick on his belt. "Turn around and cut your losses."

"You'll stay out of my business if you know what's good for you." He turned on his heel and strode toward the door. His lips curled as he glared over his shoulder at Celine. "And this isn't the end. No one treats me like that. I'm going to see that you suffer for it." He turned and threw open the door, and then he was gone.

"Ugly," Barnaby murmured. "Did you really do all that damage?"

She shrugged. "It wasn't my fault. I'd never seen him before tonight. I did what I had to do to protect myself. He followed me and then he attacked. I don't allow anyone to touch me. So I showed him that he should keep his hands to himself." She frowned. "But he might have seen me before tonight. He looked a little familiar." She remembered something else. "And he called me Celine when he made his move on me before I had to almost punch his eyes out."

Barnaby chuckled. "I'm certain he deserved it. We wouldn't want him to be too familiar. But where did you learn to mete out that kind of punishment?"

"My father was a colonel in the army. I was an army brat who traveled all around the world with him before he was killed in Afghanistan. Some of the places were fairly rough, and he wanted to make sure that I could take care of myself if he wasn't around. Everywhere we went, he made sure I learned from one of the locals before we moved on to the next place. He taught me everything I needed to know about the fine art of self-protection."

Barnaby nodded soberly, his gaze studying her face. "I can see why he'd want you to know how to protect yourself. You're so damn stunning, he probably had to contend with the entire U.S. military by the time you were grown."

"Don't exaggerate." She shrugged. "Yeah, I guess he had a few problems with me because of something like that. But he made sure I knew that the outside meant nothing if I wasn't smart enough to have people admire me because of what I'd studied and knew, not what I happened to look like. That was just window dressing." Her eyes were suddenly twinkling. "Just to remind me, he always had a photograph of Einstein set up in my bedroom at whichever base we were sent. We studied his work together."

Barnaby chuckled. "Wasn't that a bit extreme?"

"Maybe for some people. But I kind of liked it. Haven't you noticed how much Einstein resembles a distinguished grandfather?"

"It never occurred to me. All I remember is that he was very good at making bombs."

"I guess you had to have been there." She was still smiling in reminiscence. "Einstein and I became very good friends. I preferred him to any of my schoolmates' latest rock stars."

"That must have been pretty tough competition."

"But excellent training. I've found most people prefer not to have to deal with people who they might have to compete with on any level. They find it uncomfortable."

"They find it uncomfortable? Or you do, Celine?"

"Let's just say I've been taught to appreciate the value of staying in the background from all those years of learning how to protect my independence. It's much easier to keep a low profile by ignoring conflict."

He grinned. "You make the attempt, but you don't succeed. You obviously can't even walk down the street without causing a riot." He held up his hand as she opened her lips to protest. "But it's not your fault. The world is just full of scumbags who think they have a right to reach out and grab when they see something they want. I hate to see him just walk away." He frowned. "Will you at least let me walk you back to the subway and then call me when you reach the hospital? It will make me feel better."

She hesitated. "I think you've intimidated him. It's probably not necessary to—" She saw his expression and stopped. Why not let him be the hero who chased the villain away? "Of course. Thank you, Barnaby."

"Good. Wait here until I go tell my boss I'll be gone for the next thirty minutes or so. But it's really you who intimidated that bastard."

"It's not too late. I find I'm very curious why he went to the trouble of finding out just who I was." She was already reaching for her sketchbook. "I'm also a pretty good artist, remember? I'm not nearly as good as Jean Paul, but there's no reason why I can't do a fairly decent job of sketching that asshole. His face is practically engraved on my memory." She suddenly giggled. "Particularly his eyes! Lord, he was angry! I bet that I can have this sketch done by the time I finish my shift at the hospital tonight. I'll drop it by here tomorrow night, and you can turn it in to your friends at the police department and see if you can get a name for us. Okay?"

He nodded and headed down the hall. "I'll look through the mug books myself. We'll get him, Celine."

She smiled wearily as she watched him hurry down the corridor. Barnaby to the rescue, she thought. It was good to know that after those moments of ugliness that she could turn to a man as solid and good as Barnaby and have him there to help. It was almost like having her dad back again. It just went to show that the ugliness would fade away, but men like Barnaby would still be there.

She opened her sketchbook and then closed her eyes for an instant, trying to remember every detail of that face. Then her lids flicked open and she started to draw…

THE DEATH MASK

Ezra Caldwell gazed at Jossland with disbelief as he threw open the door of the suite and stormed in. "What the hell happened to you? I sent you to get the Kelly woman. You look as if you've been mauled."

"Shut up." Jossland was still trying to stanch the flow of blood seeping from his nose. "You'll have to choose someone else. Celine Kelly isn't going to be available."

"The hell she's not," Caldwell said. "She's perfect. Do you know how long it took me to find exactly the right woman to complete the mask? The minute Zakira saw her photo, he said he had to have her."

"Ask me if I care," Jossland said. "You said I was your partner. It's my money, too, and I have something to say about this choice. You can't have Kelly."

"Why can't I?"

"Because I'm going to kill the bitch. Very slowly."

Caldwell gave a low whistle. "She did this?" He started to laugh. "I thought there was a real problem. We can solve this. Let's talk about it."

"There's nothing to talk about," Jossland said. "I told her that she was going to suffer, and I'm not going to let you talk me out of it. She broke my damn nose," he said between set teeth. "And she almost clawed my eyes out."

"I didn't say that you weren't right," Caldwell said soothingly. "Of course we'll take care of her, but let's not rush it.

Perhaps you haven't thought this through." He smiled. "Yes, that must be it. I've let you go through this terrible experience and not explained the importance of what we're doing and why every piece of the puzzle has its place. That ends right now, because you have to realize how important you are to this job." He was nudging Jossland toward the library. "Let me get you a drink to soothe the pain, and I'll show you the entire picture. Do you want to clean up a little and get rid of that little whore's bloody marks on you before I show you how rich you're going to be if you just have a little patience?"

Jossland jerked his arm away. "Just talk to me and tell me when I can have the bitch. And why can't I have her now? Why do you have to use that damn bitch. Why her?"

"Because she's perfect," Caldwell said simply as he threw open the door of the library to reveal a luxurious room with the walls covered by photos and portraits. "Why do you think I've spent so much time here in Boston making sure that I've found the right women to give Zakira what he wants?" He pulled Jossland over to the far wall and gestured to the two photographs framed in ornate gold. "The Eve Duncan choice was easy. No one compares to her in her field. But Celine Kelly was a headache. I'm lucky I found her. Admit it, have you ever seen a more beautiful woman? Those almond-shaped violet eyes, the cheekbones, that single, shining black braid, those lips...She takes your breath away. It took me a long time to find Celine Kelly. Not only is she exquisite, but she bears a slight resemblance to that statue of Nefertiti. Though she's much more stunning. Plus no one really knows much about her and the details of her background. She keeps a very low profile these days, and that might prove valuable if I decide I need to have her disappear into the great beyond."

"Now I'm interested," Jossland said grimly. "How is that going to make us lots of money?"

"Because in this day and age, the entire world is fascinated by Egypt and Rome and Greece and any other ancient place you can name. And that means riches enough to make both of us billionaires if we work it right." He crossed the room and pointed to a photo of Tutankhamun. "Do you remember what I told you about that young pharaoh they discovered in an Egyptian tomb surrounded by gold on every side? They say his golden death mask alone is valued at over a billion dollars." He smiled. "And no one is entirely sure where all that gold in his tomb came from. But I'm certain that an enterprising man such as myself can find a way to make an accurate enough guess and make us both happy. I already have a few ideas how I can accomplish it."

Jossland doubtfully shook his head. "You told me that pharaoh died thousands of years ago."

Caldwell shrugged. "But gold can last forever. I've been studying how we can best get our hands on an identical jackpot."

"You're talking about that boy-king," Jossland said impatiently. "We don't need this Kelly woman."

Caldwell sighed. "Trust me. Before this is over, we're going to need all the distractions we can manage to beg, borrow, or steal. Celine Kelly will be a major distraction. We're going to find a way to force Eve Duncan to state that she did the forensic sculpting to create a statue of a queen who was more beautiful not only than Nefertiti but than the forensic work she did herself on the Helen of Troy tomb. That work took the art world by storm. Celine Kelly will be world-famous. They'll be standing in line to get into a museum to see her."

Jossland scowled. "And you know the bitch won't cooperate."

"I didn't say that we'd ask her to do that." Caldwell smiled. "Perhaps I'll let you have your way after we squeeze as much publicity as possible from Kelly's disturbance into our lives. There will definitely come a time when we no longer need her."

"I'm not going back to get that bitch for you," Jossland said belligerently. "Not unless you promise to let me have her right away."

"I wouldn't ask that of you. I'll get someone else to do it. I believe you need a little cool-down period. I have another job for you." He was gazing at the picture of Eve Duncan on the wall. "Though I'll have to do some advance work to prepare the way. But there can be no mistakes when you go after our distinguished forensic sculptor. She's the key to everything. She's a genius as a sculptor and smart as a whip and she's married to Detective Joe Quinn. He's not in the country at present, but she has friends and family, so you'll have to be cautious."

"You don't have to tell me that. The Kelly woman surprised me or I would have put her down with no problem."

"I'm sure you're correct," Caldwell said. "But let's make absolutely sure, shall we? Otherwise, I might have to replace you. How I'd hate to do that." He reached out and gently touched the face of the woman in the Eve Duncan photo. "You agree, don't you, Eve?" he asked softly. "I won't waste your valuable time by ignoring doing what must be done to assure your work is without a flaw."

Jossland was gazing at him impatiently, as if he thought Caldwell was crazy. "You're not listening to me. I'm not going to just let that Kelly bitch think she got the best of me," he said bitterly.

"You'll do what I tell you." Caldwell gave one last lingering glance at the Eve Duncan photo. "We'll discuss it and I'll make sure you're satisfied. But it's not going to ruin my plans. That isn't going to happen." He paused but didn't take his gaze from the portrait. "Are you ready for me, Eve Duncan?" he murmured softly. "In spite of this little setback, I believe I'm almost ready for you..."

CHAPTER

2

The answer is no, Professor Fallon," Eve said firmly into the telephone. "I realize I promised you I'd work with you on the new project, but this is entirely the wrong timing. I don't want to have to worry about another reconstruction for the next month. My son is coming home from school for the summer and I want to have family time with him and Joe until he goes back to Scotland."

But Eve could tell Claude Fallon was not giving up. She had known when the FedEx package arrived from him yesterday morning that she would feel guilty as the devil if she didn't keep her word to him after he'd pulled all those strings to get her special permission to examine the ruins of that Herculaneum volcano last year.

"I wouldn't ask you to change your plans if I could avoid it," Fallon said quietly. "But it seems I'm behind the proverbial eight ball. I have to return a favor myself, and I don't have a

25

choice. Dominic did me an enormous service that had nothing to do with the university, and now I have to give him what he needs."

"This Dominic is another professor at your university?"

"No. That would be much easier to refuse. Alex Dominic is a man of vast and unique experience, and he has contacts who have helped me several times in the past. On a dig three years ago, he even managed to save my life."

"Then I can see why you'd be grateful," Eve said. "And if you could delay this job for another couple of months, I'd be glad to try to help you. But creating a death mask would be difficult and time consuming. I'd want to be extra careful and make certain I didn't make any mistakes."

"You don't make mistakes, Eve," Fallon said. "Even if you didn't have the reputation of being the foremost forensic sculptor in the world, I've watched you work and I've seen the finished products. If you agree to do this mask, it will be what I want because I know you won't accept anything but perfection." His voice became coaxing. "Look, read all the information that I enclosed in the shipping box about how this new tomb was discovered. It was discovered by a colleague of mine, Dr. Dale Sherwood of Trinity College. The tomb was located high in the mountains of Central Africa and was found sealed in a temple surrounded by almost impenetrable jungles and shrubs. The hieroglyphics on the wall identified her as Queen Folashade, which was a name she took herself when she became pharaoh of her kingdom and loosely means 'honor confers my crown.'"

"Central Africa?" Eve said. "A bit far from home for an Egyptian pharaoh, wasn't she?"

"Indeed. Which makes it even more historically significant. We knew Egypt had distant trading partners, but this find suggests their reach went farther than previously thought. It's no wonder the sarcophagus was only discovered a few months ago—that territory is a virtual maze of tunnels, waterfalls, and caves." He added quickly, "However, I understand the working conditions would be excellent. As I said, this new tomb was moved to a small temple in a nice little village that's not too far from the original burial site. The headman of the village is Masini Zakira, a priest whose ancestors have lived and worked there for centuries. He also seems to have a good deal of influence with other chiefs in the area. I've been assured that it's well guarded, and you'd be welcomed with open arms. You'll find it interesting if nothing else. I believe it will persuade you to at least think about doing the mask once you visit and see how cooperative the villagers will be to you. There's even supposed to be a statue in the temple of a queen that bears a resemblance to Nefertiti. Perhaps she's some relation? You've always been fascinated by the Egyptian queens."

"Yes, I have," Eve said. "But you're using words like 'supposed' and 'perhaps.' Do you have proof? Somehow I don't think so."

"Not yet. But we're expecting a confirming report from Dr. Sherwood. I'll get it to you as soon as possible."

"That's a little too vague for me to even consider committing myself, Fallon. Particularly since I also know that we have DNA records that show quite a few relatives have already been found linked to Nefertiti." She smiled. "You can see why everyone wants to stake a claim to being related to the glamour girls of history."

"Does that include you?"

"The glamour doesn't really appeal to me." Eve thought about it for a moment. "But the strength and the intelligence of those queens who had to fight to keep their thrones and their lives against all odds makes me want to pitch in and investigate how they managed to do it. I believe they had to struggle much harder than the pharaohs. For instance, the tale you told me about how Folashade named herself to tell everyone that honor conferred her crown on her fascinated me. It made me want to know more…"

"Then are you certain you wouldn't want to see what you can do about trying your hand at creating a fantastic death mask for perhaps one of the most beautiful and intelligent queens who ever existed?"

"Now you're really reaching, Fallon," Eve said dryly. "You're trying to meet my every wish? It's not going to get you what you want."

"Sorry about that. But you have to admit that statue of Nefertiti at the Berlin museum is absolutely wonderful. It's incredibly beautiful. And, according to what I've heard about this new bust that's been found with the mummy in the mountains in middle Africa, both the mummy and the statue are even more fantastic and authentic than the one in the museum in Berlin. Tell me you'll think about it. We'll make sure you have everything you need in the village so the death mask won't take more than three or four weeks to complete; then you can get back to your husband and child. I don't believe you'll regret it." His voice became almost coaxing. "It will be an exciting project, and I'll be very grateful."

"Three or four weeks? That's still too long."

"Think about it. It's really the chance of a lifetime to bring something that will last an eternity back to life. Wouldn't your son be proud of you?"

"Michael is proud of me whatever I do," Eve said. "Just as I'm proud of him." She was looking down at the box at her feet. "I admit it's an interesting job and a challenge that would be exciting. I'll discuss it with Joe and Michael when I call them tonight. But I can't promise you that I'll do it. I'm sorry if that's going to interfere with your being able to repay your friend for services rendered."

"Just think about it. Suppose I call you in the morning?"

"You are determined," Eve said. "By all means, call me tomorrow. But it may be for nothing."

"I'll be willing to waste a little time if it might mean getting what I want in the end. You're definitely worth it."

"But then so are Joe and my son," Eve said gently. "They're pretty terrific. I'm sorry, Fallon, but you're up against exceptionally heavy competition. Like I said, I'll let you know tomorrow, but don't be surprised if I decide to stay here and just enjoy being with them. Find someone else to give your queen her death mask. I'm very much into enjoying life right now."

———

Fallon hesitated for only a few minutes after he hung up from Eve to start dialing again. Alex Dominic was definitely not going to be pleased with Eve Duncan's response. He might as well break it to the man right now.

"Duncan is probably going to tell me to go to hell," he said as soon as Dominic answered the phone. "She's going to talk to Quinn tonight, but tomorrow she'll probably give me the bad news. I used every argument I had at my disposal, but she wasn't buying it. She didn't offer much hope. Her family are coming to visit, and they mean too much to her."

"I'm sure you understand," Dominic said. "You're a family man yourself, Fallon. But I was hoping you would have been able to strike a sympathetic note."

"Maybe I didn't want to," Fallon said bitterly. "I like Eve Duncan. I also like the idea of letting her stay home with her family instead of turning her over to you and hoping that I'm doing the right thing."

"You are doing the right thing," Dominic said. "It's much better that you let me handle this and try to keep Duncan's family out of it. I guarantee that she'll be much safer with me. Trust me."

"I do trust you. Why else would I have let you talk me into this?" Fallon asked sourly. "But it would help if you could tell me that you're certain that the information I was giving Eve Duncan was at least close to the truth. Look, do you think that I'd just blindly go into deceiving Eve if I hadn't realized who and what you are? Over the years, my university has done quite a bit of investigating with some of my friends at Scotland Yard. I found out that you're rather a mystery man, Dominic, but you're not a crook. You own several casinos in Africa and Europe, and you also have quite a prosperous farm near Johannesburg. You appear to have contacts all over the world. You've had dealings with not only Scotland Yard but also the FBI, the CIA, and several other similar organizations. Yet no one at any of those places seems to have in-depth reports on you. Or at least none they'd reveal to us. Which probably means you're some kind of secret agent."

"Does it?" Dominic chuckled. "I guarantee you didn't find out I was James Bond, and I'm sure none of your sources would have hinted in that direction. They're much too cautious of being ridiculed. You did your probing very well considering what an upright and straitlaced scholar you are. But then I thought you would."

Fallon scowled. "You seem to think this is amusing. All I really want to know is where the hell you heard about either that village I was describing or the tomb that's supposed to be its pride and joy. You promised me that at least that part of your story was true."

"As far as I know, it was not a lie. As you say, I have certain contacts," Dominic said. "And most of the time, you wouldn't want to associate with them, Fallon. But sometimes information filters down that can be useful to even a learned professor like yourself and brilliant forensic sculptors like Eve Duncan. I don't believe you regretted my interference when I stepped in last year and took out that thief at the trade conference in Johannesburg who was trying to put you down."

"You know I didn't," Fallon said. He was still remembering that moment when Dominic had appeared out of nowhere and quickly and efficiently destroyed the attacker. "I was out of my depth until you showed up and saved my neck. I don't think I would have gotten out of there alive. But then you were there, and I was very grateful."

"But now I've given you a way to return the favor," Dominic said. "And you've done it. So we're even. And since all you wanted to know was where I found out about the tomb, naturally I'll tell you. I had a tip from an informant who frequents one of my casinos in Morocco, who mentioned that Duncan was going to be asked to work on a recently discovered tomb in a mountain range near Kilimanjaro. Since Eve Duncan's reputation was absolutely sterling, I decided it might be wise to take a look at the situation and bring the two of you together."

"Not that it will do you any good. As I told you," Fallon said, "she's going to turn me down."

"Perhaps. But at least you've prepared the way. I'll follow up with someone that may be able to persuade her to go the rest of the distance."

"And who will that be?"

"You needn't worry about that. I have someone in mind." He added, "If it makes you feel any better, she won't be a stranger to Eve and will have only her well-being at heart. Trust me. Okay?"

"I suppose it's got to be." Fallon grimaced. "Though I wish you actually were James Bond."

"Well, you can't have everything." Dominic chuckled. "Thanks for your help, Fallon. I'll call you in the morning and keep you updated."

"Do that," Fallon said. "You know that if it does work out, I want to be involved? This entire project could be magic for any archaeologist or educator." He hesitated and then asked the question he'd tried to avoid. "Don't lie to me. I know you promised to take good care of Eve. But this could be dangerous for her, couldn't it?"

"You want the truth? From what I've found out in the past few days, some very nasty characters are weighing in on the hunt for that sarcophagus. I know I can promise that she'll be safer with me and my team. I'll try to make sure that it doesn't turn out in a way that we'd both regret. All I can do is watch out for her, and you can bet I'll be doing that. Thank you for your efforts. Goodbye, Fallon."

Dominic cut the connection before Fallon could ask any more awkward questions and sat there for a moment. He wasn't eager to make this next call. The last person he wanted to involve in this potential mess brewing ahead of him was Catherine Ling. But it wasn't something he could leave her out of considering her relation with Eve Duncan. The fact that Dominic knew she and his partner, Cameron, were lovers made the assignment more difficult, though not impossible. Hell, it was always his job to do whatever made the impossible turn out as close as he could to reality, he thought recklessly. It wasn't Catherine's fault that this particular job was shaping up to be a nightmare. Just do what was necessary to put together the right elements and then keep them moving in the correct direction. He'd already checked and knew that Catherine was in Rome at the moment. He quickly dialed her number. "Catherine? Alex Dominic. I may need your help. Are you busy? Or can the CIA survive without you for a few days?"

"I'm always busy, Dominic," Catherine said sarcastically. "It's only you and Cameron who belong to an agency that permits you to schedule your own assignments to work toward your special Shangri-La. I'm just a poor peasant striving to preserve democracy." She paused. "Though it seems I haven't heard from Cameron in a long time. How is he?"

"He's well," Dominic said. "We've been working on different continents, but we still manage to keep in touch on the important goals. I may have to call him in on this new job I've been pulled into. Particularly if he knows that you might be involved in it. That's always a lure for Cameron."

"Bullshit. You know I stay out of Cameron's world as much as I can," Catherine said. "We walk our own paths."

"Yes, you do," Dominic said. "And ordinarily I'd keep far away from the fireworks that surround the two of you. I don't know if Cameron told you that we've now split up the territories our teams monitor. I drew Africa, which is fast becoming a hot spot. But Cameron is tied up in Nova Scotia trying to keep Diane Connors's medical miracle from being hijacked, so I have to run the risk of being the one to drag you away from the CIA for this small job…because you may be the only one who can do it."

"What a blow to your ego," Catherine said mockingly. "The great Alex Dominic, who manages to manipulate almost everyone to do his bidding and can persuade dictators to stop wars, has to rely on me to do a job for him? Why?"

"It's a matter of persuasion. You've worked with Eve Duncan and I haven't. Plus I can't make any mistakes in this. Since you care about her, neither can you. She's your friend."

Catherine inhaled sharply. "What's that supposed to mean? Is she in trouble?"

"Not yet. But she may be heading in that direction. In fact, it may be our task to guide her toward it for the greater good."

"Go to hell."

"I thought you might feel that way. I'm glad that I can accept that venom and protect Cameron from it. Anything for my best friend."

"Keep your damn machinations away from Eve."

"I'll certainly try. Now listen, and I'll tell you what I know and don't know. But I should first mention that this problem centers on someone we all know very well. One Ezra Caldwell, whom you want to nail as much as we do."

"Caldwell!" Catherine muttered a curse. "Oh, yes. Espionage, gunrunning, human trafficking, murderer, high treason… The CIA has had him on their most wanted list for years. What's the bastard up to now?"

"You didn't mention grave robbing. It seems he's trying to open a few new doors in that area. I have a hunch he might be using his gunrunning to get into local African politics, placing himself in the best possible position to go after the big bucks."

"And he's involving Eve? How on earth could he be doing that, Dominic?"

"Easily. He probably couldn't resist making the attempt. Antiquities and ancient tombs can bring in billions these days. And Eve made herself a target by doing that work on the Helen of Troy tomb a few years ago. My bet is that Caldwell has been planning to go after a big score in that direction for quite a while. It's not as if he lacks confidence." He paused. "You've heard about the Karimu massacre?"

"How could I not? They're comparing it to Rwanda. We're sending out an investigating team."

"Well, when they get there, you'll find that the weapons used to destroy the village were furnished by Caldwell."

"Shit! You're sure?"

"I found the main weapons cache. It wasn't too difficult. So will your agents, unless he's managed to destroy the evidence by then. Whoever purchased those weapons wasn't being too careful. They were probably too high on drugs and bloodlust to think at all." He added wearily, "Whatever your reports told you about that massacre, prepare to multiply it. My bet is that Caldwell sold the weapons to one of Karimu's rival chiefs, who didn't care if the women and children got butchered. I've been studying the possible customers, and it's probably Masini Zakira—his village has been Caldwell's African headquarters for some time. It's so far up in the mountains that it's practically unapproachable. It's surrounded by jungle and caves like a giant maze. Caldwell would feel very safe there. He's probably thumbing his nose at the local armies on the coast right now."

"That bad?"

"There's no one more arrogant. He doesn't think any of us can catch him."

"Tell me about it," Catherine said bitterly. "We've had some our best CIA agents hunting for him. I've been as frustrated as hell."

"Don't blame yourself," Dominic said. "It's probably the same way he's managed to avoid being caught by me and any other of Cameron's teams. He's very smart and makes enough money to keep his men loyal and very well paid working on his various game plans. We've just got to concentrate on not letting the bastard slip through our fingers again."

"And I suppose you've got a way to do that? How did you even know that Caldwell was pulling the strings on this job?"

"I recognize how he marks the weapons he sells to his clients, and I tracked down a few cases at the ruins at Karimu. I'd just gotten wind that Caldwell was involved in a new scheme from Jim Hastings, one of my informants, who often frequents one of my casinos in Algiers. He's one of Caldwell's lesser scumbags so he obviously didn't know that much, but after Karimu I went back and primed the pump with a special truth serum that usually works very well on him. I got a few names, one of them Eve Duncan. Considering that Duncan is extremely unlikely to be working with Caldwell willingly, my next supposition was that she might be a victim or a tool."

"I don't like any of this," Catherine said. "You couldn't get anything else out of this informant?"

"Not yet. But he might find out more about Caldwell's plans later. I thought it best that I release him so that he would go his merry way and no one would suspect me. Naturally, I have a twenty-four-hour tail on him."

"Naturally," she echoed caustically. "You never take chances, do you?"

"All the time. But hopefully never fatal ones." He added, "And I'm trying not to take any chances with your friend Eve. Caldwell wants her to do this mask, and I won't deny it might be dangerous. Hell, of course it will. Shall we go into the fact that Caldwell will probably find an excuse to kill Eve, because she'll inevitably get in his way? Individuals like Eve will always go after the bad guys to find a way to save the world. The only way to save her is for us to step in."

"Or send in a sniper with an AK-47 to get rid of all those bastards," Catherine said harshly. "Eve is a great person. That would simplify everything."

"What a wonderful solution." Dominic laughed with pure delight. "I can see why you're so near and dear to Cameron. Would you mind if we explore a few less radical answers first? I promise that the prime offenders won't receive undue mercy that might annoy you. May I talk now?"

"By all means," Catherine said. "In detail, please. Start with more about Caldwell."

"Who is up to all of his usual ugliness and clearly starting to move upward to even greater and more profitable crimes. But Hastings couldn't tell me many of those details you're going to want to know, Catherine. I just got the broad strokes. He was raving about how Caldwell had discovered a secret pharaoh's tomb in a village in the mountains of Central Africa that was filled with gold and treasure, and everyone who helped Caldwell to retrieve it was going to be a millionaire."

"And Hastings believed him?"

"I didn't say he was bright. Why do you think Caldwell only told him the basics? That's why I have to move fast, before Caldwell discovers that Hastings is one of my informants and he ends up dead."

"And you're still asking me to persuade Eve that she should get involved with this assignment? She has a lot to live for and a hell of a lot to give," Catherine said. "Of course I won't do it."

"Yes, she has a lot to give. And she's shown in the past that she's willing to do it. Did I mention that there's an excellent chance that if we can't finesse Caldwell out of the picture, then he might very well find it necessary to burn half that village and all its citizens to the ground?"

She was silent a moment. "Damn you, no, you didn't. But I know he's fully capable of it. If you need someone to play his game, then set me up to go after the bastard. I'm a fully trained CIA agent. You know I can handle it."

"And risk Cameron going after me if anything happened to you? That would be suicidal. No way." He paused.

"Besides, you don't have Eve's unique qualifications. I guarantee your name wasn't on Caldwell's list that I squeezed out of Hastings."

"What were the other names?"

"Masini Zakira, an African chief. And one Celine Kelly, an artist's model from Boston."

"What the devil is he up to? That combo is as weird as hell," she muttered.

"Yes. Will you talk to Eve?"

"I'll talk to her, but I won't try to con her into doing this. I'll advise her against it."

"I thought you might. But you'll tell her the entire truth. That's all I ask of you. We'll let her make up her own mind."

"And you've probably studied Eve in depth and figured out how to get her to do exactly what you want. I've seen you do it before. Cameron says he thinks you're some kind of witch doctor."

"I'll have to tell him that's very much like the pot calling the kettle black." Dominic was laughing. "Actually, I'm just a student of human nature trying to get along as best I can and survive this complicated world we live in."

"And adding an entire collection of puzzle complications yourself."

"But that's why Cameron usually keeps me on the other side of the world when we have to find solutions. I like puzzles much better than he does. We all realize that Cameron has some psychic abilities that make puzzles a bit boring for him. You're the only puzzle he never gets bored with solving." He added thoughtfully, "Or maybe you're the only puzzle he can never solve."

"We're not talking about me or Cameron," she said curtly. "We're discussing Eve."

"Yet I was sure that it was you who mentioned Cameron first...Oh, well, it doesn't matter. I'll be in touch with you after I get back from Boston and let you know if I've learned anything."

"You're going to Boston to see that artist's model? She might not have anything to do with Caldwell's current plans. She could just as well be his mistress, you know."

"Perhaps. But I somehow doubt it. Hastings wouldn't have been tempted to talk about a woman Caldwell was sleeping with even under my less-than-subtle questioning...He would have been too frightened. This Masini Zakira appears to be a chieftain and priest in Central Africa. That could prove intriguing, since Hastings mentioned a payoff in gold, and Africa has been known for its gold mines for centuries. I've already sent out a team to see what more they can find out about Zakira. In the meantime, I called Rashid and told him I needed him to start initiating a few inquiries about Celine Kelly. I should have a complete report by the time I land in Boston."

"Ah, Sam Rashid, your favorite bloodhound," Catherine said. "I should have known that you'd put him on the trail. He's quite the expert. I'm sure he'll give you whatever you need about that woman, including her DNA and fingerprints."

"That sounded a little bitter, Catherine. You're right, Rashid is an expert at the many tasks I give him, and I'm lucky to have him. Did I tell you that we got together in his home country of Tanzania, where he was heading the ranger unit that practically eliminated poachers in that area? He was so good, I persuaded him to come work for me, and I'm quite sure the CIA would like nothing better than to hire him or any other of my team members away from me. Isn't that true?"

"Yes, it's true." She was silent a moment, then added wearily, "I'm more than a little bitter, but I shouldn't have taken it out on Rashid. Most of the time, I like him. I think you know I just don't like you pulling his strings when it comes to anything that involves Eve. You're too damn good."

He chuckled. "Oh, that must have hurt to confess. But you said you were going to talk her out of even becoming interested in taking the Fallon job. What chance would I have?"

"Don't give me that bullshit. Even if I hadn't seen you work, Cameron thought you were good enough to trust with his damn Shangri-La theories, and that means you're dangerous as hell."

"But never toward you, Catherine. We're on the same side," he said gently. "Even if you won't admit it."

CHAPTER

3

Catherine sighed in exasperation as she pressed DISCON-
NECT, but she wasn't about to put off talking to Eve.
She knew she'd only be on edge until she could actually get in
touch with her. She dialed the Lake Cottage and put the call
on video.

"Catherine?" Eve's smiling face appeared on the screen. "I
was just thinking about you. I received a few pictures of the
baby from Jane, and they're absolutely priceless. You haven't
seen any photos since Jane had the baby so you can't complain
I'm one of those relatives who constantly bombard all their
friends with pictures." She made a face. "And Cira is positively
enchanting and we haven't had a baby around for a long time,
so I figure I deserve a few bragging rights. Michael is almost
twelve now."

And Catherine could see that Eve was positively glowing as
she spoke about her family. Perhaps those photos would help to
give Catherine the opening she needed. But blast it, she didn't
want to break this mood. Eve worked so damn hard that she
deserved a little downtime. "And how is Michael?" she asked.
"Does he mind playing big brother to Jane's baby?"

"Nah, he's crazy about Cira. They've seemed to have a kind

of bonding since we introduced them to each other. So Jane says. I haven't seen them together as much as I'd like lately. Jane is still supervising the repairs on the castle in Scotland, and I had to come back and get to work myself." She was suddenly smiling brilliantly. "But I'll have all of them here soon for a visit. That will be fantastic."

"Yes, it will," Catherine said. "And may I see those photos now?"

"Soon." Eve's eyes were narrowed, and her gaze was suddenly searching. "I believe we should discuss what you really called me about first. I think you'll enjoy it more after you stop worrying about anything else." She smiled. "And I know I will. What's going on? Does it have anything to do with that assignment Professor Fallon wanted me to take?"

"Oh, shit," Catherine said in disgust. "Your son isn't the only one in the family who's a little psychic."

Eve chuckled. "You're a magnificent CIA agent, and I'd trust you with my life. But deception is not one of your gifts. Not when it's anyone you care about. For that matter, Professor Fallon wasn't very good, either. You should both remember that I stare at forensic sculptures that I've created every day, and most of the time I can read what's in front of me. What's happening with the good professor?"

Catherine sighed. "I don't know for sure, but you shouldn't take that job Fallon offered. There's a very bad actor involved. It's better if you're not connected with it at all. I was relieved to hear you didn't seem tempted to leave the Lake Cottage."

"Fallon was lying?" Eve frowned. "That's disappointing. I've known him for years, and he's always been honest with me."

"No, Fallon may have just been manipulated. He was probably telling the truth as he knew it. Alex Dominic can be
very clever, and he convinced Fallon that you'd be better off
with him and his team if you decided to take the assignment."
She shrugged. "And that could have been the truth, too. He's
Cameron's partner, and they don't make mistakes."

Eve gave a low whistle. "I know they don't. And it must
have been difficult for you to go against them."

"No, it wasn't," Catherine said sharply. "Cameron and I
have different viewpoints, as you know. He thinks the politicians are ruining the world as we know it, and that we should
have a Shangri-La ready to run to if they manage to destroy
this one. I told him that it's our job to try to save the world we
have. And I clearly warned Alex Dominic that I was going to
be honest with you, but I promised him that it would be the
entire truth as I know it." She added reluctantly, "Though if
you'd actually needed someone to help you survive that trek
up the mountain while you were searching for that very elu-
sive village, I suppose you could have trusted Dominic and his
team to come and rescue you."

Eve started to laugh. "That was a trifle grudging. I guess
I'm lucky I've already decided to not go looking for that sarcophagus." She tilted her head wistfully. "Though Fallon made
creating that queen's death mask sound like a very tempting
challenge. If I only didn't already have my family coming…"

"Don't even think about it," Catherine said flatly.

"I won't." Eve was grinning again. "No contest."

"Good," Catherine said. "Now show me those photos. I
need a reward."

Eve was already posting them on the phone. "But I warn

you, you'll want to have one just like our Cira. She's almost eighteen months and she's…"

"Adorable," Catherine finished for her as she gazed at the photos. "Those huge eyes are fantastic…like amber crystal… She looks a little like Jane."

"Only a little. She looks far more like her father." Eve was gazing critically at the photo. "That intensity is all Caleb…"

"Really?" Catherine hesitated and then lifted her gaze to meet Eve's. "And that doesn't bother Jane?"

Eve understood immediately what Catherine wasn't saying. "You're talking about the baby possibly inheriting Caleb's mental gifts as well as the physical?" Eve asked. "Jane knew that was a possibility, and she accepted it. She knows what a hellish time Caleb had growing up—and he still turned out to be a man she could love with all her heart. She told me she could only imagine what he would have become if his parents had shown him any affection instead of total rejection." She smiled. "You can bet that little Cira is going to have all the love in the world heaped on her to balance any lethal inheritance she might have gotten from Caleb. Jane isn't worried in the least about that problem when she's sure she has the solution."

"And I trust Jane's judgment," Catherine said. "But the head of MI6 once told me that Caleb was the most deadly agent they'd ever contracted. What do you think, Eve?"

"I think that we're all lucky to have Cira in the family, and I'll love her as much as her parents do." She paused. "And I'll trust them to make the right decisions, and I'll always do what I can to protect them. Okay?"

Catherine nodded. "Absolutely. And I hope you realize that

I wasn't being nosy or interfering. I only wanted to know if I could help in any way."

"That goes without saying. You've known our family for a long time." Eve's eyes were twinkling. "Or you wouldn't have called me and tried to save me from Professor Fallon. If I accept one service, then I can't complain about you worrying about Jane and the new baby."

Catherine nodded. "But I regard it a privilege that you let me even see those photos. Cira is gorgeous. I hope I see her in person sometime soon."

"They'll be here in a few weeks," Eve said. "I'll let you know when they get here, and you can come for tea. I can't wait."

"Neither can I," Catherine said grimly. "But I'm mainly eager because I'll be able to call Dominic back and tell him that you're definitely not interested in accepting Fallon's death mask assignment. I guarantee he won't like it, but I'm delighted." She straightened as she added, "And if you don't mind, I believe I'll say goodbye to you and call him right now."

"That's up to you," Eve said absently. "At the moment, I need to enlarge these photos and then find frames that will do Cira justice..." She was suddenly smiling. "You're right, family is the only thing important to me right now. All I want to do is talk to Joe so that we can admire this younger generation together!"

———

"Yes, Jane sent me the new photos of Cira." Joe interrupted Eve almost as soon as she reached him by phone. "They're wonderful, and she's absolutely giddy about showing the baby off to you as soon as possible. She and Caleb are talking about taking his Gulfstream and starting out this weekend instead of waiting until Michael finishes his finals and gets out of school next week so that we could all travel together. She said she wants a little alone time with you so she can show you how clever Cira is becoming if she doesn't have to constantly compete with Michael. Though neither one of them appears to mind it. And Cira seems to have Michael wrapped around her finger. You'd be amused how serious and intent he is whenever he's with her. It's as if he's listening to her every word."

Eve threw back her head and laughed. "Good for Cira. I knew from the moment she was born that she was going to be a very special little girl. I'm glad Michael appreciates her. And I don't care how you arrange the travel, as long as I get you all here as soon as possible." Her throat was suddenly tight, and she had to clear it. "Look, I know setting up all those labs in Europe to distribute the silver bullet cure-all medication is important. But Lord, how I miss you, Joe."

"You think I don't?" he asked roughly. "I'm damn tired of trying to save the world. All I want is you. Is there any chance you can come back with me to Scotland when this little vacation is over? I know your work is important, too, but I'll move heaven and earth to clear the way to set up a workshop here that will give you everything you need."

"I'll try. We'll work on it." She made a face. "But so far the only interesting new offer I've had is that Fallon death mask sculpture that he said would make me eternally famous and also make Michael proud of me. I told him Michael and I were always proud of each other, and I wasn't about to go trekking through the wilderness when I had the chance to see you and the rest of the family instead. He was not pleased. But I didn't give a damn at the time. I owed Fallon a debt for helping me out with red tape several times in the past. But it wasn't worth giving up even one day with you or the rest of the family."

He smiled. "And we're all humbly grateful when anyone offers to give up eternal fame for us."

"Stop it," Eve said. "I just had to give you the background to let you know how difficult it's going to be to get what we both want. All the opportunities seem to lie in the depths of the Nile River, in erupting volcanoes or ancient burial tombs."

"Or trekking through the wilderness?" Joe asked gently. "And you've already given up one job from Fallon."

She nodded. "Gladly."

"And where do they want you to 'trek'?"

She shrugged. "Somewhere in Africa. I didn't get all the details. But he was persistent. When I turned him down, he must have called Catherine Ling and asked her to give me a call."

"Catherine?" Joe's eyes narrowed intently. "She tried to talk you into going on that trip? What's the CIA got to do with that sculpture?"

"Nothing, evidently. She told me not to consider it. She said that there were bad people connected to the job, and I shouldn't get involved. She acted relieved when I told her that I had no intention of taking the job because I didn't want to miss one minute with my family." She grinned. "And then we went on to more important matters. Like the photos of Cira. We both agreed they were much more interesting."

"And so they are." Joe was silent for an instant and then

asked, "Did Catherine mention the name of the 'bad people' connected to the Fallon job?"

"No, and I didn't ask since I had no intention of taking the offer." She smiled teasingly. "But since you're a detective, naturally you'd be interested in knowing. I'm sure that Catherine will be willing to give you all the information your heart desires when she comes for tea. I invited her to come and see Cira in the flesh as soon as you all get here. Is that soon enough, Joe?"

"Maybe. Maybe not. I'll have to think about it. But in the meantime, Michael just strolled into the room and wants to talk to his mother. Imagine that. So I'll turn the videophone over to him while I make a few other calls. Bye, Eve. I'll see you soon, love." Then he was gone.

And Michael's face was there before Eve on the screen. He was grinning at her, and she took an instant just to look at him. She spoke to him often on the phone, and yet he seemed to change every time. He was almost twelve and he'd be a teenager soon, with Joe's close-cut chestnut hair and brown eyes. But that puckish smile and the intensity of the way he stared deep into her eyes was all Michael.

"Hi, Mom. I guess I'll be seeing you soon, but I thought maybe we should talk for a little while now." He smiled. "I've missed you."

Was his voice lower than it had been a few months ago? He was growing up and she was missing so many changes, she realized with a pang. "I've missed you, too." She tried to smile. "But you're doing very well in school, and you seem to have made a lot of new friends. And it's positively amazing how many sports teams you belong to now. I'd like to have you home again, but you've been happy, haven't you?"

"Sure I am. And it's not as if I don't see you and Dad much. We go back and forth a lot on vacations like this one coming up." He was silent a moment. "And it was better that I left that school at the lake. Sometimes it was getting kind of hard to be around my friends there. Most of them knew about me, you know."

She stiffened, and her eyes narrowed on his face. "Michael?"

"It's okay, Mom." He was smiling gently. "They just thought I was kind of weird. Let's face it, psychic stuff can be kind of scary to kids, and I wasn't old enough to realize I should keep that stuff to myself. You knew about a couple of things that happened with them and even tried to help me out. But I could see that it was hurting you."

"It wasn't hurting me," she said fiercely. "Nothing about you has ever hurt me. You've always been a wonderful son. And I'm certain that you were just as terrific to those students at the lake school."

"Well, some of those kids didn't think I was all that wonderful," he said dryly. "When I was trying to help a few of them, I made clumsy mistakes. But when you enrolled me here at my school in Scotland, I made sure I started fresh and I was very careful." He grinned. "Plus I kept myself busy here to keep out of the other students' business. Most of the time that seemed to work."

"But not all the time?" Eve was gazing searchingly at his face on the screen. "I know you, Michael. You can't resist helping when someone is hurting or in trouble."

"Neither can you, Mom." He tilted his head as if considering before he added teasingly, "Gee, do you suppose I inherited it from you?" He shrugged. "You taught me that I have to give where I can. I still do that, but if possible I do it discreetly."

"Discreetly?" She made a face. "That's such a grown-up, sophisticated word. It makes me a little sad."

He laughed. "It shouldn't. I've been growing up for a long time on your watch, Mom. You do it very well."

"Not such a long time. But every time I turn around, it seems as if you're changing or thinking deeper or in a different way." She was staring thoughtfully at him. "And all this talk about your school and what you went through as a little boy. Where is it leading? Why did you really want to talk to me today, Michael?"

He chuckled. "Perhaps to tell you that you're the wisest mother on the planet? It's true, you know."

"Why?" she asked again. "May I help?"

"I don't know. But I thought I should make sure that you knew what I know about Cira."

"Cira?" Eve was immediately alarmed. "Has something happened to Cira? Why didn't Joe tell me?"

"Easy," Michael said. "As far as I know, Cira is fine. It's just that you should know."

"Know what?" she asked in frustration.

"She knows things. I think she's been trying to tell me about it for the last few times I've been playing with her." He was frowning. "Only she hasn't wanted to play. She's been too worried."

"Michael, she's only eighteen months old."

"But maybe that's why she's worried. I've been studying

about psychic phenomena lately because I wanted to see if I could find out some answers about myself. But I'm afraid most of those books are wrong. They don't make sense to me. But one thing that did make sense was that a lot of those doctors think infants have shown signs that they've had psychic experiences. It shows up more clearly than in older children because their brains are much cleaner and better defined."

"And what is Cira supposed to be worried about?" Eve asked. "She looked very happy in those pictures."

He shook his head "Well, she seems anxious when Jane isn't in the room."

Eve gave a sigh of relief. "Michael, I'm afraid that those books you read may be wrong, too. Though I applaud you for trying to pierce the veils of science on the subject. But most babies are uneasy when their mothers aren't around."

"But I felt it, Mom. Cira was worried."

"Then we'll all keep an eye on her and Jane and anyone else that you choose. But do me a favor? Skip relying on science and just use your own instincts. You have tried-and-true experience in that area that works just fine."

Michael was still frowning. "It seemed like a good idea."

"And it was. All of your ideas are good, and I'm happy you wanted to have this talk." She smiled. "And I'm also glad you're having your chats with Cira. Keep on doing it. I'm sure she probably does like being with you. Big brothers always make their sisters feel safe."

"Don't worry," he said soberly. "I'll take care of her."

"I know you will."

"And you too, Mom." He shook his head. "You're laughing but it's not funny. I'm getting old enough to take care of you now. Dad says we all have to take care of each other, but you have to be special because that's what you are to us."

"I sincerely thank you," she said solemnly. "But don't be so eager to grow up, young man. I told you how I feel about that. And we both know how brilliant and knowledgeable your dad is about most things, but he can get a little sappy sometimes. I like his idea about everyone taking care of each other much better. Suppose we just make a pact about that?"

"Whatever you say, Mom." Michael was grinning again. "But that's between you and Dad. He's always pretty definite whenever he speaks about you. I wouldn't want to be disrespectful." Then he winked. "And I think I should tell you that I really agree with him on this particular subject. I don't see anything at all sappy in his judgment in this case."

She tried not to let him see how touched she was. "What do you know? You're just a kid."

"But you just told me not to be in such a hurry to grow up," he said softly. "You can't have it both ways."

"I can have anything, any way I want it. As long as I have you and your dad to back me up." She had to change the subject. She was getting too emotional. "But now tell me all about your friends in your classes at school. Do you have a special buddy that you hang out with? And how about the rowing team? Are you strong enough to hold your own with those older boys?"

———

"You sound very satisfied with yourself, Catherine," Dominic said quietly when she finished reporting back to him. "Thank you for making the attempt. I'm sure you did the best you could."

"No, you aren't," Catherine said. "You knew I'd do exactly what I told you I'd do. As it happened, I didn't have to even try to persuade Eve to change her mind about the Fallon offer. She was intelligent enough to read me before I got the opportunity. You'd appreciate that talent because you have it, too. But this time you didn't have a chance to get your way, did you? Her family means too much to her, and they'll be knocking on her door very soon."

"Then I'm glad for her," Dominic said. "There was always that possibility. I guess I'll just have to go down a different road."

She stiffened. "You don't appear to be very upset. Why?"

He shrugged. "Because, though I may not be able to follow Eve on a trip up to those mountains to see what Caldwell is up to, he had a reason why he particularly wanted Eve Duncan to create that mask. And since he doesn't give up easily, maybe he'll decide to stay close to the Lake Cottage to persuade her to do what he wants himself."

"'Persuade'?"

"Don't start spitting fire at me. Did I mention that I'll send a team to watch over the house and the occupants?" He smiled. "And of course, you're such a smart, savvy agent that I'm certain you've already planned to keep an eye on Eve and her family yourself. Isn't that true?"

"Yes." She was still frowning. "But between Joe Quinn and Seth Caleb, they're not exactly lacking in powerhouse help."

"I've heard rumors to that effect. But I believe we'll both feel better with our own people in place. Right? Let me know if you need me for anything."

"I will." She added caustically, "But I believe we can survive. You're off to Boston?"

"Why not?" he asked. "You've just robbed me of one of those very valuable names Caldwell had on his list. Maybe the most valuable. Because if Eve was to make the death mask, she would have to be taken to the tomb, and I could follow her. It might wrap this nasty business up a bit faster." He went on before she could speak. "Though I can see your reasoning. I realize how hard it might be to trust me, but it's still a loss. Because now I'll have to see what I can find if I dig hard and deep enough in that revolutionary hotbed, that cradle of liberty, Boston town..."

CHAPTER

4

Y ou've got a letter on your easel." Jean Paul was scowling as Celine walked into the studio that evening. "The
receptionist brought it by a couple hours ago and asked me to
tell you about it when you showed up for your sitting. If it's
another one of those loser artists trying to hire you away from
me, you can just tell him to go to hell. I've got enough to compete with since you won't quit that damn hospital job."

"Poor you." Celine put down her sketchbook as she reached
for the envelope taped to her easel. "And we all know life is
only about you and what you need."

"No, only the most important things." His eyes were narrowed on the envelope she was opening. "Go ahead and put
me out of my misery and then let me know how much more
I'll have to pay to keep you posing for—"

> Did you think you were free of me, bitch? I
> told you, I'd make you pay.

Celine stiffened as she read that first line scrawled on the notepaper. "My God," she muttered. "Be quiet, Jean Paul. This isn't what you think."

"Of course it is," Jean Paul said. "You should at least let me talk to you about—"

But she was no longer listening. She was reading that damn letter.

> But it seems I can't reach out and bloody you as you did me yet. You have that to look forward to, and it will come. But that doesn't mean that I won't punish everyone around you to show you that you can't expect help from anyone. Did you really think that I'd be scared of that stupid rentacop? It's too bad you can't ask him if he was scared of me. I made certain that he was before the end...

The signature was a scrawled *Jossland*.

Before the end...

Perhaps he'd only meant to frighten her.

But she stood there remembering every line of that bastard's face. Celine felt ice-cold. His meaning couldn't be more clear...or fatal.

Barnaby!

Jean Paul was frowning at her. "You're not listening to me, Celine."

"You're right, dammit. I've got to go talk to Barnaby." She

turned and whirled toward the door. "I didn't see Barnaby when I came into the studio. Did you, Jean Paul?"

He shook his head. "I'm busy. I don't keep track of the help."

"Maybe somebody should." She was already darting out of the studio and down the hall toward the back entrance. There was a uniformed policeman on duty there, but it wasn't Barnaby. What was his name? Charlie…Something. "Charlie, isn't Barnaby on duty tonight? I forgot to tell him something."

Charlie was shaking his head. "He called me because he wanted to trade shifts tonight. He said he had something important to do." He grinned at her. "I think it probably had something to do with those mug shots he was trying to track down for you. Didn't he tell you that he'd zeroed in on the bastard? He warned me to keep an eye on you until he could get the cops to bring him in for questioning."

"Oh, shit," she whispered. She closed her eyes for an instant. This was a nightmare. "Look, I have to call Barnaby's wife, Judy, and see if she has any idea where he went tonight. Will you do me a favor and call the local police department and ask the same thing? He told me he used to be a rookie cop at that precinct before he resigned because he wanted to spend more time with his wife and kids. But he knows most of those officers, and he'd probably talk to them if he got a lead about that mug shot."

"Sure," Charlie said. "But I don't want to get Barnaby pissed off with me. He really wanted to help you. He said you both were working to get that guy off the streets. Should we wait and see if we hear from him?"

Jossland promised he'd made sure the guard became afraid of him, she thought to herself. *Before the end.*

"No, we shouldn't wait." She shook her head as she reached for her phone. She was terrified it might already be too late. "Let's just make those calls. Okay?"

———

DOMINIC'S GULFSTREAM
SOMEWHERE OVER THE ATLANTIC
FIVE HOURS LATER

"I've found Celine Kelly, Dominic," Sam Rashid said when Dominic picked up his call. "And I have to admit I'm finding this particular job very interesting. You do like to keep me on my toes, don't you?"

Rashid was definitely sounding amused, which automatically made Dominic wary.

"I wouldn't want you to get bored," Dominic said. "What's wrong? All I asked for was information. Couldn't you find out enough about her to give me a decent report?"

"Oh, I found out quite a bit. According to the people around her, the woman is usually very understated and hard-working, but her life appears to be an open book. She grew up as an army brat. She earns her living as an artist's model and is also working part-time as a physician intern. She shares an apartment with two other models who also work at the art institute. But she appears to have no close friends or lovers, probably because she's so busy."

"Then why do you find Celine Kelly so interesting? Not much to keep you on your toes from that report."

"I didn't tell you the best part," Rashid said. "The interesting part is that you said you wanted to interview her as soon as you landed, and that I'm supposed to make her available to you."

"That's what I said. What's the problem?"

"The problem is that I'm having difficulty doing that," Rashid said. "Because at the present time she's being held for questioning by the Boston Police Department, and I can't even get to see her."

"What the hell?" Dominic murmured. "On what charge?"

"I've been trying to determine that, but they're not being forthcoming. I thought you might know. But evidently she's not as pure as you might guess from that report."

"Possibly," Dominic said. "But I want to know definitely. I'll be landing in about an hour. Until then, I want you to talk to everyone connected to her and find out why the ministering angel turned out to be a demon in disguise."

"Of course. I'm on my way to the art studio now. I thought that's what you'd tell me. It was just too bizarre to resist poking the bear a little. I'll pick you up at the airport?"

"I can hardly wait," Dominic said. "And in the meantime, I'll make a few calls on my own and see if I can nudge a few answers myself from those noble officers of law and order..."

INTERROGATION ROOM
BOSTON POLICE DEPARTMENT
FOUR HOURS LATER

"I don't know where Barnaby is," Celine said wearily. "Why do you keep asking me?" She turned to Lieutenant Jacobs, who was leaning against the wall across the room. "If I knew the answer to that, why would I have asked Charlie to call you and see if anyone at the precinct could let me know what had happened to him? You're treating me as if I'm guilty of some kind of crime."

The lieutenant shook his head. "No, we believe the only thing you're guilty of is being a little too persuasive to Barnaby. It's understandable. It would be natural for him to want to please a lovely woman like you. You were angry that some thug had tried to attack you and you wanted the man punished, so you sent Barnaby after him."

"It wasn't like that." She stiffened. "I'd already punished him myself. I only ran back to the studio so that I could have Barnaby fill out a report and warn the other students to keep an eye out for him."

Jacobs smiled slightly. "Yes, Officer Charles said that Barnaby told him that rather unusual story, but I'm afraid I took it with a grain of salt. Particularly after I caught sight of you. You don't look nearly lethal enough to be able to cause the kind of damage Barnaby described. I'm sure you must have many other weapons available to you."

She was getting too impatient to go on with this. Why wouldn't he listen to her? "I'm sure you do, too. But it's always a question of choice, isn't it, Lieutenant? Please could you just tell me what you know about Barnaby being missing."

He nodded. "We just have a few more questions that we have to ask you to verify your story. Barnaby told a couple of his friends here at the precinct that he was doing a favor for you when he asked to check the mug books. He said you'd been assaulted and needed to check the identity of the perpetrator. Evidently he thought he'd found what he was looking for and just wanted to locate the man for a final confirmation of ID before he asked you to file a report. Was that true?"

She nodded. "Part of it. I gave Barnaby a sketch, and he was hoping he could find the man in the mug books. I never asked him to hunt him down. I thought he was just going to file a report and then turn the case over to the police." She moistened her lips. "Tell me he didn't do that."

"I'm afraid we can't tell you any such thing," the lieutenant said coolly. "And you told the officers we sent to pick you up at the art studio how helpful and friendly Barnaby had been to you, but you were afraid that something terrible might have happened to him. Is that correct?"

"You must know it is. I gave the officers that letter I'd received." He'd even signed a name. Surly that should have helped. Her hands were clenching nervously into fists. "Now may I ask a few questions? Did you find Barnaby? Is he okay?"

He was silent for a long moment. "We're not sure." The lieutenant shook his head. "We have a body in the morgue that hasn't been identified yet that was discovered down in the warehouse district. But it may take some time before we know if it's definitely Barnaby." His lips tightened. "There was severe torture involved."

Celine inhaled sharply. "Dear God." She felt as if he'd struck her. "Have you told his wife, Judy?"

"Not yet. We hope to have something more definite to tell her soon."

"Yes, that would probably be better," she said dully. "But

when I called to check with her about him earlier, she said he'd been gone from the house for most of the day and she couldn't reach him by phone. She must be frantic by now."

"You're friends with Barnaby's wife?" The lieutenant looked surprised. "How...cozy."

The inference was too clear to miss. Celine pulled herself together and stared him in the eye. "I was good friends with Barnaby, and I liked her and the kids. I'm just thinking that you should have one of your department heads find one of Judy's close relatives and have them go and keep her company until you know something definite about Barnaby. I hope we're both wrong, but there's a chance she might need someone."

He nodded and for a moment almost smiled. "I was going to see to that. Is there anything I can do for you?"

"I want to know the minute you find out about Barnaby." She rubbed her temple and tried to think. "It's too late for me to go back to my job at the hospital. I'll have to call and cancel for today. Could I just stay here for a little while and see if you get any news?"

"There's a waiting room next door that we use for witnesses. It has a couch, but you wouldn't be very comfortable," Jacobs said. "And if that letter wasn't just a threat, it might be better if you're also with your family."

"No family," she said. "And I can take care of myself, but I'd rather stay here until I know about Barnaby, if you don't mind."

He shrugged. "I guess it will be okay." He was still hesitating. "Can I have them bring you coffee or something to eat?"

She shook her head. "No, thanks. That letter was signed

Jossland. Do you know the name of the man in the mug shot that Barnaby found?"

He nodded. "Leon Jossland. British citizen. He worked for several criminal organizations over the years and had a very nasty track record."

"Can you find him and see if he had anything to do with Barnaby's disappearance?"

"We're already doing that," Jacobs said. "But so far he appears to have disappeared himself. At least as far as Boston is concerned. We've checked all his previous addresses and known acquaintances and no sign of him. And Jossland isn't one of the big bosses, but he's well known in the mobs. He wouldn't waste his time harassing a woman on the street or writing an incriminating letter like the one you gave Charles."

"Then it seems I gave him cause," Celine said. "I made him very angry, Lieutenant."

Jacobs nodded. "According to that letter, you caused quite a disturbance. But we don't know yet if he acted on those threats."

"But we don't know that he didn't." She tried to stop shivering. "We just have to pray that he only wanted to frighten me."

"That may be true. But we should still keep an eye on you to make sure that he doesn't try to bother you again. Or perhaps you already have someone to do that. You said you have no family, but that doesn't mean you don't have powerful friends who might want to help you."

She frowned. "What are you talking about?"

He shrugged. "We've had a few inquiries about you since

you were brought in for questioning. Some of them from people with a good deal of clout. Not surprising. After all, a woman like you must have a good many men you can call on when you need backup. It's natural you might want to pull a few strings if a situation was becoming difficult for you."

"A woman like me?" Her lips tightened. "How do you know what kind of woman I am? I don't have any high-powered friends. Most of my friends are artists or doctors, and they're just as hardworking as I am. Even if I had any strings I wanted to pull, my 'influence' is nonexistent." She turned back and pulled her coat around her as she sat down and leaned back against the wall, trying to get comfortable. "And I'll take care of myself as I always do. But you're right, the situation is difficult, and I'll be grateful if you'll just let me know about Barnaby." She closed her eyes and tried to close him and the rest of the world out.

She heard the door close behind the lieutenant.

That's right, go away.

She didn't want to face the thought of this police station or that lieutenant, who had been struggling to be polite but probably thought she was some kind of temptress who had been using Barnaby.

And most of all, she didn't want to think that somewhere in this complex was the morgue where Barnaby might be lying.

No, don't think of that. It hurt too much. Don't accept it until someone came and told her that it was true.

Let it all go…

TWO HOURS LATER

"These papers seem to be in order." Lieutenant Jacobs pushed them aside and looked up at Dominic. "And the call I received from the commissioner was very specific," he said dryly. "He told me I was to be completely accommodating on all points."

"Then I'm glad we understand each other." Dominic smiled. "The lawyer I retained was a little bit upset that I wasn't being allowed access to Celine Kelly. But I'm certain that was just a misunderstanding."

"She had a lot of questions to answer," Jacobs said. "Barnaby was a good man and a friend of many of the officers in this precinct. We weren't sure that she didn't have something to do with his disappearance. But she was more than cooperative, so we allowed her to stay here when she requested it. She was a bit upset and wanted a final report on Barnaby. Should I arrange for a police escort to take her back to her apartment?"

"Not necessary. I'll take care of it. Now that I have your report and the Jossland file, that's all I need. Where is she?"

Jacobs nodded at the door of the interview room. "It was either there or find her a vacant cell. I figured that a cell would be a trifle lacking in hospitality. You are going to furnish her with security? I might be able to authorize a few days for a couple officers to keep an eye on her."

"Evidently she managed to convince you that she was worth saving," Dominic murmured.

Jacobs shrugged. "Have you seen her? It's kind of hard not to appreciate that kind of appeal. It's like not wanting to see a beautiful masterpiece destroyed. I could almost see why Barnaby went to so much trouble for her."

Dominic chuckled. "Almost?" He was heading for the door. "Don't worry, I'll see that your masterpiece remains intact."

The lights were off in the room. Presumably Jacobs had thought it might help the woman relax enough to sleep. In the dimness, he could barely see Celine Kelly curled up on a couch. She seemed to be wrapped in a dark-colored coat of some sort.

He moved carefully, silently, toward her. Trying not to startle her. He stopped when he was a few feet away, lit the light on his phone, and said quietly, "My name is Alex Dominic, and Lieutenant Jacobs released you into my care. I came to have a talk with you, Miss Kelly. Would that be all right?"

"I have no idea." She was sitting up on the couch. "It depends on who you are and what you're going to be able to tell me. Lieutenant Jacobs wasn't at all helpful. He said he'd let me know about Barnaby as soon as possible, but he's left me here waiting for hours. Has there been an arrest yet?"

"Not as far as I know. I'm sure he didn't mean to disappoint you. He seemed genuinely eager to help you. But perhaps he decided to leave it up to me to fill you in. Would you mind if I turned on the overhead lights so we can have our discussion?"

"Why would I mind? I told you, I have to know what's happening." She got to her feet and moved toward the wall switch. Suddenly the room was full of light. "That's better. Now maybe I can at least see if you're telling me the truth. It seemed as if Jacobs not only didn't believe me but was playing games with me as well."

Holy shit!

Dominic almost said the words aloud as he stared at Celine

Kelly in the bright light that now fully illuminated her. That shining dark hair framing the fantastic features...those cheek-bones...those almond-shaped violet eyes. All he could think of in that moment was the word with which he'd mocked Jacobs a short time ago. *Masterpiece...*

He jerked his gaze away from that face and concentrated on what she had been saying. "He was probably doing his best. But I'll tell you the full truth so you won't accuse me of the same thing. Now, where would you like me to start?"

"You must know," she said bluntly. "Everyone at this precinct must know. I couldn't have been more clear. Barnaby. Tell me about Barnaby." She was obviously bracing herself. "What did you find out about Barnaby?"

"I'm sorry," he said gently. "The results were indisputable. The victim the police are holding in the morgue is your friend, Gary Barnaby."

She flinched as if he'd struck her. "Dear God in Heaven." She closed her eyes. "You're absolutely certain?"

"It's him. After I heard the results, I went down to the lab and questioned the medical team myself when I got here. They did a thorough job, and I wish I didn't have to tell you this."

"I wish you didn't, either." She opened her eyes, and he saw them glittering with tears. "Does his wife, Judy, know? Does she realize he's been identified?"

"I believe the lieutenant told her before I arrived at the precinct. Naturally, he didn't choose to let her view the body. She didn't request it. It will have to be a closed casket."

"Because of what that monster Jossland did to him?" She began wiping her wet cheeks with the backs of her hands. "He managed to cheat Judy and her two kids of a final goodbye?" Her eyes were suddenly blazing. "My God, I hate that bastard. Have you arrested him yet?"

"Not yet. There seems to be some difficulty finding him. I thought perhaps you might be able to help. Do you remember anything that might lead us to any of his associates?"

"How could I? He was a blank page as far as I was concerned. How many times do I have to tell you? One moment I'd never seen him before, and the next he was following me and putting his hands on me. Was I supposed to meekly bow my head and let him do it? People like that think they can get away with anything if you don't fight back. My father taught me that, and he made sure that I was able to do it in the most efficient way possible. There was nothing wrong with him doing that."

"Shh." He reached out and touched her hand. "No offense. I just thought that there might be something that you'd forgotten to tell us. I've read your dossier, and your father seems to have been an exceptional man."

"A dossier?" she said. "I don't have a criminal record. Where did you get that?"

"I have connections."

"Obviously, but you're not a cop. The Breitling wristwatch you're wearing tells me that. Who are you?"

"Someone who wants to help you. As for your father, he taught you well; you should be very proud."

"You're damn right." She reached up and rubbed her temple before she added wearily, "But what he couldn't teach me was that there would always be choices I'd have to make. I made one that night, and Barnaby is dead."

"Choices?"

"During that last minute I was trying to decide whether to run toward the subway or back to the art studio. I chose to go back to the studio. If I hadn't, Barnaby wouldn't have been involved at all." She shuddered. "And he wouldn't be down in that morgue, he'd be home with Judy and his children. So it is partly my fault that all this happened."

"Bullshit," Dominic said. "You were making perfectly good sense until you came up with this nonsense. I'm going to assume it's just shock and that you'll be back to semi-normal behavior in no time. But don't expect me to accept it. I came here to get information that will get me to Jossland, and neither of us have the time to waste on self-pity."

Celine stared at him in shock. Then she blinked, and her lips curved in the faintest smile. "I'll remember that. I'm glad you made your position clear. And I promise you, no more self-pity."

"Perhaps I could tolerate a small amount of it," he said. "As long as you don't mind me warning you not to let it get in the way."

Celine shrugged. "You'll have to take what you can get. I may just tell you to go to hell. But you're very...unusual."

"So you may allow me to stay around for a while?"

"Until I decide if you're trying to manipulate me. I don't like people who do that." She shook her head. "But right now I think I may need you. You said you went down to the morgue when you first got here. Can you take me down there right now?"

"I don't see why not," he said. "Tell me why?"

"I don't want Barnaby to be alone down there tonight." She shuddered. "I want to tell him that we'll never stop until we find the person who did this to him. I want him to know that I was there for him, and I don't care how he looks."

"You realize that's not at all reasonable, Miss Kelly."

"It's Celine. And I don't care if anyone thinks I'm reasonable or not. What do we really know about life or death? What if he somehow did know? I'm not going to take the chance. Will you see that they let me in to see him? I'm studying to be a doctor. I promise I'm not going to scream or faint on you."

"I didn't think you would." He was taking her jacket and wrapping it around her before fastening it. "They keep it pretty cool down there. I just want to make sure you'll be warm enough." He took her arm and led her toward the elevators. "Stay as long as you want. I'll be there to make sure no one bothers you. I wouldn't want you to have to get in a brawl with any of the staff. Okay?"

"I'll try to restrain myself." She barely heard him, but she was grateful for the strength of his grip on her arm as she watched him punch the button for the morgue.

I'm coming, Barnaby. Somehow I'll find a way to help. You're not alone.

FOUR HOURS LATER

"Time to leave now, Celine?" Dominic asked as he watched her stiffly get to her feet. "The M.E.'s will be grateful. They've been pretty patient, but I'm afraid they don't quite understand your philosophy. And you look as if you're so exhausted that you're close to passing out yourself."

She shook her head. "Don't be ridiculous. I'm okay." She

was heading toward the elevator. "I was just sad…and angry. So very angry."

"I could see that you were. But do you feel any better now?"

"No, all I feel is more determined." She didn't speak again until they were walking down the steps of the precinct to the parking lot. It was almost dawn, and she found herself studying him. Until this moment she had only been aware of Dominic as the man who could help her fight against the rules so that she could stay with Barnaby during this last night. She'd been vaguely aware that he'd brought her a cup of coffee twice; once, he'd taken her hand when he'd noticed it was shaking. Now she could see he looked to be in his middle or late thirties, and she noticed the weathered tan of his skin, his gray-green eyes, and the single streak of white that threaded his dark hair. He was dressed casually, but his shirt and trousers were beautifully tailored and undoubtedly expensive. She was sure none of the other detectives at the precinct wore clothes like that, and she gave him another searching glance as she added sharply, "Along with a strong dash of curiosity about you that I intend to have satisfied. There are a lot of things that make me uneasy about you, Dominic."

"By all means, I could see that coming. I even left a trail of breadcrumbs leading to the witch's castle, but you're not in any condition now to cross-examine me. Take my word that I'm a fairly tough nut to crack, and you'll be better off if you get a long nap and face me later." They had stopped beside a black limousine; a tall, dark-skinned man got out, opening the passenger door and giving her a warm smile. "And since the Boston Police Department have put you in my hands for the time being, I don't like the idea of sending you back to the apartment you

73

share with those other models to keep you safe while you get that rest that you need. This is Sam Rashid, who works for me, Celine. He's going to take you to a very fine hotel where you'll be secure and very well fed, if I remember correctly." He turned back to Rashid. "This is Celine Kelly. Take no chances with her. Keep her safe, and don't let her skip out on you because she thinks she can take better care of herself than you can. Understand?"

He nodded. "No problem."

Dominic turned back to Celine. "Get that rest, and I promise we'll have a long talk when I meet you at the hotel later today. But don't think you can squeeze any answers from Rashid. Though you may be his greatest challenge to date." He stepped back and tipped his hand to his brow in a salute. "It's been a unique experience, Celine. I look forward to dinner."

He turned and walked away.

CHAPTER
5

BOSTON RITZ–CARLTON HOTEL
7:40 P.M.

S am Rashid was waiting in the hall in front of Celine's penthouse when Dominic got off the elevator and made a face as he walked toward him. "I hope you had a good day," he said sourly. "Personally, mine sucked. That gorgeous guest of yours started off with cursing me and trying to jump out of the limo. She evidently didn't like the idea of you marching off into the sunset and not giving her a chance to state her wishes. By the time we got to the hotel, she had quieted down a bit; I checked her into the penthouse and ordered her breakfast. Then I explained that you sometimes have difficulty with the simpler things of life, like courtesy, but it generally comes out all right in the end."

"How kind of you to soothe and reassure her," Dominic said sarcastically. "Do tell me more."

"Hey." Rashid shook his head. "I was the one who compiled that dossier on her. According to reports, she could do serious damage to me, and I thought that you wanted her to calm down and rest."

"And did she do it?"

"Not right away. But after the third time she tried to escape from the suite, she probably became discouraged. Or maybe she just admired the fact that I was alert enough to catch her doing it each time." He added thoughtfully, "But she's very good with locks. Once, she managed to get off the balcony to the next penthouse."

"Interesting. Locks and skipping over roofs and balconies..." Dominic paused. "But she didn't appeal to any hotel guests or employees for help? Yet you must have run into several. It's a busy hotel."

Rashid nodded. "It never occurred to me. Of course, a good many people were staring at her. Who wouldn't? But she wasn't afraid of me. I'd say it was just the opposite."

"I've done some staring myself. But perhaps it was a weapon that she didn't want to use..." Dominic stepped closer to the door and rang the bell. "Maybe I'll ask her."

The door opened, and Celine Kelly stood glaring at him. "You took your time, Dominic." She looked beyond him to Rashid. "Not you. I've had enough of you to last me for quite a while."

Rashid nodded. "But I believe you'll find I'm much more agreeable than Dominic." He glanced at Dominic. "I ordered your favorite wine. I thought that it might mellow her a bit."

"I don't believe wine could do that," Dominic said. "But maybe if I'm humble enough..."

Rashid was smiling slyly. "Oh, may I stay around and watch that?"

"No," Celine said definitely. "He couldn't be humble enough to make me feel in the least mellow. He was rude and ignored me when I told him I needed to talk to him. He treated me the way Jossland did that night he followed me. Like a...thing."

"You're right, I'll make myself scarce." Rashid turned and moved toward the door. "I hope our next meeting is more to your liking. I'll check in with you later, Dominic." The door slammed behind him.

Dominic turned immediately back to Celine. "I see that Rashid also ordered you a pot of coffee. May I pour you a cup if I promise not to treat you as anything but the woman you've shown yourself to be since the moment I walked into that office last night?" He smiled. "And that's definitely not 'a thing.' I can see why you'd be angry with me—I was abrupt."

"Rude," she substituted.

"Rude," he repeated. "But I'd given up all night to sit with you in that morgue even though I had business to take care of that could have been important to both of us. I couldn't allow myself to become distracted."

"I never asked you to sit with me and hold my hand," Celine said coldly. "All I wanted was for you to arrange to get me permission to go there. I thought you were someone important in the police department."

"And now you don't think that?" He poured her coffee and was carrying the cup across the room to her. "Please don't throw this at me. It would please Rashid too much if he heard about it later. If you spare me, I'll tell you what I was doing at that precinct tonight. And then I'll tell you a few more interesting facts about Jossland that you'll need to know."

"This isn't a game."

"No, it's dead serious. With the emphasis on *dead*."

She looked at the coffee and then slowly took the cup. "You're not a regular policeman, are you? In addition to the watch, you don't dress like a cop, and you scoot around town in a limo with a driver. And yet you seemed to have the run of the precinct. You knew that lieutenant. But those M.E. agents at the morgue had to call someone to verify you had the authority to let me view Barnaby."

"All very true."

"But they practically snapped to attention after they called for permission. So you're someone who wields a lot of power. Who the hell are you?"

"As I said, Alex Dominic."

"And why did you come to see me tonight?"

"I had to question you in case you had information I needed. It was necessary."

"And why did that lieutenant and those other cops welcome you with open arms?"

"You might say politics entered into the picture. I'm a very good friend of the commissioner. I asked him to give me carte blanche with this particular case."

"And he did it? Just like that?"

Dominic shrugged. "I assured him I'd clear the matter up to his satisfaction."

"Satisfaction! Barnaby's dead."

"Don't worry. The commissioner is a politician, and he only wants a clean slate. But it will be done exactly as it should be...as you'd want it to be."

"And how do you know how I'd want it to be?" she asked fiercely. "You don't really know anything about me."

"I know much more about you than most of the people in

your life," he said. "Because I've been doing a bit of research on you lately, and though I can't claim to know you intimately, I believe we came a little closer last night. We're no longer strangers."

"Research?" She shook her head. "Why would you be doing research on me? What kind of research?"

"As I said, I had to make myself completely familiar with you. Therefore, it had to be rather in-depth."

She was looking at him in bewilderment. "Because of that monster Jossland?"

"No, it didn't start out that way. He's just a minor part of the puzzle."

"Minor?" she repeated harshly. "He's a very big part of the puzzle. He killed Barnaby. Or was that a lie, too?"

"No lies, Celine. I told you I'd tell you the truth." He shook his head. "It's just a damnably confusing truth at the moment. The first thing you should know is that Jossland is a very nasty thug who works for an underworld boss named Ezra Caldwell. If Jossland tried to hurt or kidnap you the other night, it was almost certainly at Caldwell's orders. As far as we can tell, Caldwell has a plan to steal gold from a mine in Central Africa, and it involves at least three people who have been brought to our attention: Masini Zakira, Eve Duncan, and you, Celine."

"What?" Celine shook her head emphatically. "That's crazy. It sounds like something from a kid's comic book."

"Except it wasn't a kid who killed your friend Barnaby," Dominic said. "And if they showed you Jossland's police file, you'd notice that his past crimes usually involved torture and dismemberment." He paused. "You do remember what you saw in that morgue last night?"

Celine inhaled sharply as that memory jolted back to her. "I could hardly forget," she said bitterly. "Damn you!"

"I didn't want to have to remind you," he said softly. "But you had to accept it. Because it wasn't really Barnaby he wanted to kill. It was you."

"As I said, it doesn't make sense." She sat down on the couch and stared into the amber depths of the coffee in her cup. "Why would anyone want to kill me? And I don't know anything about gold mining. Who were those other two people you mentioned? Masini Zakirar..."

"Zakira," Dominic said. "At least you'll agree he makes some sense. He's a chieftain living in an African village named Shafira. He's also a priest who has been causing a good deal of trouble among the other villages in the area. Eve Duncan is the other woman who could be involved, and she—"

"Eve Duncan?" Celine interrupted. "Of course I know who she is. I didn't catch the name when you were reeling off all that information. It was just a blur."

"I thought you'd recognize the name since you're both artists."

"Don't be disrespectful. I'm only a part-time artist who works to keep the landlord at bay and put myself through med school. She's a genius. I saw an exhibit of her work at a science show in New York and it blew me away." She was trying to remember the details. "So...alive, but not really quite...here." Then she suddenly frowned. "And that makes what you told me even more absurd. Why would someone like Duncan be involved with a crook like this Caldwell you told me about? I could see how he might think I could be lured to the dark side. I'm small potatoes as far as income is concerned. But it's not as if he'd think he could offer her anything she doesn't have now. You can't get higher in your field than Eve Duncan. There's absolutely no comparison between the two of us."

Dominic smiled wryly. "You're wrong. I'm sorry, but there may be a very significant similarity as far as Caldwell is concerned."

Celine lifted her chin defiantly. "And what's that?"

"My guess is that he may now be regarding you both as tools. And if you don't prove useful to him, that designation will change to targets."

Her eyes widened. "And on what evidence do you base that opinion?"

"None. Except that I've studied Caldwell's behavior in the past, and he's very efficient when he goes after something. Since he's also completely ruthless, he doesn't waste any time with people who don't function as he wishes. He rewards the men who please him and punishes those who don't." He paused. "But for some reason he wanted to keep Jossland alive even though you'd done all the punishing yourself in the encounter. Perhaps he has plans for you later." He thought about it. "But in that note that he sent you, he indicated that the Barnaby killing had been done because he wasn't free to get you in his sights."

"Yes, he did," she said hoarsely. "I've got the damn thing memorized. And he wanted me to know that he was going to hurt him and that it was my fault."

"So allowing Barnaby to be killed was done to pacify Jossland when he wasn't permitted to go after you? He was obviously saving you for something special."

"You've got it all figured out. Except that it doesn't make any sense."

"It makes a great deal of sense," Dominic said. "You've just got to adjust to the idea that Caldwell is the central scumbag who arranged the killing of your friend Barnaby, though he used Jossland as the weapon." He reached into his wallet, pulled out a photo, and handed it to Celine. "I decided that it was safer if you had an idea what Caldwell looked like. I'm afraid the chances are that you'll be getting to know him very soon. He's almost six feet tall and in his forties, with slicked-back gray hair and blue eyes."

"And before the other night, I never saw this man you say could be in charge of whether I live or die." Celine tossed the photo on the coffee table. "Would you care to tell me how you know so much about him?"

"He's an assignment I took on when I found out what a son of a bitch he was. You might say I do vigilante-type work when I deem it necessary."

"I don't remember ever hearing about vigilantes working with police commissioners," she said caustically.

"It happens under special conditions. My work is entirely legal and acceptable to law enforcement, or I wouldn't have such influential backup." He smiled. "I can give excellent references."

"I saw that last night. It doesn't mean you're telling me the entire truth."

"No, and you may not believe totally in me, but I think you have faith in yourself, and you'll have to decide how far and on what grounds you'll let me help you."

"Help me?" she repeated warily. "I haven't asked you to help me do anything. Just because you practically kidnapped me and brought me to this swank hotel doesn't mean that I want you to do anything else."

"No, you haven't asked me for anything else," he said. "I don't think you've made up your mind yet, and I can understand that. I just want you to know that I'm available to you. I have more knowledge about Caldwell than you do, and I have people who will help in whatever we decide is best to do to him. Right now, you're upset and it's difficult to decide which way you need to go. I've checked you into this hotel for the next week, and Rashid will be on hand in case he's needed. That will keep you safe while you get a chance to think. You'll be alone except for Rashid. You won't hear from me unless you call me and tell me you want to see me." He handed her one of his cards. "Or if there's anything I can do to make your way easier."

She looked down at the card. "I won't call you. I can take care of myself. I'll probably go back to work in a couple days." She grimaced. "If I still have a job to go back to. I'll have to call them and see. The hospital doesn't tolerate its interns not showing up for duty."

"I don't think you'll have too much trouble," Dominic said with a slight shrug. "The surgical director of your unit would fight to keep you. He says your first two years of internship have been remarkable; he thinks you may become the most brilliant brain surgeon the hospital has ever turned out."

She was staring at him. "You actually talked to him?"

"I told you I had to know who you were. I thought your hospital director would be one of the best people to ask." He smiled. "I was going to talk to the head of your art studio next. Do you think I should?"

"It would be pretty much a waste of time. He'd only tell you I have strength and stamina and an interesting face. Nothing important."

"I disagree. All of those qualities have an importance to the right person."

"Then maybe I'm not the right person." She gazed at him with narrowed eyes. "But I think you know quite a bit about people, don't you? You work at it?"

"I find most people very intriguing," he said. "And some are extraordinary. For instance, it was a pleasure to explore you, Celine." He smiled. "And at no time in the process did I ever consider you 'a thing.' There are some people who would consider referring to you in that way as almost a sacrilege."

"Bullshit."

He chuckled as he nodded goodbye as he headed for the door. "And that remark exactly illustrates my point. Goodbye, Celine."

"Wait."

He looked back at her.

"I should probably say thank you."

"Not if it particularly pains you."

"Oh, be quiet. I'm trying to say something." She met his eyes. "I was hurting last night. I would have felt really alone and sad if you hadn't stayed with me. That was a good thing that you did. Thank you."

"You're welcome." He grinned. "Since you're obviously destined to be a phenomenal brain surgeon, perhaps you can return the favor someday. Rashid is always telling me that I don't think like other people and I need some serious work up there to straighten me out."

She smiled faintly. "You'll have to wait a bit before I qualify."

"I'm a patient man."

She frowned. "And besides, I'm not sure that what you did for me will make up for how rude you were when you virtually threw me into that limo with Rashid."

"Then that's another thing you'll have to decide, isn't it?" he said. "What a lot of decisions." He paused. "And here's another one for you. I checked and found that Barnaby's wife has arranged for his funeral, since his body has been released. It's going to take place three days from now. Why not stick around here in the hotel until after his funeral to honor him and perhaps comfort his wife?"

He opened the door and the next moment he was gone.

———

Celine didn't move for a long time after Dominic had left. She stayed sitting there, staring at the door and remembering everything he had said and all the agony and bewilderment those words had brought. She wanted to reject all of it, but how could she when she was living with the thought of Barnaby's death and her own part in it. Dominic's s explanation was no more crazy than a complete stranger attacking her that night for no reason and what had followed afterward. And somehow Alex Dominic had made his explanation about the involvement of Caldwell seem almost logical with his knowledge and documentation of the man. For heaven's sake, he'd even given her a blasted photo! Of course, Dominic could be rigging some kind of scam, and there was no doubt he was the most unusual individual she had ever run across. But she couldn't accept that the man who had sat with her all night in that morgue just to keep her company would be anything but what he presented himself to be.

Oh, she just didn't know, and she was too weary and depressed right now to figure anything out. As Dominic had said, there were too many decisions to make, and she wasn't capable of facing them right now. She'd go to bed and try to sleep; maybe in the morning she'd be able to put everything together and come up with answers.

Dominic had said something about answers, she remembered, as she climbed into bed and closed her eyes. He'd said that he could better help her because he knew things she didn't...Was he right?

CHAPTER

6

The tears were stinging Celine's eyes and running down her cheeks as she moved quickly down the road toward the cemetery gates. Just a few more yards and she'd be on the street and away from this place. She passed a white marble tomb with a huge angel statue guarding the doors. So sad...It seemed the entire world was sad today.

"Do you need a lift?"

She looked up to see Dominic, who had pulled his Lexus to the side of the road and stopped. He reached over and opened the passenger door for her. "I know I promised you wouldn't hear from me if you didn't call, but Rashid phoned me from the church and said you might be having a bit of a tough time."

"So you decided to come to my rescue again?" She was wiping her eyes with a tissue as she got into the car. "Well, I'll let you. I just want to get out of here as quickly as possible." She was still wiping her eyes as he started the car. She caught a glimpse of herself in the mirror and shook her head. "Lord, I look hideous."

"I don't believe hideous is possible for you. And it doesn't matter to me how you look. Just sit back and relax and push everything away while I complete this rescue. You wouldn't want to spoil my technique."

"Heaven forbid. But you can let me out in the next block after we leave the cemetery. I just didn't want to run into Judy or the kids again."

"Am I allowed to ask why?"

She didn't answer for a moment. "Judy didn't want me there. She was very…cold. She looked at me as if she hated me. Whenever the kids came over to talk to me she'd call them away. It was as if she didn't want me to touch them. I think she blames me for Barnaby." She swallowed, hard. "Who could blame her?"

"I could," he said sharply. "Do you want me to go and talk to her about the fact that you had nothing to do with it, and it was Barnaby who took the action that killed him?"

"No, stay out of it. She's suffered enough. And those kids are all she has left. I shouldn't have even come here to the funeral. I just wanted to say goodbye and tell her to call me if I could help."

"Just what I suggested you do," he said grimly. "I should have kept my damn mouth shut. I didn't even need to do it when I knew you were almost there anyway."

"You're saying that you think you were responsible?" She gazed at him in disbelief. "Screw you."

"I'm saying that I've been known to be very persuasive on occasion. I'm sorry if it backfired like this. I should have thought it through and kept my mouth shut."

"And you shouldn't have had the arrogance to think that

just because you suggested something, I'd be weak enough to just fall into line. I'll always pick and choose." She held his gaze. "And don't ever think because you saw me shed a few tears that you can step in and try to solve all my problems. I own them, just as I own all the good things that happen to me. Do you understand?"

"I believe you've made yourself clear." He was smiling. "And now you may know me a little better, too. Would it be all right if I take you back to the hotel and we have dinner? Then you can ask me anything else you care to. And maybe you can forget all about Judy Barnaby and have a glass of wine."

"But I don't intend to forget about her. I can't forget anything that's happened to me. I told you, she wasn't to blame. I have to remember everything so that I'll know how to find those men who killed Barnaby. That's what I learned during these last three days. That nothing matters if I can make Jossland and Caldwell pay for what they did." Her lips twisted. "We shouldn't have had to bury a great guy like Barnaby today. Yes, you can bet I'll ask you questions. One of them I couldn't get out of my mind in the past few days was about Eve Duncan…"

Dominic nodded. "Then that's where I'll go first. Dinner?"

She nodded slowly. "Dinner."

SHAFIRA, AFRICA
TWO HOURS LATER
"The Kelly woman was picked up at the cemetery after the Barnaby funeral," Jossland said when Caldwell answered his

call. "It was the same man she was with when she left the precinct a few days ago. You said you knew him."

"Oh, I do," Caldwell said. "Dominic's been a thorn in my side in the past, and he can be extremely dangerous. But that only means we'll have to be very careful not to let him get in my way on this job. The stakes are much too high. Is she still with him?"

"He took her back to the hotel, and neither of them has left the suite. He's probably too busy fucking her. It's all a whore like her is good for," Jossland added sourly. "I've cased out the penthouse. I could go back later tonight and get rid of both of them."

"But that's not what I want, Jossland. I was worried you'd get overeager when I permitted you to leave the village and go back there. However, I've noticed you're definitely good at taking care of certain lethal duties that I've given you in the past. Since I'd heard rumors that Dominic was making his presence known among certain of my employees, I thought it would be wise to have you handy."

"But I don't want to take care of anyone but that Kelly woman," Jossland said obstinately. "And I certainly don't want to have to hang out in those stinking, steamy jungles while you try to talk Zakira into showing you where all that gold is supposed to be mined. Leave me alone with the priest for thirty minutes, and he'll tell you anything you want to know."

Caldwell chuckled. "You have no subtlety, and there's no way I would risk you injuring a prime source of income. Now stop complaining and count your blessings. Didn't I let you get rid of Gary Barnaby and play your mind games with Celine Kelly? But here you are trying to dive in and spoil everything for me. Wasn't that Barnaby death enough for you? You told me how much you enjoyed it." He added critically, "And you did some really excellent carving on the poor man."

"But it wasn't Celine Kelly." Jossland's teeth were gritting with rage. "You told me I could have that bitch."

"Patience. I have other work for you to do first. So keep an eye on Kelly while I go and have a discussion with our client, Zakira. He's beginning to get a little restless. It's about time we got ready to start working on the main event…"

An hour later, Caldwell was entering Zakira's palace and trying to look appropriately humble as he inclined his head before the son of a bitch's elaborately carved teak throne. Zakira had fooled his followers into thinking he was some kind of god, and visitors had to perpetuate the charade. The chieftain was as usual dressed in army camouflage gear and flaunting brilliant ribbons on his chest, and he frowned coldly as he turned to face Caldwell. "You're moving much too slowly, Caldwell. Do you think I paid you all that gold to watch you stay here and just fornicate with my women?"

Caldwell forced a smile. "No, though the women you send me are exceptional. I think you forget that I furnished you with enough arms to wipe out Karimu and all the enemies there who insulted you," he said. "That's an entire village who will no longer trouble you."

"They've seen my power. But it's not enough. They've got to know that as the supreme priest, I have the right to be respected by all the villages, and they have to obey me. They won't believe that until they see the proof. When do I see the rest of my payment you promised me?"

"There's been a slight delay. It's on its way."

"I do not accept that answer," he said softly. "I want everyone who sees me to know I was meant to rule this entire land. They cannot be certain of that without the mask. It's a symbol that's a part of our history that they'd understand. You've made many promises. You've even made suggestions that I've accepted because I thought them worthy. How long do you believe you'd live if I find you've been trying to lie to me? You'd be wise to give me what you promised. You understand?"

"Yes." What Cardwell understood was that he might have to kill this arrogant asshole sooner than he planned. There was no question Masini Zakira was a deadly adversary. He'd watched him make brutal public executions of his people in this village when they displeased him. But Zakira was not about to back off before he got the next and last shipment of gold. Caldwell had to give him the tribute he'd promised him for his damn temple, and he couldn't wait much longer to do it. "Of course I do. I'll get right on it." He made a sweeping gesture that he hoped the bastard thought was humble and started to back out of the throne room. "You won't be disappointed…"

PENTHOUSE SUITE
BOSTON RITZ-CARLTON HOTEL
8:40 P.M.
"You were right when you told me that I'd be well fed at this hotel," Celine said as she dabbed at her lips with the linen napkin. "I wasn't in good enough shape to appreciate the cuisine before, but the Ritz obviously has a spectacular chef." She shrugged. "Not that I've been familiar with fine cuisine lately. My father would take me out on special occasions, but most of the time we both enjoyed the local foods of whatever country we were visiting. My dad was a great cook."

"And your mother?"

"She died when I was eight. My dad and I were on our own after that." She met his gaze across the table. "But you probably know that. You said you have all those dossiers stashed away somewhere."

"They don't tell everything." He was pouring her wine. "For instance, I don't know your preference in wine. I had to guess."

"If you had thought it important, you would have known. You probably thought an occasional misstep or lack of information makes you seem more vulnerable. You're something of a perfectionist, aren't you?"

"Mistakes do annoy me if they're caused by either laziness or ego."

She smiled. "Then I have to agree with you. I chose a specialty that doesn't tolerate either of those faults. Either one can cause death in brain surgery."

Dominic shook his head. "You're far too intense to let anything distract you."

"But I've allowed you to distract me ever since you brought me to this penthouse today."

"I guarantee I didn't regard that as a distraction." His eyes were twinkling. "I'm really much better than that. And if you did allow me to casually amuse you for a few hours, I'd guess it was because you'd had a bad couple of days. This afternoon was particularly painful, and you needed to put it behind you for a short time."

How did he know that about her? Her gaze flew to meet his own. Warmth. Intelligence. Intensity. She inhaled sharply and glanced quickly away. "Perhaps you're right." She moistened her lips. "At any rate, I no longer need to hide away and avoid facing reality. Tell me about Eve Duncan and why she and I are on the same list."

"Caldwell evidently has a reason to believe he can use both of you for whatever he's planning."

"Something to do with a gold mine?"

"That was the general idea of the plan I uncovered with one of Caldwell's men. I'm still trying to find out all the details. I've sent a team to do research in the general area where it was found. Word of mouth is everything when it comes to searching out archaeological sites. Stories and legends passed down from generation to generation until you find the mother lode."

"Or you don't," she said curtly.

"Caldwell believes it's there or he wouldn't have decided to go after it." He paused. "Or Zakira might have already taken it over, and Caldwell is only waiting for his opportunity. And if Caldwell has gone mine hunting, then Jossland will be tagging after him."

"And what does Eve Duncan have to do with looking for this gold mine?"

"Perhaps nothing for the search itself." He paused. "But it could mean everything if she created the death mask. The gold in the mask itself is probably worth at least a billion dollars. If it was created by a famous sculptor like Eve Duncan, it could possibly bring in double that amount."

"Incredible," Celine murmured. "It seems impossible."

"Not if you look at the history of other burial areas. Five thousand or so gold treasures were found in Tutankhamun's tomb alone. Which included six gold chariots and many priceless weapons. And according to scientists, there are still other burial places without number beneath the sand in Egypt and other surrounding countries in the Middle East. Remember, those ancient dynasties had thousands of years to establish their traditions and build their belief in the afterlife before the world even knew they existed."

"Like those mountains in South Africa?" she asked skeptically.

He nodded. "It wouldn't be beyond belief that an ancient tomb might be found in those mountains. The priests were always on guard to hide the pharaohs' tombs in out-of-the-way places to protect them from grave robbers. From the recent reports I've had from the team I sent scouting those mountains, that area is damn well impassable." He shrugged. "Another thing that attracted the pharaohs was that they were always looking for rich gold fields that were fairly close to where the tomb was being built so that the gold for their afterlife was easily obtainable. They're still not entirely certain where the gold from Tutankhamun's tomb originated, but they think it may be from a long-lost mine in the Sahara Desert. It must have been extremely difficult to transport, and for the laborers to build the treasures for the tomb." His lips tightened. "But that's evidently not Caldwell's problem. He's making deals and he'll go through hell and high water as well as murder to get his hands on his own private gold mine." He lifted his glass of wine to her. "But then you know that. No one could know it better."

"You're wrong," Celine said bitterly. "Barnaby died because Caldwell wanted that damn gold. And there's no telling how many other people will die because of that greedy bastard." She put her glass down on the table. "But the one I'm most worried about is Eve Duncan. I was just a young med student when I went to one of her seminars and saw the sculptures on display. I was too intimidated to even speak to her, so I just found a seat in the back and watched her talk to the other students and tried to learn as much as I could."

Dominic smiled. "I can't imagine you being that withdrawn. It's not the woman I know."

"What can I say? I admire her and I didn't want to get in her way."

"Ah, I see the problem." Dominic leaned back in his chair, his eyes slowly traveling over her face. "You didn't want to risk overshadowing your heroine."

"Don't be stupid," she said curtly. "I've just told you how wonderful she is. I couldn't do that."

"But you were afraid anyway." His eyes were narrowed on

her face. "Because it's caused you so much trouble in the past? Yes, that's probably what it is. You take the backseat, you avoid drawing attention to yourself unless it's perhaps a written exam or you're masked and operating on a patient. Because that's sufficiently anonymous to be comfortable. Unfortunately, there's always someone ready and willing to take potshots at someone as wonderfully endowed as you if they get the chance."

She shrugged. "Guesswork. I'm not so vulnerable, Dominic."

"No, you're extremely tough. But you've probably been hurt many times before the way you were today—by people who think you've gotten everything you've ever wanted because of that really incredible face."

"Really? I wasn't even sure that you thought I was anything special. You're different from anyone else I've ever met. You've probably run into other women with similar problems with people who didn't understand they weren't just a pretty face. Most of the time, I was just relieved that you didn't seem to have any problems with it and accepted me as I am."

"Oh, I'd have to be blind not to notice how unusual you are. But I choose to regard it as a gift, and I enjoy it every time I see it. There's no way I'd ever resent that gift." He smiled. "But I don't pity those idiots who do resent it. Instead I'm tempted to clobber them."

Her lips twitched. "Don't bother. I can do that myself."

"That's been established."

"And it was my fault I didn't go talk to Eve Duncan when I got the chance. I wasn't that shy. I just didn't want to spoil a wonderful experience." She sat up and looked him straight in the eye. "But I think I have to go talk to her now. I'm afraid for her, Dominic. I have to tell her what happened to

Barnaby and warn her that Caldwell might want to hurt her." She paused. "Though you've probably already discussed this with her, haven't you?"

"Why do you think that?"

"Because it would be the intelligent thing to do, and you're extremely intelligent. She's much more important than me in the scheme of things. Naturally, you'd try to enlist her help in going after Caldwell."

"Not more important. I just had to divide up my efforts." His smile deepened. "And I assure you that you're just as important as Eve Duncan as far as I'm concerned now."

"I would think so. Since you know that you have me primed and willing to go after Caldwell and company." She added quietly, "And you've also even succeeded in getting me to trust you. Which was a major accomplishment considering everything you've thrown at me during the past week. Yes, you're very clever, Dominic." She leaned forward. "You were going to use Eve Duncan to lead you to either that gold mine or the priest who ordered the massacre at Karimu village so that you could set a trap for Caldwell?"

He nodded. "I knew Eve would be the key for Caldwell to get what he wanted from Masini Zakira, and it would have made my job simpler."

"But it didn't work out, so you decided to come here and use me for the same purpose?"

He shook his head. "You were a completely unknown quantity. I knew Caldwell wanted you for some reason of his own but I didn't know why. I still don't."

"Then you'd better find out, hadn't you?" Her voice was suddenly harsh. "Otherwise you're going to be wasting my time, Dominic. Because I want to go back to living my life, and I won't have Caldwell or Jossland interfering with it." She lifted her chin defiantly. "You needed bait and I'm willing to provide it." She got to her feet. "But first I want to go see Eve Duncan. She's got to know everything, and I want to make sure that she's protected."

CHAPTER

7

Y ou're going to owe me, Dominic," Catherine Ling said as she watched Dominic and Celine come down the jet-way to the gate. "You couldn't have arrived at a decent time and let me get some sleep?" She turned to Celine. "You're Celine Kelly? I'm very glad to meet you. Dominic called me from the cockpit when you were en route here from Boston. He said that I was going to be required for a character reference and to bring my documents." She flashed her ID and then thrust it back in her pocket. "I'm with the CIA and I'm a good friend of Eve Duncan."

"He didn't tell me to expect an official greeting at three in the morning," Celine said dryly. "I'm sorry that you were inconvenienced."

"No problem," Catherine said. "All was really forgiven when he told me that you were here because you agreed with me that Eve was right to stay home with her family instead of going on the hunt for Caldwell." She turned back to Dominic and made a shooing gesture. "Go away. I've got a room for her at the airport hotel and I'll take care of her. We'll talk and maybe have time for a short nap until it's time for you to deliver her to Eve."

Dominic looked at Celine. "It's up to you."

Celine tilted her head thoughtfully. "Now, that's rare. I don't remember that I've had that option lately."

He shrugged. "I was worried you might get edgy about Catherine and start to worry when you should be relieved to be with her so that she can fill you in on anything you want to know about Eve." He made a face. "Or anything else that you might be curious about and might not trust me enough to tell you the truth."

"Most of the time I've found you've told me the truth." She turned to Catherine. "But I'll appreciate anything you can tell me. I'm a little starstruck about Eve."

Catherine shook her head. "Don't be. No one is more human or warmer. We'll see you later, Dominic."

"I'll be around." He was heading toward the doors to the parking lot. "I'll just escort you back to your hotel. But I won't get in your way until I pick Celine up in the morning. She goes in alone to talk to Eve, Catherine. She's had some nasty firsthand experience with Jossland, and she's earned the opportunity to warn Eve by herself." He moved ahead of them down the escalator.

"My, my," Catherine murmured. "Our Dominic is being very protective, isn't he? From what he told me about what you did to Jossland, I would have thought he'd have a little more faith in you."

"He's right, I haven't been at my best around him since I

met him." Celine grinned. "But he'll have to adjust. I have to do my part when we go after Caldwell."

Catherine's brows rose. "Do what you wish, but don't feel guilty about trying to keep up with Dominic. He's one tough bastard. So let me get his recommendation over with. I'm sure you must have already realized that he's a powerhouse with his contacts and the influence he can wield if he chooses to. The organization that he and Cameron run is possibly the strongest one that I've ever come across. At times they make the CIA look like amateurs."

"What kind of organization? He told me that those contacts were legal."

"And they are...when he wants them to be. It's a private security company, but their client list includes half the governments in the Western Hemisphere. Dominic and Cameron also delve into everything from high finance to toppling renegade governments when they believe they've found anything that could do damage to life as we know it. That's why they can pull all those strings when no one else can. They don't trust the way our governments are running things, so they make rules of their own on occasion. As far as I know, neither of them has done anything that could be termed criminal, but I've told both of them they should step very carefully and not try to solve every problem on their own."

"And this is what you call a recommendation?" Celine asked.

"I haven't finished. All that power can be mind-boggling, but you had to know about it. But you can also trust Dominic's word and the fact that I'd rather have him in my corner than anyone but Cameron. And I've seen what he can do when he brings in a team to take down a smuggling or poaching gang. It's pretty much a massacre. He used to be in special forces, he's an expert sharpshooter, and he can handle himself in any situation I can think of. I was glad when he told me he was going up against Caldwell. If anyone can bring him down, it will be Alex Dominic."

"I'm glad to hear that," Celine said jerkily. "But it won't stop me from going after Caldwell, too. I couldn't bear it if those bastards managed to walk away after they killed Barnaby."

"Dominic told me about his killing," Catherine said gently. "I'm sorry for your loss."

"I'm sorry, too. He had a wife and children," Celine said bitterly. "And he died because he was my friend." She drew a deep breath. "But if you don't mind, I prefer not to talk about it. It seems as if I can't think about anything else right now. Why don't you tell me instead about Eve Duncan. How long have you known her?"

"Years," Catherine answered. "But I've never seen her happier than she is right now. A few days ago, she was showing me photos of her ward Jane MacGuire's baby…"

LAKE COTTAGE
NEXT DAY, 9:40 A.M.
"It's charming," Celine murmured as they drove down the road from the freeway toward the Lake Cottage. She gazed at the staircase leading up to the covered porch overlooking the deep-blue lake. "It looks like everyone's dream house.

Certainly mine. I grew up on army bases all over the world and my father tried to get the nicest houses possible, but we always knew we'd have to move on soon, so we just planted beautiful flowers in the front yard and left it at that. My dad made sure there were always books and games in the cupboards, and he made time to play them with me."

"Sounds like a great home to me," Dominic said. "And a very decent father."

She nodded. "He was wonderful. It nearly killed me when he died in a terrorist explosion in Kabul. I didn't know what to do without him for a long while. But then I got hold of myself when I realized that the only way I could honor all the love and care he'd given me was to become the person he'd wanted me to be."

"So that's what you did?"

"That's what I'm trying to do," she corrected. "I've got a long way to go. That was the reason I became so angry when Jossland tried to attack me that night. It was difficult enough working two jobs to make ends meet without that asshole getting in my way."

"I can see that."

"Can you?" She was gazing at him curiously. "Perhaps you can. You don't allow anyone to know enough about you to judge. All I know is that you have a hell of a lot of contacts all over the civilized and uncivilized world. And that Catherine Ling believes you're some kind of super warrior, and she's glad that you're going after Caldwell."

"Super warrior?" He grinned. "I'm sure she didn't use those words. She's much too pragmatic, and she's one tough agent herself when the chips are down. We've known each other through a number of very difficult engagements, and she seldom agrees with my solutions."

"Because they're too ruthless?"

"Sometimes. I don't stop until I've completed my objective, and I try to get it any way I can. I'll never be as kind or basically decent as your father, but I do have my own code."

"My father?" she repeated, startled. "I would never compare you with my father."

He chuckled. "Thank God for small miracles." Then his smile faded. "But to reinforce that divine intervention, I'd better make sure that you realize how far apart we are in every way. I was born in the slums of Rome. My father was a gambler, and my mother had the good sense to leave us when I was four. I was on the streets of half a dozen European cities from the time I was nine—at least when I wasn't working in a casino or the nearest bar. The only reason my father kept me with him when he moved to Las Vegas was that he found that I was better at numbers than him. He was grooming me to be a gambler and probably destined to support him. Unfortunately, after a client became irritated when they caught him cheating, he was found in the back room of the casino, very dead. Needless to say, I was not heartbroken. I didn't want to end up in a foster home, so I took off and hit the streets again. I surveyed the possibilities, and they didn't look good. But there was one way that I could see a way to control the world around me. So I ended up lying about my age and joining the army."

"What? Like my father?"

"I assure you, I was nothing like your father. He was evidently an exemplary human being and father. I, on the other hand, was a self-serving sixteen-year-old kid who was willing to take on the whole world to get what I wanted. But while I was doing it, I ran into a good many people whom I admired. I'm very competitive, so I couldn't bear not to study and work until I was better than them at their particular specialties. I regarded my time in the service as a good decision, and I used it to pattern the way I operated when I moved on to other endeavors."

"What endeavors?"

"Now, that would be another tale, and I believe I've told you enough about my troubled childhood to content you for the time being."

And it had been a sad yet fascinating story, she thought. But there had been no hint of self-pity in his words. It had been told with casual acceptance and hard cynicism. What a life he must have had. She found she wanted to hear more about those "endeavors" that had shaped him. "But I haven't heard anything about this so-called code you were telling me about. I'm particularly interested in how it applies to those guards you supposedly put out here to protect Eve Duncan. Were you lying to me?" Her gaze raked the lakefront property. "I don't see any guards."

"There're two on the rear of the boathouse." He pointed at the woods. "One near that pine tree at the edge of the woods." He added, "And there were two on guard right after we left the freeway. As for that code I mentioned, I keep it very simple. I tell the truth to those I know will tell it to me. And I do unto others as I would have them do unto me." He paused. "Naturally, there are exceptions. And I admit that my temper does explode on occasion, and then I say to hell with codes. But I work on it, and it's much rarer now than it used to be."

He'd reached the Lake Cottage, and he parked near the staircase that led up to the covered sunporch. "Here we are." He turned off the engine. "I had Catherine call Eve to introduce you. I would have called her myself, but I wanted you to have a chance to be welcomed by someone you admire and appreciate. She knows that I was behind Fallon and Catherine trying to persuade her to do the death mask. I'd be lucky if impatience is the worst thing she feels toward me at the moment. So I'll wait for you here. Take your time. I hope you get what you want."

"That's very generous of you considering you told me that you don't stop until you get what you want," she said dryly.

He smiled. "And that hasn't changed. If I decide that you'll turn out to be a hazard, I'll just go in another direction. But there's nothing wrong in hoping perhaps we can both get what we want."

She was already climbing the flight of steps leading to the sunporch. "I'm not a hazard, dammit." Then she added over her shoulder, "Though I admit I'm a little nervous right now."

"Don't be nervous," he said. "If she attacks you, I'll come running."

"Don't you dare. This is my battle." She winked and was already knocking on the door. "If you try, I'll knock you down and stomp on you."

The door was opening…She drew a deep breath as she saw the woman standing there smiling at her. "Hello, Eve. You probably don't remember me, but I attended one of your New York seminars. My name is Celine Kelly."

And then Eve smiled warmly and held out her hand. "Catherine already let me know you were coming. But I told her those seminars were such a crush, it was difficult for me to remember any of the students." She pulled Celine into the room and tilted her head as she walked around her, examining every detail of Celine's face and body. "But I can't believe that I didn't remember you. I make my living doing forensic sculptures, and I wouldn't have forgotten you. You're quite incredible." She wrinkled her nose. "It makes me wonder if I'm losing my touch."

"Oh, no," Celine said quickly. "You're absolutely wonderful. There's no one like you. I didn't want to bother you, so I stayed out of your way and just listened and tried to learn."

"You're an artist?"

Celine shook her head. "Not like you. I just dabble when I'm not posing. I'm in med school. I was most interested in how you prepared the Helen mummy before you did your work on her. It must have been fascinating."

Eve nodded. "And breathtaking and terrifying. One of the most exciting assignments I've ever undertaken." She frowned. "But it also led to having to ward off having artists and museums try to talk me into doing other similar projects." She paused. "What I couldn't explain is that there aren't any similar projects. The closest I've come is the death mask that Professor Fallon wanted me to sign on for—but that has far too many questions that couldn't be answered to my satisfaction." She gave a half shrug. "And now you show up out of the blue. I assume they all think I'll be tempted by your spectacular face to use you as a model for the death mask? Just in case they haven't found the genuine mummy." She was shaking her head. "I admit you even look enough like the bust of Nefertiti in the Berlin museum to make that offer very alluring." Her eyes narrowed on Celine's features. "And since you're probably even more beautiful than that queen, I could show the world what this new discovery that Fallon told me about must have looked like when she ruled her world. Do you know how rare it is to have a queen step out of the history pages and have a face right before me that I could use as an exact model? It's a sculptor's dream." She sighed and shook her head reluctantly. "But the answer is still no. I have a life of my own; I don't have to live vicariously just because it's a career challenge. So I'm afraid you've paid me a visit for no good reason, Celine. But good luck to you in the future."

It sounded like a dismissal, but Celine couldn't allow that to happen. Not yet. Not until she said what she'd come to say. "Thank you," she said quietly. "But it seems you've made a mistake about my intentions in coming to see you. I'm surprised, because I know Catherine is your good friend. She probably wanted to be sure I'd be allowed to talk to you myself, since that's why I made this trip from Boston. But I didn't come here to persuade you to make that death mask. I'm sure you could do it splendidly, but I think it's too dangerous. I came to talk you into turning down any opportunity you're given to do that assignment. My friend Barnaby was tortured and murdered because he went after a killer who attacked me on the street last week. I have it from a very reliable source that you and I have both been targeted. And I came here to tell you that you should be very careful. I understand you're married to Joe Quinn, a fine detective. It might not be a bad idea to bring him into the picture." She didn't know what else to say. "Every word I'm telling you is the truth." Her hands were clenching at her sides. "I'll leave now, but just tell me you believe me. And that you'll do what I'm asking."

"I think I do believe you," Eve said slowly. "I've been in trouble too many times before myself not to recognize the truth when I hear it, even when it's packaged in such a bizarre story. But I'm not going to let you go anywhere until I hear the entire tale from the beginning." She turned away. "Sit down on the couch while I put on a pot of coffee. You might have to be here awhile."

———

TWO HOURS AND TEN MINUTES LATER

"Eve wants to talk to you," Celine said curtly as she marched down the flight of steps and stopped beside Dominic's car. "Right now."

Dominic nodded as he got out of the car. "I was wondering why your little chat was taking you so long. I was hoping she wasn't giving you a hard time." His gaze was raking her expression. "Was I being too optimistic? You're looking pretty grim."

"Because I feel as if I've been picked up by a tornado and thrown into the Grand Canyon." Celine turned and was climbing back up toward the sunporch again. "You're damn right she was giving me a hard time. She's a cross between an army drill sergeant and that lieutenant who questioned me at the police precinct. She only softened when she decided you might be partially or fully to blame for everything that's been going on."

He grinned. "So you threw me to the wolves?"

"No, I tried to defend you. It was Joe Quinn who told Eve she should get the full story from you. I asked her to call him and tell him about the threat to her, and she thought it was a good idea." She was already knocking on the door. "I suppose you can guess he didn't like what was going on."

"I can imagine. I expected it would set off fireworks if she decided to bring in Quinn. It was a chance I had to take if I let you come here."

"Let me?" she repeated. "You couldn't have stopped me."

"That's debatable. But we won't discuss—"

Eve threw open the porch door. "You're Alex Dominic?" she demanded. "I have a few questions I need to ask you. And I'm afraid my husband, Joe, has a couple dozen more." She stepped aside and gestured for them to come in. "Celine seemed to think you'd be willing to answer anything I threw at you. Which one of us do you want to try to tackle first?"

"Since Celine compared your tactics to a drill sergeant's, I thought that Quinn might be gentler on my delicate psyche. I've heard many interesting things about him."

"Don't expect any gentleness from Joe at the moment." Eve was already punching in Joe's phone number as she spoke. "I've put you on speaker. I'm sure you won't mind. It seems he's heard quite a few interesting things about you, too."

"I'm certain that's true." He spoke into the phone. "I'm happy to talk to you, Quinn. I was certain we'd get together soon."

"Not soon enough," Joe said. "Believe me."

"I'm afraid he didn't like the idea that you were involving me in your plans," Eve said. "Neither do I."

"But I wasn't the one involving you," Dominic said quietly.

"That was all Caldwell. When I heard that Caldwell had his sights on you, I decided it was better to take control of the situation myself rather than try to hunt you down after he'd arranged for one of his teams to bring you to him. Because that was what would have happened. It's the way he operates. And it seems he wanted this particular plan to go off without a hitch. But I thought if Caldwell found out I might be interfering, it might escalate his actions, so I did arrange protection for you. You both have to agree that was the correct thing to do, right, Quinn?"

"The hell I do," Joe said roughly. "The correct thing would have been for you to come to me and tell me everything so that I could arrange protection for her myself. It's not as if she doesn't have family to stand by her."

"I wouldn't presume to assume any such thing," Dominic said. "You're a force to be reckoned with, Quinn. And I've run into Seth Caleb a few times in the field when I had dealings with MI6. I was so impressed, I offered him our unit's protection if he ever decided he needed it. As I expected, he only laughed at the idea."

Joe muttered a curse. "He might have done more than that if he'd known that you'd stumbled on this nastiness that could possibly affect Eve. You know that Jane MacGuire is our ward and the mother of Caleb's child? He wouldn't like the idea of there being a danger to anyone close to our Jane. He knows how Eve considers Jane her daughter and has since we took her in when she was a little girl." He added grimly, "Caleb would dislike it so much, he might cause you a good bit of trouble."

"There was always that possibility," Dominic said quietly. "Naturally, I researched all the drawbacks when I made the decision. But the stakes were very high, and an entire village had already been wiped out. The longer I waited, the greater the chance that Caldwell would be able to deliver more weapons with greater firepower to Zakira, so they'd be encouraged to attack other villages. I had to weigh the checks and balances. You can't say I've been trying to hide anything from you. I sent Catherine Ling to let you know that there was a problem so that the CIA would be able to take action if they could find an opening. I also assigned some of the best guards in my unit to Eve. You might have heard how good they'd have to be for me to say that, Quinn."

"Yes," Joe said reluctantly. "But you didn't turn the massacre over to the CIA to solve."

"No," Dominic said. "I've learned that stepping into the politics in Africa can be frustrating, so I generally let them know about the crime and then go after the perpetrators myself. That entire area has a lot of potential warring factions and a number of religious and power-hungry dictators who want to take over entire countries. I have quite a bit of experience with most of them, so the territory was assigned to me with orders to keep the peace in any way I could. I have the contacts, and I know the countryside pretty damn well. Besides, I was the one who saw the carnage in that burned-out village. It made me angry as hell. Those villagers were good, peaceful people who didn't deserve what happened to them. I couldn't trust the CIA to be quite as thorough as I would be." He paused. "Is there anything else you'd like to know?"

"Not that I can't find out for myself," Joe said. "And I think you know I'll be having a chat with Scotland Yard?"

"Good luck to you," Dominic said. "However, I think

you'll find they're a little too involved dealing with the local African governments to be effective. If you don't mind, I'll still keep my team in place to protect Eve. My contact with her has probably deepened any threats to her, so I'd prefer to make sure she's still safe even though you insist that you'll take over."

"Why not?" Joe asked. "There's no such thing as being too safe where a murderer like Caldwell is concerned."

"My thought exactly," Dominic said. "And while you're at it, you might arrange to take care of Celine Kelly. I'll still have surveillance on her, but I don't know if I'll be around for the next few weeks. She's extremely emotional at the moment and may be prone to taking unnecessary risks if she's not watched carefully."

"Bullshit!" From across the room Celine spoke for the first time. "Go to hell, Dominic. If you want to opt out of helping me find those bastards, that's up to you. But don't try to push me on someone else."

"You see what I mean?" Dominic sighed. "One can't blame her, but let your conscience be your guide, Quinn."

"I will," Joe said grimly. "And that also goes for any future action toward you, Dominic."

"Then that seems a good exit line for me," Dominic said. "It's been very good talking to you. Take care. When I wrap this up, I'll let you know." He pressed DISCONNECT and was heading for the door. "I'll see you later, Celine."

Joe pressed his own DISCONNECT button after he heard the door slam behind Dominic. "Arrogant son of a bitch."

"But you took him up on that offer to keep his men on guard here," Eve said. "So you must respect him."

"When he's not trying to run the world," Joe said sourly.

"Yes, he's smart as a whip and an expert at tracking down the assholes and bringing them to their knees. And I'd bargain with the devil himself if I thought it made it safer for you. But it doesn't mean I should let him run the show."

"Well, you've clearly made up your mind," Celine said as she got to her feet. "I don't believe you need me for anything more, Eve. I'm sorry that I had to be the one to give you such an upsetting day." She was heading for the door. "It was a privilege to meet you even under circumstances like this."

"None of this madness was your fault," Eve said gently. "You're also a victim. Where are you going? Sit down and we'll talk about how we can make sense of all this."

Celine shook her head as she opened the door. "Nothing we can say would make sense of what happened to me, or my friend Barnaby, or his family. I'm just glad that those monsters didn't get their hands on you." She raised her voice to make sure that Joe could hear her on the phone. "Take good care of her, Joe. You were right to take the offer Dominic made you. Because I think that he may be the only one who can stop all this. He's not only smart...he knows things about Caldwell and his thugs. We might be able to get him that way." She paused. "And I'm like you, Joe. I'd bargain with the devil himself if he could give me what I have to have."

The door closed behind her.

CHAPTER

8

Celine ran down the flight of stairs, but Dominic was already out of the car and opening the passenger door for her by the time she reached the bottom. "I wasn't sure you'd still be here," she said as she ducked into the seat. "You were so eager to get rid of me when you were talking to Joe Quinn, I thought you might take the opportunity to ditch me."

"I wouldn't be that rude," he said as he got into the driver's seat and started the engine. "Though I won't promise not to find a way to rid myself of you if the going gets rough. You're too damn determined. I could see you hitchhiking across the country and working your way across the Atlantic on a cruise ship."

"I hadn't thought about the cruise ship." Celine smiled. "I know enough languages that there's a good chance a cruise line would hire me. Maybe I should thank you for bringing it up."

"Please don't, because I meant it when I said I'll get rid of you if I have to. According to the reports I've been getting from Rashid, this is shaping up to be a very ugly struggle, and you shouldn't be anywhere near it."

"And yet you were thinking about using me as bait before

this," Celine said quietly. "Because after you saw that burned-out village, you wanted to stop it from happening again. What is it you said to Joe? Peace at any cost? Well, it's not your choice any longer. I have my own dead to revenge. So you're not just taking me along for the ride. We'll get a plan together and find a way to take Jossland and Caldwell down."

He slowly shook his head. "You're impossible, and you're obviously going to cause me a great deal of trouble."

"You sound almost resigned." Her gaze was searching his expression. "Does that mean I won't have to get a job on a cruise ship?"

"It doesn't mean I've changed my mind. We'll see how it goes. I rather like the idea about you just going along for the ride." He was suddenly smiling. "Because I can imagine what a hell of a ride it would be for both of us."

For a moment she couldn't look away from him. Then she finally jerked her gaze away and looked straight ahead. "Then are you going to tell me what that report said you received from Rashid?"

"I wouldn't think of keeping you in the dark. But we have plenty of time to go into details once we board the jet to my place in Africa. Rashid is going to meet us at the airport there. Why don't you sit back and get a little rest? You've had to go through hours of the third degree from Eve and Joe Quinn. It's been a rough day for you."

"No, it hasn't. Eve was very kind and helpful toward me before I left. It's not as if she could react any other way after what I told her."

"So you forgive her for being a drill sergeant?"

"I did say that, didn't I?" She made a wry face as she looked back at the Lake Cottage over her shoulder. "She was tough and smart and just what I thought she'd be. I'm glad I came here, Dominic. I had to be sure that she knew everything that was happening. Between the guards you sent and Joe, she'll be safe now…"

———————

"I'm worried about her, Joe," Eve said into the phone as the taillights of Dominic's car were lost to view. She dropped down on the couch on the sunporch. "It took a lot of courage for her to come here just to make certain I'd be safe. Someone else might have just gone into hiding after all that's happened to her. It's all crazy, Joe. I had to come out here on the porch to make sure that Dominic had given her a ride and was going to take care of her. I'm still not sure he will. He obviously didn't want to be bothered by her."

"But he's not reckless," Joe said, "or he wouldn't have tried to rope me into watching out for her. He just wants to get the job done, and now he has to keep that woman alive while he's doing it. We've got to hope he'll do it at top speed. There's a good chance. I called Caleb, and he said Dominic is one of the best agents he's ever run across." He paused. "Though after I hang up from talking to you I'm going to call Scotland Yard and see if they've got any more info on the massacre in Karimu and see if the authorities have traced it to Zakira as Dominic told us."

"Of course you are," Eve said. "That goes without saying, just as you'll verify the qualifications of exactly who is guarding this house. Right?"

"It's the sensible thing to do," Joe said. "I trust Dominic's men, but we can't be too careful."

"I agree," Eve said. "People I love will be staying here soon. When will I get to see you and Michael?"

"Michael has two more finals, and I'll be able to take him out of school on Wednesday. Three days and we'll be on a plane heading for Atlanta."

"Hallelujah!"

"And Jane may be there before us. She can't wait to show off Cira."

"I can't wait to see her! I'll be surprised if Michael doesn't skip school and tag along with them. The last time I talked to him, he was being very protective about her."

"Yes, he is. But you know there's no one more disciplined than Michael. I think I can talk him into staying at school another day and coming with me." He paused. "I'm the one who's having trouble with discipline at the moment. I want to come running to you. And all this business with Dominic isn't making it any easier."

"I know. Me too," Eve said. "But keep busy and the time will pass like lightning...I hope. I love you. I'll see you soon, Joe..."

———

"I've never ridden in a plane like this." Celine settled more comfortably in the passenger seat of the Gulfstream. "Though a lot of times my father would arrange to get me a lift on one of the Air Force jets when I had to go back and forth to school.

Nothing near this luxurious. But then you told me about all your contacts. Is that where you got this beauty?"

"No, though our organization does have donors that contribute equipment to our work. We have several planes that we use on different jobs. But this particular plane I acquired on my own." He grinned. "I won it in a poker game. I do a good deal of traveling, and I like to move with speed and comfort."

Her hand stroked the suede material of the armchair. "I'd say you probably manage to do that. What's our flight plan?"

"I'm not sure. Sometimes it changes midflight. But our first stop will be Sardwa airport in Africa. That's about thirty miles from Bon Jaka, my estate. I figured it would be a good place for meetings, and I'd be able to check in with my farm manager about the workers and what they might know about what happened at Karimu village. Most news moves by word of mouth in these country areas."

"I would have thought you'd check in with your workers as soon as you found out about the massacre."

"There was too much to do. I was heading for Morocco almost immediately."

"Ah yes, your contact who had both my name and Eve's."

He nodded. "I picked up Caldwell as a connection in the village and had to follow up."

"You said that you were virtually in charge of this area with your agency. You must be very familiar with all of the villages and mountains?"

"I do a lot of hiking in the mountains and talking to the chiefs." He grinned and nodded to a pile of books and maps on a shelf beside the galley. "And I read a lot. I have quite a few trails memorized just from locating them on the maps. It's beautiful country, but it's not easy to get around in. The mountain and lower ravines are networked with trails where it's a maze of jungles and caves along with quite a few waterfalls." He grimaced. "If you're not careful you'll lose your way and we'll have to send out the bloodhounds. I recommend you keep the maps close to you if you decide you need to know a bit more about the surroundings once you reach Bon Jaka."

"I'll keep that in mind."

"Or you can just ask me. You won't find me at all secretive."

"Well, I can't say you've been entirely open and above board on all occasions," she said dryly.

"Maybe I'm trying to change my wicked ways to please you?"

"Somehow I doubt that. When are we going to take off?"

"When I have a final decision from you." He handed her a cup of coffee. "I'm still not happy about your decision. I don't want any regrets."

She straightened in the seat. "You have a final decision. I thought we'd already said what we had to say."

"Not quite," Dominic said. "I told you almost everything about what you might have to face. I even showed you photos of Caldwell and Jossland so you could prepare yourself."

"Yes, you did. That didn't change anything."

"But I didn't tell you quite everything. You'd already gone through a hell of a lot, and I thought it might not be necessary. But I won't let you go with me if you don't know every single thing." He reached into his wallet and brought out a stack of photos. "These are photos of the massacre at Karimu. I sent copies to Catherine so that she could show them to her bosses at the CIA. I kept my own copies to help me remember how much I want to kill Caldwell, who supplied the weapons, drugs, and firepower to the natives who attacked that village." He set the stack in front of Celine. "Be sure you examine every one. Don't miss the women and the kids and the babies. Because that's what you might see if you decide to come with me tonight."

She stared at him in horror and then slowly started to go through the photos. She was pale, and every now and then she flinched as she saw a particularly terrible photo. But she kept going until there were no more photos for her to see. Then she sat back in the chair and took a deep breath. "That was… hideous." Her voice was trembling. "The babies were the worst. Their whole life in front of them and then to be murdered like that…" She closed her eyes for an instant. And then she shuddered. "What am I saying? There is no worst. It's all terrible and senseless." Her eyes opened, swimming with unshed tears. "And I just saw the photos. What must it have been like for you to be there to see them lying there and have to—"

"Shut up." He was suddenly in front of her and pulling her up into his arms and holding her. His voice was hoarse. "This isn't how you're supposed to react when someone deliberately puts you through hell, Celine. Now tell me you don't want to go through anything like that again and particularly not with me, so that I'd have to see it. Let me send you somewhere I can keep you safe."

"But those people in that village weren't safe. Barnaby wasn't safe, and who knows who those bastards will zero in on next. I have to stop it." She pushed him away. "We have to stop it. Did you really think that showing me those nightmare

123

pictures would keep me away? They killed my friend, they killed all those people in that village. And it made you so angry, you tried to hurt me so I wouldn't be another victim. Why do you think I'm studying to try to save lives if I could just walk away after seeing what happened in Karimu? I realize what you're trying to do—mold the situation to suit yourself." Her eyes were suddenly glittering in her taut face. "But maybe you're not as ruthless or tough as everyone thinks, because what you did might have hurt you as much as it did me."

"There's that possibility." He reached out and cupped her face in his two hands and gazed down into it. "I admit I took a chance on manipulating you because I wanted the end result so badly. I didn't expect you to be able to strike back with such...anger. It startled me."

"I wasn't striking back at you. I was just expressing the very real anger that was boiling inside me. I imagine that could translate to attack in your world." She stepped back away from him again. "But I believe that I passed your rather painful test, didn't I?"

"If I can't talk you out of being reasonable about it." He took another step back. "Yes, you managed to pull the rug out from under me." He turned and headed for the cockpit. "So fasten your seat belt in about another five minutes, when we'll be taking off. You might get yourself a fresh cup of coffee first. The one I gave you before I tossed those damn photos at you has to be stone-cold."

"I'll do that," Celine said as she turned toward the galley. "I'm feeling a little chilly myself at the moment."

"I wonder why," Dominic said grimly. "When I've been such a kind and considerate host."

"You did what you thought you had to do," she said quietly. "I realize I'm not the only person who feels they have a job to do and is trying to do it with the least collateral damage."

He looked back over his shoulder. "You're being very generous."

"I expect a return in kind," she said. "I know I'm going to need you when we start to hunt for Caldwell and Jossland. I'd already started to use you when I asked you to take me to Eve Duncan. I'm sure it will increase when we reach Sardwa airport in Africa. I want you to be willing to give that help and not just look for a way to get rid of me. Will you do it?"

He nodded curtly. "I'll do it. I had no more questions from the time I realized that you'd taken away my best weapon and turned it against me. Anything else?"

"Only one thing. Will you be my friend, Dominic? There have been moments since we came together that I felt as if you were. I might need that."

"Friends?" He stared at her for a long moment. "That might be more difficult to promise. I think you realize why. Suppose I just promise to try very hard, Celine." He turned and disappeared into the cockpit.

Yes, she knew why friendship would be difficult. That moment when he had held her face in his hands and she'd looked into his eyes, she had felt her breath leave her body and her breasts swell. She wanted him to touch her. Sex might be heady and filled with dangerous sensuality with Dominic. Friendship would be safer. Friendship would be best.

Work toward it. Don't let those random moments of intense desire overtake her. Think of the work to be done in catching Jossland and Caldwell. Keep busy. She picked up the pile of

125

maps and books Dominic had given her and settled down in her seat. By the time she reached the African territories Dominic knew so well, she had to be prepared.

She unfolded the first map on the top of the pile.

Keep busy…

CHAPTER

9

SARDWA AIRPORT, AFRICA

I was expecting something a bit cozier," Celine said as she jumped out on the tarmac and glanced around at the modern runways and multiple hangars. "I saw at least three jets as we taxied down that runway." She grinned. "What? No control tower?"

"Of course there is." Dominic gestured at the tall stone building on the edge of the east runway. "It's fully equipped, but I don't have personnel manning it unless it becomes necessary. I prefer that from the air, the airport appears understated. But there are three men who have been fully trained to do the job if called on." He took her arm and led her toward the parking lot. "Rashid will be picking us up and taking us to Bon Jaka. He got in yesterday and has been doing the preliminary questioning of the workers." He smiled. "I hope you're hungry, because I also told him to tell Kontara to make us one of her special meals. You're in for a real treat."

"Kontara?"

"She's the cook who helps me keep the other workers happy

so they won't wander away to the big city." They had reached the jeep, where Sam Rashid was leaning on the fender. "Ask Rashid. He's a big fan. Tell her about Kontara, Rashid."

He smiled. "Magnifique. She makes the cuisine at the Ritz taste like it came from a fast-food joint. She's taken a lot of the local delicacies and made them her own. She's an amazing chef."

Dominic opened the car door for Celine. "Prepare to be dazzled and a little intimidated. But I think you'll like her. She reminds me a little of you."

Rashid chuckled. "I get that." He started the car. "Or at least I remember it from that miserable first day you inflicted on me."

"You deserved it," Celine said. "You shouldn't work for someone who would treat a strange woman like that."

"You weren't at all strange. You were just pure hell."

"Did you get the workers' questioning done?" Dominic asked.

Rashid nodded. "Jason, your overseer, helped a lot. There were a few good leads. But I think you should talk to Kontara."

"Why?"

He shrugged. "She wouldn't talk to me. She just said she wouldn't talk to anyone but you."

Dominic nodded. "Then she must have a good reason if she knew you were questioning everyone else. Take Celine inside and get her settled while I see what Kontara needs."

They were drawing up to a twelve-foot iron fence, and Rashid got out to open it. "Whatever you say. Celine?"

But Celine was gazing at the massive white columned house beyond the gates. "It looks very grand. It reminds me of that old classic movie *Gone with the Wind*. Did you build it to resemble it?"

"Not guilty," Dominic said. "I actually bought the place from a Dutch planter who was returning to Amsterdam because I needed a permanent base in this area. He inherited it from his grandfather. It's older than it looks. Sometimes I like the feeling of age and substance. Probably because I never had either when I was growing up."

"Well, it's lovely anyway." She was about to get out of the vehicle when she stopped and turned to face Dominic. "All of this questioning has to do with Caldwell, doesn't it?"

"Yes," he said warily. "From now on, everything we talk about is probably going to have to do with Caldwell."

"Then may I go with you when you talk to this Kontara?"

He grimaced. "So this is where it starts?"

She nodded jerkily. "This is where it starts."

He took her hand and drew her toward a smaller gate a few yards away. "Then come and meet her. She has her own quarters at the back of the main building of the estate. It was the only thing she asked when she came to work for me. But don't be surprised if she's rude to you. She hasn't had a great life. One of my workers found her in the jungle unconscious a while back. She'd been brutally beaten and raped, and we weren't sure that she'd live. She bounced back, but she wouldn't tell us her name or who had done that to her. She said we could call her Kontara. She speaks English, French, and several African dialects. The moment she was able to get on her feet, she started to take over the kitchen and boss everyone around."

"Including you?"

"We came to an understanding. I thought that anyone who

had been through the hell she had should get a say in her own future."

"But evidently her life has been better since she met you?"

"One could argue that it's our lives that have been better. But then you haven't tried one of her gourmet dishes." He was knocking on the door. "I'll let you judge."

The door swung open and a tall, red-haired woman was scowling at Dominic. She was in her late twenties or early thirties with a voluptuous body and olive skin; she wore her red hair in a thick single braid that fell down over her breasts. Her huge, dark eyes were glaring at Dominic. "It's about time you came. I needed you. I have a problem." She glanced at Celine. "Who is this? Another one of your damn rescues? Just look at her. She's not going to be anything but trouble. And I told Rashid I didn't want to talk to anyone but you."

"But it seems Celine wants to hear what you have to say and she's earned the right, so be polite, Kontara. Now tell me what the problem is."

She hesitated. "Rashid was asking all the workers if they knew which villagers were responsible for the attack on Karimu." She paused. "I know who they were but I can't tell anyone. I won't tell anyone."

"Then we may have a difficulty," Dominic said. "Because I have to know, Kontara."

"No difficulty," she said impatiently. "Because you're not anyone. I trust you. You saved my life. You're just Dominic." She paused and then said in a rush, "The massacre was probably done by the Shafira tribe. It's a village high in the mountains, and the people have been on the verge of war with the Karimu for years. The Karimu had rich grasslands that support herds of cattle, and the high priest of Shafira must have gotten tired of just toying with them and decided to send his army to take over their village."

"It was destroyed," Celine said bitterly. "And so were all the men, women, and children who lived there. It was a bloodbath."

"Of course," Kontara said. "I told you that the priest regarded them as enemies. I knew it was going to happen someday. He was only waiting for the right time and place after he took over the gold mines in the lower valley. Then he knew he could have anything he wanted if he dangled enough gold in front of the right people."

"Slow down," Dominic said. "Give me names. Though I'm beginning to guess a few of them. The name of the high priest wouldn't be Masini Zakira?"

She nodded. "Zakira."

"And who were the right people he was dangling that gold in front of?"

"The human traffickers who sold women like me to the highest bidders. I was a dancer in a nightclub before the traffickers sold me and at least sixty-five other women to Zakira to be his concubines. He'd give us to workmen, merchants, soldiers, anyone he wanted to reward or bribe. He was also building an army by recruiting young men and boys from his village, and he found us useful to reward them if they pleased him." Her lips twisted. "Sometimes he'd have festivals where they made us perform unspeakable sex acts for hours on end. And every time I'd try to run away, they'd hunt me down and bring me back and beat me. But they were careful not to damage me too badly." She added bitterly, "After all, I was valuable property. Otherwise, they would have probably killed me. But I kept on running away, and I got to know the trails and caves where I could hide. One day I found a cave where I hid for almost a week and then set out again. I don't know how long I ran, but I must have gotten far enough away so that I was near this property, and one of your workmen found me." Her lips tightened. "But even then, I knew someone would come after me if they knew I was here. Because Zakira liked to make examples, and he would have paid someone to bring me back to him." She met his gaze. "And you were kind to me. I didn't want to cause you trouble."

"Dear God," Celine murmured. "It's a wonder you managed to live through that horror."

"Of course I lived through it," Kontara said fiercely. "Do you think I'd let those beasts get the best of me? There was no way I wouldn't escape. I only wish I'd found a way to send them straight to hell."

Dominic chuckled. "There you are. Plain as day. Rashid was right. You can see why she reminds him of you." He turned back to Kontara. "She didn't mean to insult you. We're all in complete agreement regarding Zakira. And when you get to know Celine a little better, she may even be able to give you a few lessons on how to send them to those lower regions. I'm sure she's not nearly your equal as a cook, but she's very talented at what she does." He was reaching for his phone. "But since you had an up-close-and-personal experience with some of the men in Zakira's camp, would you look at these photos and tell me if they're familiar?"

She took the phone and checked out the photos. "The man with gray hair is Caldwell. Zakira sent me to him quite a few times. He wanted to please him. They had some sort of deal going on. The other man is Jossland. He works for Caldwell." She shuddered. "He and Caldwell both like to cause pain, but Jossland almost killed one of the women he was sent. Caldwell had to apologize to Zakira."

"What kind of deal with Caldwell?" Dominic asked.

"Weapons and drugs for gold," she said absently as she turned to look at Celine. "What could you teach me that I don't already know?"

She smiled. "Nothing that I wouldn't be happy to show you. I did have a recent experience with Jossland. I believe I broke his nose. Perhaps we could come to an arrangement."

"But in the meantime, I've been promising Celine that she could try out some of your fantastic cooking," Dominic said. "Would you oblige?"

"A broken nose..." Kontara repeated thoughtfully. Then she slowly nodded. "Yes, I think I'll definitely oblige, Dominic."

She closed the door behind her and headed for the gate. "Let's go around to the kitchen. I'll let you talk to me while I make preparations. I want to ask you a few questions..."

"Probably more than a few," Dominic murmured in Celine's ear as they followed her through the gate toward the front of the mansion. "I have a number of questions for her myself, and I'd appreciate it if you'd let me have my turn first. Your discussion may be a little more complicated and drawn out. She appears to need a good deal of reassurance after all those memories that came flooding back."

"I can see why," Celine said grimly. "She must have felt terribly helpless most of that time. I don't think I could have stood to go through that. From the time I was a child, my father saw that I was able to take care of myself in every way possible. There's no question that I would do anything I could to help Kontara."

"I didn't have the slightest doubt that you would. Just remember that she's a woman who wouldn't hesitate to put down an opponent permanently if you give her a weapon. She must have an enormous amount of stored-up rage brewing within her."

"You're warning me?" Celine shook her head. "That's another thing my father taught me. Never hesitate to go all the way if you see an enemy is heading in that direction. You just have to decide how far they intend to go and then adjust."

He chuckled. "My admiration for your father continues to increase with every bit of wisdom you unfold for me." They had reached the large scullery kitchen, and he pushed her gently down into a chair at the table. "Stay here and let me have my little chat with Kontara and then I'll leave the two of you alone to come to terms. Okay?"

"Not really. She's upset and I think you should let her have time to recover before you start interrogating her."

He ruefully shook his head. "And now you're tucking her under your wing to protect her from me? She's managed to survive working here for months with no permanent damage so far."

"How do we know that?"

He chuckled. "Ask her." He turned and headed across the kitchen toward the sink where Kontara was standing washing vegetables.

"I figure I have at least ten minutes before our friend Celine comes over here and interrupts us because she's afraid I might be browbeating you," he said. "Though I tried to tell her that you've survived me very well during the time you've been here at the estate. Isn't that true?"

"You've been kind." She turned and stared him in the eyes. "Even when you were angry with me because I wouldn't answer any of your questions after I regained consciousness. You still did nothing to me to force me to talk. It took me a while to realize that you weren't like those men I'd become accustomed to at Shafira village. Even after I began to trust you, I was afraid for anyone to know where I'd come from in case they came after me again."

Dominic nodded. "But when you heard Rashid asking questions about the massacre at Karimu, you realized that those bastards might be getting too close and you needed to know where you stood with me?" he said quietly. "Where you stand is a place of safety. I would never turn you over to that priest or his gunrunning friends who tore that village and its people apart." He paused. "But I might want you to help me get rid of all of them and find a way to release the other women, who you say have suffered as much as you did under Zakira."

"How?" she asked warily.

"I've had teams of trackers trying to locate both the gold-fields and Zakira's village stronghold. But from what they've told me, that mountain country is like a giant maze. They couldn't locate either one. But you said you escaped many times. Could you find your way back to that village?"

"I don't know. It's true, that country is worse than any maze. Even Zakira's guards who went searching for me had trouble finding me and bringing me back to the village. That's why they were so angry and the punishment was so severe," she whispered. "I remembered some paths and a cave or two… Maybe I could find it again. But I swore I'd never go back to that nightmare."

"Even if it means destroying the nightmare for all those other people at Shafira? Even if it means preventing Zakira from turning Caldwell loose on other villages?"

"I don't know if I could find it again." She shuddered. "I feel sick just thinking about it."

"I'm not going to push you right now. As far as I know there's no urgency at the moment," Dominic said quietly. "I just want you to consider whether it's possible, and if you'd be willing to lead a team back up to the mountains to save all those lives. If I promise to keep you absolutely safe, will you do that for me?"

"I'll think about it," she said slowly. "No promises." She suddenly looked across the room at Celine. "Why is she here? You're not thinking of taking her up to those mountains? Zakira would love to get his hands on her. The pretty ones are always more valuable to him to barter. And she's more than pretty…He could get anything he wanted for her."

Dominic grimaced. "I may not have a choice. She's very stubborn, and she lost someone because of what's going on in those mountains. She wants them punished." He paused. "And she doesn't have to think about it."

"She's the one who will probably be punished," Kontara said harshly. "Don't let her go near them!"

"You're perfectly free to tell her that," Dominic said. "She wants to talk to you anyway. I'm sure she wants to set up her lesson plan to help you become a deadly scourge to anyone who tries to hurt you."

"Dominic, listen to me," Kontara said fiercely, "I repeat. Don't let her go near them."

"I'll let you get on with preparing your meal. You've had such great reviews from Rashid and me that Celine can't wait to try it." He was moving toward the door. "And Kontara… Don't worry."

CHAPTER

10

Hi, Dad!" Michael ran out of the main testing hall and gave Joe a quick hug. "You're right on time. I just finished my last final. I'll run back to the residence hall and get my computer and suitcase. Are Jane and Caleb already at the airport?"

"You bet they are," Joe said. "Jane called me while I was on the way here and told me that I should get you to Caleb's plane as quick as I could. She needs you to distract Cira while she finishes that portrait she's doing to give to Eve when we get to the Lake Cottage. She said Caleb's busy filing the flight plan, and the baby is so restless she won't stay still."

"But Cira's okay?" Michael frowned over his shoulder as he reached the steps of the residence. "They're both okay?"

"Fine as can be. Cira may be a little too energetic for Jane at the moment. You seem to be the only one who's able to keep that little girl occupied for any length of time."

"It's because I'm her big brother." Michael grinned mischievously. "Maybe she knows that I've been through all the

139

IRIS JOHANSEN

things she's going through now, so I can give her tips on how to handle all of them."

His dad gave a mock groan. "That's all we need—two of you to contend with."

Michael's grin faded. "I told Mom that I thought Cira was worried about something. Maybe about Jane. But you said Jane is fine."

"And she is," Joe said. "Now stop borrowing trouble. If there's any problem, we'll manage it. Enjoy this vacation, and we'll see if we can't talk your mom into coming back with us when it's over. I'm tired of being without her, aren't you?"

"Yeah," Michael said gruffly. "Nothing's quite the same. I know what you're doing is important, but she's…Mom. We need to be close so that we can take care of her."

"My thoughts exactly," Joe said. "Though we both are going to have a tough time convincing your mom she needs taking care of. But we'll worry about that later now that we're on the same page. Go pick up your computer and other belongings. I'll pull the car around in front so that I can pick you up. Let's get to the airport so Cira won't drive Jane crazy."

"I'll be right out." Michael took the stone steps two at a time and then disappeared through the tall front doors of the residence hall.

Joe pulled the car over into a parking spot and turned off the engine. The lot was mostly empty, and the usual number of students weren't sitting outside on the steps studying and chattering. They were all probably going home for school break, like Michael. It was a fine school, and Michael had made the most of his time here. It would be good if he could continue to attend, but if that wasn't in the cards then he would

140

adjust as he always did and come out on top. Because that was Michael.

Joe leaned back in his seat and started to wait.

Ten minutes passed.

Fifteen minutes.

Something might be wrong. Michael was super efficient. He would have had his bags packed and ready to grab when he ran back from the testing hall.

Another five minutes passed.

No Michael.

Joe was out of the car and running up the entrance steps and down the hall toward Michael's dorm room. "Michael!" He flung open the door. Michael's neatly packed suitcases were lying tossed on the bed.

No computer case.

But there was something else…

Just inside the bathroom door…

Blood!

———

"Caleb? It's Joe. Something's happened. I need you to come out to Michael's school right away. Will you do it?"

"Of course I'll do it," Caleb said. "Why wouldn't I? But what the hell's wrong? We've been waiting for you and Michael. Jane just asked about you again. Is Michael having trouble getting out of school? You said he had to finish his last final."

"And he finished it," Joe said hoarsely. "Then he ran back to his quarters to get his computer and suitcases. But that was over half an hour ago, and when I went to pick him up, he'd disappeared."

"Is this some kind of joke?" Caleb was swearing softly beneath his breath. "It's not funny. What am I supposed to tell Jane? She's nuts about the kid."

"Do you think I don't know that? No, it's not a joke." He paused. "There was blood, Caleb. Not much. Just a thin rivulet on the floor in the bathroom. But how am I supposed to tell Eve that our son is missing when I saw that damn blood?" He took a harsh breath. "But I don't have time to talk to you any longer. I've just called security and they're forming a group to see if we can locate Michael on campus. Before they get here, I need to search Michael's room to see what I can find. Though I don't have much hope. We both know Michael isn't the kind of kid to just decide to run away on a jaunt with one of his buddies when we had plans. Call me when you get here. I hope to God I've found him by then. I'm not going to call Eve until I have something definite to tell her."

He cut the connection.

He looked around the room. *Search. Clear your head and see if there's any hint of what could have happened to Michael in the short time that he was here before he got whisked away.* Joe had no doubt that was what had happened. He trusted Michael would not have left this building on his own. And that meant Michael had been taken for a reason—and one that almost certainly had to do with the fact that he was Joe and Eve's son. Joe was involved in the distribution of a lifesaving medical miracle that was often targeted by criminals. Eve was even now being protected because of her status as a premier forensic sculptor. Hell, even Caleb and Jane might be targets, because of all the enemies Caleb had gained as a top MI6 agent. Okay. No doubt that it had been a crime. Now he had to try to forget that it had been Michael who was the victim. Smother the rage and the panic. Treat it as if a stranger had been taken. Find out why and when.

Find a motive and a clue. He blocked out everything but the purpose that he had to cling to at all costs. He started to carefully, methodically, go through Michael's things to find that clue.

———

Joe received a call from Caleb forty-five minutes later when Caleb's helicopter landed on the heliport by the executive offices of the administration building. "We're here," he said curtly. "Any sign of Michael?"

"Not a word. We're still searching. We're in the hill country on the other side of the lake. I called Jessup with Scotland Yard, and he's on his way with a team. Did you tell Jane?"

"Of course he did," Jane answered for herself. "Do you think I'd let him come without me? It's Michael, for God's sake. I put Cira in her chair and brought her with us," she said shakily. "I think she knows something's very wrong. She keeps holding my hand and won't let it go. And she keeps calling for Mikey." She swallowed, hard. "I know I won't be able to go on the hunt with you. But give me something else to do. Anything, Joe."

"Be careful what you wish for," Joe said. "I haven't told Eve yet. But there's no way I'd ask that of you."

"You wouldn't have to ask. We all have to do our part. It

might be easier for Eve if I tell her when she can see Cira at the same time." She shook her head. "No, nothing can make it easier. But we can share it." She turned to Caleb and gave him a quick kiss. "I'll see you later. Now go find Michael." She got out of the helicopter and took Cira toward the administration building. "Be sure to call me when you find out anything."

He didn't answer as he headed off the tarmac in the direction of the lake.

———

"No sign of him," Joe said curtly as he came to meet Caleb coming down the hill. "We found two farmers who've been here most of the day, but they didn't notice anything unusual. One of them thought he'd heard a helicopter about the time Michael disappeared. But he didn't see anyone or anything near here."

Caleb frowned. "But when I flew over this lake and fields, I was low enough to scan the entire area. There were quite a few places where a helicopter could have landed and not been seen from the school. Probably the most likely place would be on that field on the far side of the lake. Have you checked it yet?"

"Not yet." He gestured to the security team and the student volunteers and then started off at a fast trot toward the heather field Caleb had indicated. "But we will now. Cross your fingers..."

Caleb didn't answer. He'd already streaked past Joe into the field, brushing aside the heather to examine the ground. "Signs of a landing," he called out. "Check out the entire area."

Joe was already carefully making his way through the heather. He waved the security teams aside as he carefully examined the ground for clues. "Keep them away until we can get a closer look."

Joe and Caleb each took a separate section of the field and moved through it carefully, stopping now and then to examine their entire surroundings.

But it was Joe who caught sight of the gleam of metal that was lodged half beneath a rock on the side of the hill. Then he was digging frantically for it. Seconds later he freed the computer, which had MQ engraved on the cover. "Michael's computer," he muttered as Caleb ran toward him. "But it wasn't Michael who buried it here. Whoever did it didn't want it to be found too quickly. They didn't want it to be noticed until they'd gotten safely away from this area." His hands were shaking as he opened the lid of the computer. "But the bastards wanted to be sure we got the message loud and clear." Then he froze as he read the first line scrawled on the computer screen. "Only this isn't addressed to me. The son of a bitch is trying to leave me out of it." His fingers bit into the laptop as his gaze flew over the message. "He's using Michael to get to Eve." He closed his eyes as the rage swept over him. "I'm going to kill the asshole."

"Who is it?" Caleb asked. "May I read it? And may I help you rid the world of him in the most painful way possible?"

"It's Caldwell," Joe said "And he starts the message, 'Hello, Eve Duncan. How wonderful we can be together at last. I'm enjoying your son's company, but he's really no substitution.'" Joe looked up and met Caleb's eyes. "I'll let you read the rest later. But right now I've got to go over this with Eve and try to keep her sane and away from doing something crazy to get him back. That's not going to be easy. As for letting you help me get rid of him, I reserve that pleasure. But I might call on you if the situation changes. At the moment, you can thank those searchers for me and then go back to Jane and give her the bad news."

"She'll want to go to Eve right away and help her get through this," Caleb said. "And that's not a bad idea."

"Let me talk to Eve first. She may not be able to make any rational decisions about what she wants until she gets over the first shock." He paused. "And Caldwell had a reason for taking Michael. We may have to negotiate."

"Ransom?"

"He had a reason," Joe repeated. "I've already told you how you can help." He was moving deeper into the banks of heather and dialing Eve. "Let me get back to you, Caleb. In the end, you know all the decisions have to be made by Eve and me…"

"I know. I know." Caleb was frowning as he turned away and headed back toward the administration building. "But don't close us out. Remember, we love Michael, too. Let us know as soon as you need backup."

Yes, everyone cared about Michael, Joe thought. From the moment of his birth, he had reached out and touched all of them with his warmth and special presence. But no one more than himself and Eve. And now he had to tell Eve that their son had been taken and might be in deadly danger. The pain twisted inside him at the thought.

"Joe?" Eve was on the line. "I've been trying to call you. Have you reached the Atlanta airport yet?"

"Not yet." Dear God, how he hated to hurt her. "Something has happened that I have to tell you about..."

———

"Gone?" Eve repeated dazedly. "Michael's gone? But he can't be gone. You all were coming here. I was so happy, I was almost giddy. And he was with you, Joe. He's always safe when he's with you."

"Not this time," Joe said huskily. "I failed you. I failed him. I was waiting right outside the residence hall and Caldwell and his men managed to go in the back emergency exit and bring him out that way."

"You said it was Caldwell?" She was trying to think through a terrible, painful fog.

"Yes, and he left a message for us. Caldwell had a helicopter he landed on the lake side of the hill, and I found the message on Michael's computer. I'm emailing the letter to you. He made it very clear that his message and orders are aimed at you. He obviously thought going after you directly was too risky with all the guards camping out at the Lake Cottage. So he settled for Michael, whom he must have considered easy pickings. An eleven-year-old kid that you love with your entire being. Naturally, you'd do anything that he wanted to keep Michael from being hurt or killed."

She was already reading the email Joe had sent. It wasn't long, but it could not have been more clear.

Hello, Eve Duncan. How wonderful we
can be together at last. I'm enjoying your

son's company, but he's really no substitute. It was really quite rude of you to
refuse to give me that death mask that
I requested you make. You're such an
artist. It would have been such a little thing
for you, and it meant quite a bit to me.
You've put me in an uncomfortable position, and I really must insist you change
your mind. Otherwise, I'll have to demonstrate to your son how uncomfortable I can
make him. It would be a shame because
I have employees who are exceptional at
that skill. I permitted my friend Jossland
to show the Boston police how good. I'd
hate to have to put your child through
that agony. Children are so fragile, aren't
they? So I will assume that you will have
a change of heart and be prepared to give
me what I require.

I will be in touch very soon. Please be
ready to act promptly on my orders.

—Ezra Caldwell

Eve was shivering with panic when she finished reading
the letter. "He's a monster. I think he'd actually do that to
Michael."

"We won't let him," Joe said harshly. "We'll make sure he
doesn't get the chance."

"How?"

"I'll bring in every organization I'm connected with to help catch the son of a bitch. I'll be out there myself until I find where he's keeping Michael. So will Caleb."

"What if that's not enough?" Eve asked. She couldn't get over the sheer evil of Caldwell's thoughts and words. "I know that no one could have done any more than you to watch over Michael, but he was still taken. And that horror of a man might be able to somehow hurt him even more if we can't stop him. There has to be some way to—" She could feel the tears running down her cheeks now, and she had to stop. "Michael is so smart. He won't just take this lying down. He'll be fighting to help us if we give him the chance. We've got to find a way to give him that chance."

"I know that, Eve," Joe said. "I wish I was there with you now. I'll get on the road as soon as I can, but I need a little time to see if I can get Scotland Yard stirring to try to locate that bastard."

"Forget about me. Don't try to rush home to hold my hand. I've got all kinds of guards to take care of me. Finding our son is more important anyway." Eve added dully, "Get here as soon as you can, but I'd rather you take every opportunity you can to find Michael. He's the only thing we should be worrying about now." She had to get off the phone before she totally broke down. "Call me as soon as you find out anything." She pressed DISCONNECT and just sat there almost in a stupor for a moment, staring at the empty screen.

It seemed incredible that she should feel like this. She needed every bit of her mental acuity not only to keep going in a world without Michael but also to bring him home.

I'll take care of you, Mom.

Michael had said that. But now they had to take care of him. First they had to find him, and then they had to discover that magical way to bring him home.

So clear your head. Go over the possibilities. What did Caldwell say he wanted? What might really be his objective? The problem was that she didn't know enough about him or his plans or why he wanted her to create that death mask. She would be a fool to believe anything she'd been told; it had probably been meant only to lure her to do the mask. Still, she had learned quite a bit from her talk with Celine Kelly and Alex Dominic. What Celine had said about Dominic's contacts and his knowledge of the backgrounds of all the players in this ugly game had also struck a chord. It was obvious that she had meant what she said about Dominic being the only one to trust in that game. Eve would have to think about how all the pieces fit together. Only one thing was certain right now. She couldn't afford to indulge in self-pity or discouragement when there were so many places this puzzle could take her and so much work to do. The essential thing was to do what she needed to do first.

Hold on, Michael. Your Dad and I are trying everything we can to bring you home. You try, too, and I promise we'll get there.

THE DEATH MASK

"You did very well, Kontara," Dominic said as he strolled over to the mat where Celine had Kontara in a headlock. "Much better than yesterday. How did you feel about your progress?"

"Oh, splendid." She struggled to turn her head so that she could look Celine in the eyes. "She only got me in a position where she could have broken my neck three times today. Will you please release me so that I can see if you've broken any bones?"

"I haven't." Celine grinned as she moved away from Kontara. "I was careful. I didn't want to stop when you were doing so well. The only reason I gave you a sprained wrist yesterday was to teach you a lesson about getting cocky. All you need is one slip and you end up in the hospital."

"How kind of you to show me the error of my ways." Kontara added sarcastically, "Do you know how difficult it is to handle those cast-iron skillets I use in my cooking with a sprained wrist?"

"I can imagine." Celine sat up. "But you did it, just as you did what you were supposed to do today on this mat. If it's too much for you, why don't you quit?"

"You know why I won't do that." Her eyes were suddenly glittering. "Because I love that feeling of power it gives me when I do something right. And one of these days I'm going to get you down in a headlock or knock you down with a single kick."

"Yes, you will." Celine was smiling. "It's only a matter of time."

"And did I really do better today?" she asked eagerly.

"You had me worried." Celine laughed. "I was wondering if I should sprain your other wrist."

"Don't you dare," Kontara said. "Or I'll draft you for kitchen duty."

Dominic was smiling with amusement as he helped Kontara to her feet. "Celine, you've built a monster in your own image."

"I did not do any such thing," Celine said. "I wouldn't dare. For one thing, I know very little about cooking, and you'd have a mutiny on your hands if I tried to take Kontara's place. She's superb and your entire staff knows it and worships at her feet. All I did was give her a few lessons so that she'd feel more confident when a situation became too difficult to handle." She glanced at Kontara. "I believe I did that very well. You agree?"

"I agree." Kontara winced as she limped toward the door. "But now I believe I need a hot shower to unstiffen some very sore muscles or I won't be able to function to cook dinner." She glanced over her shoulder at Celine. "And I've got to have all my strength by our session tomorrow." She smiled slyly. "Because tomorrow is the day I take you down." She ignored the laughter from Celine and Dominic and gave them the finger as she strode out of the exercise room.

"I like her," Celine said when she finally stopped chuckling. "I don't believe I've ever met any woman I've liked more. Usually women don't seem to like me, or they say one thing and mean another. Kontara always means every word she says. Tomorrow I'll have to be very careful."

"That goes without saying," Dominic said. "But you should consider that most women probably have a deep fear that you'll successfully compete with them over either a mate or a job. And the fact that they seem to mean one thing and yet say another is a sign of insecurity. Either way, it's a little sad. You should feel sorry for them."

She made a face. "I'm too busy trying to protect myself." She tilted her head. "But there are two women I've met recently that I like besides Kontara. I liked Catherine Ling very much." She smiled. "And of course, I liked Eve Duncan."

"Of course," he said. "Your heroine. I liked her, too."

"But you seem to like most women. I don't remember you talking badly about any of them."

He shook his head. "I'm not that forgiving. You just conveniently forgot how angry I was at Barnaby's wife, Judy, that day in the cemetery. But that was purely an individual antagonism. She'd made you cry, and I automatically wanted to punish her if I could."

"She had reason."

"No, she didn't. You'd done nothing wrong. If she thought you had, it was probably all mixed up with how she felt about you being friends with her husband and his wanting to save you at any cost." He shook his head. "Stop trying to take the blame for how people feel about you. It annoys the hell out of me. It's all surface judgments, and you should ignore them."

"But it didn't stop you from becoming angry at poor Judy."

"'Poor Judy' attacked you. You'll have to forgive me if that ruffled all my protective instincts. And that's another thing. The male sex hasn't been very fair toward women in the last few thousand years. If someone steps up and tries to protect you, it's rare enough so that you should accept it gracefully."

She blinked. "Yes sir, Dominic. Duly noted." She was trying to keep from smiling. "You appear to have strong feelings on the subject. I wouldn't want to upset you."

"Liar," he said. "Sometimes you do. It comes and goes with you. You just happened to tap a subject that I've been thinking about lately."

"Thousands of years of mistreated women?" she asked teasingly. "What a heavy issue to be carrying around."

"Well, your situation actually brought it to mind. I found myself thinking of how women had been used by men as chattels all through the centuries and weren't even allowed to vote or be issued their own credit cards until very recently. It kind of pissed me off. After all, fair is fair."

"And yet you told me that your mother had left your father and you when you were little more than a small child. Evidently, she didn't stick around to be mistreated. Didn't you resent her leaving?"

"What's to resent? If I hadn't been too young to figure out how to leave my father and survive, I'd probably have done it, too. Who knows what she might have gone through before she decided to strike out on her own. Like I said, most women were treated as chattels."

Her smile faded. "You're a very unusual man, Alex Dominic. I don't appreciate the fact that you seem to think of me as some kind of victim. Considering that I had a fantastic and understanding father who raised me and tried to run interference to keep me safe, it's completely misplaced. You should have chosen Kontara if you're looking for someone to save. I can take care of myself."

"I've noticed. But so can Kontara now that you've taken a hand in her development. I've enjoyed watching that process enormously." He shook his head ruefully. "And I'm afraid it's not a question of selecting what I feel or which person I feel it for. Which is very frustrating considering that I'm usually such a cool and calculating individual. So you'll have to accept it until you decide you can't tolerate it any longer." His gaze was suddenly holding her own. "But you may have to be the one to walk away since I appear to be having difficulty with it. You'd better prepare yourself to assume the responsibility."

Heat. Electricity. Celine could scarcely breathe. The intimacy had come out of nowhere, and she couldn't look away from him.

"I want to touch you," he said softly. "May I?"

Dear God, she wanted it. The pulse was pounding in her wrists and her breasts were taut, the nipples hard and burning. Her lips trembled as she tried to smile. "Are you asking because you want to prove you don't think of me as a chattel?"

"I'll think of you any way you want me to think of you. You set the pace. Whatever you choose. Let me inside you and I'll make sure you won't regret it."

He wasn't even touching her yet and her muscles were tightening as she thought about how it would feel to have him over her, in her. It was so intense, she could scarcely keep from trembling. "I can't be sure of that. Because you're a very complicated man, and you told me yourself that you take any means to complete a mission. I might not regret it today, but I might tomorrow when you decide you need to go down another path. I think that Kontara is even afraid you'll talk her into using her to find those men who brutalized her." She searched his expression. "And she has a right to be afraid, doesn't she?"

"Yes, but I'd take care to keep her safe. Though I won't lie to you—if I can persuade her, I'll do it if it means saving all those lives."

She nodded. "And I can even understand it. But I'd have to think long and hard over whether I'd be able to watch you do it now that I know and care about what happens to Kontara."

"It's never easy," Dominic said. "It's always much simpler to risk your own neck than someone else's. That's why I've been putting off taking action for the last few days and hoping I'd get a break that would keep me from having to make the decision."

"Which must be rare indeed for you," Celine said. "Since you seem to have no trouble at all running the entire show."

"Evidently, I do," he said wryly. "Or this conversation would have had a much more positive ending. But I'll continue to persevere on all fronts." He turned to leave the gym. "I'll see you at dinner. I hope that your session with Kontara won't cause her to—" He stopped as his phone rang and he glanced down at the caller ID. He gave a low whistle. "Or perhaps you might want to stay around for a bit. It's your old friend Eve Duncan."

"What?" She stiffened. "Why would she be calling you?"

"I have no idea. But I'm going to find out." He pressed SPEAKER and then answered. "Hello, Eve. How delightful to talk to you. I trust there's not been any trouble with the team

I assigned you? I'm sure they would have let me know if there had been a problem."

"You're wrong. There's been a big problem here," Eve said grimly. "I'm surprised that no one has let you know yet. But then why would they if it didn't involve your damn guards that you were so sure would make everything okay for me." Her voice was suddenly shaking. "Well, shock and surprise. They didn't, Dominic. Your friend Caldwell came knocking on the door today and turned everything into a nightmare."

"Caldwell?" Dominic repeated. He heard Celine gasp next to him as he stiffened on the stool. "Are you all right? What happened? Were you hurt?"

"No, I'm fine. Because he didn't knock on *my* door, Dominic. He went straight to what would hurt me the most. My son, Michael, was kidnapped from his school in Scotland today, and Joe found a note written on Michael's computer from Caldwell that described the damage he'd do to my boy if I didn't do exactly what he told me to." She was obviously trying to keep her voice steady. "My son is only eleven years old, but I could tell Caldwell didn't give a damn. Joe said there was blood on the floor of Michael's room."

"Shit," Dominic said under his breath. "What's the story, and how can I help? I know Quinn, and I know whoever he has on the job is doing everything possible. But sometimes I can manage to turn a couple corners that they didn't see."

"Your contacts that Celine was telling us about?" she asked wearily. "I'm in no position to question anything that will bring Michael back to me. I could tell that Celine believed in you and wanted to help me."

"Yes, I did." Celine took a step closer. "I'm so sorry this happened to you, Eve. We all thought any danger was to you."

"I only wish it had been," Eve said. "So you're still with Dominic? That must mean that you haven't lost faith in him."

"No, I trust him," Celine said. "I believe he won't stop until he catches Caldwell and his men. He's totally dedicated to that goal. As I told you, we all thought any danger was to you. No one dreamed Michael would be a target..." Then she remembered something and whirled toward Dominic. "Except perhaps you. After we left the Lake Cottage, you mentioned something about going down another path." She was gazing at him in horror. "Did you realize that this might happen?"

"Do you expect me to deny that I thought Caldwell would go to any lengths to get what he wanted? No, of course I won't. But we both realized that we'd given the warning, and Quinn and the rest of Eve's very capable family wanted us out of the mix and to leave it in their hands. I even kept the guard unit I'd put in place on duty when Quinn sent his own team to watch over her. Did I know they'd target an eleven-year-old child? Of course not. But I probably should have." His lips twisted bitterly. "I saw the children who'd been butchered at that massacre at Karimu. So if you want to blame someone, Eve, by all means, blame me."

"Don't be foolish," Eve said curtly. "I'm not blaming anyone but Caldwell. And the only reason I'm calling you is to tell you that I'm going to get my Michael back and you have to help me, if you can think of any way in heaven or hell to do it. Joe and I can't do this by ourselves, so I'm calling in everyone who cares for us or him to make that happen." Her voice was suddenly fierce. "Do you understand?"

"Of course I do," Dominic said quietly. "Celine is right, I was going to take Caldwell down anyway, but you've given me a reason to make sure that the emphasis is on urgency. That should be no problem. Since I returned to Bon Jaka, things have been moving very quickly as far as information is concerned. But I need to know what Caldwell said in his note."

Eve nodded. "It wasn't much. He still wants me to do the death mask. He said that he'd phone me very soon and I had to be ready to move when he did." She moistened her lips. "Other than that, it was just a threat about what they'd do to Michael if I didn't cooperate. He mentioned how talented his men were when they demonstrated their technique for the Boston Police Department."

"Barnaby," Celine murmured. "Vicious bastard."

"I thought that was who they were talking about," Eve said. "But all I could think about was the threat to Michael and how sick it made me feel."

"We won't let that happen to him," Celine said. "We'll find a way to get him away from those butchers."

"Tell Joe I'll be in touch." Dominic paused. "What are you going to do when Caldwell contacts you?"

"Whatever I have to do. Say whatever I have to say. Anything to keep Michael alive. Now you talk to me. Do you know where Caldwell might be keeping Michael?"

"I know that his principal hideout in Africa for the last few years has been in the mountains fairly close to the territory where I have an estate. That mountain country is a maze of trails and caves. Caldwell feels safe because he's also been under the protection of Masini Zakira, a priest who's almost as corrupt as himself. Since Caldwell will know that he'll have me on his trail, he'll probably want to keep Michael there—he'll believe it safer. That gives us a head start."

Evidently that wasn't enough for Eve. "But if you know so much about this hideout, surely you'll be able to locate it quickly. Those people are murderers. Your damn head start may not keep Michael alive."

He shook his head. "But they want something from you. They're not going to be in a hurry to get rid of their ace in a hole if they can find a way to make this kidnapping pay dividends. We'll just have to find a way to work at super speed to get your Michael away from Caldwell before he gets impatient. Is there risk? Yes, we'll have to find a way to stall him. There's nothing sure about any of this except that we'll get Caldwell eventually. The rest is luck and how good we are about tracking through those caves and that damn jungle. But I'll start working on bringing him home safely the minute I hang up the phone. I want you to call me as soon as you hear Caldwell's terms. Will you do that?"

"Of course. I told you, I have no choice but to get all the help I can. I'll shout it from the rooftops."

"I know you'll call Joe as soon as you hang up," Celine said. "Tell him that we'll be doing everything we can to make certain everything goes well. We're not going to let your son be hurt like Barnaby was hurt. You're not alone in this, Eve."

"Thank you. I know I'm not. But right now it feels like I am. It's just me and Michael. I'm feeling very helpless. I'll be back in touch." She pressed DISCONNECT.

Celine closed her eyes. "I hate this for her. She's going through hell, and there's nothing we can do." Her eyes flicked open, shimmering with tears. "But we've got to change that, don't we? Dominic? This is about a little boy who could die if we don't stop them. So start thinking and reaching out to all those contacts you have tucked away."

"I will," he said gently. "But you know where we have to go first."

Yes, she knew, and that was why the pain was so intense. "Kontara," she whispered. "You're going to try to persuade her to lead you to Shafira."

"I'm not going to have to persuade her. She's known it's coming, and she's been preparing herself for it. You've been preparing her for it, too, whether you realized it or not. All that's left is the commitment. When she hears about Michael being held by those sons of bitches, the commitment will be there."

"And you can see it coming. You set the stage and the action happens." Her lips twisted. "Don't you get bored with always being right?"

"I'm not always right. It's just a question of logic and knowing human nature. And there are some things I don't want to be right about." He paused. "I don't want you to insist on going with the team to Shafira. I find it's killing me to think about it. I'd like to lock you up somewhere on the estate to keep you safe and away from that blasted mountain. But you're going to go because you won't let Kontara go back there and stay behind yourself."

"There are other reasons."

"I know. Eve and her son."

"Which is reason enough. But you're right, regardless of the reason, I've got to go. And I'd advise you not to try to stop me."

He shook his head. "You'd only find a way to get loose and follow us. I'm better off keeping an eye on you." He was heading for the door. "And now I'd better go and talk to Kontara. I don't believe you'd like to come with me?"

"No, I'll talk to her later. I don't want her to feel I'm putting pressure on her either way." She watched him walk out of the room before she headed out of the gym to go to her room to shower. No, Dominic wasn't always right. He hadn't been right today when he'd gone through the reasons why she'd insist on going to Shafira.

Kontara.

Eve.

Eve's son, Michael.

But he'd left out one very important name…

Alex Dominic.

CHAPTER

11

No, I haven't heard from Caldwell yet," Eve told Joe when she picked up his call. "The bastard is probably trying to insert a little more tension to torture me with. As if I haven't been going through enough." She added through set teeth, "But I mustn't let him see that he's getting to me. The weaker I appear, the more powerful he thinks he is. Dominic said that we have to stall him at all costs, and I think he's right."

"So do I," Joe said. "And I was grateful when he called me and said he was doing everything he could to locate him. But I'm trying to arrange to trace your call and get another possible address in case Dominic is wrong about where Caldwell is keeping Michael. I wish to hell it wasn't so risky to try to get him to call me instead."

"No," she said quickly. "He has to think I'm only a weak woman trying desperately to negotiate for my son. Everyone knows your reputation as a detective. He'd probably bristle or balk if he had to talk to you when it's me he's trying to pressure. The best I can do is to record the call and let you hear it later."

"That's not good enough."

She was suddenly hearing another call come in. "Wait, that might be him. I'll include you on the call, but you need to just listen, okay?"

"Got it."

She took a deep breath, pressed the CONNECT button twice, and then took the new call. "Eve Duncan."

"You sound a little upset, Eve." The voice of the man on the line was mocking. "Ezra Caldwell here. Did I keep you waiting? What a pity."

"Isn't that what you meant to do?" Eve asked bitterly. "There was no need for you to put me through all this worry if you didn't hope I'd get a little hysterical and easier for you to manipulate."

"Yes, that was my intention. But you disappoint me. You don't seem at all hysterical. You're even stronger than I thought when I chose you to do the mask."

"No, I'm not hysterical. But I'm angry as hell that you took my son and let me go through this hell of not knowing if he's alive or dead."

"Oh, he's alive. It would be very stupid of me to kill him after all the trouble I had acquiring your services."

Incredible relief soared through Eve. But she couldn't let it be revealed in her voice. "I don't know if I should believe you. Perhaps you're bluffing. I want to see him. Talk to him. My husband said there was blood at the school."

"And so there was. He did a very good job of fighting off my men before they were able to give him the hypodermic. But they knew I would be most displeased if they did anything fatal to him. They had their orders. Now, shall we discuss the terms of his return to you?"

"Not until I see him and talk to him."

"You are stubborn." His voice was impatient. "You do realize that I'm in charge here? I would have no problem disposing of the boy."

"I've been told that's true, and it sickens me." She let him hear the fear in her tone. "But I won't give you something for nothing. There has to be a strong reason why you went to all this trouble to get me to create that mask. Probably because you realize I can do it better than anyone else. But it takes dedication and intensity as well as skill, and it won't turn out the way you want it if I have to worry about my son when I'm working on it. Every time you hurt him or threaten him, you'll see the difference in my work on the mask."

Silence. "Now you could be the one bluffing," he said softly.

"No," Eve said. "I'm just fighting with every weapon I possess. You said you chose me. That must mean you studied my work. I could be bluffing, but it's more likely I'm telling you the truth, isn't it?"

Another silence. "Damn you, yes, it is." He looked over his shoulder at someone and barked, "Bring in the kid."

The next moment, Michael's face appeared on the screen. He had a bruise on his lip, and his eyes were wide with concern. "Mom? They want something from you? Don't let him do this to you. I'll be okay."

"Yes, you will," she said. "We'll both be fine, but I'm going to have to go along with these people for a little while. Have they hurt you?"

"Only a little. I'll find a way to make sure they don't."

"No!" she said sharply. "Don't fight them. We'll both be

okay when we can be together. I have to go now. I'll see you soon, Michael."

"Satisfied?" Caldwell came back on the line. "You gave him good advice. If he takes it, it may keep him safe."

"No, I'm not satisfied. He had bruises. But I can probably keep him from getting any more if I'm there to talk to him." She drew a deep breath. *Don't hesitate. You knew it was probably going to come down to this from the beginning.* She said a swift prayer as she tossed the dice. "Because even if I agree to do your death mask, you won't let him go, will you?"

"Perhaps...when it's finished."

"I can't count on that. I can't count on anything to do with Michael unless I have him with me where I can see what you're doing to him and negotiate his safety along with every step I take in the creation of the mask. That way we'll both get what we want. You'll get the high quality you want for the mask, and I'll get the opportunity to make sure no harm comes to my son while I'm doing it." She added caustically, "Perhaps I can even find a way to persuade you to let us both go after I've turned that mask over to you. I'll take whatever I can get."

He chuckled. "Because you're a very clever woman. You can never tell what I'll do in any situation. I detest being thought predictable. But what you've asked isn't unreasonable from my point of view. And it happens I have a partner in this project, and Zakira is becoming very impatient to get you started on the mask. There's a celebration coming to commemorate the anniversary of his arrival here. I tried to get him to just pay someone else to do it, but he insisted on you and only you. You've had such good luck on your projects in the past, and he's a superstitious man."

"As superstitious as his gullible followers?" Eve said.

Caldwell chuckled. "He can be very bad-tempered, so I try to accommodate him. I found it convenient to stash the boy in his village when I took him from his school in Scotland. I'm sure he won't mind keeping your son in his village for a little while longer if it means that we get you to work on the mask sooner."

"All I want to know is how do I get to Michael? My husband is a remarkable man, but he wouldn't approve of my taking this risk. He'd want to try anything else first. I know you realize there are guards here on the property, and you won't be able to get to me."

"Do you think I wouldn't have taken that into consideration? That's why we had to take the boy instead. You had to be the one to come to me, so I gave you a reason to do it. I've taken care of that problem. We can't come to you, but those guards won't stop you leaving the safety of your home in your own Toyota that you use all the time. As it happens, I've had one of my men slip onto your property and make some GPS adjustments to your Toyota; once you get on the highway, it will take you straight to the field where my helicopter is waiting for you. It should work beautifully."

"Maybe not so beautiful. Those guards will still notify Joe that I've left the property."

"Too late. Unless you let them know what you've done. But you won't do that, because you'll know that your Michael would be the one to pay. And you think perhaps you'll find a way to save him. Who knows? Maybe you will. Anyway, we'll be over the Atlantic before Quinn catches up to the fact of what you've actually done."

Eve knew he was right. And dear God, Joe might never forgive her for the deception even if everything went well in this hideous scenario. They had always been together in every endeavor all these years, and now she was risking Michael's life because she couldn't see any other way he could survive. She hadn't even been able to tell Joe what she'd planned because she'd known he'd try to stop her.

"Second thoughts?" Caldwell asked. She could hear the mockery again.

"No second thoughts. I just want it over."

"Your wish is my command. All you have to do is go and get in the Toyota right now and I'll see you very soon, Eve." He was still chuckling as he hung up.

And Eve sat there for a moment more as she tried to recover from all the painful emotions that had bombarded her as she had talked to Caldwell.

Joe...

No, she couldn't think about Joe now. It was Michael who was still threatened. She had to do what was necessary to save him. But she could only do that if she made sure that she was where he was being held captive.

However, there was one thing she could do before she devoted herself totally to their son.

She got to her feet and tapped out a text to Joe.

Joe,
It had to be this way. Forget about me. I'll
be safe as long as I can give them something they want. Michael is well enough
and being held by Zakira somewhere near

his village. I'll do everything I can to send
him to you. Be ready.

Then she tossed a few items of clothing in a knapsack and was leaving the Lake Cottage and heading down the steps toward the Toyota in the driveway.

———

BON JAKA, AFRICA

Dominic received a call from Joe Quinn four hours later. His voice was harsh and explosive the instant Dominic picked up the phone. "Tell me that you've already sent that exploratory team up that damn mountain to find Shafira."

"By the tone of your voice, I'd better answer in the affirmative," Dominic said dryly. "So it's a good thing that I can do so truthfully. The first team left for the mountains forty minutes ago. I'm taking another tracking team up there myself in about an hour. But I've already told you how difficult it's going to be for them to find that village. It could be a matter of days or weeks."

"I don't know if we have days or weeks. So you'd better find them a hell of a lot sooner than that."

"You know we'll do what we can." Dominic paused. "You've heard from Eve? Is the boy all right?"

"Yes, I've heard from Eve. And Michael is okay." Joe added, "It seems Eve is going to make sure he stays that way. She decided to agree to give Caldwell the mask he wants so that she'd be there with Michael and be able to protect him. We found her abandoned car near a field near the woods at

169

Lanier, where there were signs she must have boarded a helicopter. Do you realize how difficult it's going to be for her to keep both of them alive? It will be like walking a tightrope. I could lose them so easily," he whispered. "That can't happen, Dominic." He cleared his throat. "So I'm not going to let it. I've called and arranged for a team of my own, including your old acquaintance Caleb, to meet me at Sardwa airport. We'll set out from there toward that blasted mountain and join you."

"I'm not waiting for you. I'll leave a man at the airport to give you the latest directions we manage to find on the trail. As I said, it's a maze."

"I heard you the first time," Joe said bitterly. "But Eve got a confirmation from Caldwell that Zakira was definitely holding Michael for him at his village. That means it's a maze that's going to lead to Eve and Michael. So we'll damn well get through it!"

———

Dominic found Celine in the library fifteen minutes later. "We'll be leaving the estate within the hour. If you're going to come, get your backpack and meet me at the jeep in the front."

"You know I'm going to come." She gazed searchingly at him. "You said you had arrangements to make and we weren't leaving until this evening. Why the rush?"

"The picture's changed a bit. I can do what needs to be done on the road. I don't want to waste any time."

She was frowning in puzzlement. "How did it change? What happened?" She stiffened. "You heard from Eve? Did they hurt the boy?"

"No, I heard from Quinn. The boy's still okay. But Eve took the deal to do the mask so that she could find a way to protect her son." His lips tightened grimly. "She's probably heading in the same direction we are. Only she'll be getting there faster, because Caldwell knows where the hell he's going. They know how to move in and out of this jungle without being seen. I just hope she's still alive when we catch up to her."

"She's very smart. She should have a good chance." Celine added thoughtfully, "But I can see why she'd do it."

"Of course you can," he said. "You'd probably do the same thing."

"No question. After all, it's her child. Family is too important not to accept being willing to sacrifice to save them. You can understand that."

"Don't be too sure." He smiled sardonically. "Remember, I didn't have a father like yours. I grew up being taught that I couldn't expect anything from my family but a life of survival of the fittest. That was okay for me. I was tough enough to take care of myself. But most kids don't stand a chance when bastards like Caldwell push them around. I saw that again at that massacre at Karimu." His lips tightened. "I'm not going to let him do that to Eve's Michael. I don't know anything about all this family dynamic business, but I know right and wrong and how to stop that bullshit in its tracks."

"That's what I've been told," she said quietly. "And I believe you know more than you admit about how families operate. You may not have had any close family members around you or supporting you, but you've made up for it by the way you've drawn people to you through the years. I've only been with you a short time, but I've met Sam Rashid and Kontara and Catherine Ling, and every time I turn around, you're giving orders or calling one of your contacts. I'm sure there are many more that you reach out to. In a way, all of them are your adopted family. You've just selected them yourself."

He smiled. "I appreciate you trying to furnish me with a ready-made clan, but aren't you reaching?"

"No more than you are by choosing to surround yourself with those particular people."

"But you forgot about one Celine Kelly," he said softly. "Have you decided not to consider yourself one of the chosen ones?"

"Our relationship is…different."

"Yes, it is. And if you decide to come with me today, it may change again. Are you prepared for that?" His voice was suddenly rough. "I don't know if I am. I want this too much. I don't want to back you in a corner, dammit. Why don't you just stay here at the estate with some of my so-called family you've chosen for me and let me go take care of what I do best."

She was backing away from him. "Because it's my business, too. Barnaby made that clear. So did Eve Duncan when she risked her life for her son. So did you when you showed me those photos of those little children at Karimu." She turned on her heel. "I'll go pack my backpack as you told me, but first I've got to go talk to Kontara…" She was running quickly toward the kitchen.

"We're leaving earlier than expected," she said as Kontara turned away from the refrigerator to face her. "Dominic said

there was an emergency situation and he'd take care of doing
the prep work on the road."

"Emergency?" Kontara frowned. "This entire trip is one
big emergency. What is it this time?"

"We told you about Eve Duncan. Caldwell has managed to
persuade her to come to the village to do the death mask. He
promised to keep her son safe if she agreed."

"He lies," Kontara said flatly.

"But it buys time to keep her Michael alive," Celine said.
"That's all she cares about. And that's why we have to move
much faster to help her. I know you didn't want to do this."
She grimaced. "I didn't want it for you, either."

"I know you didn't." Kontara shrugged. "But you worked
very hard to keep me as safe as you could by teaching me all
that you could on those damn mats. I'm grateful to you for
that. But now you've done what you set out to do, I don't need
you any longer." Her voice was suddenly harsh. "So for God's
sake stop being stupid and tell Dominic you're not going to go
trekking up that mountain and get yourself killed. He won't
argue with you. You're not important to him in this particular
scheme of things. He needs me to find those bastards, and he
told me he's practically got an army to take them down once
he zeroes in on them. You're not needed, dammit. You'll just
get in his way."

Celine shook her head. "Then he'll have to find a use for
me, won't he? Because I don't believe you. You haven't wanted
him to take me with him to help bring down those monsters
since the day I came here. It's clear you wanted to protect me.
You've seen enough ugliness and horror to last you a lifetime,
and you want to be done with it." She smiled as she shook her

head. "But then the worst thing possible happened. Lo and behold, now we've actually come to like each other. What a predicament."

Kontara was scowling. "That's not funny. It is the worst thing if it means you're going to do something that could get you killed."

"We'll just have to take care of each other to make sure that doesn't happen." Celine's smile had vanished. "As well as find a way to help Eve." She turned away and headed out of the kitchen. "No more arguments. It's a done deal. We both have to start packing."

"Wait."

Celine glanced over her shoulder.

Kontara was smiling at her with almost catlike satisfaction. "You're getting a little too cocky. It's probably because you've been taking me down too often in our gym sessions. But never count me out. It's not a done deal until I tell you it is." She turned away and began scraping the food she'd cooked into plastic freezer bags. "We're in this together."

BON JAKA COURTYARD
ONE HOUR LATER

Celine gave a low whistle as she saw the number of jeeps, trucks, and helicopters in the courtyard. She said to Dominic who was coming out of the main house, "Kontara said that you practically had an army to help you take down Caldwell's thugs. She wasn't exaggerating. No wonder she thought I'd believe her when she said you didn't need me."

"I can call on considerably more assets than I discussed with her," Dominic said. "Though it took considerable persuasion to convince her that an attack on Zakira and Caldwell could be successful after the chaos they've caused." He shrugged. "And even after she decided to trust me to get the job done and agreed to try to lead me to their village, she still kept nagging me to leave you behind." He was watching Kontara crossing the courtyard toward them. Her red hair was pinned back, and she was dressed in jeans and a loose brown shirt, carrying a backpack. She was ignoring Celine and staring straight at Dominic.

He sighed. "And, by that determined expression on her face, I believe she's going to make a final attempt to get me to order you to do exactly that. I've sent drones out in search of the village, but it's too well hidden." He smiled as he took a step forward. "I'm putting you in the lead jeep with Rashid, Kontara. I thought you should familiarize yourself with the surroundings as you see if you can recognize any landmarks from your trip down from the mountain. It may save us a few false moves through the maze if you can catch them ahead of time. Does that make sense to you?"

"I told you that I'd try," she said curtly. "There won't be anything to watch out for until we're several miles from the estate. The last thing I remember was a creek near a ditch. After that, I woke up near his temple, which is where we want to go." She shrugged. "But yes, when I was on the run, I'd remember things from the last time I'd escaped from the village. That does make sense." Her lips tightened as she looked him in the eye. "What doesn't make sense is that you're still letting Celine come with us. I thought surely you'd change your mind. You don't want her along. I can feel it. It's all wrong that you pay any attention to what she says. They'll kill her. I know it."

Dominic shrugged. "If you feel that deeply about it, then you should have persuaded her to your way of thinking. I did my very best. She's damn stubborn." He turned back to Celine. "She's actually very convincing. You wouldn't care to change your mind?"

She shook her head. "It's natural that she would believe I wouldn't stand a chance with those bastards. She's seen too much death and torture in that village. But she should realize I can take care of myself now. I told her that she should drop trying to convince you. It's a done deal."

Kontara whirled to face her. "Zakira doesn't think you can take care of yourself. Neither does Caldwell." She was spitting the words out. "They both think that you're just something to use and abuse like the rest of the women in that camp. But they have something special in mind for you. I've seen it. Give them a chance and they'll show you."

"Seen it?" Dominic repeated thoughtfully. "Now what have you seen that's upset you? That's the first time you've mentioned any personal connection between Celine and those assholes. I believe you'd better elaborate."

"I didn't want to elaborate." Her eyes were blazing. "Do you think that I wanted to frighten her with all that ugliness? But she wouldn't listen to me. It's all your fault. All you had to do was make sure she didn't go up there with us and I wouldn't have had to say anything else."

"But you did say it, and now you can't unsay it," Dominic said. "Because Celine won't let you." He added, "And neither will I. I thought you were a little fanatical about insisting that I not bring her, but evidently you weren't telling us everything. What is the special thing Caldwell and Zakira have in mind for Celine?"

She didn't speak for a moment. "It was mostly Zakira," she finally said grudgingly. "At least the priest was the one who got angry because Caldwell didn't have the two women he wanted yet. I've heard that he's often yelled about Caldwell breaking the bargain they'd made. The entire village heard him, and everyone was afraid because Zakira did terrible things to the women and soldiers in the village when he was in a temper, and he was definitely furious when Caldwell said he was having trouble getting hold of the women he wanted." She moistened her lips. "Caldwell got a lot of phone calls and he kept making excuses. But then one day he took one of his helicopters out of the village because he said he'd arranged to give Zakira exactly what he wanted."

"And I can hardly wait to hear what Caldwell said he'd give Zakira," Dominic said grimly.

"The women in the photos," Kontara said simply. "The ones in the temple. Caldwell had brought two large photos framed in gold as a special gift to Zakira at the same time he shipped in boxes of guns and bombs in exchange for the bars of gold Zakira had given him. Zakira seemed to be very happy with the photos. He hung them on special walls of the temple he'd had built for himself." She smiled bitterly. "And he brought all the concubines to the temple to have one of his sex festivals in honor of his fantastic new gifts. I needn't tell you that we didn't appreciate that particular honor. Or the ones that came after it." Her gaze shifted to Celine. "But I could hardly forget any detail of that night, and you have a very memorable face. I knew the minute I saw you that Zakira and Caldwell would want to get their hands on you. It brought everything back to me, and I just wanted to hide away again." She shook her head. "I wasn't even sure that I wouldn't be a part of any bargain that anyone made with those bastards. I couldn't bear the thought of it. Even when I realized that Dominic wouldn't betray me, I still wasn't sure you wouldn't try to save yourself, Celine. Some of the women in the camp would do anything to make the abuse go away."

"We all tried to tell you that we'd keep you safe," Celine said gently. "I'm sorry you couldn't believe us."

"It took a little while," Kontara said wryly. "I only knew part of what was going on while I was at Shafira village. I learned the other part from you and Dominic once I came to the estate. I didn't know what Eve Duncan's role was going to be in Caldwell's plans. I thought the two of you were going to be just other women for the priest to use for barter. But then I was told why Zakira was so eager to get hold of Eve Duncan to do the mask. I was still puzzled about you, Celine, and I thought maybe I'd been right the first time and they just wanted you because your looks made you an asset. But it was unusual that they'd wanted you bad enough that they'd actually argued about you. So I went back and tried to remember everything that happened in the temple so I could puzzle it out."

"And did you manage to do it?" Celine asked.

"Yes, and it didn't take that long. But it scared me. And then after I got to know you I realized I couldn't let you go when I knew what they probably intended to do to you. There was a chance Eve Duncan might come out of it alive if she negotiated. But they weren't going to let you go until you fulfilled their purpose." She shook her head in frustration. "And you wouldn't listen to me."

"And what was that purpose?" Dominic asked sharply. "Talk! What the hell did you remember, Kontara?"

"It was the placement of those framed pictures in the museum." She turned and looked at him with something like desperation. "I told you they were hung on separate walls. The Eve Duncan photo was on a wall by itself, and it looked like a place of honor."

She moistened her lips. "But the Celine photo was on an entirely opposite side of the temple. Her picture was the only photo on that wall, but there was a statue and some other objects on the fancy decorated gold shelves surrounding it. It was those objects that were being honored on her wall."

"What kind of objects?" Celine whispered.

Kontara looked her straight in the eye. "You've probably guessed. Weapons. Daggers. Torches. Guns. Weapons of medieval torture. Even some kind of modern water torture gadget."

Dominic was cursing softly and vehemently.

Celine reached out and touched his arm. "I see that we agree on what they intended my fate to be. Zakira evidently decided he needed a human sacrifice to go along with Eve Duncan's death mask." She smiled wryly. "Not very complimentary. It makes me want to spit in their eyes and spoil all their carefully laid plans."

"And all I want to do is keep you here and go after them myself." Dominic added grimly, "I intend to use every one of those weapons to do serious damage to those bastards."

179

"I won't object." Celine shivered. "As long as you don't try to cheat me out of my share of the action." Her lips were trembling as she tried to smile. "Though maybe I should thank Zakira for choosing me for such an important role. And here I thought he only wanted me to be another pretty face in his slave harem. I didn't realize he wanted to make me a star."

"I don't find that amusing," Dominic said harshly. "And I'll lay odds that the statue on the shelf with the weapons is a copy of the Nefertiti statue. He wants to ceremoniously replace it with one that you model for before your sacrifice, to show his followers how much more important and splendid his entombed queen is than any other in history."

"And glorify his own splendor by doing it," Celine added grimly. "I admit I didn't think about the significance of the statue at first. But then I was a little bit overwhelmed. I believe I may be starting to dislike Zakira even more than Caldwell."

"It's not a contest. They'll both be dead men before this is over. I promise you." His voice was absolutely implacable. "And now that you know what you're facing, will you please stay here at the estate and let me take care of this?"

"It's because of what they're making me face that I can't do that," she said. "My father taught me that no one has the right to make a victim of me, and if they try I have to fight back."

"I didn't think so." He was gazing at her with a mixture of desperation and helplessness before he threw up his hands in frustrated disgust. "Get into my jeep. I'm not letting you get more than a seat's distance away from me until this dirty charade is over." He turned to Kontara. "Front jeep. Keep sharp. Don't take chances. Your job is to track, find, and report.

When you've located the target, I'll take a team in to do the rest. Understand?"

She nodded absently but her gaze was still focused on Celine, and she took a half step forward. "This is wrong. I didn't mean to—"

"Give it up," Dominic said. "Drop it. I believe she's had enough of a shock for the time being. She knows your intentions were good." He gave Celine a gentle push toward his jeep. "I'm sorry as hell you weren't successful, Kontara."

"So am I." She grimaced as she turned and headed for the jeep at the front of the column. "This isn't a good idea. I hope she doesn't regret it."

"I'm getting a little tired of being spoken about as if I'm not here," Celine said wearily as she got into the jeep. "You're right. I'm going to do this, so resign yourselves. Now let me see if I can find something to keep me busy besides thinking about some weird creep of a priest who's trying to pick just the right ceremonial spot to slit my throat." She unzipped her backpack and pulled out a few of the maps she'd been studying during the last few days she'd been at Bon Jaka. "I'm going to ignore both of you and check out the trails on the first several miles from the estate that lead toward the falls..."

CHAPTER

12

How delightful to meet you, Eve Duncan." The silver-haired man who was walking toward the helicopter had to be Caldwell, Eve thought. The helicopter pilot who had flown her from Angola to this heliport in the mountains and the man who'd been guarding her from the moment she'd left the Lake Cottage had almost snapped to attention when they had seen him. He was smiling as he opened the helicopter door and helped her out to the tarmac, which was covered with massive fan-shaped banyan leaves, obviously placed there to prevent detection from above. "Though I feel as if we're already the best of friends. I can't tell you how many hours I've spent with you smiling as you looked down at me."

"Then you're hallucinating," Eve said bluntly. "Because I know I've never met you and I'd never willingly smile at you."

"Well, perhaps it was a forced acquaintance." He gestured for her to precede him down the rough jungle path toward the thatched roofs of the distant village. "But that doesn't matter, since I'm the one who created you in Zakira's eyes, and if you want your son to live, you'll do exactly what I say to keep Zakira happy."

"Created me?" she repeated scornfully. "You flatter yourself."

He shook his head. "Perhaps I should say I created the image of the scenario Zakira wants his followers to believe is true. And I've worked hard to bring a facsimile to him to use as he sees fit." He added softly, "But if you destroy that image, he will probably try to reach out and crush us all. You have a lot to lose, Eve."

"But then so do you. It appears to be to your advantage to keep this Zakira happy, and I've already agreed to do the death mask. But you'll have to help me to make it what he wants it to be." She added fiercely, "And you'll have to keep him from harming Michael or I won't give a damn if he's happy or not. I don't want to see any more bruises on my son. Give him a cot wherever you put me so that I can keep an eye on him."

"You're being very demanding." Caldwell was frowning. "You'll take what I choose to give you."

"But if I'm unhappy, my work may suffer," she said quickly. "You wouldn't want that. I'm not asking that much."

"True. As long as you don't make waves with Zakira that I have to correct."

"Let's face it, I'm not going to be able to call the shots here. You proved that when you took my boy," Eve said. "All I can control is my skill in my profession. I'll try to make my dealings with that priest as incident-free as possible until we can come to an agreement."

"You're going to get the opportunity very soon." He nodded at a bald man who was coming toward them from the direction of the village. "It seems Zakira is honoring you with his presence." Wearing sandals and dressed in camouflage pants and shirt with brilliant ribbons decorating his chest, along with a bejeweled dagger in the holster at his waist, the priest looked like a character from a B movie to Eve. Almost as if he'd read her mind, Caldwell murmured, "Don't make any mistakes. Zakira may look a bit bizarre, but he attended Oxford University, and he can be sharp as a tack when it suits him. It might be better to leave the negotiating to me. He doesn't have very much respect for women."

"Yet he chose me to do this death mask."

"I chose you. Don't forget that fact." He stepped forward and bowed before Zakira. "How kind of you to honor us, Zakira. This is the woman I told you about. A little pressure and she agreed to come here to serve you. She only begs to be permitted to care for the child until the mask is done."

Zakira took Eve's chin between his thumb and forefinger and lifted it to look at her face. "She does not look like one who serves."

Caldwell said quickly, "She's been spoiled a little by the fame I told you about. But she will cause no problem if you do as I instructed regarding her training. I've already prepared everything for the first lesson. Will she do?"

"I'll examine her work. We will see." He shrugged. "But you still haven't given me the other woman you promised. When do I get the one with the violet eyes?"

"Soon. Don't be impatient. This woman can give you what you immediately need. You agreed she was an expert when I showed you a few of her sculptures. Her work will impress everyone."

IRIS JOHANSEN

Zakira shrugged. "But what I do with the other woman will show the entire world that I'm master of all I survey. She will be a token of the power I wield. You promised me I would have both."

"Violet eyes..." Eve murmured. "You're talking about Celine Kelly? May I say that I'm happy you may have to make do with my humble services. From what I know about her, she seems too clever for Caldwell to use in his games." She gave a mocking bow. "But then I can't guarantee that he gave you the correct information about me, either. I don't even know if I'll be able to create this mask if the tomb wasn't kept at the proper temperature and ventilated." She heard Caldwell mutter a curse but didn't look at him. There was clearly a conflict between the two men that she might be able to use if she could handle it correctly. "Caldwell said you were both educated and intelligent, but I wasn't certain he'd let you know that those preparations were necessary. I don't want my son to suffer because Caldwell was careless about giving you what you need."

Zakira was gazing at her with narrowed eyes. "You might be adequate after all. For your information, Caldwell didn't have to tell me about those advance preparations. I told him everything and ordered him to get me both the equipment and the people I'd need to create the mask. I've been planning to do this since I was a boy at my father's knee and he first taught me about our destiny. He knew we were meant to lead, to gain power by giving the masses a compelling connection to the ancients. I've already begun that journey, but you will help me complete it. You will have everything you need, including the services of a worker in gold

186

and choice of gems to complete the mask. Does that sound satisfactory?"

"I'd have to examine the jewels to be used in the mask," she said. "Did you choose them, or did you rely on Caldwell?"

"I chose them," Zakira said impatiently. "I wouldn't leave such an important choice to anyone else. Caldwell serves me. I do not serve him. Tell her, Caldwell."

"Of course I do," Caldwell said. "I obey his every command."

"Sarcasm, Caldwell?" the priest asked. "I let you share many of my most exquisite treasures. You have only to ask. I do not appreciate sarcasm."

"You misread me," Caldwell said without expression. "It was not sarcasm. And I appreciate your generosity. Would you like me to take her to the temple and show her the jewels that you've chosen for the mask?"

"No, I will take her," Zakira said. "There are other things in the temple I wish to point out to her. You go and get the boy and bring him to her hut so that she will see that I've not seen fit to damage him...yet."

A brilliant smile lit Caldwell's face. "What a splendid idea. Just what I'd expect of you. As it happens, I've already set up the arrangements for that lesson I mentioned in the museum. We do think alike on the important things. Enjoy seeing all those lovely treasures Zakira will show you, Eve." He turned to leave. "I'll see you after the grand tour."

The museum where Zakira took Eve was not large, but the glass cases it contained were almost overflowing with precious jewels and finely wrought golden objects and ornaments. It was also guarded by three uniformed guards, who stood to attention the minute the priest entered the room.

Zakira gestured toward the treasures as he led her down the first aisle. "Are they not wonderful? I gathered the finest craftsmen I could find to work on my museum. This is only a small sample of the treasures I found when I discovered the tomb where those foul traitors had hidden the queen when they stole her from the palace after her death. I've secreted most of those safely away. But I had to have a suitable display to show my importance to my subjects, so I had them create a special museum just for me and fill it with offerings."

"Offerings?" Eve tried not to let him see how distasteful she was finding this. "That's a strange word to use. I'm sure the treasures you took from that queen's tomb were offerings, but you said that you ordered your people to create and give these treasures to you."

"They were offerings." His eyes were narrowed on her face. "Because I am both chief and priest here, and it was their duty to obey me. I deserved their worship and obedience. Just as I deserve your total obedience." He added deliberately, "I'm beginning to see why Caldwell decided you needed to be shown respect. You're not pleasing me, Eve Duncan." His smile was not pleasant. "But before I let you go to your son, I know we will come to an understanding." He gestured for her to follow him down another aisle. "First, though, I have a few other things to show you." He stopped before a wall where there was a photo of Eve. "As you can see, I chose to honor you here in my museum."

"I prefer you appreciate my work, not anything to do with me personally."

"But I don't care what you prefer." His face was suddenly twisted with anger. "I *chose* it. And what I choose comes to be." He grabbed her arm and shoved her down another aisle so that she was facing the opposite wall. Another gold-framed photo was on that wall. "Here is another choice I made, but Caldwell hasn't been able to give her to me yet. Is she not beautiful? She's the one I chose for you to use as a model for the mask."

Celine Kelly! Eve stiffened but tried not to show any expression. "I guess she's attractive enough. But why her, of everyone in the world? How did you know she even existed?"

"The miracle of modern technology. My advisors used online search engines to find close modern matches for Nefertiti. This young woman's face kept popping up. Caldwell did a good job finding her."

"Hmm. Naturally, I'll do whatever you wish."

"Of course you will," Zakira said. "Because you know what will happen to you if you don't." His gaze was raking her face. "You recognize her, don't you? She actually attended one of your seminars. Fate may have played a hand, but Caldwell was there. He photographed you both."

"I'm usually busy at my seminars, and I don't remember ever seeing her or Caldwell before."

"Well, naturally Caldwell had to check with me if she'd be adequate. so there was an annoying delay. But he told me that his men had recently seen her visiting you at your cottage."

He frowned. "He made a mistake in not finding a way to get her for me then. Though if you please me, I might forgive him." His voice lowered to a silky murmur. "And you have a much better chance of surviving than does that violet-eyed Kelly woman." He smiled. "Because I've already made a definite choice regarding her fate. While you might still be able to convince me you may be useful."

Eve moistened her lips. "What fate?"

"Why, look at the beautiful toys I've given her to play with. Don't you think she'll enjoy them?"

Eve's gaze dropped to the glass case below the photo.

She inhaled sharply and looked quickly away so he wouldn't see her horror and repulsion.

"I see you recognize what some of those toys are." He laughed. "Since I'm sure you've done a good deal of research on ancient weapons in your career, I'm not surprised. I'm particularly fond of the machetes. Don't you believe they have a certain deadly style? A lovely weapon to show my power over an equally lovely symbol that any man would want to possess. The idea has a certain flair."

She still didn't look at him. "I'm afraid I don't understand the concept. I don't like the idea of any beautiful object being destroyed. It seems an incredible waste."

"Not if I choose to make it happen." His lips twisted. "Not if it gives me pleasure. You have no concept of the rush of power it would give me if handled properly. But you seem surprised I'd want to use them to make my point. You obviously have no respect for me or my position." He frowned. "I'll have to correct that immediately."

She shrugged. "It will be difficult. I'm afraid I have real

problems with people like you. I'll try to do what you wish, but I usually don't get along well with people who have a penchant for destruction."

"You will learn." He took a step closer to her. "Because you have a son."

She inhaled sharply. "I told you that I'd do what you wanted."

"I find that's no longer satisfactory." He reached out and touched her throat. "I have to know that you respect me. I'm afraid that I have to teach you."

She stiffened. "I've agreed to do what you wish. Caldwell said you'd leave my son alone."

"For the time being. I've decided I'll only take the first step and see how you respond. Anything else would be down the road if you fail to show me that you're not the skilled sculptor Caldwell promised."

"First step?" She didn't like the way the bastard was smiling like a cat about to eat the canary, and she hated the feel of his touch on her throat. "If you don't mind, I'd like to go and see my son, Michael, now."

"Presently. As it happens I do mind. You haven't had that lesson Caldwell went to the trouble of arranging for me." He turned and snapped his fingers at one of the guards. "Fetch the child."

"Child?" Eve's gaze flew to his face as the guard ran out of the room. "You're bringing him here?"

He chuckled. "That's not the first step. It's not your son. He has a certain value to me. I chose to use the girl child of one of my soldiers to give you that lesson. I believe they call her Nieva. He wasn't pleased that her mother didn't give him a boy. He wanted a son who would serve me in the army as he does. He knows that women are useful for only one thing, and since she's only ten it will be too long before she can be sold to be used in that way."

Eve suddenly heard a piercing scream and her gaze flew to the door. It was being flung open and a young girl was being dragged into the room by two of the guards. Her long dark hair was flying around her face; she was sobbing uncontrollably, and her eyes were wild and frantic. She was shaking her head in bewilderment and panic as the guards forced her to kneel at Zakira's feet.

"Hello, Nieva." Zakira tangled his hand in her long hair and jerked her head back. "Stop fighting. I've decided you're to be chosen."

"What are you doing?" Eve asked as she saw Zakira reaching for the ornate jeweled knife in the holster at his hip. She had a horrible feeling that she knew, and she started toward him. "Let's talk about this. It doesn't make sense. She's only a child."

"A useless child." He shrugged. "Except for one purpose. To demonstrate that only I control what happens to those who serve me. Her father will be relieved that I have rid him of this burden, and she'll show you that you must never question me."

"It won't happen again. I didn't understand." Eve was running toward him. "I'm sorry if I offended you. I'm sure that the little girl has some use." She pushed herself between him and the child. "Perhaps I can teach her. I have a ward I raised from the time she was very young, and I'm sure you won't be sorry if you let me try. Jane turned out very well." The child was screaming again, and Eve reached out and frantically grabbed Zakira's wrist. "Please. Don't do this. How can I stop you?"

He looked down at her hand gripping his wrist. "You cannot. I told you, I'm the one who chooses." He motioned to the guards. "Hold her!"

"No!" It was too late. The guards were gripping Eve's arms and dragging her from between Zakira and the child. She watched Zakira draw his dagger.

Now it was Eve who was screaming as he stepped toward the girl and lifted the dagger.

He looked back at Eve, and his smile was cruel. "Now you understand. Choice!" He plunged the dagger into the little girl's chest.

Blood spurted. The knife went down again. This time there was no doubt the child was dead. Eve watched in horror as the girl fell to the floor. It was too much. She bent over clutching her stomach, fighting nausea. She looked back at Zakira and gasped, "Why? You didn't have to do it. I could have helped her. Why didn't you let me?"

"I told you, it was the first step. Caldwell said you needed a lesson, and I agreed with him." He looked at her appraisingly. "But you must be even softer than we thought. You look as if you're ready to faint. I thought someone of your experience would be a bit tougher."

She wanted to scream—no, she wanted to *kill* him. "She didn't have to die! Yes, and it does make me ill to have watched you do it."

"Then get over it. I'm done with you for the time being. I'll let you have a little time to recover before I show you the sarcophagus." He gestured to one of the guards. "Take her to Caldwell."

———

Caldwell was leaning against the door of a hut a few yards from the temple when Eve ran out of the arched teak entrance of the museum a few minutes later. "You seem to be in a hurry." He motioned to the guard following her to let her come toward him. "And you look a bit under the weather," he added mockingly. "Now, I wonder why?"

"You know very well why," she said fiercely as she glared up at him. "He's a monster, and so are you. He was the one with the knife, but you sent me to see him use it." She swallowed, fighting the overwhelming sadness and nausea again. "That poor child...What you did was hideous and without reason. There was no excuse for it. Zakira has to be mad and totally without conscience—but I don't know which one of you is worse. You're the one who evidently set up that entire scenario and persuaded Zakira that he should execute it. Do you deny it?"

"Of course I don't. It would be foolish of me to try," he said coldly. "But you're not in a position where you can demand admissions of guilt, are you? However, I feel in the mood to pamper you since I don't want you to make any other mistakes that would affect my relationship with Zakira. It's to my advantage to have you perform well for him, since I was the one to bring you to his attention. And I did have a reason to order that lesson for you. I could see you have a tendency to be very willful, and I was afraid it might get in the way of you giving Zakira exactly what he wants. The fact that I have your son is a powerful weapon, but there was an off chance that you might occasionally not remember that. I had to remind you exactly what the stakes are." He smiled as he added softly, "So I did. Will you ever be able to look at your boy without thinking about what you saw in that museum tonight?"

"I wouldn't let myself connect any of that horrible ugliness to Michael. He stands alone." She looked him in the eye. "The only time I'll let myself remember it is the day that I see you die."

For an instant, Caldwell frowned, and then he suddenly chuckled. "And that only proves how right I was about you. I realized you could be a dangerous woman."

"No, you were wrong. I'd never be careless enough to endanger my son. All you did was hurt me and kill that innocent child and make me want to find a way to hurt you." She was wearily rubbing her temple. "Now I'd like to see Michael, please."

"Not quite yet," Caldwell said. "You leave when I permit it. I'm finding you as interesting as I thought I would. What else did Zakira show you before he decided I was right that you weren't quite worthy of his respect and attention?"

"What do you think? That damn priest showed me all those jewels and treasures, but what he really wanted me to see was that photo of Celine Kelly, so he could explain exactly what they might do with all those torture devices and weapons when they decided they wanted a sacrifice. He obviously wanted to see my reaction." She was trying to keep her voice from shaking. "Isn't that what you also wanted, because I wasn't the meek captive you were expecting me to be? I didn't realize that was only going to be the beginning."

195

"I figured you'd probably say something to anger the son of a bitch." He smiled maliciously. "After I warned you, I figure that you deserved it if you shot off your mouth to our good priest. Did you do it?"

"No, I didn't. I did say something that annoyed him, but it wasn't really an insult. But he was watching me very closely, and I'd realized by that time how you were trying to punish me. I couldn't let him see how much it bothered me. Besides, Celine Kelly is safe and hopefully far away. Nothing that I said or did would affect her as long as I just ignored what Zakira was planning on doing. But how I antagonized him might make a difference to what happened to Michael."

"That's very wise of you. But how you treat me might also be factored in. I've had reports that the Kelly woman may be more accessible than you'd believe. Be very nice to me, Eve."

"I'll do what I promised. But Zakira has already told me that you're nothing and he's all-powerful. I could see it pissed you off. I'll treat you as you deserve to be treated." She couldn't take much more of this right now. She was gazing eagerly at the door of the hut. "Did you bring Michael? Is he here?"

"I brought him. And as long as you convince Zakira that it's valuable to keep him with you, he'll be permitted to stay. But the minute you attempt to help him escape, or caring for him causes your work on the mask to slow, then he'll be taken away from you and I'll be forced to find another use for him until you convince me that you'll not cause me difficulties. Do you want me to describe what those uses might be?"

She wanted to kill the son of a bitch. "That won't be necessary. I've already proved that I'd be too afraid to let anything happen to Michael that I could possibly prevent. As for

Michael slowing me down, that won't be a problem. He can be a big help. You may not have noticed, but he's very intelligent. He's grown up watching me work on my sculptures, and he thinks it's fun to help me with doing minor tasks on them."

"Really?" Caldwell said thoughtfully. "I wasn't around the boy for very long, but I did notice that he was probably a very smart kid. He fought like hell when he was taken down, but after he woke up from the hypo and realized what was happening, he was very quiet and just watched and listened." He grimaced. "I wasn't aware that we had a budding forensic sculptor on our hands."

"As I said, he just thinks helping Mom is great fun. Kids pick up all kinds of skills if you make them available." She should drop the subject. It was much better that he continued to think of Michael as a fledgling sculptor than have him start wondering about the skills Joe might have taught him over the years—which had included extensive training in martial arts. "Look, is that all that you wanted to discuss with me? Zakira said that he's sending someone to take me to the workroom where they want me to work on this Queen Folashade so that I can examine the equipment. But I want to spend a little time with my son and get him settled before I have to dive in and work."

"You see? Your Michael is already interfering." He smiled and waved his hand magnanimously. "But as long as you continue to know and admit that I'm the one from whom all gifts flow, I'll allow you an hour with your son before I whisk you to the workroom."

"You're too kind." She couldn't keep the sarcasm out of her tone and she was already running toward the door of the hut.

Then she turned back. "I'll take the hour. But there's one more thing I want from you. My husband is going to be very worried about what you'll be doing to me. Which means he'll tear this entire country apart until he finds me and punishes you for what you've done. Neither of us wants that to happen. You because you want to keep your useless life, and me because I'm afraid any conflict will endanger my son. So I need to keep Joe as calm as I can until I earn Zakira's trust and admiration and stand a chance of making a deal with him."

"Then you should make the deal with me," Caldwell said mockingly. "You have a much better chance that I'll be in control at any given time. What are you asking?"

"All I want is that you permit me to call and talk to my husband occasionally so he'll know for himself that we're safe. I've seen all the electronic computers and phones you have at your disposal, and I'm certain that you can make sure he won't be able to track you by a simple phone call."

"And what am I supposed to get for doing it?"

"Your life and Zakira's gratitude for keeping me content enough to give him exactly what he wants from his death mask."

"It may not be enough," he said slowly. "I'll consider it after you show us what magic you can work on that blasted mummy."

"Show a little respect," Eve said. "I'm sure that she worked hard to deserve it when she was queen. None of them had an easy time of it. I guarantee that you won't be able to recognize Folashade when I finish my first few weeks of work." She watched him shrug and walk away.

Then she took a deep breath and leaned her head against

the door. She had to take just a moment before she faced Michael. She had to be strong and not let him see what she'd gone through since she'd left the Lake Cottage and yet try to be honest with him about any threats to come. He mustn't worry about her if she could find a way to avoid it. Today had held too much agony and death. She prayed nothing would touch Michael.

And Nieva…Poor bewildered child caught in all this wickedness and pain through no fault of her own. Eve closed her eyes and murmured a swift prayer for her.

Then she straightened her shoulders and lifted her chin. Stop worrying. She had to concentrate on what was happening now to make sure they'd survive this.

Then she was inside the hut and slamming the door.

———

"Mom?" Michael was on his feet and heading across the room toward her.

"Hush!" She was grabbing him close and hugging him. "Are you okay? Lord, I was worried about you." She pushed him away and looked down at his face. "How badly did they hurt you?"

He shook his head. "Not bad after that first day." He was frowning. "You shouldn't be here. You shouldn't have done this. If I'd had a little time, I would have found a way to get away from them. Dad's going to be crazy worried."

"Yes, he is." She hugged him closer. "But I couldn't think of any other way to find you so that maybe together we could figure out how to get us both out of here."

Michael shook his head. "Dad won't like it. He'd be scared for you."

"Then you'll have to run interference for me with him." He felt so good. She couldn't hold him tight enough. "You're sure you're okay? No one really—"

"Mom." He chuckled. "The only thing wrong is that I'm having trouble breathing. You can take care of that, can't you?"

"Maybe. I'll consider it." She loosened her grip. "I guess just looking at you will be almost as good." She drew a deep breath. "But Caldwell gave me less than an hour before I have to report to Zakira's lab to do some work, so we'd better talk and get the ground rules straight so that we don't screw up the master plan."

"And what is this master plan, Mom?"

She made a face. "I have no idea yet. But I'm sure there will be one since two such brilliant minds are facing the problem together. Right?"

He nodded solemnly. "I'm sure it will only be a matter of time before we can loose this master plan on the world."

"I knew you'd agree with me." She added, "So until the master plan occurs to us, we'll just make a few preparations to keep trouble at a minimum. The first thing is assuring our privacy when we need to discuss anything. The best place would obviously be this hut, because we don't know anywhere else that could be bug-free. So I'll just spend a few minutes checking to see if Caldwell has already installed any bugs in this hut."

Michael shook his head. "You don't have to do that. I took care of checking it when they brought me in here. But we should probably do it again at least once a day."

"Good thinking. I should have remembered that your dad taught you to be an electronic whiz when we built the new boathouse on the lake. But I was only worried about Caldwell recalling that your dad was a SEAL and might have taught you martial arts. So I also told Caldwell that you'd be helping me with that death mask, and he now thinks you're a hotshot wannabe sculptor. I wanted to make sure he knew how valuable you'd be to me and no threat to them."

"So you decided to pick and choose," Michael said solemnly. "I hope Caldwell was impressed."

Choose. She tried to keep from flinching at the word Zakira had used so recently before killing that poor young girl. *Block it out.* She couldn't let Michael know about that moment. "Of course he was," Eve said. "And I didn't have to do much picking and choosing. He'd already noticed you were a smart kid. You're a young man of many talents."

"Yes, thanks to you and Dad, I have quite a few talents besides what comes naturally," he said soberly. "Martial arts, guns, weapons of all descriptions. And I'm getting better and better all the time. Because I always knew that sometime I might have to be ready to help someone fight against bad people, like Dad does."

Eve flinched. "And yet I'm the one who's brought you to some of the worst criminals. It doesn't say much for our raising you if we can't keep you safe at home to have an ordinary childhood."

Michael smiled ruefully. "You know that wasn't meant to happen. I would have been bored if I couldn't reach out and learn what the whole world could teach me. You're great parents. You shouldn't blame yourself if sometimes I take a wrong turn—like I did when I didn't realize I was the one Cira was worried about and not her mother. When I looked back, I realized that she was scared because she thought her mother could protect me and she didn't want her to leave me alone. If I'd thought of that, I would have expected Caldwell's men to be in my dorm room that afternoon, and Dad and I would have been able to find a way to take them down."

"Shades of Batman and Robin?" Eve asked.

"Something like that," Michael said. "I wouldn't have made another mistake. Because you have to be able to trust me, and I failed you that day." He added gently, "It was my duty to keep you safe, and I didn't. You shouldn't be here, Mom. But now that you are, don't try to protect me. I won't fail you again. I'll find a way to get us out of here. Trust me to help save us."

She was terribly touched. "How the hell am I supposed to do that?" Eve asked huskily. "You've got it all wrong. Any mother will tell you where the duty lies. I'm here because I belong here." She turned on her knees to face him. "It's my duty and privilege to help you get through this, just as we've helped each other through the years. So I'll tell you how it's going to be. We're going to try to get out on our own—but that may not happen. As I was being flown to the heliport here, I got a look at the jungle terrain and the mountains and waterfalls. Escape seems like a damn hard proposition. We might be able to do it, but if we can get help it could make it easier. So, we look for a way to break away from this village on our own. But there's a good chance that before we manage to do it, we'll have old friends and family knocking on the door trying to help. You know your dad and Caleb will never stop trying, even if they have to blow this village to kingdom come.

Plus Dominic and Celine and I'm sure many others whom you haven't met yet will try to find us."

Michael was frowning. "What is this leading up to? We're not just going to sit and wait to be rescued? That would be too dangerous for you."

"No, it wouldn't," she said quietly. "Unless you were still here. I told your dad before I left that I was going to try to send you to him, and when he came after us he should be ready to whisk you away if he was able to do it."

"No," Michael said sharply. "He'd never do that."

She nodded. "He'd hate it. But it would buy time we might need. He'd know that I'd be safe if I was still working on the tomb. If you were still their prisoner, though, their first instinct would be to kill you, and we'd probably both end up dead before it was over." She paused. "Of course, if you were with your dad, then you could help him with an attack on the village and save me like the heroes you both are." She struggled and finally managed to give him a sunny smile. "It will all work out."

"I won't do it."

"I think you will. Because you're so very smart. You'll think about it, and in that last moment you'll realize that I'm right." She shrugged. "And maybe that last moment won't come to exist and it will happen some other way. But I want you to be prepared...just in case."

He was still shaking his head.

She had to be careful not to upset him. This was all very difficult for him. "We won't talk about this any longer right now. We've got to work hard and survive and maybe even work on our master plan." She checked her watch. "And I've got only twelve minutes left before Caldwell comes to take me to that lab to look at the priest's refrigeration equipment. So I'd like to sit here and stare at you and think how alive and wonderful you look during that twelve minutes. I suppose I'll have to beg forgiveness from Folashade, but I have to admit how much better I find it than gazing at even the most intriguing B.C. queen..."

———

It was very cold in the workroom where Zakira was waiting when Eve was escorted there by one of Zakira's guards a short time later. She'd worn her jacket because she'd expected it after working to restore other mummies under similar conditions. But she almost felt sorry for the guard, who was pretending not to feel the chill. Zakira himself seemed not to even notice it. "You kept me waiting," Zakira said impatiently. "Don't do it again."

She could barely manage to look at him without remembering the last time she had seen him with that damn bloody dagger. But she couldn't let him see any response that might endanger Michael. Zakira wanted meekness, and that's what she'd give him. She nodded. "I'm sorry, I thought I was right on time. But I'll make sure I don't inconvenience you in the future." She moved nearer to the golden sarcophagus across the room. "This is beautifully carved. It looks ancient. How old is it?"

"At least four thousand years. The holy rituals were performed on Folashade during the time of the great transfer of power. But before the priests could complete her removal from the palace, her body and all her treasures for the afterlife were stolen and hidden away in the mountains. They weren't found until I took over the search myself." He patted his chest. "It was clearly meant to be. I was the chosen one."

That word again. "If you say so."

He stiffened. "You should speak to me with more respect. You do not believe me?"

"I don't know enough to decide whether or not to believe you, because I don't know enough about this Queen Folashade's history to judge." Her eyes narrowed on his face. "But you appear to know a good deal about her. I usually study my subjects if I can, because it helps me to define their characters when I start work. Would you be willing to tell me what you know about her? I guarantee it will make my work cleaner and better." She paused. "Or perhaps I'm wrong and you don't know that much about her?"

He lifted his chin like a striking snake. "I know everything about that bitch." His voice was filled with scorn. "Why shouldn't I? I've heard all the stories about Folashade that have been passed down from the time my ancestors were priests serving at her palace. What do you want to know?"

"Whatever you want to tell me. However, you don't appear to have a very good opinion of this royal queen you're so eager for me to restore."

"Why should I? The council of priests were not considered royalty though we're the ones who actually ran the country and should have been revered by the pharaoh and peasants alike. Instead, we were almost ignored, except on special days or when a pharaoh died and had to receive the special death rites. We were never properly appreciated, but our treatment became a constant insult when the pharaoh Hadabam the Third decided to take Folashade as his queen. It was a disaster. The only thing she had going for her was that she was also of royal birth from a distant branch of the family and had been brought up with Hadabam at the palace. She would have been an adequate match for some unimportant court official. The council tried for weeks to talk the pharaoh out of marrying her; he should have taken a bride from one of the royal families in Egypt or Persia. It would have been the only way he might have increased the power of not only the throne but also the priests' council." His lips curled. "But he wouldn't listen to them as usual."

"A love match?" Eve asked.

"Don't be ridiculous," Zakira said in disgust. "The council could have understood if lust had been the driving factor and taken care to supply him with a suitable alternative. This girl was plain as a post and had no skills, and yet the pharaoh seemed content to spend time talking and reading with her and the scribes of the court. If sex was even a factor, the council wasn't aware of it. Though she managed to give birth to a healthy enough boy a few years after she became queen. The pharaoh had been a sickly child all of his life and there was some doubt about his virility, but she was able to at least furnish him with an heir." His face twisted. "It might have all gone well if Hadabam hadn't gotten a fever and died. He ruined everything the council had planned."

"I'm sure he didn't intend to cause an upset," Eve murmured. "What was the problem?"

"The pharaoh had named his queen as regent to her son until he reached the age where he could assume the throne.

The child was only three years old. He should have put the priests' council in charge of the child, not that stupid girl who was still almost a child herself." His lips curled. "And that was the most terrible mistake of all. Because the minute she took the throne, she became a nightmare for the council."

"In what way? I believe I heard somewhere that she changed her name to Folashade when she became queen. It had something to do about honor and the crown...Is that right? Why did she do that?"

"Because she was a vain, power-hungry bitch. She told the entire council of priests after the death of her husband that as long as she was in charge, she'd rule with honor and justice; that was why she'd agreed to obey the pharaoh in this. Then she dismissed the council and told them she would never accept their guidance again. She called them thieves and butchers and said they had no idea of the meaning of honor. The whore made the council powerless. She made all the decisions, even made war on other villages and city-states and conducted them herself for the next twenty-four years."

"And how did that work out?" Eve asked quietly. "Didn't you mention a disaster?"

"The country people may have thought they were prospering during that period, but they were only ignorant peasants. The council should have been brought in to guide the palace. The priests deserved their worship and respect."

"And after that time her son took over as pharaoh?"

He shrugged. "No, he was as stupid and useless as his mother. All through his life, he was only interested in his horses and books. Then one night he took his finest chariot and his favorite horse for a ride down to the seaport and sailed away into the sunset as if Shafira no longer even existed for him. When the council questioned his servants and guards, they only said that lately he'd been talking about wanting to see Greece or Macedonia. But he never returned here to Shafira."

"Then perhaps he wasn't as stupid as you might think. Did anyone talk to his mother when he sailed away?"

"They tried, of course. She was unavailable. She'd been ill for the past few days, and the day after he left she died unexpectedly."

"And he didn't come back to attend her as she was taken to her tomb?" Eve shook her head in bewilderment. "But that's against all tradition. Something must have happened to him."

"There were problems," Zakira said harshly. "She was a troublemaker all the years she had lived, and her death was just as much of a nightmare as her life. When the priests came to take her body to the place where they were going to prepare it for the tomb, she and all her worldly treasures had disappeared. The council questioned and even tortured some of her servants, but they swore they knew nothing."

"My goodness," Eve said. "How puzzling. Whatever did they do?"

"Am I amusing you?" Zakira's tone was filled with menace. "Perhaps I should put a stop to that immediately. Shall I send for your son?"

She moistened her lips. "You're too smart not to realize that I would protect him at all costs." She had been careless, and she had to make sure he was convinced. "I was being honest when I told you it would help me to get an idea what kind of person I was sculpting. But I'm not sure I have the full story. It was clear that she'd been fighting this priests' council all through her years on the throne. Why? What did she think they did?"

"What does it matter?"

"I need to get a complete picture."

She waited.

Then he smiled recklessly. "I repeat, what does it matter? You have to give me what I want regardless of your thoughts or opinions." He paused. "Folashade had discovered that the council had been helping themselves to the treasures in the tombs of several pharaohs. Well, why shouldn't they? It should have been my ancestors who were honored in that fashion. They should have been the ones to live in those palaces. They were just a little ahead of their time." Eve could see his cheeks flushed with anger as he gestured to himself. "So I decided to take it all back and use her to do it. This will bring attention from all over the globe. Your participation will help ensure it. My power will reach farther than this small pocket, to the entire planet. It's how world religions are born, can't you see?" His eyes were glittering as he stared at Eve. "And I'll use you to do it. Do you understand, Eve Duncan? Are you going to give me what I want?"

"I'm going to give you exactly what I promised," she said quietly. "You've told me everything I need to start my work. I believe I can give you and the rest of the world a true picture of your queen. I think you might find her…riveting." She gestured toward the door. "Now if you'll let me get to work, I need to check to see that the prep work your experts did is in order."

He started for the door. "It will be in order. They realized what would happen if they displeased me. Just as you do."

The door swung shut behind him.

She was glad to be rid of him. This entire day had been a terrible time of stress and just trying to keep both herself and Michael in some kind of balance. It had been helpful to concentrate on Folashade and her story. She closed her eyes for a moment, thinking about the queen who had lived thousands of years ago—and yet, while Zakira had been talking about her, Eve had felt as if she had known Folashade. Still, she had been a complicated person. Well, then it was her job to find out more about the woman who had controlled a country and perhaps had held the dogs of war at bay for her people for at least a short while.

Eve opened her eyes and stared for a moment at the gold sarcophagus across the room. So stately and beautiful that it seemed impossible that it had been hidden in the mountains for all those thousands of years.

She started to move slowly across the room toward the sarcophagus. "Hello, Folashade," she whispered. "My name is Eve, and I hope we're going to become good friends. Because I think perhaps you're a person that I'd want to know if we could have met at another time and place. If you don't mind, I have a lot of questions I'd like to ask you. If the answers don't come to me, I might have to guess, and that's okay, too. But the first thing you should know is that I'm one of the good guys and I'm on your side. And I promise I always will be..."

But she needed to finish this initial examination and then get back to Michael and try to sleep so that she could start working on Folashade as soon as possible. It was the only sure way she could keep her son safe.

"Mom! Wake up!"

Michael's voice. Michael's hand on her shoulder shaking her. He needed her!

Eve jerked upright on her cot, instinctively reaching for him. "What's wrong? Are you hurt?"

"No! You scared me. You screamed. I guess you were dreaming." His hand was touching the tears on her cheek. "You're crying."

"Am I?" She covered his hand with her own. "It must have been a really bad dream. A nightmare. It's a good thing you woke me."

He nodded. "But you don't usually have nightmares."

"No, I don't. But it's been a kind of worrisome day, hasn't it? But now that we're together, everything is going to be better." She gave him a hug. "Now go back to your cot and we'll both try to sleep. We'll have to start work on the queen early."

"Okay." He got to his feet. But she could tell he was still troubled. "You didn't tell me the queen's name. Was it Nieva?"

Eve froze. "Nieva? No. It's much more unusual. It's Fola-shade. She named herself when she took the throne. It's an interesting story, and I'll tell you about her while we're working. Why did you think it might be Nieva?"

"Because that was what you were screaming when you were having the nightmare," Michael said simply. "I thought maybe what the priest had told you about the queen had scared you."

"Not at all. I have an idea she was a good and extraordinary person." But she knew she couldn't just leave it at that. Not with Michael. "But I did also meet a Nieva, and sometime I'll tell you about her, too. But not right away. Because she wasn't scary either. She was only very, very sad. And we've got enough sad things to think about right now, haven't we? So when we think about Nieva, we'll just hope that she's not sad any longer."

He nodded though he was still frowning. "And you'll try not to be sad, either?"

"You're worried about me having any more bad dreams? I'll work on it." She smiled. "And we'll probably be so busy working on the queen that we'll both collapse at the end of the day."

He smiled back at her. "Sounds good to me."

"I thought it would." She added thoughtfully, "Maybe somewhere in that master plan we're going to concoct, we'll manage to find a way to heal some of the sadness and make any nightmares vanish into the great beyond…"

CHAPTER

13

ROXANNE FALLS

TWO DAYS LATER

I t's beautiful…" Celine jumped out of the jeep, strode over to the edge of the cliff, and breathed in the mist as she gazed out over the thundering falls that cascaded down to the rocks below. The roar of the water was so intense, she had to raise her voice to speak to Dominic, who was coming forward to stand beside her. "It's perfectly gorgeous, isn't it?"

"I had a reason to stop here, but I thought you'd like it. That's why I gave the order to set up tents and overnight here. Two days on the road is enough, and I need to connect with Quinn before I go any farther into this damn jungle."

"That's fine with me. This is the first waterfall that had a name in those maps that you gave me to study." She was looking at the map again. "It's Roxanne Falls. And there's some historical reference…"

"It means 'princess,'" Dominic said. "And the reference is to the daughter of Darius, the Persian emperor whom this waterfall was named for quite recently. Roxanne later married Alexander the Great of Greece and helped save Persia. After that, there were a lot of monuments named after her, including this waterfall."

"I'm impressed. How did you know all that about her?" She glanced down at the map. "It's very interesting, but I wouldn't think it was quite your cup of tea."

"History usually fascinates me…particularly when I start to see it possibly leading to a use that's very modern indeed." His lips tightened. "And there's no one more modern and up to date than you, Celine. I needed to see why Zakira seems to be so fascinated by the queens of Egypt that he chose to sacrifice you to honor one of them. If Kontara remembered that temple wall correctly, that statue she spoke about was the one he had the most fondness for. I'm betting it was Nefertiti. Though he had a few other powerhouse queens from whom to choose. There was Cleopatra, who was a great strategist. Hatshepsut, who ruled for years as pharaoh and even went to war to protect her throne. And Arsinoe, Ptolemy's queen, who extended Egypt's trading power and made it the richest country on earth."

"But you still think he chose Nefertiti? Why?"

"Because Zakira has the reputation for being the complete egotist. The reports I've gotten on him indicate that he not only has ambitions to be in complete control of this section of Africa, but he also can't bear to have his orders questioned. Which means he probably couldn't tolerate the thought of having to compete with a woman who insisted on standing on equal footing with him. He'd prefer to have her as a beautiful toy so that other men could envy him his possession."

"And that was Nefertiti? You mean she wasn't that smart?"

"I didn't say that. She was very intelligent. A scholar and

linguist who was also very good with diplomacy. She just preferred to stay in her husband's shadow. Since that pharaoh was
Ramses the Second, and quite the egotist himself, it was more
comfortable for her to stay beautiful and adored and not get
in her husband's way. Some call her the perfect trophy wife.
That's why Caldwell had to find a stunning woman like you
to please Zakira as the ideal sacrifice to satisfy his followers.
He managed to get the surface stuff right, but there's no way
your personality is anything like Nefertiti's. Zakira would
have been disappointed the minute you opened your mouth
to speak. There's nothing in the least self-effacing about you."

She made a face. "Good. I take that as a compliment. I'd
just as soon forget about those particular plans."

"I wish I could," he said grimly. "I'm having a good deal
of trouble not imagining and reimagining that entire scenario.
And I can't even try to dismiss it, because I have a hunch that
statue was just the tip of the iceberg. I doubt if Zakira has
given up on you yet. I think he's still clinging to any plans he's
made for you. According to what Kontara has told me, once he
makes a decision, he sticks to it in every detail." He gestured
to the waterfall. "I contacted the geographic mapmaking
organization and found out that it was Zakira who recently
insisted that the name of these falls be changed from the original African one to honor the wife of Alexander the Great.
Evidently he also spent most of his life searching for this tomb
of a lost queen that he'd heard about from his father since his
childhood. When he found it, he immediately started to plan
how that discovery could make him famous and rich. But he
wanted to make sure every step was right and that anyone who
came to the village would feel an emotional connection with

not only Folashade but with other famous queens throughout history. But I'd bet that he gave Caldwell specific orders to go along with his fantasies." His gaze went back to the thundering waterfall. "This waterfall is fairly close to the village of Karimu, where the massacre took place. We know Caldwell was involved in that massacre. It wouldn't be difficult for him to set up a command and lookout position down there in that tangle of caves and brush that let him control the attack. I've been wondering if they might have also hidden something of interest in that cave. He's definitely an opportunist. Caves are traditionally great hiding places for things you don't want found. Or maybe the path through the cave leads somewhere else where we need to be—like Zakira's village." He was suddenly heading down the cliff slope as he spoke. "I think I'll go see if I can find anything intriguing down there in those caves…"

"Wait." Celine jumped to her feet. "Why didn't you tell me we need to go there? I'll come with you!"

He didn't stop. "No, not now. I've already told Rashid to watch out for you. Maybe after I check it out…" He disappeared around a bend in the cliff and she could no longer see him.

But she saw Rashid strolling toward the cliff and settling on a boulder a few yards away.

"Dammit!" Her hands clenched into fists at her sides. It was clear Dominic had known he was going to those caves and had made arrangements to keep her safely here while he explored them. She wanted to hit him.

She was still angry when he hadn't returned after over two hours. But by that time she was also beginning to panic. Where the hell was he?

"It's beautiful, isn't it?" Kontara was strolling toward her, but she was gazing at the waterfall. "Dominic told me that we'd be spending the night here. I wonder if that roar will keep us awake?"

"Did you recognize the waterfall?" Celine asked.

She shook her head. "No, as I told Dominic, there are several waterfalls along this stretch of cliff, and they all look pretty much the same to me. Yes, it's beautiful. But when I was on the run, it was just a hazard to work around so that I could save myself. There's only one waterfall that I remember well at all, and that was the huge one on the far side of Shafira village. I'd recognize that one because I almost drowned when I slipped out of the village and into the waterfall itself. I was trying to reach the currents downstream, and I was lucky enough to find a limestone ledge on the edge of the bank. I sheltered there until the soldiers gave up the hunt a few hours later. I was sopping wet and almost froze when the temperature dropped that night." She made a face. "I decided I'd rather face the punishment the soldiers were handing out than get hypothermia. You can see why I'd prefer to skip the spectacular waterworks show and stay warm and cozy at Bon Jaka."

Celine nodded soberly. "For any number of reasons. You're being very brave, Kontara. If I can help, let me know. I realize it's a nightmare for you."

"Yes, it is. But the only way I would have refused to come was if you'd let me talk you out of it. I wasn't doing this for you. I owed Dominic, and I pay my debts." She gave a slight shrug. "And maybe I wanted to stick it to Zakira and Caldwell and give all those women they were torturing a break. By the way, where is Dominic? It's been two days, and until now he hasn't let you out of his sight."

Celine tried not to show how upset she was. "A couple hours ago, he took off to explore those caves he noticed on the hillside beside the waterfall. He's looking for a path to where Caldwell might have hidden more arms or anything else. Or maybe another way to Shafira village." Celine couldn't keep from scowling as she nodded at Rashid sitting on the bank several yards away. "And he turned me over to Rashid, dammit. When I asked why I couldn't go along, all he said was that he'd take me back there if anything proved interesting. Then he was gone before I could start to argue with him." Her lips twisted. "But I'll guarantee he'll hear about it when he gets back."

Kontara gave a low whistle. "I can tell you're not pleased with him."

"To put it mildly. He went in that cave alone. He didn't think it was dangerous enough to take a team with him. But it was too dangerous to take me when he knew I'd want to go. That wasn't fair."

"Then I'll make sure not to be around when he appears on the scene." Kontara grinned. "Actually, I'm glad we're stopping for the night. I made preparations for a few decent meals while we were on the road, but I've been bored to tears with what I've had to serve to those poor men so far. I didn't want my reputation totally ruined."

"Those meals were very good," Celine said. "Excellent."

Kontara shook her head. "You ain't seen nothing yet. I'll invent something completely unique now that I've got the time. It will be a relief to try to forget about that blasted village and what Zakira and Caldwell did to all of us." She added soberly, "And I'd think you'd want to try to do a little forgetting yourself, considering what I've heard you've gone through lately."

Celine shook her head. "To each her own. I don't have your gourmet talents, so I won't be able to lose myself in that kind of escapism. All I can think of right now is Eve Duncan and her son, who are still being held by those bastards who killed my friend Barnaby. I'm feeling very helpless at the moment. There must be something I can do." She looked back at the entrance of the cave beneath the waterfall. "And I'm thinking about maybe exploring there if everything looks safe enough."

"Oops." Kontara grimaced. "I believe that may be my exit line. You've got the same expression on your face that I see right before you take me down on the mat and get me in a headlock." She waved her hand as she turned away. "I'm going to go get my supplies, and I'll ask Rashid to help me set up my kitchen. It'll keep him busy for a little while, but not for long—then he'll notice you're gone and be on your trail. He'll catch up with you in no time because he'll know where you're heading." She shook her head at Celine. "If I thought there was any danger at all connected to this, I wouldn't be doing it. But since Dominic brought you with him, he doesn't have the right to smother you just because he wants to take care of you. We both know how well you've been trained to do that all by yourself." She turned on her heel and started toward Rashid. "Get moving!"

Celine got moving!

She was down the hill and around the cliff in seconds, heading for the cave opening she could see just beyond the mist of the waterfall. She made her way through the first prickly patch of the maze bordering the cave, but then she was caught by the spray and had to cling with her back to the cliff as she carefully inched herself down the rocky pathway into the cave. Where was Dominic? She could see a flashlight dimly glowing in the distance; she lit her own flashlight and headed toward it.

Cockroaches on the uneven stone floor…She hadn't even known there were cockroaches in the African wilds. Of course there were, she thought impatiently. They were everywhere. Didn't some scientists say that cockroaches would eventually supplant the human race?

But personally, she'd bet on the human race every time. As far as she knew, cockroaches had never painted a *Mona Lisa* or invented a new lifesaving operation to save anyone from brain disease.

But where there were cockroaches, could snakes be far behind? She had no fondness for reptiles. Enough was enough.

She stopped on the trail and shouted, "Are we going to play hide and seek all day, Dominic? I'm tired of this."

"It's no game, Celine." Dominic was suddenly standing before her, a dark shadow outlined in the soft luminosity of his flashlight. "It was more of a demonstration to show you that you should have waited until I was ready to come back for you as I asked."

"You didn't ask, you just told me and then disappeared," she said curtly. "Demonstrations can be good if they teach something. The only thing I learned by having to follow you is that

I dislike cockroaches almost as much as I do snakes. Also that I hated having to worry about you in here by yourself when I could have been watching your back."

"You wanted to protect me?" He paused. "How unusual. Most people decide that I'm capable of taking care of myself. After all, it's what I do for a living. I believe I'm touched."

"Stop making fun of me. Did you find what you wanted in this cave or not?"

"I found it. I'll show you in a few minutes, but right now I want to explore the fact that you were disappointed that you couldn't watch my back." He took a step closer to her. "Why?"

She could feel the heat from his body, and she was suddenly tense. There was something different about him. She could almost feel the electric excitement he was radiating. Excitement and...something else. "Because we've become...partners, and I'd never leave a partner to face people like Caldwell and Zakira alone. I don't care how well he thinks of himself."

She inhaled sharply as he bent forward and she could feel his breath on her ear.

Then his lips were on the hollow of her throat.

She shuddered and found herself pressing closer to him. Where was the anger? Just the feel of him was making her dizzy. Oh, to hell with it. This was more important..."Though I don't think...this is the right time to..." He was unbuttoning her shirt, freeing her breasts, and rubbing her nipples slowly, sensuously, against his chest. She gasped as she arched up against him.

"No, you're damn right, it's not the right time." His hands were cupping her hips and bringing her to cradle tightly against him. "But we both knew it was going to happen sometime, didn't we...?" He bent his head and pulled at her nipple with his teeth. "Wrong time. Wrong place. But if I don't get you out of here soon, it's going to happen anyway. Because I have to be inside you."

And she wanted him inside her. He had her pinned to the stone wall, and the muscular tension of his body combined with the surrounding darkness and the rhythmic sound of the waterfall outside was absolutely erotic. "I don't care if it's the wrong time." She was breathing hard, and every breath was another caress against him as she tried to move closer. "I need you to—"

He was pushing her away!

"No!" She tried to hold on to him, but he was picking her up and putting her back on the path. She could see he was also trying to get his breath as he brushed his cheek once more back and forth against her breasts and then pushed her toward the cave opening. "Get out of here. You may not care right now, but you might if you look back on it later. I refuse to be the man you'll remember with the cockroaches and the snakes. Though I didn't see any snakes."

"Neither did I. Maybe there aren't any." She pushed her hair from her face as she looked back at him. Her body still felt on fire, and she didn't want to leave him. She vaguely remembered something he'd said. "But didn't you tell me you wanted to show me something?"

"Later. I promise. Everything later. Just get out of here. I can't touch you right now. I'm trying to be the kind of guy whose back you'd like to watch tomorrow as well as today. I'm having dire trouble with the whole concept at the moment."

"No, you aren't," she said quietly. "Even when I barely

knew you, I realized that you were different from anyone else. From the moment you took me down to see Barnaby that night at the precinct and held my hand and didn't let me face it alone. How could I not know it?" She was heading back toward the cave opening. "I was thinking that my father would have done something like that."

"Dear God, don't compare me to your father even mentally. I couldn't stand the comparison."

"No, you couldn't." She'd reached the waterfall. "But you wouldn't have to. You manage to set your own standard that works just fine for you and the people around you." She turned and said over her shoulder, "Kontara said she's going to fix a special meal tonight. You won't want to miss it." She smiled impishly. "And you particularly won't want to miss the dessert." She disappeared under the mist of the waterfall.

———

CAMPFIRE, ROXANNE FALLS
9:40 P.M.

The fireside dinner was everything that Kontara had promised it would be. A delicious beef bourguignon. For dessert, she'd prepared a special African dish that was delicate and yet totally and wonderfully cinnamon-spiced.

Dominic had a call from Joe Quinn that kept him busy after the first few courses, and he stopped by to tell Celine that Joe's team had reached the estate and would be joining them soon. But he also made a point of stopping beside where Celine was sitting by the fire after dessert was served. He bent down and whispered, "This wasn't the dessert you were talking about?"

223

She chuckled and shook her head.

"Thank God." He went on with his call as he strolled away from the fire.

Rashid took his place and knelt down beside Celine. "That wasn't a good thing that you did, you know. I caught hell from Dominic about you slipping off to that cave. Did you get hell, too?"

"Something like that." She was remembering that heated moment in the cave when it had seemed the entire world was turning upside down. Best not to elaborate on that particular reaction. "But he was happy with what he found in the cave, so I think that it ended up all right."

"Just don't do it again," Rashid said, shaking his head. "I know he was worried that Caldwell might have left one of his men in the cave to pick off anyone they ran across who was obviously on the hunt. He'd be damn upset if anything happened to you."

She wasn't going to sit there and take that nonsense. "But he wasn't so afraid that he'd take a team with him? You should have been worried about him. Someone should have been watching his back."

Rashid frowned. "He wouldn't thank me for tagging after him. Besides, he's an expert sharpshooter. He almost always works alone."

"Bullshit." But she wanted this over. "Don't lecture me, Rashid. Dominic and I might be able to work something out once we get a chance to talk. I don't want to cause any trouble."

"Since when?" Rashid asked sarcastically. "You haven't objected to trouble on the horizon since I first met you." His eyes narrowed on her face. "But maybe you actually mean it this time." He got to his feet. "We'll see. May I walk you to your tent?"

"No, I think I've caused enough bother for one day. I'll go by myself." She stood up. "It's a beautiful night, isn't it? And the waterfall looks fantastic in the moonlight."

He nodded. "That it does. And now Dominic won't have to worry about trouble with any of Caldwell's sharpshooters hanging out down there. He said he took care of the problem."

How had he done that? Celine wondered. Then she dismissed the question—at the moment, she couldn't have cared less. She knew by now Dominic would be waiting for her, and that was all that was important "Yes, we wouldn't want poor Dominic to have to worry." Then she walked swiftly away toward the spot Rashid had set up her tent in the trees overlooking the waterfall.

Her heart was starting to pound as she ran toward the tent.

Dominic was there waiting in the darkness of the tent as he'd been waiting for her in the shadows of the cave earlier today. But it wasn't the same. Because she knew exactly what was coming. No more waiting. Her body was readying, preparing to receive him. And she could feel him, hear the sound of his breathing.

Then he was pulling her into the tent.

"You took forever," he said roughly. "I was about to come after you."

"Rashid..."

But he wasn't listening. Then she was in his arms and he was dragging her down to the bedroll on the floor as his hands moved over her, taking off her shirt and then swiftly, almost frantically, getting rid of the rest of her clothes. She could feel his skin, the bristle of his cheek rubbing against her bare breasts that was a provocation in itself. Then she could hear the pounding of his heart as he plunged deep inside her.

"I want you too much," he muttered. "Don't let me hurt you."

She was full of him and trying to keep from screaming for more. "You won't...hurt me. I need..." Then she lunged upward and took what she needed. Deeper. Faster. Harder. Deeper again. She couldn't take it...But she did, and it was hot and insane and sometimes she felt as if she couldn't breathe but she still couldn't let him stop.

Again.

Again.

Again!

Don't stop.

Not now.

Not ever...

———

"I think I should be angry with you." Celine yawned and moved closer to Dominic's naked body. "But at the moment, I can't remember why. It was something about the way you were so arrogant about leaving me waiting and making me track you to that cave. All I know was that it was important..."

"If you can't remember why, maybe it wasn't that important." He moved her arm so that he could rub his lips over her nipple. "These are absolutely exquisite...You said I didn't hurt you, that was all that was important at the time. It got a bit wild there for a minute."

"For an hour," she corrected. "Or three...I lost track of time. You were quite...adequate."

"Ouch. You really know how to hurt a guy."

She giggled. "As if you'd believe me? You're much too confident to let a passing insult bother you. Besides, you must have noticed I'm a rank amateur compared with you. I've been too busy just surviving to get much experience."

"Then you're an incredible amateur. But if you want to work on anything particular for an advanced degree, I stand ready to oblige." He reached over and kissed her. Long, hard, yet somehow wonderfully sweet. "You're a masterpiece. Everything about you. And don't think I'm giving you bull because of that very lovely face and body. It's so dark in this tent I can't even see anything but a shadow. I repeat, a masterpiece. Every move you make, whatever you're willing to give...and take, your sense of humor, the way you perform a headlock. How could anyone resist you?"

She chuckled. "Particularly the headlock. You're right, I'm a masterpiece." She raised herself on one elbow. "And I've decided that practice makes perfect and I want to practice some more, if you don't mind. I should take advantage of you before I remember why I'm angry."

"By all means." He lifted her on top of him, and she gasped as he came into her. "Let's try a brisk little warm-up and then go for the wild frontier..."

CHAPTER

14

Wake up!" Eve's shoulder was being shaken, and she opened her eyes to see Caldwell's face above her. He was frowning as he sat back on his heels. "It's time for you to get up and get back to work. And tell that kid to stop glaring at me or I'll make him sorry."

That woke Eve instantly. She sat up on the camp bed and glanced at Michael's cot across the room. "It's okay, Michael," she said quickly. "He's not going to hurt me. He just can't resist being rude when he gets the opportunity." She turned back to Caldwell. "And I worked on the restoration until two in the morning. I do need a few hours of sleep occasionally. I'm not a robot."

"You sleep when I give you permission." He paused. "Though Zakira appears to be fairly pleased with your progress over the past few days. He said he can't judge the creativity yet, but you've been working hard."

"Good. Then I'll go back to sleep."

"No you won't. Not until I finish with you. I've found

a reason that perhaps I should give you something you wanted."

"And what is that?"

"I just got a report of my men watching Sardwa airport, and it seems that Joe Quinn and several other of his team have landed and are headed north into the jungle after checking in at Bon Jaka. That's Dominic's place, and it could mean trouble for me."

"What else could you expect?" Eve asked. "I don't blame you for being nervous."

"I'm not nervous. There's practically no chance of him being able to make his way through the jungle to Shafira. I'm just taking certain measures to slow him down and cut those chances even more. I've decided that I'll let you phone your Joe to assure him that you and the boy are well. Naturally, the call will be monitored."

"Naturally," she echoed. "When?"

"Within the next thirty minutes." He got to his feet. "And the call will last no longer than five minutes, and you'll give no information that might lead him in this direction. If you don't obey, that will be your last call." His smile was malicious. "With emphasis on 'last.'"

"You know I'll obey," Eve said bitterly. "Go get me that phone."

Caldwell was getting to his feet. "I'm on my way. I'm always happy to accommodate you, Eve."

Michael watched him as he left the hut. "Will that help us, Mom?"

"I doubt it. But it will make your dad feel better, and he

might be able to pull something out of his hat that will give him a clue where we're located."

"I'll be glad to talk to him. I've missed him."

She nodded. "Yeah, me too," she said wryly. "Though he's not going to be too happy to see this mess I've managed to get us into."

"He'll know it wasn't your fault." Michael shook his head. "And he'll just be glad to see you're okay. You know that as well as I do. Just like I was when you walked in here that first day."

"Thanks for the kind words." She smiled at him. "I guess you noticed I was pretty happy to see you, too. Though you did complain I was squeezing you too—" She stopped as Caldwell came back with the videophone. "Later..." She quickly dialed Joe's number and waited impatiently for him to pick up.

"Eve?" She could see his face on the screen. "Thank God." He closed his eyes for an instant. "Are you okay?"

"As much as I can be with the company I have to keep at present. Though having Michael with me makes up for it. You look very good to me, Joe."

"You're lying. I feel like I've been through a wringer and I've wanted to commit wholesale murder since the minute I heard that you'd left the Lake Cottage. How is Michael?"

"Okay." She pointed the camera at Michael, who waved. "Missing you. He's been keeping busy helping me with the restoration. I can't answer any questions about this place or the people here, and this call is being monitored."

"I figured. I'm just glad to hear your voice." He cleared his throat. "Just hang on a little longer and I'll be there to come and get both of you. We're all working very hard and thinking about you all the time."

"I'll be glad when that happens. Though working on Folashade has been fascinating, she doesn't come close to being with you. Those four thousand or so years have taken a bit of a toll on her." Out of the corner of her eye, she saw Caldwell get to his feet. "I think they're going to pull the plug now. I'll try to call you again soon. Take care of yourself. I love you." She pressed DISCONNECT. "I don't think I got my full five minutes, Caldwell."

He shrugged as he took the phone. "There's only so much mush I can stand. You're lucky I put up with as much as I did." He paused before he went out the door. "It's a shame he raised your hopes like that. It's not going to do a damn bit of good. No one's going to be able to save you. Your only salvation has to come from me."

Then he was gone, and she slowly nestled her head back on her pillow. "Don't pay any attention to what he said, Michael. He's wrong. We have all kinds of people who care and will be working to find us. Now go back to sleep and everything will be fine. We need our rest. Good night, Michael."

"Good night, Mom."

She closed her eyes. What she'd said had been the truth. She was lucky in that she had family and friends who would move heaven and earth to help them. They might be alone now, but that would end and people would be here for them. Joe and Caleb. Jane. Dominic Even Celine, who had been so desperate to help her when she had scarcely even known her name…

She had to trust all of them.

Just as Joe had said…

———

ROXANNE FALLS

DAYBREAK

The next time Celine woke, Dominic was gone, but he'd left a message on her phone.

"Somehow I was too occupied last night to tell you that I had to get up at dawn and set up a team to escort Quinn and his men to meet us here at the waterfall. I wonder how that happened…But I'll see you at breakfast, and I'll take you to the cave and protect you from the cockroaches while you look around. Or maybe you'll be the one to protect me. You'd probably prefer that. We'll work it out. I believe we're going to have to do a lot of that in the future. Don't panic. I'm not pushing… Maybe a little, but what can I say…I think we both know where this is going, and I won't give up until I find a way to bring it home…"

That was all, but it was more than enough after the night she'd spent with Dominic and the way her body still felt sated and contented and yet ached for more. It just showed how he'd studied her during their time together and how well he'd come to read her responses. Probably with anyone else, she would have felt a little panic at the totality of her response. Perhaps also a tiny bit of distrust that she'd yielded so much of her independence, even in that fantastic a sexual encounter? But he'd made sure that he recognized any problems and was willing to work with her to solve them. *What a wise man you are, Alex Dominic.* She was suddenly chuckling.

And definitely crafty. But at the moment, she didn't want to worry about anything while she was feeling this lovely glow. She could take care of anything the world threw at her, as she always had before, and she would tell Dominic that the next time she saw him.

But she wasn't about to go back to sleep now. Time to take a shower in that spray from the waterfall and then meet Dominic for breakfast...

But it was Kontara she met when she was walking back toward her tent after she finished her shower several minutes later. She stopped and watched Kontara standing by the edge of the cliff, frowning. "Good morning," Kontara said, then added jerkily, "I wanted to see you. I won't keep you long." She grimaced. "I feel awkward as hell doing this. But I'll just blurt it out and get my answer and then I can forget it."

Celine was gazing at her in puzzlement. "What on earth are you talking about?"

Kontara was speaking fast. The words practically tripping over each other. "The roar of the waterfall kept me awake, so I took a walk in the middle of the night. I was up here, not far from your tent." She paused. "And I heard more than the waterfall."

Celine blinked as she realized what the woman was trying to say. "I imagine you did. That's awkward. As I recall, I might have been a little excited. I'm sorry if I embarrassed you."

"Don't be stupid. Do you think that I would have mentioned it if that was all I was worried about?" She drew a deep breath. "But you're my friend, I had to be sure. I don't think that Dominic would do anything that you wouldn't like. But I've found that sex sometimes changes men. I've been hurt before. I can't tell you how many times. They can…hurt you. I had to be sure that you wanted it. Now just say yes or no so that I can stop being such an ass."

Celine could see how difficult this had been for Kontara in quite a few ways.

"Yes, I wanted it," Celine said gently. "All of it. But thank you very much for caring."

"Of course I cared." She started to turn away. "You cared enough about me to teach me to protect myself. Turnabout is fair play. I don't have many good friends, but Dominic is one of them. I'm glad he brought you pleasure." She grinned. "And I promise I won't be strolling anywhere near your tent from now on." She started down the hill. "Now get dressed and come down to breakfast." Her eyes were twinkling. "It won't be nearly as good as last night's dinner, but you might need the protein."

Celine didn't see Dominic until breakfast was almost over and he dropped down beside her in front of the fire. "You look fairly glowing this morning." He was eating a piece of bacon as he studied her. "You must have had a good night."

"Passable." She finished her biscuit. "But then I usually don't have a problem. Did you set up the escort to bring Quinn here?"

"Wicked," he murmured. "On their way. They should be

here in a few hours. But he'll be glad of the progress we've made since we've been here."

"Progress?" Her gaze flew to his face. "What progress?"

"Oh, that interests you? I hope I can offer you more than just a fleeting amusement. That cut me to the quick."

"It did not." She leaned forward. "What progress?"

He took another bite of bacon. "Which area do you want to explore with me?"

"Everything."

"Now, that's encouraging, almost promising." He was smiling teasingly. "But I'm torn which way I want to go with such an abundance of riches."

"Dominic."

He held up his hand. "I surrender. Everything it is." He got to his feet. "We'll start with the basics." He held out his hand to help her to her feet. "Walk with me. Are you finished eating?"

"Not according to Kontara. But I'll risk it." She put the plate on the ground. "Though she told me most sternly that I might need the protein."

He gazed at her speculatively. "Now, I wonder how that conversation came about?"

"Keep wondering. You shouldn't expect me to confide everything to you about my life when you kept me worrying and waiting for hours yesterday before I finally got impatient enough to go after you to see if you were still alive." She frowned. "And then you still didn't tell me anything important about what you'd found there."

"I was about to when you distracted me."

"My fault?" She went back to the original subject. "Basics? What are you talking about?"

He gestured to the maze leading up to the cave opening. "What's more basic than earth and shrubs that could lead through that waterfall and the cave behind it to a path that might take us to Shafira?"

Celine's eyes widened with excitement. "You found it?"

"I found the beginning of a trail on the far side of the falls that appeared very well kept for a wilderness jungle area. The reason that I kept you waiting so long yesterday was that I had to first search the cave and then clear some of the brush from the trail and go a mile or so into it to see if I could find any signs that Caldwell or his men had used it."

"And?"

He nodded. "I found both boot and sandal prints and a few ammunition shells coming down from the mountain toward the back entrance of the cave. They obviously used the trail to get Zakira's soldiers and Caldwell's men into position to attack Karimu."

"Then we'll be able to get to Zakira's village," Celine said. "We'll be able to find Eve and Michael."

He nodded curtly. "But it's not going to be that fast or easy when a good many nasty possibilities go with it. Ambush. Booby traps, drones. Sharpshooters the closer we get to the village." He paused. "And two hostages to threaten to kill if we make a move Caldwell doesn't like."

"I know all that," Celine said impatiently. "I'm not stupid enough to hope for easy. But we're closer than we were yesterday. You've probably already started to turn loose your most expert trackers on finding those booby traps and the best and safest way to negotiate the trail up the mountain without being seen."

He nodded. "The minute I got back to camp yesterday. I've been getting hourly reports from them today."

She grinned. "I thought so. Closer and closer. You did pretty damn well yesterday, Dominic. I suppose I have to forgive you for shutting me out of helping you make it even better. Now we only have to figure out the details."

"I might have gotten a start on doing that as well yesterday," Dominic said. "I told you I had to explore the cave before I thought about finding that trail. Actually, what I found in the cave led me to go look for that trail." They had reached the interior of the cave after they'd made their way through the maze of brush and mist, and he was lighting the lantern he'd brought from the camp. "I believe you'd have found it worth your while, too."

"If I'd been given the choice. I'd rather have been with you every step of the way. Rashid said you weren't worried about attacks from any of the men Caldwell might have left to guard his back when he was attacking Karimu. Why weren't you worried, dammit? All Rashid said was that you were very good at taking care of yourself."

"Yes, I am. As I've been trying to convince you since we met at that Boston police station." He took her hand and led her down the rocky pathway. "But you clearly don't trust anyone but yourself. However, if you're thinking that I was forced to dispose of Caldwell's sentry myself yesterday, that wasn't how it went down. Though I'd have been willing to do it if it had been necessary. But it seems that Caldwell didn't trust his sentry or anyone else and decided to make sure that no one knew about the nice little stash he'd hidden away in this cave." He was pulling her down a side passage toward a bank of boulders. He trained the light on a large brown leather chest and opened it. "Arms and explosives." He moved down the line and lifted another lid. "Gold, probably from Zakira's private hoard from the mines." Farther down the path at another passage, he opened still another chest. "Jewels. These had to be special selections to decorate his temple and possibly the death mask that Eve is working on. He probably substituted phonies for these genuine stones. There's a few more chests down the next passage, but you get the picture."

She nodded. "Caldwell is robbing Zakira blind and probably preparing for a quick getaway as soon as he sees his way clear. Can we use it? There should be a way to turn Zakira against Caldwell."

"I'm working on it."

She was looking down at the jewels in the chest. She stiffened as she had a sudden thought. He wasn't going to like this. "It shouldn't be so difficult. You're very clever. You even have the tool to do it." She lifted her eyes to meet his. "We've discussed all this before. That's why I came here, Dominic." She added quietly, "I told you that it was the smartest way to use me. We just find a way to dangle me in front of Zakira or Caldwell and then set the trap. Bait."

"Bullshit!" he said violently.

She shook her head. "Think about it. It would only be a matter of time until I'm brought before Zakira himself. Maybe insert a tracker in my arm or leg. Eve, that little boy Michael. Both have their lives on the line. I don't think Joe Quinn would think I was talking bullshit."

"To hell with what he'd think," Dominic said through set teeth. "He'd probably trade anyone or anything right now if he thought it would save Eve and his kid. Any father would do the same. But he can keep his hands off you." He reached out and grasped her shoulders. "We'll find some other way to get them away from that damn village. Promise me that you'll not mention that crazy idea to Quinn or anyone else."

"I can't do that." She smiled crookedly. "Find me a better, safer way to get Eve and her son away from Zakira and Caldwell's men, and I'll jump at it. Frankly, the idea of playing into those monsters' hands scares me to death. I have a hell of a lot of things I still want to do in my life. I said bait, not sacrifice. The entire plan would depend on how foolproof a trap you can set up. But you haven't shown me anything better yet. And that means we have to leave everything on the table until you do."

Dominic was cursing beneath his breath. "I'm close, dammit. I've stationed men on that maze that leads out of this cave and down into the next road up the mountain. We'll find Shafira and Zakira and go after Caldwell as soon as we do."

"But you haven't really found anything yet?" Celine asked. "I was hoping when Rashid had mentioned that you didn't have to worry about a sharpshooter any longer that Caldwell might have ordered Jossland to keep an eye on this waterfall and we might be rid of him."

He shook his head. "Caldwell's evidently promised you to him. Or to Zakira." His grip dropped from her shoulders to her arm. "And I think you should see what he's planning on letting Zakira do to you if you decide that you want to play Caldwell's games." He was suddenly pulling her down the path toward the back of the cave. "By all means, you need to know all the details of how our monsters operate."

"I already know," she said quietly. "You sat with me and held my hand after Jossland murdered Barnaby. I know you're upset, but you're not going to show me anything that would hurt or frighten me. We're way past that. Though all this is too new for me to be certain where we're heading, I know it would bother you far more than it would me, Dominic."

He stopped short on the path. "Yes, it would. I've already seen that I'd lose that battle," he said wearily. He turned around and jerked her into his arms. "But I still almost did it." He buried her face in his chest. "Because I can't stand the thought of letting you commit that kind of madness. I don't want anyone touching you. Forget it. It won't happen. Because I'll watch you like a hawk." He lifted her chin and brushed his lips across her cheek. "And now that we've settled that, do you want to go back to the camp and meet with Quinn so that we can tell him about the loot Caldwell has heisted from Zakira?"

"You could have told him on the phone last night. Why didn't you?"

"Because, as you've pointed out, you're my partner in this, and I didn't want to cheat you out of knowing about it first."

"I appreciate that. Just so we're clear, once this is over, the loot is going back to the people from whom it was taken. Even if we find a portion of it might have belonged to the queen who brought us here. I hope we're on the same page."

"Of course. Last night there were more important things to attend to on the agenda. Don't you agree?"

"Perhaps not Quinn," she said dryly.

"But then I've always told you that I sometimes don't follow my own code. I'm not the honorable example your father was or even our sterling, law-abiding Joe Quinn. Last night I wanted to take something for myself. So I did it, and I'd do it again." He added softly, "Wouldn't you?"

"How could I deny it?" Her voice was husky. "When I seem to have been the one to most benefit from it."

"Not true. It's all in the viewpoint." He was gently stroking her cheek.

"I'll accept that qualification," Celine said. "But my viewpoint is that you were everything I wanted so I didn't even try to persuade you to think about anything else." She took his hand away from her cheek and held it as she started back toward the front opening of the cave. "But now I want to know what you were going to show me. If you really want me to see it, I'm not afraid of the monsters."

He shook his head ruefully. "I know you aren't. That's your problem."

"And your problem is that you always want to protect me from them. But sometimes that's not possible." They'd reached the front opening of the cave, and she turned to face him. "Even my father realized that. It's why he concentrated on teaching me to protect myself. If you don't want to show me, then tell me what you were going to take me to see."

"Slaughter." He smiled bitterly. "You can't say I don't know how to show a lady a good time. I found a sheaf of papers in one of the armament boxes that Caldwell had written to Jossland with specific orders of what he was to do while he was in charge here at the cave when Caldwell was at Shafira. Evidently one of Zakira's more devoted officers had been entrusted with the hiding place for treasures here in the cave. Caldwell found out about it and 'persuaded' him to reveal it, then arranged the substitution. He tortured the officer to death as well as the other soldiers in his company. Then he built a bonfire in the rear of the cave and burned the bodies—except for a few that he planted at the massacre at Karimu so that he could return the bodies to Zakira and claim the soldiers had died an honorable death serving their priest and destroying Karimu's chief."

Celine shuddered. "It's impossible to tell who is worse, isn't it? All that ugliness..."

"I'll vote for Caldwell," Dominic said. "He's truly a self-made man. Zakira was raised by his father and grandfather before him to think he could take over the entire universe and wreck it if he chose. However, I'll be glad to remove either of the bastards from this world when I get the chance." He took her hand and was pulling her out of the cave and through the maze leading up the hill toward the camp. "But right now, we need to see what kind of help we're going to get from Quinn and Caleb..."

"And from me," Celine said quietly. "Because I won't let you leave me behind again. I can't tell you how angry I was when you left me sitting on that cliff staring at the maze. This is my job as much as it's yours. Find me a task to do or I'll find one for myself. Either way, when you start trekking through that maze on your way to Shafira, I'm going to be with you." She moved ahead of him up the hill. "Now let's go get a cup of coffee while we wait for Quinn to get here and you can tell me exactly what those trackers found on that trail when they reported back to you this morning..."

CHAPTER

15

Joe Quinn arrived at the encampment, accompanied by a very substantial team, late that afternoon. The first thing Celine noticed was that his demeanor was as taut and sharp as a drawn sword blade. She automatically tensed as she saw him coming toward her in deep conversation with Dominic. When she'd talked to him on the phone that one time, he'd been angry and impatient, but this man was cold...and deadly. She scrambled to her feet and moved toward them. "I'm glad to see you, Quinn. I'm sorry about Eve and Michael. It's terrible."

"Of course it is," Quinn said curtly. "Stop apologizing. It wasn't your fault. You did the best you could and tried to warn us. They were my family and my responsibility. I should be the one to take any blame for not stopping those sons of bitches." His lips tightened. "But blame is pretty damn hollow. I've decided to stick with revenge after I find a way to get Eve and Michael away from that village."

"I know how you feel," Celine said. "You might remember I had a friend murdered by Caldwell. I prefer to call it justice."

"Call it what you like," Dominic said. "Let's just get the action under way and get rid of them as efficiently as possible." He glanced at Celine. "Quinn just told me that Eve

245

was permitted to call him for a few minutes earlier this morning. She couldn't give him any information, but both she and Michael appeared to be in good health and will probably stay that way as long as Eve continues to work on the mask."

"Until she finishes it," Quinn said. "Then all bets are off." He smiled bitterly. "Eve will realize that, and if she were anyone else, she'd try to slow down. But she can't work that way. She's too blasted brilliant. She can't run the job, the job runs her. She might try to slow a little, but it probably won't happen."

"I'd heard that about Eve," Celine murmured. "You must be terribly worried about her. We probably shouldn't waste any time getting out of here."

"We've already started," Quinn said. "Caleb is the best tracker on the team, and the minute we heard from Eve he broke away from the unit and headed toward that waterfall Dominic told me about on the phone. He'll probably be able to report to us when he manages to rendezvous with the men Dominic sent to explore that trail through the maze."

"That's good," Celine said. "So I guess we'd better start out right away."

"No," Dominic said flatly.

Quinn shrugged. "Dominic was just telling me about the disagreement about your coming along with us. I can see his point of view. I have to tell you that Eve would probably agree with him. I remember she was worried about you when you left the Lake Cottage that day. You appear to be in a particularly sensitive situation that makes you very vulnerable."

But he hadn't come out and actually refused her yet, Celine realized. She said quickly, "I wouldn't be in your way. I'm strong. I'd be able to keep up with any of your team. I'm an excellent shot with either a pistol or a rifle, and hand-to-hand martial arts are really my specialty." She was trying to read his expression. "And I have a medical degree, and Dominic will tell you my instructors described my skills as excellent. I would be able to help on the spot if members of your family or team require my services."

Quinn was smiling reluctantly. "Impressive. But it's really Dominic who's in charge at the moment. I have to concentrate on getting Eve and Michael away from those bastards."

She shook her head. "Dominic will refuse whether you agree or not. I consider it my duty, so I'm going regardless. I just don't want to have you think I'll be a burden. It will make my presence less valuable to you."

Quinn studied her for a moment and then shrugged again. "The medical degree won me over. I think even Eve might have cast her vote in your favor since she has to think about Michael." He turned to Dominic, who was cursing softly. "My team needs at least four hours of sleep before we start on the trek. I'll meet you here then. Do what you will with Celine. I'd probably feel exactly the way you do under the same circumstances. But the circumstances aren't the same. I can't look at her any differently from anyone else who might help me save my family from those butchers. So hell yes, I'll be glad to have her along. She might be useful. In the end, that's the only thing that's important." He turned and stalked back toward his vehicle, where his team was waiting.

"Yes, I might be useful," Celine said softly. She held up her hand when Dominic whirled to face her. "No, don't start trying to argue with me. I'm going to Shafira and I won't listen.

247

React however seems right to you, but I don't have time to stay around and try to convince you that there will be times when I can't do what you want. Right now, I have to go get my equipment and then I want to go find Kontara and say goodbye. She's probably already upset by all this." She was heading toward the tents. "Like Quinn said, I'll see you in four hours…"

"Celine."

She glanced back over her shoulder.

"This isn't over," he said quietly. "I can't let it be over. You've just made it more difficult for me."

"Too bad. I only want to help. This is all kind of scary and it would be so much better if I could count on you. But regardless, it has to be done…"

She disappeared into the tent area.

———

"Who told you that I'd want to say goodbye to you?" Kontara crossed her arms across her chest and stared belligerently at Celine. "How many times have I told you that what you're doing is stupid and reckless and you don't deserve anyone to care about what's going to happen when you get to Shafira? I've described what happened to me and all those other women at that hideous camp. You probably won't even be able to find the damn place. You realize how difficult it was for me to escape? Just thinking about those bastards makes me start to shake. Why would you believe you're anything special?"

"I don't believe that," Celine said. "Probably the opposite.

I know how strong you are and what you've gone through. But that's one of the reasons I have to go." She tried to smile. "Because it has to stop and we have to punish them for doing it. And now they have Eve and that little kid, and that makes everything even worse."

"Oh, shit." Kontara's arms were suddenly around her, hugging her. "Why didn't you listen to me?" she asked fiercely. "Why didn't you pay attention to Dominic? What good is a lover if they don't keep you safe and make sure you have a chance to live a few more days? I thought better of him." She backed away from Celine. "Okay, I'm done. I'm finished. Get out of here. You've said goodbye and now you're going to do this stupid thing and expect me to be sorry and worry about you. Well, it's not going to happen. I'm going to go into my tent and go to sleep and pay no attention to when you and those soldiers of Dominic's leave the camp."

"Whatever's best for you." Celine gave her a hug. "Take care of yourself. I know it hasn't been easy for you to help lead us here. I just wanted to come and tell you how much you mean to me and how glad I was that you were my friend."

"Oh, shit," Kontara said again in disgust. "And now you pull that past-tense bullshit?" She turned back to her tent. "Try not to get killed. I hate to be right all the time."

"I'll do my very best," Celine said.

"See that you do." Kontara disappeared inside.

Celine hesitated, gazing at the door of the tent. Then she cleared her very tight throat and started up the hill toward her own tent to pack.

IRIS JOHANSEN

SHAFIRA

"You're burning the midnight oil again." Caldwell threw open the door of the workroom and strode over to the table where Eve was starting to do the repair work on the head of the mummy reconstruction. She had been using delft clay for a mold that could withstand the melting-point temperature of pure gold. "I know you're trying to impress Zakira to try to influence him, but I have a few needs that should be taken care of myself." He threw the phone on her lap. "Phone Quinn and let him know you're still doing well."

"Why?"

"What difference does it make? It was your idea in the first place. But since that first call, my men haven't been able to track down either Quinn or his men. It's as if they disappeared into the jungle after they visited Dominic's plantation. I'm uneasy. Now make the call."

She shrugged. "Whatever you say. I'll be glad to talk to him again." She dialed Joe's number. When he answered, she asked quickly, "Are you okay, Joe? It seems Caldwell is uneasy, and that made me uneasy. We're fine here, and things are just the same."

"That's good to know," Joe said. "I'm still as well as I can be without you. I'm fighting mosquitoes and cursing the entire continent of Africa at present. I just have to keep telling myself that everything is going to be fine if we just hold on. I remember what you told me after you found out Michael was taken. It helps a lot."

250

"It helps me, too," Eve said as she looked across the room at Caldwell. "And I'm glad that Caldwell is uneasy. Maybe it will encourage him to forget about Zakira and make a more reasonable deal with us that will get us out of here." Caldwell was shaking his head and she added, "He didn't like that. I'll have to hang up. Keep on doing whatever you're doing. I enjoy seeing Caldwell nervous and sweating." She pressed DISCONNECT.

"I'm not nervous and sweating," Caldwell said. "I just thought Quinn might drop a hint about where he was so that I could gather him in and have the entire family."

"Well, you've disturbed my concentration, and Zakira won't be pleased with either of us." She was wiping the clay off her hands. "I think I need to clean up and then get to bed."

Caldwell opened the door for her. "Ask me if I care. It's about time this charade is over anyway." He pushed past her and then looked over his shoulder. "Because at first I thought I saw something in you that reminded me of myself. We're both brilliant and talented and rule our own worlds. But you're too soft and could never survive in my world. That means you'll have to go, too. Enjoy the kid while you have him."

He left Eve staring after him as he slammed the outside door.

She shivered. He had only been there a few minutes, but she had noticed a change not only in him but also in Joe, and she had to accept and deal with it.

"Mom?" Michael called softly from the other room. "Is everything okay? I heard Caldwell."

"Yes, you did." She braced herself, then opened the door that led to their quarters and crossed the room to kneel on the floor beside Michael's cot. "I just talked to your dad, and he said he was still fine but didn't like the mosquitoes. It sounded as if this part of Africa isn't his favorite place. But that's probably just because he wants to be with us." She paused and drew a deep breath. "And because he was trying to tell me something and knew Caldwell was listening."

"Yeah, Dad never complains about stuff like that." Michael sat up in bed. "What do you think he was trying to tell us?"

"I think he was trying to warn me that he and the team were having a difficult time trying to locate this village, and maybe that something had gone wrong with their plans to attack and get rid of Caldwell and Zakira."

"Maybe." He was frowning. "But Dad won't stop. He'll just find another plan."

"Yes, he will. But it might take a little more time." She paused again. No, she had to tell him even though it would upset him. "And he also told me that he thought I was right about something I'd told him after you were taken. That's why I know there's definitely a problem."

Michael slowly nodded. "You want him to come and take me away from here if he can. I told you no, Mom."

"But I can't accept it. Do you think I don't realize how painful it was for Joe to even suggest it? But if there's a problem with a full-scale attack, that might mean one person might be able to slip into the village and find a way to get you out. If anyone could do it, Joe could."

"I know that," Michael said. "But I can't leave you."

"Yes, you can," Eve said. "If it would save my life." She took him by the shoulders and stared directly into his eyes. "Because there might be a situation where they started threatening you, and I wouldn't be able to stand it. I'd fight for you until I couldn't fight any longer. Until they killed me. But if you aren't here, then I could think about keeping myself alive. You realize I'm pretty smart, and these bastards need me. You and Joe would have time to come after me and take them down. Now don't tell me no. Whenever I send you outside to the well in the courtyard to get water, or for any other reason, just be prepared. Don't fight the guards, let them take you for granted. Your dad will have a plan. Don't screw it up."

"I won't." His eyes were shining with the tears he refused to shed. "Don't worry, we'll be back to get you."

"I'm not worried." She gave him one last fierce hug before she released him. "I know I'll be priority number one with both of you." She got to her feet. "What I'm worried about now is how long it's going to take me to clean all this clay off me before I can get to bed." She kissed his forehead. "Try to go back to sleep."

"I will." He lay back down. "But I might not be able to. I'll be too busy wondering what kind of trouble Dad ran across to cause him to be this upset."

That was also what Eve was wondering. There weren't many crises that stopped Joe in his tracks. "No telling, Michael. But as you told me, it just made him look in another direction. We'll follow his lead until we manage to get out and sweep all the trouble from our path…"

———

CAMP ON THE MAZE PATH TO SHAFIRA
4:15 A.M.
"Wake up, Celine." Dominic was kneeling beside her bedroll. "We've got trouble."

That jarred her awake. Which was fairly incredible, she thought dazedly, since she had just managed to get to sleep a few hours ago after over twelve hours trekking through this damn jungle. She automatically reached for her gun. "Trouble?"

He brushed the gun aside. "Not that kind of trouble…yet."

"What kind of trouble?" She was wide awake now and she could see that he was as dominant and sharp as he'd been since they'd gotten on the trail at the falls. That didn't make her feel any more kindly toward him; she felt like a wet dishrag after all those days on the trail, and he'd ignored her for that entire period and concentrated only on being the perfect commanding officer to all his men. "Is it something I've done? I told you I'd keep up with the team and I did it."

"I know you did," Dominic said. "I set a pace that a SEAL would be hard put to match, and I watched you get through it. So stop being defensive. You're not the one who caused the trouble this time. But I need to show you something so you'll stop trying to kill yourself. I'm having enough headaches with Quinn without having to deal with you."

"You haven't been dealing with me," she said coolly. "And I've been watching Quinn while he's been on this trail with us. He's faster and more efficient than anyone but you."

"I agree. Too fast and wanting to cut corners if it means finding Shafira sooner." He took her elbow and was guiding her off the trail. "If we go toward the edge of that cliff, you'll be able to see why we're going to have a disaster if I don't keep every man I have on the job working and under control. Right now we're practically tripping over each other. Caleb discovered it and called me right away, and I've been there all night setting up a plan to overcome the damage." His lips tightened. "But it might not be fast enough for Quinn."

He was climbing out on the edge of the cliff and took her hand to pull her up beside him. He gestured out at the ravine below, which was bathed in moonlight. "Yes, you can see almost everything from here..."

Celine inhaled sharply. Wreckage everywhere she looked! Below her was a narrow bridge that had been blown almost completely apart, and the rest of the valley had similar damage. The jungle foliage was burned and blackened, and several huge trees were lying over the trail, completely blocking any way to get to the path on the other side of the bridge.

"What on earth happened here?"

"Caleb said he thought the entire area was dynamited so that no one could get to that path or the cave beyond it. Caldwell did a very thorough job. He was protected at Shafira and probably knew of another trail that he could take around to the front entrance if he wanted access to the treasure he'd left in the cave. Destroying this entrance, he made sure that it wouldn't be easy for Zakira to know what happened in the cave unless he went to quite a bit of effort."

She shook her head. "Such a lot of destruction. This entire area was so lovely."

"It will be again. You can always count on the jungle to replace what's destroyed. Have you seen enough? Can I take you back to the camp?"

She shook her head. "You're not going to stay at camp, are you? You'll be going back to where all the destruction is. What can I do there?"

"Nothing." He held up his hand as she started to protest. "And I'm not trying to close you out. There are no battles for you to fight right now, so I doubt if you'll find anyone to need your medical skills. Last time I checked, you're neither Paul Bunyan nor Superman who can toss tall trees around while we try to rebuild that bridge area. The best way for you to help is to go back to bed and try to get a good night's sleep. You're pretty well exhausted, and you'll need to start fresh tomorrow." He paused. "But there is one thing you can do if you don't get to sleep right away. I sent Quinn back here to watch over the camp. If you could keep an eye on him, I'd appreciate it. Finding out that this trail had been destroyed almost sent him over the edge. He knew as well as I did that it could take weeks to rebuild, and no one knows if Eve and the boy will survive those maniacs another day, much less a week. He was as angry as a bear stung by a wasp when I told him we had too many workers down there already and couldn't use him to help with the rebuilding."

"I can see why," Celine said. "Of course I'll watch out for him."

"Good. He should be here in another thirty minutes or so." They had arrived back at the camp, and he walked with her to her bedroll. She started to lie down, but he stopped her and then dropped down and pulled her down beside him. "It's been a bad night and a lousy few days before that, because I had to keep myself from trying to help you get through this damn jungle. I just need another ten minutes to hold you." He took her in his arms and lay there cuddling her. "Don't worry, it won't be more than that since we're practically surrounded by the entire team."

She moved closer to him. "And yet sometimes you break the code."

"But never when it would hurt you..." Then he just lay quietly, holding her close for the next few minutes and stroking her hair.

Peace, safety, utter contentment...

He sighed, then lifted himself and bent over and kissed her. "Time to go." He kissed her again. "Go back to sleep. I'll be glad to think that one of us is getting a little snooze time." Then he was rolling away from her and getting up. "And in case you start worrying, I'll have an entire team down at the bridge to watch my back."

"But I'd do it better," she whispered. "I have more at stake."

He chuckled. The next minute, he'd turned and left the camp.

Celine wasn't about to try to go back to sleep. She wanted desperately to follow Dominic, but he was right about her not being any real help to the men rebuilding that bridge and trail. So, try to think...There had to be something of value she could offer besides just trying to comfort and watch over Quinn. Particularly since the Quinn with whom she had become familiar on this hellish trek was hard as nails and just as much on edge as Dominic had described.

"I saw Dominic leaving when I was coming up the trail."

She looked up to see it was Quinn himself coming across the campground toward her, his voice and general appearance just as lethal and on edge as Celine had expected. He appeared positively haggard. "I suppose he told you about Caldwell's latest disaster?" His lips tightened. "I can't let this one happen. I need you to help stop it."

"That's easy to say," she said ruefully. "You know that I'll do anything I can. But Dominic has just pointed out how useless I'd be helping with the construction."

"I got a similar response," Joe said. "And I can see his reasoning. But that just means that we have to go and do what we can in our own way. I can't let those sons of bitches kill Eve and Michael while I'm waiting around for that bridge to be repaired."

She shuddered. "I can see that. But is it too much to ask what you believe is our way?"

He held out his hand and pulled her to her feet. "Walk with me and I'll tell you, where there's not all of these eager ears ready to listen. Dominic would probably break my neck if he knew I was going to ask you to leave the team for even the short time I'm planning."

She stiffened. "Is that what you're doing? Why?"

"Because a good friend of yours took the trouble to come to see me before we left the falls. Kontara didn't like the idea of you going off to that village with our forces. She thought you might get yourself killed. Particularly if we ran into any of Zakira's troops in the jungle. But she also didn't like the idea of Eve and Michael being in danger. So she said she was going to keep on searching for a way to the village herself and let us know if she found one. She wasn't sure she'd be successful, but she said she'd try." His lips twisted. "And now I'm desperate and don't have a choice. She told me to keep you from doing anything stupid and to call her if we needed her."

"That sounds like her." Celine was shaking her head. "Even though she was terrified of going back to that village, she was still trying to protect me."

"Very laudable," Joe said quietly. "But Dominic would gather an army to protect you. It's not you who is in danger right now. I even tried to discourage Kontara from being reckless, but everything has changed now since we need to know if she's discovered any other way to get to Shafira. Preferably one that we could use to move an army—or if not, one that I could use to slip into the village and at least get Michael out. I need you to contact her for me."

Celine frowned as she suddenly realized something. "Eve?"

"I'll probably have to go back for her," he said haltingly. "We've agreed our son is in more danger right now."

And it was obviously killing him to have made that decision, Celine thought. She could see the pain he was trying to hide, and she wanted desperately to help him. She smiled gently and started to reach for her phone. "Then let's see if Kontara got lucky and found what you need." She quickly looked through her phone's directory for Kontara's satellite phone. "And hope that she didn't change her mind about trying to do it after she talked to you the night we left."

The phone rang several times but Kontara finally answered. "Celine?" Her voice was tense. "What's wrong? Are you having problems?"

"You might say that. We're having trouble following that

trail leading to Shafira and wondered if you'd managed to find an alternative."

Kontara was cursing softly. "I was afraid of that. I thought it might be either a trap or an ambush. It was too easy, and Zakira never makes anything easy. Take it from someone who knows. Which one was it?"

"Neither. Caldwell just saw fit to dynamite a bridge and practically the entire forest around it. It's probably going to take us too long to repair it; we need to move fast right now. You didn't answer me. Alternative?"

"I found a couple," Kontara said. "And I guarantee neither one is easy. It's the kind of escape exit I used when I was a prisoner there. Which makes it a nightmare. A waterfall and some of thickest maze shrubbery I've ever seen. You'd have a hard time getting through it."

"I don't doubt it, but it's Quinn who asked me to call you and ask you these questions."

"Quinn?" A pause. Then she said, "Of course, Eve and her son. Quinn could probably manage to use the maze exit. He was a SEAL. But I'm not sure about the others."

"I'm positive he'd make sure his son made it." Celine hesitated. "At present Eve Duncan's removal may have to be put on hold."

"Shit."

"I agree," Joe said hoarsely. "Where are you, Kontara? And would you be willing to help me get to Shafira to save my son? Celine told me that you were terrified of dealing with those people again. I promise I won't ask you to help with the actual rescue. You'll only have to tell me where it is or take me there.

After I find a way to get him out, maybe you could meet me somewhere and help us find our way back here."

Silence.

"You don't know what you're asking," Kontara finally said shakily. "I'll have to slip into a few of those huts and get information on where they're being held. That's not going to be easy. And it's sometimes almost impossible to avoid the guards when you're moving around the village."

Celine could hear the thread of panic in Kontara's voice, and she realized she was reliving that time when every moment could lead to attack and pain. She instinctively interrupted: "Quinn will take care of you. We'll both take care of you, Kontara. You won't be alone."

"No!" Kontara said sharply. "You don't go near the place. I'll take Quinn, but not you." She drew a deep breath. "I can do it. I just had a bad moment or two. I'm better now. It's not as if I didn't know all those huts in the village like the back of my hand at one time. I wouldn't have been able to get out as often as I did if I hadn't made sure of that. I could probably even figure how to get away from the village by using that waterfall I told you about, Celine. I can leave Quinn to wait in the maze on the other side of the waterfall until I locate where they're keeping his son."

"The one where you nearly froze to death getting to that maze…"

"That's right. But it's summer and not as cold now."

"You believe you can do it?" Quinn asked impatiently. "Yes or no? We're wasting time."

"I can do it," Kontara said "But I have to have enough time

to check out the village and make sure that I can still find all the foxholes that I managed to dig when I was prisoner there. It will take at least another three hours for me to get you to Shafira. It won't be dawn yet, and I'll still have time to explore the village before it gets light and everyone starts stirring. But I'll have to be back in the maze before that happens."

"And my son?" Joe asked.

"I'll have to wait and go get him tomorrow night as soon as it gets dark again. Hopefully we'll be able to slip him out before anyone knows he's gone and be on our way back to your camp."

"Hopefully," Joe repeated bitterly. "I'm a little low on hope for the moment."

"It's all I can offer," Kontara said simply. "Otherwise you'll have to sit around and wait until that bridge is rebuilt. I thought you didn't want to do that."

"I don't." His lips twisted. "And I'm an ungrateful son of a bitch for even letting you take this risk. All I can do is promise I'll be grateful for the rest of my life, and I'll guard you as I do my own family. If time is that important, tell me where I can meet you so that we can be on our way."

"I'm about three miles due west from your base camp near the rock spires closest to a deep creek. I'll send you a pinned map with my location. We can strike out directly for Shafira from here."

"I'm on my way," Joe said curtly. "I'll see you soon."

"I need to talk to you, Kontara," Celine said quickly. "I want you to—"

But evidently she'd not been quick enough. Kontara had hung up.

"Evidently she doesn't want to talk to you," Joe said. "She apparently has the same views as Dominic about your going to Shafira."

She nodded jerkily. "And she has reason, but I can't let her go alone. I could tell how frightened she is."

"She's not going alone. I'll be with her," Joe said. "I'll take care of both her and Michael."

"I realize you'll try," Celine said. "But what if it comes down to Kontara or your son? Who would you choose?"

"My god, Celine."

"The answer is that you shouldn't have to choose. If I was along with you, I could watch over Kontara."

"She won't let you come with us."

"I won't ask her. Just like I'm not asking you." She turned back to the camp. "Give me a couple minutes. I've got to go get my rifle..."

"You don't have any sense at all, do you?"

That was the first thing Kontara said when she saw that Celine was with Joe when they reached the rock spires. "It's no wonder Dominic watches you like a hawk. What do you think he's going to say to this?"

Celine shrugged. "I can't worry about that. He's busy doing what he thinks is right. Which is exactly what I'm doing. Besides, he won't say anything until morning, when someone tells him that Joe and I aren't at the camp. But by that time, I'll have called him and told him myself. Because it wouldn't be right to keep anything like this from Dominic. I know how

I felt about it. I was just trying to spare him worry as long as possible. From what you said, we may have a very long day until we can get back to camp."

"I'm not taking you into that village," Kontara said flatly. "You might as well go back to your camp."

Celine shook her head. "I never said I was going to tail behind you when you go into the main village. That would clearly be dumb. From what you said, I'd probably be recognized from that photo in the museum if anyone caught sight of me." She patted the rifle she was carrying. "But there's no reason I can't stay with Joe in the maze and watch your back in case you need a little extra firepower and Joe is busy with Michael. Right?"

"No." Kontara was gazing at her in frustration. "But you're obviously going to do it anyway." Then she added fiercely, "You don't show your face outside that maze. Understand?"

Celine nodded. "That's my intention." She turned toward the north. "Now can we go and help Joe get his son away from those bastards?"

CHAPTER

16

The journey to Shafira was just as rough as Kontara had told them. It was no wonder that she'd had such a miserable time breaking out of the village even after she'd reached the maze that bordered the waterfall. The jungle foliage was almost impossible to navigate, and they would have been hopelessly lost without Kontara to lead them. But once they reached the maze, Celine felt safer. The walls of the maze, made of densely clustered trees, were high and thick with twists and turns so complicated, she could see why even Kontara had trouble with them.

"Who built this maze?" Celine asked.

"No one knows," Kontara said. "It was cut into the jungle over a hundred years ago and paved with stones from a nearby riverbed." Kontara looked over her shoulder at Celine. "We've only got another mile or so before we reach the area where I dug a tunnel under the maze to reach the village wall. If you want to make that call to Dominic, do it now. I don't know what kind of high-end electronic detection equipment Caldwell might have installed since I broke out of here a couple years ago." Her lips twisted wryly. "Though I imagine I might be able to hear Dominic without a phone when you get through to him."

Celine was already dialing. "I'll make it as quick as possible." Then Dominic came on the line and she rushed into speech. "Don't say anything yet, Dominic. You're not going to like any of this, but things have happened. It turns out Kontara did some searching on her own after we left her at the camp and she found an alternative trail to get to Shafira. She agreed to take Joe there because he was so worried about his son."

"I thought that was where this might be going," Dominic said grimly. "I'm just hoping it's going to end there. Is it?"

"No. I have to tell you the rest." She quickly gave details, even though she could almost hear how upset he was getting with every word.

Then it was over.

"That's all," she finally said. "With any luck we should be back at the camp by tomorrow with Joe's son with us. How did your night go with repairing the bridge?"

"Well enough. We got a good start. We'll be able to finish quicker than I thought. If you don't mind, though, I don't want to talk about that hellish job when all I can think about is how close you must be to that damn Shafira." He was speaking very slowly and precisely. "And wondering if you're going to come back at all. Why the hell couldn't you have come to me when Joe brought up everything Kontara had told him?"

"Because you had a job to do. And I could tell she was frightened, and I thought I was the one who should help her. She didn't want to come along and try to help us find Shafira but she did it anyway because we convinced her that we needed her. I figured it was my turn to make sure she knew she wasn't alone."

"Bullshit." His voice was low and intense. "You're the only

thing important when a situation like this comes up. Now I'm supposed to sit here going crazy until I know you're safe?"

"No, you're supposed to finish the job you started, which I know you're going to do. I'm sorry this happened, but I'll be very careful and wait in the maze while Kontara and Joe do the tough work of getting Michael."

"That's not good enough. Give me the coordinates so that I can follow you."

"I'll have to let Kontara do that as soon as I've finished talking to you. This route is just as confusing as the one Caldwell blew up at the bridge. She doesn't have any trouble with it, but I'm not certain Joe or I could find our way without getting lost."

"Then let me talk to her. But I want your promise you'll stay safe."

"I never expected to do anything else. I like the idea of living a long, productive life. I've found a lot of things to educate and amuse me lately." She saw Kontara motion her to cut the call. "I've got to go now. I'll ask her to call you later if possible. I may not be able to call you again myself until after we manage to free Joe's son. Kontara is a bit nervous about whether Caldwell might have upgraded the spy equipment here. Goodbye, Dominic." She hung up the phone. Dear God, that had been hard to do. She drew a deep breath before she turned back to Kontara. "It was about what we'd both expected. But he had a right to be upset. It's not easy to be the one who has to sit and wait for someone you care about and not be able to step in. It made me very angry with Dominic when that happened."

"And this time he knows you're probably a sitting duck for

Caldwell," Joe said grimly. "I believe both of us are going to hear about that from him at a later date."

"Maybe," Celine said. "But right now all I can think about is Michael. We'll worry about the rest after he's safe."

"I'll second that motion," Joe said bitterly. "I can't do anything else." He turned back to Kontara. "Let's get going."

———

Rashid took one look at Dominic's expression as he hung up and gave a low whistle. "That bad? Is she okay?"

"How the hell do I know?" Dominic asked jerkily. "She's somewhere within spitting distance of Shafira courtesy of Kontara and Quinn, and you know what that means."

Rashid nodded. "I know it means that Quinn will do anything to get his family away from there. He almost went crazy when you told him about the wait because of the blown bridge."

"Well, Kontara evidently found a way that he wouldn't have to wait. Now the only thing we have to wait for is whether those sons of bitches will manage to catch and kill them." His lips tightened as he strode back down the hill toward the construction site. "And then we'll go after all of them and slaughter every single one of them. Until then, we go back to work and repair that bridge and the trail that will lead us to Shafira on the only path we know. Because Celine had to hang up before I could ask her to let me talk to Kontara so that I could get directions to lead us to the trail she used to get them there. I can only hope Celine will call me later...before it's too late."

THE DEATH MASK

It wasn't yet dawn when Celine and Joe Quinn saw Kontara streaking back across the village. Celine kept her rifle in readiness until Kontara reached the hedge and slid down the sloping earth. Quinn stepped immediately forward and dragged the large piece of foliage they'd cut out of the hedge to block it again. "Teamwork," he said to Kontara. "I just wish you'd let me go with you."

She shrugged. "And that would have looked suspicious as hell and probably meant we'd have both been caught if anyone saw us strolling around those huts. You definitely wouldn't have fit in. The only thing that the men here in the village are interested in doing with a woman is dragging her into the nearest hut and raping her. We were all fair game." She moistened her lips. "It all came back to me when I was slipping around the village trying to be as invisible as I could." She dropped down in front of the hedge and drew a deep breath. "But I think I've located your son, Joe."

"You saw him?" Joe asked eagerly. "Did he look okay?"

"As far as I could tell. He looked to be the right age, and he resembled you a little. He was the only white child I saw there. I only saw him for a few minutes. He was getting a pitcher of water from the well in front of the hut on the next street over, and one of the guards was practically on top of him for the entire time until he went back into the hut. I waited outside, but he didn't come out again."

"Which hut?" Celine asked. "What kind of guards? How many?"

"It was the seventh hut on the street," Kontara said. "And it was almost adjoining the workroom where Zakira has special people come to do the jewel insets, ornaments, and fancy gold trim to decorate his throne room and special museum."

"That makes sense," Joe said. "It's where he'd bring Eve to work on the death mask for the sarcophagus." He paused. "So they're probably both there. Maybe we could find a way to—"

"Stop right there," Kontara said. "I wish I could say that we'd be able to bring Eve with us when we take your son, but it's not going to happen. You asked about the guards, Celine. Caldwell has assigned five men to watch Eve and Michael. I watched them as they came on duty. Four of them were on the back side of the hut, and evidently they were assigned to patrol the entire village except when they took over to relieve the guard stationed at the well at dawn." She made a face. "Who, by the way, was your old friend Jossland, and I don't have to tell you what a vicious bastard he can be. But he's also scared of Caldwell, and he won't be careless if he's guarding Michael. The only good thing is that he's so arrogant, he won't accept any help from any of those other guards. But those odds still aren't good. I might be able to slip Michael out of the hut and over here to the maze, but if anyone sees Eve leave someone's bound to raise an outcry and she might be hurt…or killed."

"Then how are you going to manage to get Michael out?"

"Most of the work on Zakira's museum items was done in a huge room in the basement so that the craftsmen wouldn't disturb Zakira when he was playing his priestly dictator role for his loyal followers. Some worked cutting gems, one was a specialist in melting and handling gold, another made fine furniture and weapons for his new museum. It was hot as hell down there and very hard to breathe, but Zakira didn't give a damn."

"How do you know?" Celine asked. Then she answered her own question. "You were down there because you were looking for a way out."

Kontara nodded. "The craftsmen's room wasn't as guarded as the rest of the village. They were artists, and Zakira wasn't worried about them trying to get away. They were terrified of him because they knew they were only going to be alive as long as they produced what he wanted. They were right. I spent a long time trying to dig a tunnel into the basement." She made a face. "Really more like a hole I could hide with debris, so that I could use the trapdoor to get up to the museum from the craftsmen's workroom in the basement. But it was slow going. Too slow. One day I saw the workmen being herded out of the basement and into the center of the village. Then Zakira came out of his throne room and gave the order. He announced that their work was now completed and they were no longer needed. Then his soldiers raised their rifles and shot every one of them."

Celine shuddered. It was just another horrific episode that Kontara had been forced to go through that she had never known about. How many others had there been?

Kontara nodded as she saw Celine's expression. "Yes, it was bad, terrible. But the only good thing is that after they killed those poor, innocent human beings, they immediately sealed off the basement, because Zakira decided he didn't like the stench of sweat and honest labor drifting up to his precious

271

museum. I thought I might be able to get down into the base-ment, break the lock on the trapdoor, and get to the museum level when I had the opportunity."

"But you didn't get the opportunity?" Joe asked.

"No, because it had been raining, and I was afraid that my tunnel was flooded. There was all kinds of excitement going on in the village because Zakira had sent his men into the mountains searching for Folashade, the lost queen, and they had found her and were making preparations to bring her back to Shafira. I had to find a way to get out fast or I might not get another chance. It was risky, but I went over the falls instead."

"I'd say that was risky," Joe said dryly. "Michael's a good swimmer, but I'd prefer not to take him that way."

"We won't have to," Kontara said. "I checked out the tun-nel I dug on the outside of the basement wall, and it's still in place. It hasn't rained in weeks, so flooding won't be a problem. We'll be able to enter there and then go up to the museum. It should be deserted, and we can wait until we see that the guards are distracted and then make a run for the maze."

"You're saying 'we,'" Joe said. "But you're still leaving me out of this."

"You know it's safer for all of us if I do. Once I deliver Michael to you, then you can take care of everyone to your heart's content. In the meantime, just keep an eye on Celine while I do my job."

But she wasn't the one he wanted to keep an eye on, Celine thought. It must be agony to know Eve was so close and he couldn't do anything to help her. But Joe wouldn't appreci-ate anyone noticing what he was going through. She turned and spoke to Kontara instead. "I shouldn't even dignify that remark with an answer. I've behaved exactly as I promised I would, and I don't need anyone to watch over me. However, if the occasion calls for it, you know I'm always ready to help."

"That's why I want him to keep an eye on you," Kontara said. "You've always been a little too eager to help. Though it's a quality I've been grateful for in the past..." She turned away. "And now I'm going to eat a sandwich and then take a nap. I want to be fresh when I go to get your Michael tonight, Joe. If you want something to do, Celine, you might stand guard yourself tonight. Make sure that you keep a bead on Jossland and make sure that he's not drifting around too much while we're smuggling Michael out of that museum. That should keep you busy..."

"I was planning on doing that," Celine said as she positioned herself on the slope with her rifle. "By all means, get some rest. The last thing either of us wants is to have you so tired that you start making mistakes when you're leading us back through that hellish maze after we've managed to free Michael. I would have been lost a dozen times on the way here if I hadn't had you to follow."

"I know just how you feel. Why do you think it took me so long to escape from here? That's why Shafira has been so impregnable all these years. I had to teach myself not only how to escape from Zakira and Caldwell but all the tricks and turns of one of the most difficult landscapes I'll probably ever have to face." Kontara had finished her sandwich, and she closed her eyes. "But I think I've got it now. Though it's every bit as difficult as that headlock you taught me. Maybe when this is all over, I'll teach you all my secrets, Celine."

"I can hardly wait," Celine said gently. "Any of them except your cooking. I've seen how long it takes you to make some of those gourmet meals. But for the time being, I'll meekly follow in your footsteps until you get us out of here."

"Meekly?" Kontara repeated. "You've never shown me meekness. I would have thought you were sick." She yawned and then gave a weary sigh. "But maybe we'll take this up later..."

Celine didn't answer, but a few minutes later, she realized that Kontara was asleep.

———

SARCOPHAGUS WORKROOM
SHAFIRA
10:40 P.M.

Michael sat against the wall, watching Eve as she carefully worked with the delft clay, creating features where there had been only bland smoothness. She felt his gaze on her and turned her head to look at him. "I thought you were still asleep. You didn't get to bed until the middle of the night."

"I couldn't sleep." He was staring at the reconstruction. "Not since the last time I went out to the well to bring you more water to dampen that plaster. I kept thinking about how hard you were working on Folashade and how little I was able to help."

"You do all you can." She smiled at him. "And just your being here with me is an enormous help. You brighten my life. It wouldn't surprise me if Folashade turns out to be a much better reconstruction because you've been here helping me work on her."

He shook his head. "No, it's all you, Mom. We both know

that. I've watched you work on those reconstructions since I was so young I was barely able to walk, and it's always the same. They seem to know you're able to bring them home when they're a little lost, like Folashade." He looked away from her. "But I don't want to leave you alone." His hands at his sides clenched into fists. "Don't make me do it. I've heard all you've said, but I need to stay with you."

Eve stiffened. It was clear that something was very wrong. She had known that Michael had been upset when they'd had that discussion, but she'd hoped he'd become adjusted to the idea that it was the only reasonable solution. But right now she could sense his pain. "Something's wrong." She got up from her chair, crossed the room, and knelt beside him. "Something's different. When you went outside to get me that pitcher of water, did that guard, Jossland, bother you? I know what a bully he is, and I've been a little worried. Did he touch you?"

Michael shook his head. "He just scowled at me like he usually does. I think he hates having to guard us. I wanted to ask him what his problem is. But you told me not to have anything to do with him."

"But something happened out there?"

Michael shook his head. "I just got my pitcher of water, stood there a minute, and then I came back into the workroom."

"Michael?"

Michael was silent a moment. Then he looked into her eyes and whispered, "He's here, Mom. Dad's here."

She stiffened in shock. "You saw him?"

"No, but I could *feel* him. He was out there somewhere in the darkness. Close…"

275

"Are you sure it wasn't just wishful thinking? We're both missing your dad. You wanted it to be true. So do I."

He shook his head. "I'd know the difference. I could feel him. I even knew what he was thinking. You know sometimes I can do that when I try, and with you and Dad it just happens even when I don't try. This time it was just there and it was all about you and he was so sad." He added desperately, "Believe me, Mom."

"I do believe you." She reached out and took him in her arms. And because she did believe him, it was scaring her. "You're right, I never discount anything you do or say. It just means that we may have to face this sooner rather than later." She pushed him away and looked down into his eyes. "Because you know that what I told you has to happen. I can't let you stay with me, and if your dad is out there trying to find a way to take you away, then you'll have to go with him. And if you say he's sad when he thinks about me, it's probably because he knows I can't go with you right now. But you've got to be ready to go when he comes for you, because if you're not it might put him or whoever he sends for you in danger." She frowned. "Your dad would be smart to send someone else. Caldwell might have photos, and they might recognize him if he tries to come after you himself."

"He is smart." Michael was gazing pleadingly at her. "Mom?"

He was breaking Eve's heart. "No. I'll see you soon. You took care of me. Now you've got to watch over him." She gave him a quick kiss. "Go back and get some sleep. We don't know when or where he'll come for you, but you have to be ready."

He looked back at her for an instant and then ran out of the workroom. She heard the adjoining door of their hut slam shut.

Eve got slowly to her feet and moved over to the worktable to grab a towel to wipe her hands. She looked down at the face of the reconstruction. It wasn't completed enough for her to be able to start working on the expressions yet. But it soon would be.

"Sometimes being a mother is kind of rough, isn't it, Folashade?" she murmured. "I wonder how you felt when you had to send your son away across the sea?" Should she sit back down and try to concentrate? But she didn't want to work anymore right now. She was worried and probably as sad as Michael had said Joe had been. Maybe she'd go and lie down on her cot so that she could look over and see Michael for the short time she'd still have him with her.

Take care of him, Joe.

And, for heaven's sake, take care of yourself.

———

But she had only been lying down on her own cot for a brief twenty minutes when she heard a faint noise from outside the door leading to the workroom.

Eve tensed and then saw the door silently open. She swung her feet to the floor, her gaze still on the door.

A woman stood there. "Eve?" she whispered. "I'm Kontara. Joe sent me for the boy."

"Bless you." Eve was on her feet and running over to Michael's cot. "We've been waiting, haven't we, Michael? You have to leave now."

He didn't move, and for a moment she wasn't sure if he'd obey her. She gave him a swift hug and said, "Not much time. Don't keep her waiting."

"I'll be back for you." His voice was husky, and his arms tightened around her. Then he was on his feet and moving toward Kontara. "You heard her. Let's go find my dad…"

CHAPTER

17

THE MAZE BORDERING SHAFIRA
3:40 A.M.

There was the faintest hint of gray in the eastern sky, and Celine didn't like the fact that Kontara hadn't shown up with Michael when pitch darkness would have been the perfect time for her to slip out and head back for the hedge. She had told Celine that was her intention before she left last night, and that she'd keep an eye out for any moment that Jossland had left his post. What had gone wrong?

Where was Jossland? Celine had just seen him going into the commode a short time ago. But he should have come out by this time.

Celine's grip tightened on her rifle. She shouldn't be this worried. Kontara had a pistol of her own and could take care of herself. It could be that she was waiting for him to come out of the commode before she went after him.

But that wasn't what she'd told Celine, and anything different could be dangerous on a night like this.

Then Celine caught a flicker of movement at the door of the museum, which was nowhere close to the commode!

But it did lead to the workroom and Eve's quarters, where Kontara would have to go to get Michael. A trap! Jossland must have caught a glimpse of Kontara entering Eve's quarters and left the commode and slipped around behind her to wait for her to come out. And now Kontara was moving quietly out the door of Eve's hut holding Michael's hand.

"No!" Celine was on her feet and scrambling up the slope. "Stay here, Quinn," she hissed over her shoulder. "Keep an eye out for Michael and Kontara." She rolled over the hedge and picked herself up when she reached the cobbled street. Then she was flying over the ground toward the museum, where she saw that Jossland had his back to her, but he was pointing a pistol at Kontara and Michael!

Celine stopped short and held her breath.

Move slowly.

Move quietly.

It's not as if she hadn't practiced this discipline many times in the past when she'd been working on learning self-defense. Being able to come up behind an adversary and take them out was very important. But this time it could mean the difference between life and death. Jossland was pointing that pistol in Michael and Kontara's direction, and if she startled him, he might fire it.

So absolutely no sound as she moved behind Jossland to strike the blow.

She took a step forward.

Dead silence.

Yet Michael suddenly lifted his head, startled. And Celine could have sworn he'd heard her.

But the boy's motion had also startled Jossland, and he raised the gun and aimed it at Michael's head.

Celine leaped forward and crashed the butt of her rifle down on the back of Jossland's skull. He fell to his knees and then collapsed.

"Celine?" Kontara was gazing at her in shock.

"Yes. You've got to get out of here. I don't know how much time we have. I was watching him closely, and I didn't see him using his phone but I might have missed it." It was only then that she noticed Kontara's pistol was missing. Jossland must have taken it when he'd first captured her and the boy. No time to look for it. She tossed her own rifle to Kontara and then was kneeling beside Jossland and examining his wound as she took his pistol from his hand. There was a shallow cut, but he gave a low groan and appeared to be stirring.

She looked up at Kontara. "He's only dazed. He'll regain consciousness any minute. That's good. Because we need to have him able to point to a false trail when his buddies get here. Grab the kid. Take him to Joe and get out of here. I'll delay Jossland long enough to give you a head start. After I lose him, I'll catch up with you."

"I can't do that," Kontara said. "You know I can't leave you."

"Do it," Celine snapped. "You've got Joe and the kid and you've got to get them out of here before all of you are captured." She turned and smiled at Michael. "Hi, I'm Celine, and I'm a friend of your mother's. I'm sure she told you to go with Kontara. I'm telling you the same thing. Your dad needs you to help your mother." She pushed him gently toward Kontara.

"You can come back and look for me if I don't show up when you think I should, Kontara. But remember that story you told me about that winter day you almost got away from here by jumping in that waterfall? Who knows? I might think it's a great idea to follow in your footsteps. You've proved that Shafira isn't impregnable, and I bet there are all kinds of ways we can beat those assholes if we try hard enough." Her smile faded. "Anyway, you know getting Michael out of here is the right thing to do. Run, dammit!"

Kontara gave Celine one more agonized glance. Then she grabbed Michael's hand and ran toward the labyrinth.

———

Celine watched until she saw Kontara and Michael disappear into the depths of the shrubbery. Then she heard the sound of a groan and looked back at Jossland. Yes, he was definitely stirring. Now she had to decide how to lure him in the direction she wanted him to go. Her gaze traveled from the huts on the cobbled streets, to the stand of pine trees at the far end of the village, and then on toward the roaring waterfall that was cascading down the mountain to the lake in the valley below.

Another groan from Jossland. Time was running out. She had to decide. He had to feel safe, and she needed to keep any other of Cardwell's thugs from getting involved in the chase to help him.

Okay, play it whichever way instinct led her.

The first thing she did was empty the gun she'd taken from him of all its bullets. Then she put the pistol back in his hand. Now that he had a weapon, he should feel safer.

But she knew a way to stir the bastard so that he wouldn't be able to think of anything but the rage he felt for her. She knelt beside Jossland, lit the flashlight on her phone, and shone it upward to illuminate her face. Then she reached out with her other hand, grasped his shoulder, and shook it hard. "Wake up, you son of a bitch. Do you think I'm going to let you get away with just that little tap I gave you? I saw what you did to Barnaby. It made me sick."

He was fully awake now, and his eyes were focused on her face. "You!" Then his face flushed and convulsed with rage. "You did this to me?" He was looking wildly around them and trying to sit up. "Where are they? Where's that kid? I'll kill you."

"I sent them away and into hiding. You'll never be able to find them. How do you think Caldwell will like that? He'll probably decide to get rid of you. Look how many mistakes you've made since that night when you tried to attack me."

"But now you're here." Jossland's lips twisted savagely. "And he'll forgive me anything as long as he can turn you over to Zakira. You should have killed me when you had your chance."

She shook her head. "I wanted to wait and do it slowly. And I had to remember everything you did to Barnaby. I'm very angry, and you should be afraid. Remember how I hurt you the last time? It's all coming back to me now."

"You're nothing," he said bitterly. "You're just a stupid woman who got in a couple of lucky punches. I'll take you down and then make you tell me where you've hidden the boy."

She got to her feet. "We'll see." She watched him stand up and brace himself. She could see the anger and the venom, and she knew he was almost ready to attack.

Almost.

But there was still a way to make him as crazy and homicidal as she needed him to be to make certain that he wouldn't even think about calling for help before Kontara got Michael and his father safely away.

"I'm a capable woman and I don't think I'm in the least stupid." She tilted her head. "Lucky punches? Let's see if you're right."

She gave him a paralyzing blow to his right arm. She smiled as he cried out and the gun dropped from his hand. She followed the blow with another to his nose.

"You're bleeding," she said. "You do bleed easily, don't you? What a pity."

"I'm going to kill you." Jossland was now positively livid as he dove down to pick up the weapon he had dropped. "I made sure your friend Barnaby died a horrible death, but it's nothing next to what I'm going to do to you."

"Only if you can catch me." She took off at a dead run in the direction of the pine forest. "But you don't seem to be very good when it comes to attacking women." Her laughter drifted back to him. "Perhaps you need practice. I'll be glad to give you a few more lessons."

He roared like an animal in pain, and she knew he was running after her at top speed.

She streaked down the cobblestone street, keeping an eye out for any sign of Caldwell's guards or Zakira's soldiers. It was still fairly dark and the streets were deserted, but she knew the sky would lighten in the next fifteen minutes or so. All she could do was hope she could lose herself in the pines and allow Kontara time enough to get Joe and his son.

She was in the forest now, and the shadows were even more dark and intense. But she couldn't lose Jossland. She had to make him follow her. She shouted back to him, "You're slowing down. Getting tired, Jossland? Or are you just afraid of what I'll do if you catch up with me? I'm getting a little bored. Maybe I'll circle around and come up behind you. The waterfall is so loud you wouldn't hear me, and I'd be able to do whatever I'd like to you before you could stop me."

"You bitch!" He was panting but he was still screaming at her. "You're a dead woman. It's almost dawn and my relief will be checking in to see why I'm not at my post. If I haven't cut your throat before they find us, then they'll be here to watch me do it. But I'm not going to wait for them. I've been waiting too long to get you to myself. I think I just caught sight of you…"

And he might have done that. She was breathless and slowing down, while he was so full of hatred and poison that it was probably driving him to go faster. "Wishful thinking. Come and get me, Jossland." She put on more speed as she headed toward the bank of the waterfall. As long as she was on the ground, she was in danger from Jossland and those guards he'd said were probably going to check on him at any minute. The answer was simply not to be on the ground. She started to climb one of the tall pines leaning over the waterfall. There were enough branches on the pines to mask her from view, and the roar of the waterfall would keep Jossland from hearing her as she climbed up past the lower branches to the safety above. But all the time she was climbing she was aware of the sound of Jossland's curses as he came nearer and nearer.

"I know you're somewhere in this damn forest." Jossland

was moving in and out of the trees. "I caught a glimpse of you when you first ran in here. I'll find you. Maybe I should wait so I can turn you over to Caldwell. But I don't trust him, so you're mine until your last breath." He was right below her now. "And that face that Caldwell wants so badly to give to Zakira will be just a mass of scars and burns by then. Too bad. But I'll enjoy it with every slice of my knife."

Suddenly a shout came from the huts!

Jossland laughed. "Did you hear that? It has to be those fools who are trying to find me and that boy. We're going to have company very soon. They'll be crawling all over this village. But I'd better hurry or I'll be missing all the fun."

Celine could see what he meant. There were at least fifteen to twenty men dressed in camouflage uniforms streaming toward them, all carrying phone lights and lanterns beaming in Jossland's direction. But those lights weren't trained anywhere near where Celine was crouched high in the pine tree overlooking the waterfall. Which meant that if she chose, she might be able to dive down and knock him to the ground before he realized that she was in a position to do it.

But those guards were mockingly calling Jossland's name now. If she was going to do it, it had better be soon.

She started to slowly, carefully move down the pine tree. Good. He was paying more attention to his buddies than to finding her.

One more branch and she'd be in position…

Then she was there. She pushed off the tree with her feet and launched herself down to tackle him!

Contact! She struck him squarely in the neck, and he

286

tumbled down on the ground. Then she was mounting him and putting his neck in a headlock.

But Caldwell's men were getting closer and closer. She could hear them shouting at Jossland. She had to do something that would deter them.

The waterfall! She'd been joking when she'd told Kontara she might use that ploy she'd told Celine about. But it was time to be dead serious now.

"Goodbye, Jossland." She used her legs to give him a lift and powerful push that sent him off the bank and into the depths of the river. Then she followed him into the water and started swimming toward the rapids that were formed by the thundering waterfall.

She'd only gotten a few yards when she was dragged beneath the water!

Jossland! "Got you!" His hands gripped her throat as he tried to ram her head against the bank. She fought desperately and finally managed to break free, grabbed him by the waist, and pulled him under the water.

Splat! A bullet exploded in the water next to her. Caldwell's men must have gotten close enough to see what was going on with Jossland and were trying to protect him.

Splat. Another bullet…

But Jossland had broken her hold again and was trying to pull her to the surface where she'd be a clear target for the men on the bank.

No way. She wasn't going to get this far only to let the bastard get the best of her. If they wanted a target, let them have Jossland. She relaxed her muscles and let him take her almost to the surface—then at the last minute started struggling so that he surfaced first.

Splat! Splat! Splat!

Blood on the water.

Jossland was screaming. Hopefully that would cause enough confusion to make them ignore her for the time being.

Celine dove deep underwater and once more headed for the rapids, which she reached in only a few minutes.

But there was something definitely wrong. She was experiencing a sharp pain in her right shoulder. She had been swimming so hard trying to get away that she hadn't noticed until she'd actually reached the rough current of the rapids. But now the pain in her shoulder was striking her like a whip with each rush of water.

Some of that blood on the water must have been her own.

Don't panic. She would just get out of these rapids and shelter on that limestone shelf that Kontara had told her about. She would examine the wound and treat it herself and then decide what to do from that point on. Either hide if she was too weak to move or find some way back to Dominic or Kontara and Quinn. She was not really alone. It just seemed like it right now.

Ignore that defeatist attitude as well as that pain in her shoulder. First, get out of the rapids and find that limestone shelf...

And hope that Caldwell's men thought that their shots had done their deadly work and the waterfall had sent her body cascading to the valley below...

"You're a complete idiot, Jossland," Caldwell said coldly. "How could you let this happen? I should turn you over to Zakira's firing squad."

"It was the Kelly bitch," Jossland said. "None of it was my fault, but I'm the one who got shot in the arm and almost bled to death. But I stopped that other red-haired bitch from taking the kid and I thought everything was going to be all right. How was I to know that Kelly would sneak up behind me and practically smash my head in? But I ran after her and I would have caught her and forced her to tell me where they'd taken the kid." He scowled. "Before I cut the little whore's throat."

"From what I've heard from the men who were supposed to relieve you, they said you weren't doing a decent job even at that," Caldwell said sarcastically. "And you still haven't been able to get it through your thick head that I have a use for her. We may have lost the kid, but it's a lucky break that Kelly dropped into our laps. I couldn't ask for a better substitute."

"But you said we lost her, that maybe she was dead."

"We found fresh bloodstains on the path that leads past the lake to the mountains. You'd better hope she isn't dead. I sent a team out to search the village and valley for her. I also sent some of Zakira's best trackers to find her. He was very excited when I told him how clever I was to set a trap for her using the boy as bait."

"That means you're not going to let me have her?"

"That's exactly what I mean. But I might put in a word for you if Zakira needs a recommendation for an executioner."

"That's not good enough."

"It's all you'll get. You're lucky I don't hand you over to Zakira because you lost her, and now we have to go to the bother of finding her." He turned to the door. "Which reminds me: I want you to be part of the team to find Celine Kelly. It will not only cause that smashed and broken arm to hurt like hell, it will serve you right to have to turn her over to me and Zakira." He was smiling maliciously as he opened the door. "And it will make me feel tremendously better, and I know that will make you happy." He slammed the door of the hut behind him as he heard Jossland begin to curse.

A few minutes later, Caldwell was throwing open the door of Eve Duncan's quarters. "I just thought I'd drop in and give you a report on the status of your son's escape. I know you're such a devoted mother that you must be in agony about his fate." He leaned back against the door. "Of course, I was most displeased and thought seriously about telling you that the poor innocent lad had been shot and killed."

She flinched. "I can see how you might have wanted to hurt me. Now tell me the truth."

He threw back his head and laughed. "You think you can read me?"

"I've had practice reading many people who were far more complicated than you. I'm married to one, and I gave birth to another. Because you're a threat to my family, I've been studying you very carefully. It was necessary. Now tell me why you lied to me. It wasn't only to hurt me."

"I'm capable of wanting to hurt you. You've been a problem to me from the moment I saw you. I believe I have a bit of an obsession about you."

She was studying him. "But that isn't why you lied to me. No, I think it was that you wanted to increase your power over me. You felt that I'd somehow bested you when Michael

succeeded in getting away from this village. It made you feel…
diminished."

He was silent a moment. "Yes, it did. Even though you
might not have done it yourself, you've always been the center,
haven't you?"

"I try to be," she said simply. "It's my duty. Is that the reason you want me to have less power?"

"I have mixed feelings about my motives. But Celine Kelly
has reentered the picture, and I may need her as the wild card
that wins me the game. You owe her a great deal. In case no
one has seen fit to tell you, she's the one who saved your son
and gave those others involved in your little plot the chance to
escape." He paused. "We know she's been wounded, but we're
searching diligently to find her. Zakira is very eager for reasons of his own. I believe you've probably been told why. If we
find her alive, I might have reason to negotiate with you again.
By then I'll have all the power I need." He opened the door.
"I'd not waste any time getting back to that lost queen you're
working on. You'll have to show your progress to Zakira, too,
if it comes down to those negotiations."

"Wait." Eve had to ask the question. "You're right. Except
for your men coming in here and questioning me and searching the workroom, no one has told me anything. You said you
thought Celine might be alive, and I seriously doubt you'd
be here asking questions if your people had killed or captured
anyone else."

"Someone like your husband? I thought Quinn might be
involved, but he was wise enough to not show himself around
the village and let that whore Kontara take care of snatching
the kid."

"She's not a whore. She's a victim and a very brave one. She's a survivor."

"Well, I should tell you how Jossland did his usual fine work and damaged them terribly. It would serve you right for your part in this annoying mess."

"But that would be another lie." She breathed a sigh of relief. "So they're all safe except for Celine?"

He nodded curtly. "She kept Jossland so busy chasing her down that they had time to escape the village. That damn Kontara evidently knows enough about Shafira territory to help them find their way back to Quinn's team."

"That's what she told me," Eve said. "Or I would never have let her take Michael. Thank you for telling me."

"Don't be too happy about it." His lips were curled into an ugly twist. "Because I don't like to lose. I'm already planning how to make all of you suffer. I think perhaps it will have to do with what we're planning to do with Celine once we've found her. Perhaps it will involve sending her body parts to everyone who has given me an uncomfortable moment. Yes, that sounds like just what I need to top off that ceremony Zakira is planning." His brilliant smile was full of self-satisfaction. "Now I must run along. I feel inspired to get my men to find Celine with even more speed so that I can start the process right away…"

———

Eve shuddered as the door closed behind Caldwell. She hadn't the slightest doubt that he'd meant every word of that statement describing what he intended to do to Celine Kelly when she was found. The man was clearly a split personality, and one of them was this ugly savage that had been revealed only a few minutes ago. She was feeling terribly helpless at the thought of Celine out there wounded and alone with men like Caldwell hunting her down with only the intention of inflicting more pain on her. She had deliberately put herself between those killers and Michael, Joe, and Kontara. Eve wanted to rush out and help her. But she was a prisoner and could do nothing, dammit. And now that Michael was free, she was no longer of use to him, either. All she could do was pray that Joe and Dominic would find Celine before Caldwell and Zakira did.

No, prayers were all very well, but she could do something else. The only power she really had was her work on Folashade. Caldwell had been sarcastic, but what he'd said about her value being linked to the queen was true. So it had to be the strongest weapon she possessed. Yes, think good thoughts and pray that Celine wasn't in some cave bleeding out from that damn wound. But now it was time for Eve to get off her ass and go into the workroom and start working so that she might be able to negotiate a way to get Celine out of Caldwell's hands if she managed to survive everything that had already happened to her. The next moment, Eve was on her feet and heading for the door leading to the workroom.

Her hands were clenching into fists with the frustration she was feeling.

But where in the hell are you, Celine?

In the workroom, Eve moved to the golden sarcophagus. "We could use a few good wishes from you, too, Folashade. After all, you might say Celine was wounded in your service."

She sighed. "Never mind. But if you have any influence

wherever you are, we could use it about now. That's all. I'm signing off and hope we hear from you soon."

Then she drew a deep breath before she sat in her chair and forced herself to concentrate on the reconstruction in front of her.

Close everything else out. Because this was something that only she could do. *I'm trying to help, Joe. But I wish I could be with you now. I know how you must feel about losing Celine…*

———

"What do you mean you lost her, Quinn?" Dominic asked harshly on the phone. "How could you lose her when she swore to me she wouldn't think of going into the damn village?"

"A few unexpected things happened," Joe said. "Kontara told her that she shouldn't let herself be seen and she agreed, but then she saw that Jossland was threatening Michael and Kontara and decided that she could help them. I didn't even know she'd left the maze until I saw her running across the square toward the hut where Michael was being held."

"You should have known," Dominic said. "You should have been right beside her. That's where I would have been."

"Do you think I don't know that?" Quinn asked harshly. "Do you believe I don't feel like shit? I was doing a balancing act, dammit. But everything was happening very fast, and I was worried that if I moved too quickly I'd get them all blown to kingdom come. Celine seemed to have a handle on what was happening, and I was hoping that she'd be able to get them all out of a very tight spot and get back to the maze before reinforcements appeared on the scene." He paused. "But that's not how she worked it. She decided to give us some extra time to get out of the village. She didn't want me to lose Michael after we'd just managed to get him out of that hut. So she convinced Kontara to start us on our way back up toward your camp. She said she'd catch up with us."

"Dear God in heaven," Dominic muttered. "Could it get any worse?"

"I don't know," Quinn said. "Celine's strategy worked, but when we looked back after we reached the hills, the entire village was in turmoil. We couldn't tell what was happening."

Kontara snatched the phone from Quinn and spoke quickly, frantically. "But we can guess, can't we, Dominic? This was all my fault. I should never have done what Celine told me. I wanted to go back and try to find out what had happened in the village after we left, but I was afraid that Michael and Joe wouldn't be able to find their way back to camp, or that I might even lead Caldwell to you. But as soon as I turn them over to you, I'll go back and find out why Celine wasn't able to follow us." She added huskily, "What if it turns out I was the one responsible if something terrible happened to her?"

"Stop blaming yourself," Dominic said harshly. "We could all take turns doing that. I'm probably the one most likely to have put her in this nightmare. I was in charge of the team. I didn't stop her because she'd promised, and I thought you and Joe would be able to take care of her. Obviously, I was wrong. But she still wouldn't thank us. You know she's always fiercely passionate about anyone interfering with her life or what she needs to do. All we can do is get together and go after all those assholes who are a danger to her. So get Quinn and his son to my camp, and when you get here we'll talk about how you're going to help turn this horror story around. I've finished with the bridge and additional construction on the path, but the alternative path you've discovered and used will make any attack we can manage to spring that much more efficient."

"I need to go back," Kontara said. "I know what it's like to be alone in that damn village. I can't leave her there."

"I'm not going to tell you again." Dominic's voice was ice-cold. "She won't be alone, but I won't let anyone go near that village without a plan to get them out. Now get moving and take that kid somewhere I know he'll be safe. I'll see you at the camp." He cut the connection and turned to Rashid. "You heard them. Everything is going to hell. Go back to the construction camp and bring the team that's working on the bridge and trail back to the main camp. I've had them working on those repairs for almost twenty-four hours. I want to get them fed and rested before I have to ask them to take down those sons of bitches at Shafira." His smile was totally without mirth. "Though I think they'd prefer it. They were sick and tired of having that village just out of reach and were pissed off knowing that Caldwell's men had caused them all that work."

"Not only that," Rashid said quietly. "Celine became one of the team while we were on this hellish trek through the jungle. She kept up and she never complained. Word gets around, and the guys could tell you were worried as hell when she and Quinn disappeared. It's the same old mantra about never leaving a buddy behind. They're going to be ready to go after anyone who stands in their way."

"They'll get their chance." Dominic's lips tightened. "I've just got to be sure that I get mine."

Rashid tilted his head as he stared quizzically at Dominic. "Why do I sense that you're not going to be napping or making up for any missing meals yourself while you're waiting for Quinn and Kontara to arrive at camp?"

"Because you know me too well. There's no way I'd be able to nap. But as for satisfying appetites…" He smiled grimly. "There are all sorts of ways that can happen. Did I mention that we'd no sooner finished the repairs than Seth Caleb came to me and asked if he could do an exploratory trip and verify that Shafira was at the end of the trail as we thought?"

"You know you didn't," Rashid said. "You gave permission?"

"Of course. I didn't tell you because I was jealous as hell. I wanted to be the one to do it." He scowled. "But I was in charge, and there are rules. I knew Caleb could do it, and I didn't have any excuse. He's damn good when he's on the hunt. MI6 told me once he's like a ghost the way he fades in and out of the enemy lines, and I agree. I should be getting a report from him anytime now." He paused. "And he's aware that I need to know about Celine. Though he didn't realize that the situation has changed, and she's managed to slip away from Quinn and Kontara. After that, I may have to go take a look for myself."

"It doesn't sound like she slipped away. More like she didn't want to leave any buddies behind."

"I know," Dominic said hoarsely. "Because that's what she'd do. It's still hard for me to accept. That's why I might have to go looking for her myself."

"If you decide you want company…She's my friend, too."

"I'll call you. Don't I always?" Dominic asked as he headed

back toward the camp. "But first we have to find out what's happened to her and how much damage we're going to have to contend with." He added through set lips, "And how many of those bastards we're going to have to punish or kill for even daring to touch her."

CHAPTER

18

Celine could hear voices outside the cave again. They were speaking English; it had to be Caldwell's men. It was the third time they had come this far into the valley, so they must suspect that she was hiding here. She'd tried to clean up all the bloodstains on the trails outside after she'd doctored the wound in her shoulder, but she'd had to keep moving; the hunt was on by both Caldwell's and Zakira's men, and their separate teams appeared to be getting closer all the time. She'd thought she might be safe here in this shallow cave, because there was another opening on the upper level that she might use to escape if necessary. So far, she hadn't had to use it; she'd just waited it out when she heard the search teams and hoped they'd get discouraged. But she might have to change her plans, because they definitely were not getting discouraged. The next time Caldwell's men left the area, it might be better for her to leave the cave and head down to the lake to find another hiding place.

But they weren't leaving the area!

And a voice boomed out that was chillingly close to her. "This is Caldwell, Celine. You should be flattered that you're important enough to get my personal attention. We know you're somewhere near here, but I'm getting bored with this game. So come out and give up and I'll promise not to turn you over to your old friend Jossland anytime soon. He's very eager for me to do that. But he has such crude ideas, and Zakira might get upset—he has elaborate plans for you himself."

She froze in place and held her breath. Maybe it was a bluff and he had no idea where she was.

Don't move.

She was silent. Waiting.

Then she heard Caldwell cursing and then the sound of the movement and clink of weapons and departing footsteps.

She might have been right about it being a bluff. Still, she'd take her time and be very sure...

She waited for fifteen minutes. Caldwell's men did not return.

But that didn't mean she was safe here.

She began slowly crawling up to the outer opening. It was slow going. Her shoulder was throbbing with pain as she used her elbows to pull herself over the rocks up to the second level. When she finally reached it, she was panting and had to stop to get her breath before she managed to push aside the rock she'd used to barricade the opening.

Then she was peering outside and wriggling out onto the trail and looking around.

Silence.

No Caldwell.

No sign of Zakira's soldiers.

Now to get down past the waterfall to the lake in the valley...

"If you make one more move, I'll blow your head off." Caldwell stepped out of the trees pointing a rifle at her. "I'm tempted to do it anyway. You've caused me far too much trouble in the last twenty-four hours. I do admire ingenuity and endurance, but not when it gets in my way."

"I'm glad I got in your way," Celine said fiercely. "I'd do it again. Anyone who hires scum like Jossland should expect any decent person to know that they're a pitiful loser and not worth bothering with. Michael will be safe by now, and you won't be able to get near him."

"I'm afraid you're right. But I'll have you, and that may upset Dominic enough to keep me happy. We've had a long-standing and extremely unpleasant relationship, and he deserves any pain that I can inflict on him. In the meantime..." He raised a whistle to his lips and gave a piercing blast. "I'll let Jossland have a little fun with you. Nothing too fatal. He has his orders."

Jossland appeared out of the forest and came eagerly forward as he saw Celine.

"Take her back to the village," Caldwell ordered. "I think we'll show her to Zakira first and then decide what else to do with her."

"I have a few suggestions," Jossland said. He grabbed Celine's bandaged arm and yanked her after him as he started back toward the village.

She bit her lip to keep from screaming from the pain.

"No marks, Jossland." Caldwell was frowning. "I warned you that Zakira wouldn't like it." He sighed. "But it seems I'll have to accompany you, Celine. You've given him a few too many nasty wounds in your short acquaintance, and I can't trust him..."

———

Dominic received a call from Caleb at just after two that afternoon.

"We were right," Caleb said when Dominic picked up the call. "From the bridge, it's about twenty miles before you get to the trail that leads directly into Shafira. Pine forest, huge waterfall, very structured little town with its own museum and palace. Quite a few guards and soldiers around. Most of them are teenage boys and young men who are vicious but also very well disciplined. Evidently Zakira is a tough taskmaster. Though he keeps them happy with drugs and the chance to torture any enemies they manage to capture. I also spotted twenty or thirty of Caldwell's thugs around, and they're fairly lethal, too."

"Celine Kelly," Dominic said. "What did you find out about Celine?"

Caleb was silent for an instant. "At first, I didn't hear anything at all, except that there was a rumor that she might have been shot and killed during a fight with Jossland, one of Caldwell's men."

"For God's sake, don't give me rumors," Dominic said harshly. "Tell me what the hell happened."

"Easy," Caleb said. "I'm trying to give you the complete

picture. But then when they were searching for the body, they found bloodstains on the shrubbery in the mountains overlooking the lake and decided she'd been wounded but not killed if she'd managed to make it that distance. They've been searching the entire village and mountain all day trying to find her." He paused. "She did a great job of avoiding them, but if she was wounded it was only a matter of time before she was caught. I just heard before I called you that Caldwell has captured her and is bringing her to Zakira."

"Shit!" Then Dominic tried to control himself. "But maybe that's not as bad as it might be. At least she's not somewhere in those mountains bleeding out. There's a good chance that Caldwell will see that her wound is tended so that she'll be a proper gift for Zakira. We'll just have to move very fast and not make any mistakes."

"No problem," Caleb said. "It's what we've been waiting for since this crapshoot began." He added, "And we have one more plus on our side. Though I guarantee that Joe won't agree. Eve is still at Shafira, and when she finds out that Celine has been captured, she'll find a way to help. According to what Joe told me, Eve's in a rather unique position with Zakira, and Eve can be a force to be reckoned with. She's like my wife, Jane, in that."

Dominic nodded. "I believe that's a proven fact where Eve is concerned. But let's hope she won't have to display it and can leave it to us. Do you have anything else to report?"

"No, except that I've done enough reconnoitering to know how to blow this place into outer space if we need to do it."

"Then start back here right away," Dominic said. "I want

you and Quinn in the planning meeting that I'll convene as soon as possible."

"I'm already on my way," Caleb said quietly. "I knew once you heard about Celine that you'd be ready to start the fireworks. I'll see you soon…"

———

EVE'S QUARTERS
SHAFIRA

Eve threw the outside door open when she heard all the shouting and hubbub outside. She'd been waiting for hours; the entire village had been in turmoil since Jossland was brought back with a broken and splinted arm. She wasn't surprised to see Caldwell standing there with a decided smirk on his face.

"Hello, Eve," he said. "How nice of you to come to greet us. Particularly when you can see that even though you managed to free your brat, I'll still get what I want." He stepped aside to reveal Celine being held upright by Jossland so that she wouldn't fall. She was pale, her eyes sunken deep in her face, and her shoulder was bloody with a leaf binding the wound. Her hair hung lifelessly around her filthy face, and she looked as if she could barely stand. "I thought I'd bring her to Zakira first, but I changed my mind on the way here. I decided that it would be much more satisfying to let you see your failure first."

"She didn't fail," Celine said hoarsely. "We got her son away from you. And I didn't fail, either. I kept your men too busy to go after them. You're the one who failed."

"Tell me that when Zakira gets through with you." Caldwell's lips curled. "I'll be there to watch it and applaud."

Eve couldn't stand any more. "Oh, for heaven's sake, Caldwell. Does it make you feel more manly to beat up on a woman who can't protect herself? She looks like she's gone through hell."

She ran to Celine and stared her in the eyes. "How bad is it?"

"Not good. But don't feel guilty. It was my choice." She tried to smile. "And I did protect myself. I did most of the damage to Jossland here, and he can't wait to return the favor." She glanced at Caldwell. "But I think maybe this one is worse. He's in another league."

"Yes, he is." Eve turned back to Caldwell. "May I take her inside and let her lie down?"

"I'll think about it. Though I kind of like to see her weak and unable to spit at—"

"Where is she?" Zakira was coming down the cobbled street from the palace, his expression alight with eagerness. Then he saw Celine and he stopped short. "She is not what she should be." He gazed accusingly at Caldwell. "This isn't the woman you showed me in the photo, Caldwell. My people should not see her like this. What kind of symbol would she seem to them? She's filthy and almost...ugly. I'll not even have her in my village. Get rid of her, Caldwell." He turned to Eve. "You are not to make the mask to resemble this creature. Do you understand?"

Unfortunately, Eve did understand. Zakira had no foresight or imagination as far as anything connected to Queen Folashade was concerned. There was only intense resentment bred by his upbringing and the stories told him about his ancestors.

She saw Celine start to open her lips to speak and quickly shook her head. She could see what direction she'd have to go if she was to have a chance at keeping Celine alive even for a short time. "She's not as ugly as you think. She does have potential and only needs to have a talented professional artist to bring it out."

Zakira's eyes were suddenly narrowed on Eve's face. "And you're that artist?"

"You chose me, and you've been pleased with my work so far. I've barely started on the sculpting, and I believe you can see the progress I've made."

"I admit I was impressed," Zakira said slowly. "I thought I could see signs that I might have a mask that everyone would compare to that of Tutankhamun, the boy-king."

But he was still looking skeptical, so Eve added quickly, "Yes, and I can give you what you want now that I have a model to use to help me get through the basics. Just allow me time to do the work and get her in shape so that she looks like a queen and not an uncivilized gutter slave. Caldwell obviously doesn't have any idea what you really want in the mask."

"Yet he tried to convince me that he did," Zakira said. "I wonder why?"

Eve shrugged. "I have no idea. That's between the two of you." Time to insinuate a thread of suspicion? "And I also have no idea why he decided to hand my son over to you when you wanted a queen to show your power to everyone who doubted you. Does that make sense?"

Caldwell was cursing beneath his breath. "The boy was just a temporary fix for a bad situation. Don't listen to her."

Zakira stared thoughtfully at Eve for a long moment. "But I think I should listen to her. I'm a reasonable man, and she's offering me what I want—while you appear to be failing miserably at it. So I'll give her the time she needs." He turned back to Caldwell. "I've decided you don't have to get rid of that woman yet. We'll keep her around and let our sculptor do what she does best. Just make certain she's well guarded."

"You don't have to worry about that," Caldwell said. "I'm just as eager as you to prove that our Celine will prove a success for you."

Eve said quickly to Zakira, "Of course, I'd be a fool if I didn't understand about the guards. But I can't promise success unless you let me work with her without interference from Caldwell or his men. They're a disturbing influence. Naturally, your presence will be welcome at any time."

Zakira chuckled. "Did you hear that, Caldwell?" He turned away and headed back toward his palace. "Cease to be a disturbing influence until I tell you it's needed."

Eve took advantage of his departure to shove Jossland aside, put her arm around Celine's waist, and help her into her quarters. "You heard him, Caldwell. Keep Jossland away from her and send someone with soap, a bowl of water, and a decent antibiotic right away."

"Do you think that you're going to get what you want?" Caldwell asked. "Zakira can change his mind a dozen times a day. I've known him for a long time, and I've seen him do it. All I have to do is wait."

"But at the moment, you're not on his list of favorite people. Maybe he's looking for a replacement. I thought I'd volunteer."

She slammed the door shut behind her and turned to

Celine. "Bastard," she muttered. "Sit down before you fall down."

Celine dropped down on the cot. "Willingly. I'm a bit weak in the knees at the moment. Though Jossland was concentrating on doing more damage to my shoulder. He was royally pissed off because I put his own arm in the way of those guards' bullets while I was getting away from them."

Eve frowned. "How bad is your wound?"

"Not too bad. It's only a flesh wound. It would have been a lot better if I'd been able to treat it and rest it, instead of having to go on the run from half the soldiers here in Shafira." She smiled wearily. "But then I guess that's what I have to expect when I have the reputation of being an uncivilized gutter slave."

Eve frowned. "You know I was just trying to make it safer for you here."

"I knew exactly what you were doing," Celine said quietly. "And I'm forever grateful. I wasn't thinking too clearly after they dragged me here from the mountain. It was a great relief to have you in my corner today."

"How could I do anything else?" Eve asked simply. "You helped Joe and Kontara get my son away. I hope I would have done it anyway, but there was no way I could turn my back on you after that." She smiled. "I'm sure that we'll have plans to discuss in a little while, because neither of us is going to be content to let those bastards get their way in this. But right now, I'd like you to close your eyes and try to rest. You've had a long, hard time. I'll wake you when Caldwell sends his errand boy with the antibiotic and water that I requested."

"It was more like an order," Celine said. She found herself

yawning and tried to fight the exhaustion. "Again, thank you very much, Eve. When I attended your lecture last year, I would never have dreamed that I'd be here saying that to you. You can never tell where fate is going to take you, can you?" Then she could no longer battle against the weariness. She closed her eyes and let the darkness flow over her...

———

It was two hours before Eve woke Celine gently but firmly. "Sorry about this, but Caldwell took his time about sending you that antibiotic and I didn't want you to have to wait any longer before you took it." She handed her the medicine vial and watched her examine the ingredients carefully. "From the limited experience I've had with wounds, I don't think the bastard was trying to poison you," she said dryly.

"I wouldn't put it past him." Celine made a face. "But he'd probably be more likely to give the job to Jossland as a reward for services rendered. That seems to have been his modus ope-randi since he came into my life." She lifted the vial in a toast to Eve. "But this time he seemed more concerned about pleas-ing Zakira, so I think I'm probably safe for the time being." She swallowed the antibiotic in the vial and handed it back to Eve. She smiled as she gazed down at her hand. "I believe you've been doing a little cleanup. When I passed out a couple hours ago, I remember thinking that I looked so filthy dirty, I couldn't blame Zakira for wanting to toss me on the near-est trash heap." She turned her hand appraisingly to the left and right. "Now it's pristine clean and you've even given me a manicure. I suspect you couldn't stand seeing me like that?"

IRIS JOHANSEN

Eve shook her head ruefully. "I couldn't do much because I was afraid of waking you, but I thought you might rest better if I could get off a little of that surface dirt. You'll have to use my shower to get rid of the rest."

"I can't wait," Celine said as she swung her legs to the floor and braced herself to get to her feet. "Where is it?"

"Far side of the hut." Eve helped her to get across the room. "I'll help you undress and turn on the shower. Do you need me to help you with the shower itself?"

"No." Celine moved stiffly until she was underneath the spray of the shower, and then the heat was a cure in itself. "But you can lend me something to wear and help with bandaging my shoulder again. I've got to make sure it's totally clean."

"Coming right up." Eve disappeared for a moment, and then she was back. "Are you sure you don't need any more help? I'm something of an expert at reconstruction, and I don't usually get a chance to use my skill on live subjects."

Celine chuckled. "I'm sure. No one knows better than I do what an expert you are. But I've got to get my strength back, and I can't do that if I let you wait on me. Just give me a towel and help me over to the cot, and I'll let you bandage my shoulder."

Eve handed her the towel. "If you insist, but I do have to remind you that I'm the one who owes you a debt. You helped my son, and I'll never forget that."

Celine shrugged. "We were both caught in the middle, and neither of us really had a choice. We just have to remember who was responsible for putting us there and how we can help each other to survive it." She met Eve's gaze. "Agreed?"

Eve hesitated and then slowly nodded. "Agreed." She helped Celine to sit down on the cot and then moved closer to bandage the wound. "Now hush, and let me do this. If I'm not mistaken, we're going to have a good many more difficult things to handle together than this wound. I want you to be strong and capable. Let me finish this task and then we'll try to come up with a game plan."

Celine nodded. "Any suggestions will be welcome. Now I believe I'll stop pretending to be so damn tough and take a few deep breaths while you finish bandaging my shoulder. It smarts a little."

"Then I'd better try to distract you." Eve handed her the bra and shirt she'd brought from her own backpack before starting to carefully clean the wound. "You realize that you shouldn't have run the risk of coming here to Shafira?"

Celine grimaced. "It wasn't supposed to work out this way. I promised everyone I was going to be so careful and not take any chances. But then I thought Kontara might need me. She was so frightened about coming back here. I'd already lost one friend to Caldwell's men. I didn't want to lose another one." She paused. "You knew it would be a danger to me?"

"I found out the first night I came here," Eve said dryly. "Zakira couldn't wait to show me his damn museum. I couldn't miss the photo of you, and all the weapons in those cases told their own story. I was glad that Dominic was taking good care of you." She hesitated. "But maybe not too good if he let you come here."

Celine shook her head. "Don't blame him. I made my own choices." She added ruefully, "And my own mistakes. I'm glad one of them wasn't your Michael."

"So am I," Eve said. "But now we have a few more problems to solve. Will Dominic be coming after you when he finds out that Caldwell has you?"

Celine nodded. "You and your son were here and we couldn't let that continue. Dominic was already halfway to Shafira when we had to change trails."

"Then he'll be here very soon? When I met Dominic at the Lake Cottage, he seemed to want you to arrange for someone else to protect you. Did the situation change? We have to know who we can count on."

"We can count on Dominic." She stared directly into Eve's eyes. "Yes, the situation did change. He's been there for me since the moment he picked me up at that police precinct in Boston. It took me a little while to realize I could trust him, but now there are no limits."

"I see." Eve's gaze was searching. "You seem to be very sure."

"You could say that," Celine said with a smile. "I know he'll be there when I need him. Like, to hell and back. And since he has Joe, Caleb, and an entire army with him, you should also feel a bit more comfortable."

"That might be good," Eve said absently. "I don't think there's any question that they'll make an attempt to attack Shafira. It will only depend on when and where. With any luck, we'll only have to stall for a short time."

Celine chuckled. "You don't ask for much."

"As I told my son, I'm not the one who has to worry. I'm safe as long as I haven't completed the sculpture. It's you who must keep a very low profile whenever Zakira and Caldwell are anywhere near you. I don't want them to notice that you no longer resemble a refugee orphan. Spend as much time as you can in my workroom. If I had a closet in which to hide you, or a famous rug like the one Cleopatra used to fool Caesar, I'd give it to you in a heartbeat. You understand where I'm going with this?"

Celine nodded. "Yes, head down and definitely low-profile. I won't screw this up for us. Could I at least help you with your work?"

"You can pose for me so that if Zakira drops by he'll see you're worth keeping around."

"I can do that. And otherwise you want me to sit and just wait to be rescued?"

"By George, I believe you've got it." Eve added, "Much as I'm grateful for your help with Michael, I believe you've managed to stir up enough trouble for the time being." She stepped back from Celine and was helping her to her feet. "And now before I call Caldwell and start nagging him to get you some dinner, I think I should take you into the workroom and introduce you to your hostess, Queen Folashade. Since you'll probably be spending a good deal of time together, it's only polite. And I did ask her to intercede for you if possible and not let you bleed out."

"Then by all means I should do what's courteous," Celine said with a smile. "Lead on. I wouldn't want to offend her. I've been wanting to make her acquaintance since the day I was told you were going to be doing the forensic sculpting on her."

"I'm just starting the baby steps," Eve said. "But she's going to be very exciting."

"I don't have the slightest doubt," Celine said. "On the

whole, I approve of baby steps, but lately I seem to have hurled myself headlong into the depths at every point."

"But you don't regret it?" Eve asked curiously.

"Not for a minute. I might have missed too much. The only thing I would have regretted would have been if I'd had to do without Dominic when he needed me. That would have been a true nightmare." She gestured toward the workroom door. "Now let's go and I'll explain all of that to Folashade."

———

DOMINIC'S CAMP
LATER THAT DAY

"You asked me to tell you when Quinn showed up," Rashid said as he came down the cliff toward the bridge. "He's up at the camp with Kontara and the kid. He wanted to come down here, but I could see that they are all pretty well exhausted. I told them to grab something to eat, and you'd be up to see them right away."

"They're all okay?"

Rashid shrugged. "As good as they could be. If they'd had their way, they would have turned around and headed back toward Shafira." He looked at the recently completed repair work on the bridge. "They did this in record time. I'm impressed."

Dominic nodded. "So am I." He started back up the trail. "And we'll get there pretty damn quick once we decide which route we want to use for the attack. I just have to talk to Kontara to be sure we'll have those bastards in our sights…"

"Well, then I believe you're going to get what you wanted." Rashid was glancing over his shoulder. "Looks like she followed me. Sorry about that." He nodded as he pushed past Kontara. "Hello. I do know how worried you are. I'll see you both later back at the camp. I did give him your message."

"I thought you would, but I needed to see him," Kontara said, then focused on Dominic. "Because it's my fault Celine isn't with us, and I can't stand it. I never should have listened to her, but she was so certain I had to save the boy and Joe Quinn. I don't know how much time we have now, but I have to know what you're going to do."

"I'm going to go get her. What did you think I'd be doing?" He grabbed her by the shoulders and gave her a little shake. "And you're going to be there with us. So don't give me that self-pitying bullshit. All I'm going to need from you is a map that will lead me down the eastern maze and position me where I can set up a trap for Caldwell. Do you think you can handle that?"

"No." She was frowning. "Not unless you have a way to take care of Zakira and his soldiers, too. Do you?"

"I might have a few ideas." He nodded at the bridge. "I sent in Seth Caleb well equipped with firepower. He'll do some reconnoitering at Shafira and coordinate with the forces I bring in from the eastern maze you're going to tell me about. Satisfactory?"

"If you can promise me that you'll move fast enough." Kontara shivered. "I'm having problems forgetting that statue in the museum where I first saw that photo of Celine. Zakira used to stop and stare at it whenever he was anywhere near it."

She turned on her heel and headed up the hill. "Don't let him touch her, Dominic. I'll do anything you tell me to do. Just promise me that you'll keep her safe."

"Absolutely. She'll be safe even if I have to burn down the entire damn village to keep her that way."

"I think you mean that," Kontara said wryly. "But there are a limited number of people in that village for whom I feel a certain sympathy, so please not everyone, Dominic."

"I'll try to restrain myself," Dominic said. "But since I don't believe there are many people in that category, you'll have to point them out to me." He shook his head. "Now go get some rest and a decent meal and draw me that map. After I give everyone on the team their assignments, we'll be assembling the equipment. And we'll be leaving the camp before midnight."

She nodded. "I'll go back to camp and see if I can manage to get a decent meal down Michael. I'd make a bet that if I don't, he'll be on his way to find out where I went. The last thing he asked me was when we were going to go back to get his mom. I told him I'd tell him after I talked to you."

"Is he causing you problems?" Dominic asked. "I can designate one of the men to keep an eye on him if you like."

She shook her head. "Not what you'd call problems. He's just not like any kid I've ever run across. From the moment we managed to get him away from Shafira, he's barely said a word. He just does what Quinn and I tell him to do, and sometimes he's even ahead of us in that." She frowned as she gazed back up the trail toward the camp. "But he's worried about Eve, and you can tell how much he's hurting." She shrugged. "But then so is Quinn. So any plan you've devised had better work."

"It will work," Dominic said. "Because it's damn well got to. Just keep an eye on that kid so I don't have to watch out for him, too."

"I'll do my best." Kontara started up the hill. "But the only thing that may help us is that Quinn isn't about to lose his son again now that he's managed to get him back. I'll try to have a few words with him…"

———

Michael was waiting by the path when Kontara reached the camp. He took a step toward her, his gaze on her face. "When?"

She knew he wouldn't be evaded. "Tonight. Midnight. But there's no way your dad is going to let you go back to that place again. He'd consider it entirely too dangerous, and so would your mother. It's the last thing that she'd want, Michael."

"I know that," he said soberly. "We talked about it. But that was when I was still a prisoner. What she said made sense. It was safer for both of us. But everything is different now. I can't let her stay there. I always told her that I'd take care of her. She laughed about it, but I meant it."

"I'm sure you did, but your dad still wouldn't permit it. Trust him to take care of your mom."

"I do trust him. But now it's also my job, and I can't do anything else." His lips tightened. "My dad has taught me a lot, and there are other things I already know that will help me do what has to be done."

She frowned. "I don't know what you're talking about."

"I know you don't. But my dad will, and even if he doesn't

like the idea of me going with him, he'll understand that I might be able to help us get Mom away from them." He suddenly smiled gently. "I thank you for all you've done for us, but I can't do what you want, Kontara. And now I have to go and talk to my father."

"By all means." She gestured to where Joe was sitting talking to Rashid. "That's probably for the best anyway. Perhaps he can talk some sense into you. I don't seem to be doing very well."

"You've said everything you should have said," Michael said as he started across the camp. "Mom would have agreed with you. But it's just something I have to do."

He stopped a few yards before he reached his dad and stood waiting. Joe must have felt Michael staring at him because he suddenly broke off what he was saying to Rashid and then stiffened as he met Michael's eyes. He got to his feet and strolled over to him.

"Kontara said tonight at midnight," Michael said quietly.

"I know. Rashid told me." He was gazing at him searchingly. "And you have something to say to me?"

"I don't have to say it, do I?" Michael asked. "I have to go with you."

"You don't have to do anything. You're a kid and that takes you out of the game."

"It's Mom," Michael said. "And that puts me right back into it. But if you don't take me with you, I'll follow you and be there when I'm needed."

His dad muttered a curse. "You know I don't want you to do this?"

"I know that she's special to both of us, and we should do

it together. Which way do you want it? Do you take me with you, or do I follow you?"

He sighed. "I take you with me. But you obey every rule I've ever taught you, dammit."

Michael grinned. "Of course, you're always the boss. I'm just along to aid and assist."

"I had my doubts about that for a few minutes."

"No, you didn't. It's just hard for you to realize that it's time for you to look at me in a different way. Though you're not like Mom, who seems to want me to stay a kid."

"Because she doesn't want to let you go," he said gruffly. "Nothing wrong with that."

"Nothing in this world or the next," Michael said. "It's kind of wonderful." He was walking away. "I'm going to get something to eat and then I'll come and sit down with you and listen to all the words of wisdom that will be swirling around you and Dominic. I promise I won't interfere."

"You'd be better off taking a nap."

"Whatever you say...I'm only here to listen and to please you..." He glanced back over his shoulder. "And admire that you're clever enough to listen to me and pay attention even when you don't want to. It's no wonder I respect you as much as I do."

"Because I'm doing what you want me to?"

"Perhaps a little. But mostly because you trust what you've taught me and you know I won't do anything to let you down. That's kind of wonderful too, Dad..."

———

EVE'S WORKROOM

SHAFIRA

TWO DAYS LATER

"Did you think I'd forgotten about you?" Caldwell asked as he threw open the door leading to Eve's quarters. "You're not that lucky. I was busy, so I gave you a couple days to let our Celine recover before I brought her to Zakira's attention again."

Eve stood and stepped toward him as he searched the room. Caldwell was obviously more stressed than he had been earlier. "Where the hell is she? I want to make certain that she's progressing just the way Zakira would want her to." He smiled maliciously. "You might say I have a vested interest in their future relationship."

"So I've heard," Eve said coldly. "She was wounded, remember? I've just been giving her a chance to rest and heal. I'm sure you realize I wouldn't be able to whisk Celine out of this place without you knowing it. Not with you sending Jossland in here every few hours to check that she was still firmly under your thumb. He sometimes glares at her like a starving man would a prime rib steak."

"I assure you, Jossland enjoyed those visits enormously," Caldwell said. "That's why I assigned him as her sole jailer. I knew he'd still be hoping I'd change my mind and turn him loose on her. I had to reward the poor guy in some way for all he's gone through since she came into his life."

"You're both cowards to gang up on a wounded woman." She paused. "Why were you so busy? Were you trying to hunt down my son?"

"Naturally, I was hoping to find a way to get him back. I liked the situation I'd set up with the two of you." He shrugged.

"But this damn country frustrates the hell out of me. I couldn't find any trace of him after that first day. Don't be too pleased with yourself, though. I'll go on the hunt again as soon as I take care of this business with Zakira. In the meantime, I'll let Zakira's soldiers try to find Quinn and that bitch who brought him knocking on your door. Though having Celine may turn out to be even more valuable and satisfying. Jossland was sure Alex Dominic was sleeping with her before she left Boston. I might be able to make an even more profitable deal…To the victor belongs the spoils, and I'm almost always the victor." He frowned. "Now stop making excuses. Do I have to tear this place apart, or are you going to tell me where she is?"

Eve nodded toward the connecting door to the workroom. "She spends a lot of time with me when I'm working on Folashade." Her smile was almost catlike. "You can tell Zakira that even when I'm not actively working on the mask itself, I keep her on hand to inspire me."

"Enjoying yourself?" He was already striding toward the door. "Well, that has to stop, and I have a few ideas what I can do to replace it." He threw open the door and then stopped as he saw Celine sitting in a chair beside the gold sarcophagus. "Ah, there you are." He strode toward her. "Hello, Celine. I believe Eve was trying to hide you away from me. I wonder why she'd do that?" He lit his phone flashlight and shone it on her face. "Do you have any ideas?"

"I'm sure you think that you do," Celine said. "Why should I help?"

He was turning her face from side to side and then examining her throat and torso. He gave a low whistle. "You must have a very good constitution. You've healed amazingly well during the past few days. A little bit on the pale side…but only a little, and the rest is very close to that photo I gave Zakira. As soon as I add a few other embellishments, you'll be ready to go on display." He took a few steps back and gazed at her appraisingly. "You're absolutely what that fool Zakira thinks you should be."

"Hooray," Celine said sardonically. "Just what I always wanted."

Eve was suddenly standing beside Celine. "But that will only convince Zakira that he should allow me more time to complete the death mask."

"We'll have to see about that," Caldwell said. "He has a vision, and I've been feeding it with my own inimitable skill. But I'm almost ready to close the trap now." He reached out and patted Celine's cheek. "And you're such an incredibly enticing bait for that trap."

"Why are you in such a hurry?" Eve asked. "You appear to be a little uneasy."

"Nonsense." Caldwell shrugged. "I'm just a very careful man, and I might have heard that there have been sightings of strangers in the area in the past few days. Nothing definite, but I've decided to give the priest what he wants and take what I want in return." He turned on his heel. "Take good care of her, Eve. I have to go gather those embellishments I mentioned. I'll send Jossland with them a bit later. I guarantee he'll enjoy that just as much as he has his other visits with you."

The door slammed behind him.

"Damn him," Eve murmured. "I was hoping to buy more time. I still may be able to talk Zakira into giving it to me."

"If not, then we'll just have to think of something else," Celine said. "I know you did everything you could. Caldwell is getting impatient." She grimaced. "And a lot of it was my fault for stretching him to the limit when I was on the run." She turned and stroked the gold sarcophagus. "Thanks for the company, Folashade, but I think I might have to be on my own from now on."

"We can't be sure of that," Eve said. "In spite of what he said, Caldwell hasn't been able to find a definite trace of Michael or anyone else that we know would be on the hunt for you." She smiled. "Or me. He's getting very frustrated. I'm afraid I wasn't sympathetic enough. I was too happy when he mentioned those strangers that might get in his way. The poor man evidently doesn't realize what he's going to have to face when he does catch up with them."

"I don't feel at all sorry for him," Celine said. "He's a little too pleased with himself, and he gave the orders to kill Barnaby. I can't ever forget that." She wearily shook her head. "And I want him out of our lives so I don't have to worry about Dominic."

"Point taken," Eve said. "But from my experience with you, I don't believe that you won't bounce back when you get a chance."

Celine blinked and then she found she was chuckling. "I can't, either. I must still be a little under the weather. But I suppose I'll have to make an adjustment or two if those 'embellishments' that Caldwell is sending turn out to be troublesome."

"It might be just as well to keep that in mind," Eve said. "Caldwell seems to have an affinity for troublesome situations."

She paused. "But I'll wait here with you and we'll see what he has in store for us this time…"

"In store for me, not you, Eve," Celine said gently. "You and Folashade might have to sit this one out together."

Eve smiled. "Like I said, we'll have to see what he has in store for us."

CHAPTER

19

It was close to midnight when they heard a loud knock on the outer door. But Jossland didn't wait for Eve to answer him. He was cursing as he pushed open the door and carried in a huge white wardrobe box and threw it on the floor at Celine's feet. "A present from Caldwell," he said with a grin. "I told him I approved of it, and he gave me special orders about what to do with it once you unwrapped it. He thought I'd enjoy being the one to give you orders. He wasn't wrong." He threw himself onto a chair and waved a royal hand. "Go ahead. Open it. It probably cost Caldwell a small fortune."

"Not interested," Celine said. "And I don't take orders from you. Open it yourself."

His lips twisted as he leaned forward. "But I want to see you do it. Caldwell gave me orders and told me if I had trouble making you obey me, I could use a bit of force to help you to remember that you're just a prisoner and I call the shots. I think he's getting tired of having to kowtow to you and Eve Duncan."

"That could be interesting," Celine said. "But not enough to waste my time on. Go to hell, Jossland."

"Don't be rude, Celine." Eve was pushing past her and

325

scooping up the box. "I know that designer label, and I'm curious to see what's inside." She slipped down the black velvet ties and opened the lid. "There! It seems to be a fairly innocuous-looking garment. Not worth causing a fuss over."

"That's a matter of opinion." But Celine was looking down with revulsion at the gown, and then she took it out of the box shook it. "I have an idea what it is, though I have to admit it's really exquisite." She dropped the gown on the floor. "But tell Caldwell I said no thank you."

"You don't have a choice." Jossland was scowling. "I have my orders. He said you were to put it on and that I was to take photos and bring them to him. I think he wants to show them to Zakira and prove that you're ready for him. So you have a choice of putting the damn thing on yourself or leaving it up to me." His smile was very nasty. "I'd enjoy it, but I doubt if you would."

"You underestimate me," Celine said. "I'm always wide open to new experiences. I might be able to make even that bearable."

Eve stepped between them and gave the gown to Celine. "But I really want to see it on you. I'm sure that deep-violet silk would show off your eyes beautifully." She pushed Celine toward the workroom. "Try it on, and while you're doing it, imagine where else a gown like that might lead you. I can't wait to see you in it. You should thank Jossland for giving you this opportunity."

She slammed the door of the workroom.

Leaving Celine alone to get over the anger and terror of the moment when she had seen that gorgeous gown that she knew was meant to be her shroud. Okay, forget it. Just decode those last few sentences of Eve's and use Jossland and this gown to save both of them tonight. Simple? No way. But she already had an idea how she might be able to do it.

Think.

Make a plan!

Her hand moved exploringly over the folds of the gown. The fabric was inset with glittering amethysts, brilliant emeralds, and gold. She looked down. The second emerald in the inset was loose enough for her purpose.

She quickly slipped on the gown, fastened it, and then took a deep breath and turned to leave the workroom and face Eve.

"You look stunning." Eve gazed at her in astonishment as she walked slowly around Celine, taking in every detail. It was a clinging Roman toga design, but the bejeweled fabric glittered. The necklace and earrings Celine had on were also studded with amethysts and emeralds.

"I'm glad you think so," Celine whispered. "But it's not exactly what you'd call a festive occasion, is it? Though I might have come up with a way to make it bearable."

Eve went still. "Have you indeed? Interesting."

"I hope it will be." Celine suddenly grinned. "Though I admit I intend to try to enjoy it. I want to make sure Zakira and Caldwell don't get off too easily after what they inflicted on Kontara and the other people here at Shafira. She deserves to see them suffer."

"What are you two women whispering about?" Jossland was gazing at them suspiciously. "Get away from her, Celine. I don't trust you."

She turned to face him. "Really? When I'm such a gentle, peace-loving person."

"Shut up!" he hissed. "I have to report to Caldwell." He was dialing his phone as he spoke. "I made her put on the damn gown just like you said, Caldwell. Yeah, I guess she looks okay. She wasn't happy about it, but I bet the priest will like her in it. Do you want me to bring her to you now?" Evidently he got a negative response, because he shrugged. "Okay." He hung up and turned back to Celine. "He's going to talk to the priest and then come here and check you out himself before he lets him see you. He said he didn't trust me to give an opinion. since he knows I want him to give you to me like he promised."

"He's more intelligent than I thought," Celine said. "And you're clearly much more stupid to think he'd bother trying to please you."

"Bitch!" He took out his Glock and pointed it at her. "I'm getting tired of putting up with your smart talk. You don't even know that Caldwell is almost through with his games with you. He wouldn't have gone to all that trouble sending you that fancy gown if he hadn't been ready to make a move on Zakira." His teeth were clenched with fury as he took a step closer. "And I might just make a move myself after what you made those guards do to my arm in that damn river. I can't wait to get my hands on you."

"You're making that obvious," Celine said. "But you're clearly too scared of Caldwell to do anything but talk big. You'd better put that gun up before you hurt yourself." She smiled mockingly. "Caldwell seems to think of you as some kind of errand boy. Why else would he send you here with this gorgeous gown? Oh, that's right. He wanted you to take photos." She twirled around in a circle. "That's all you're good for, according to Caldwell. By all means, do what he's ordered you to do."

"Shut up!"

He started taking the photos but she could tell he was getting more angry with every moment as she continued twirling and mocking him. "You're slowing down," Celine called. "Caldwell will be getting completely disgusted with you. He'll never trust you again."

"I'll show you how much he trusts me." His cheeks were flushed as he grabbed her wrist and pulled her toward him. "I'll break you apart!"

"Stop it." Eve was suddenly standing between them. "This isn't what Caldwell would want and you know it, Jossland. I was promised her as a model for my death mask. Do you want me to complain to Zakira?"

"Do what you want." Jossland tightened his grip on Celine's arm. His eyes were glittering wildly as his other arm lashed out and his fist struck Eve in the jaw with brutal force. "You're nothing to me."

"No!" Celine watched Eve fall to the floor unconscious. Then she was fighting desperately to jerk her arm free and do a Muay Thai kick aimed at the gun in Jossland's hand. It flew across the room, away from Jossland!

Celine tensed as Jossland circled around her. She was making a mistake, she realized. She was instinctively sizing him up as she would a Muay Thai opponent in class, but this was no training session. Here, her opponent would gladly kill her. There was no elegance to play by. This was a fight for her life.

No rules.

With a slight hop, she swung her left leg up and brought

it down on his neck with an ax-kick. He screamed, and his knees buckled.

Good. His head and shoulders were now lower, so the next kick would be easier.

She hopped again and swung her right leg up. Shit. The stupid dress was inhibiting her range of movement. Jossland grabbed her ankle and flipped her over. She hit the floor hard. He was on top of her in an instant.

He smiled. "Got you. No more tricks."

She cursed. This damn dress. The sharp-edged jewels were cutting into her torso, making it almost impossible to move.

She closed her eyes. Her old Muay Thai master had always told her to turn every weakness into an advantage. Right. He'd never been shoehorned into a ceremonial dress like this one, she wagered.

Jossland closed his hands around her throat. "This won't be quick, but I'll enjoy the hell out of every minute, my dear bitch."

She tried to gasp, but her airway had been totally cut off. She tried to wiggle free, but the bejeweled dress sliced into her.

Turn every weakness into an advantage...

She had to make this count; she'd only have one shot at it.

She reached down and gripped an emerald that had been cutting into her. She yanked it free of the gown, swung her arm upward, and sliced Jossland's throat!

His eyes bulged as his carotid artery opened. Celine rolled out from under him and held the emerald protectively before her as she would a knife. Then she realized there was no need. He was bleeding out quickly. His hands closed around his own throat as blood gushed over his fingers.

He lost consciousness in seconds.

He was dead in less than a minute.

"Eve…" Celine crawled over to where Eve was still lying and started to examine her. "Eve…it's over…We have to find a way to—"

Eve's eyes were opening! Celine took a deep breath. "Good. I was worried for a minute. But I think you're okay. How do you feel?"

Eve made a face. "Like that asshole punched me in the jaw. I hope you managed to return the favor."

Celine nodded. "I made sure that you came out on top of that particular battle."

Eve's eyes narrowed as she caught a certain nuance in Celine's voice. "How far on top?" Her gaze wandered around the room until she caught sight of Jossland's crumpled, bloody body. "Oh, I'd say that put me quite a distance on top."

"It couldn't have happened to a more deserving person," Celine said. "And I don't regret a minute of it. Cutting his carotid artery seemed a perfect ending for one of the emerald icicle insets on the gown Caldwell so generously gave me." She was helping Eve to her feet. "But we've got to get out of here. We don't know how long it will be before Caldwell will start worrying and decide to bring Zakira to see me and those photos. Thanks to Jossland being such a thorough bastard, we've bought ourselves some time to try to lose ourselves here at Shafira until the people we want to find us show up here."

"And you have an idea where we can go?"

"I thought we should head for the hills where they caught me before," Celine said. "I became very familiar with that area while I was hiding out, and I can probably avoid Caldwell's

331

thugs. And I've trekked through enough jungles with Dominic and Quinn to realize they both have the skill to track us there."

Eve nodded. "I know Joe does, and I'd bet that Seth Caleb is probably somewhere near him." She grabbed Jossland's gun and phone from the floor and headed for the door. "Okay, you've convinced me. Let's head for your hills, Celine. But first we should try to phone Kontara to see if she can give us any hints about how to safely get out of this damn village. If anyone knows, it would be her. And I've seen enough of the weapons Caldwell gives his thugs to know that they're rarely what they seem. Along with the phones and radios, the weapons he gives them are lethal and high-tech. But we might be able to find a way to break the codes and turn them against them."

Celine shook her head skeptically. "I admire high-tech but I'm no expert."

Eve smiled. "Neither am I. But I've been surrounded by a good many people who are, and one of them is Seth Caleb, if we can find a way to get the weapons to him...All we can do is try..."

———

JUNGLE MAZE NEAR SHAFIRA

"What is it, Dad?" Michael took a step closer as he saw Joe's sudden tension. His father was looking down at the village below them. "You said we were almost there."

"I thought we were." Joe lifted his binoculars, and his gaze scanned the cobbled village streets and outlying farms of the

332

lush acreage that was Shafira. He hadn't wanted to alarm his son, but his every instinct was telling him that something was very wrong. "But there's no harm in taking it slow and easy and being absolutely certain. You're sure this is the exit Kontara took when you escaped from the village?" he asked Michael as he lowered the binoculars. "It's familiar to me, too, but the entire village looks deserted from here."

"I'm sure. I wouldn't forget that, Dad." Michael shook his head. "But it does look kind of strange. Whenever I went to the well to get water, there were always people around. Soldiers or Caldwell's men or quite a few women who visited the men in their quarters. It looks empty." He frowned. "I'm sorry that Kontara isn't here to tell you more. I guess she was the only one who really knew what was going on here."

"It's not your fault, Michael." He grimaced. "If anything, it's mine for being too cocky because I had the map Kontara drew for us. When Dominic said he had to send her to meet with Seth in the hills to give him directions for the attack, I told him that we wouldn't have a problem. After all, I had the map. Evidently I forgot how easy it was to get turned around in this nightmare of a maze."

Michael frowned. "Well, you got us here, Dad. You didn't get turned around."

"Are you defending me?" Joe smiled wryly. "Then I'll have to admit that, for a moment, I wasn't sure I'd brought us to the right village. Something's very strange here. But there's at least one good thing about the fact that the village seems deserted." He pointed to a thick acreage of corn and grain that ran along the north fence. "It's almost dark now, and we might be able to slip into that field if we're careful. And the field has the same thick vegetation as the rest of Shafira. Maybe, once we're actually in the village, you'll recognize something about it that looks familiar. Or perhaps they moved your mom and Celine to a different house or farm."

"Maybe," Michael said doubtfully. "But they didn't do it any other time after they brought me here."

"It could be the very reason they'd do it this time…" He looked down at Michael. "Stop worrying. Things seldom remain the same in situations like this. You're sure about the exit, and I'm sure that I trust you. But things here have changed, and we'll just find out what and why. The important thing is that we have to be close to your mom. So it's not going to stop us." He smiled. "Nothing is going to stop us. Right?"

Michael nodded. "Right, Dad."

"Stay close." He lifted his binoculars again. "We'll give it a few more minutes and then we'll go for it…"

———

Joe checked his phone screen as he and Michael moved through the dense vegetation. "If Mom was moved after we got you away from this area, they almost surely took her this way. Any other path would have been too risky for them…Too easy for them to be spotted."

Michael nodded. "The guards were always worried about that when I was with them. Anytime someone talked about moving us, they decided not to do it. I guess they knew people were looking for us."

"Well, when you got away, it didn't leave them much choice. They had to move." Joe pointed ahead. "And this way offered them the most cover. Does anything here look familiar to you?"

Michael looked around. "Not really. It's not like our house at the lake where everything is warm and homey. Everything at this village kind of looks the same after a while."

"I know what you mean." Joe stopped and crouched on the overgrown trail. "But I can tell someone's been here recently. Look how the grass is pressed down and the lower tree branches are all pushed in the same direction. I'd say that a group of four or five people moved through here."

Michael nodded. "You're a great tracker. I wish I could do that."

"You can. It's all about practice. And lots of training."

"Is that what the SEALs taught you?"

"Them and the FBI."

"Maybe you can teach me?"

Joe looked at his son. He'd grown up so much in the past year—maybe a bit too much. "Sure. But I hope it's a skill you won't need after today."

"It's a skill that you still use when the chips are down." Michael paused. "Though I wish I'd stayed with Mom. Maybe I could have helped her."

"I don't think so, and I know that isn't what she wanted."

Michael nodded. "I know that she told—" He froze. "Stop!"

Joe whirled toward him. "What is it?"

"Someone is watching us." Michael crouched in the tall grass. "Get down, Dad."

Joe crouched next to him. "Where is he?"

"I—I don't know. But I could feel it."

With Michael, Joe knew it was always more than just a feeling. The boy *knew.*

"Any idea what direction?" Joe asked.

"No. But I think he recognized me."

"If he saw your face, he was probably on the trail ahead of us." Joe felt for the spearpoint knife in his belt sheath. "Remember those boulders we passed? I need you to go back there and wait for me. I'll be there in a minute or so."

"What are you going to do?"

"Just do it, Michael."

"I want to stay with you."

"I'll be back in a minute. It'll be okay. Just hide behind those boulders."

Michael's eyes were wide as he stared at his father. "You're going to kill him, aren't you?"

"Only if he tries to kill me first."

"You know he will." .

"He came after our family, Michael," Joe said quietly. "And right now, he's standing between us and your mother. Wait at the boulders."

Michael nodded. "What if you don't come back?"

"I promise you I'll be back. Don't worry."

But Michael was clearly worried. Joe hugged him close and then motioned for him to leave. Michael finally pulled away and started back down the trail.

———

Joe ducked low and moved through the brush, trying his best not to disturb the thick branches. If someone had indeed been

watching him and Michael, he was probably twenty yards farther along the trail, where the path was slightly elevated. Joe
found a hiding spot and looked around. There was no one to
be seen. Maybe Michael was just mistaken, though his "feelings" had never failed him before. But it was possible that his
emotions had caused him to—

Wait. There was something up ahead…

Joe shifted position to get a better look. There was definitely a
man up ahead. He was also crouched in the bushes. He had a gun
in one hand, a phone in the other. He was punching a number.
After a moment, he spoke just loud enough for Joe to hear.

"Strickland here. The kid is back, and it looks like he
brought Quinn with him. I lost sight of them, but they can't
be far." He jiggled the phone. "Hello, why aren't you talking?
Is something wrong with my phone? If you send a few guys
back, we should have no problem rounding them up." The
man paused. "Hello? Are you there? Hang on, I'll send you my
location coordinates."

Whippp!

Joe's knife sailed through the air and sliced cleanly into the
man's chest. He slumped to the ground, dead.

Joe dragged the man several feet off the trail and covered
him with two large bushes. Then he checked his phone. No
response. Another indication that something was disrupting
cell phone service. Evidently these guards hadn't been in contact, so he'd just continue as planned. He moved back to the
boulders, where he didn't immediately see Michael. Oh, shit!
He'd never forgive himself if anything happened to—

"Dad!" Michael popped up from behind the largest boulder
and ran over to greet him. "What happened?"

"You were right. There was a man ahead who spotted us."

Michael was gazing at him intently. "What did you do to him?"

"Only what I had to, Michael. He was about to report our position. We never would have found your mother if I'd let him do that."

Michael thought about this for a moment and then nodded slowly. "I understand. You had to weigh what was best. We have to take care of Mom."

"That's right." Joe put his hand on Michael's shoulder. "And I hope we don't have to make another decision like that anytime soon. But it was my decision, not yours. Remember that."

"I will," Michael said. "But you always give me a choice in what I do," he added soberly. "And I have to remember that, too."

"I'm not sure I like where this is going," Joe said. "Let's save this discussion for a time when we're not so stressed." He patted him on the shoulder. "Come on, let's go look for your mom."

They walked another quarter mile until they approached the shed that Michael must have known all too well because he froze in shock when he saw it.

"Michael?" Joe murmured.

"This is it." Michael moistened his lips. "I know it. It's bigger than the other houses in the village, and there's the well where I'd go for water. If we go in that main door, it will connect with the bedroom and the room where Mom worked on the queen."

"Stay here," Joe whispered. He unholstered his automatic and fired up his pocket flashlight. He went inside.

Blood.

Joe inhaled sharply.

Blood everywhere!

Please God, no. Eve…

"Joe?"

He went rigid with shock as he heard that voice he knew so well. "Eve?"

Then he was bolting back to the door and running outside. Eve was kneeling on the floor against the far wall with her arms around Michael. Joe crossed the room in a heartbeat and then she was in his arms. "Eve…I thought…"

"I know what you thought." She kissed him and then hugged Michael closer. "I was hiding down in the basement. I had to be sure that it was you before I took a chance on showing myself. Caldwell's men have been through here. All that blood. Not my fault. Celine did it." Tears were running down her cheeks.

It seemed almost too good to be true that not only was Eve now with him, she was holding their son tightly in her arms, both safe after all the horror he'd been imagining could happen to them today. "It was Celine? Talk to me." Joe didn't want to let them go so he threw his arms around both Eve and Michael. "I saw all that blood in there, and it scared the living hell out of me." He kissed Eve once, twice, three times before finally drawing back. He was trying to think. "You said Celine? Is she okay?"

She nodded. "That bloody mess is Jossland, Celine's handiwork. Caldwell's men were here less than an hour afterward, and I'm sure Caldwell has been tearing this jungle apart looking for us ever since. After we escaped, we called Kontara to

339

tell her where we were heading. She was already in the hills tracking Caleb, but when she heard I had something I wanted her to take to him to decipher, she came back and took the weapons and phones with her. She told us you were heading in this direction and to hide here on the property until you made contact with them." She paused. "But that wasn't an option for Celine."

"Why not?"

"Because the first thing that Caleb had told Kontara when he saw her was that Caldwell had sent word to all his soldiers that he'd put a bounty on Celine's head because he'd found she'd killed his old friend Jossland. He was going to give her to the priest for punishment."

Joe gave a low whistle. "Which would give Caldwell exactly what he wanted: the chance to please Zakira, take over his guerrilla armies, *and* steal him blind."

Eve shook her head. "Do you think that Celine didn't realize that the minute she heard what Kontara said? I was supposed to go with her when we escaped to the hills, but as soon as she heard what was going on, she helped me find this hiding place. And she refused to let me go with her because she was afraid that I'd be compromised."

"And you would have been," Joe said.

"I don't care," Eve said. "They'll find a way to kill her. We have to do something to help her. She'll have to be smuggled out of Shafira or she's dead." She was rubbing her temple as she tried to see a way out. "But we'll have to wait until it's safe to do even that."

"Maybe not as long as you might think," Joe said. "Things are looking a bit more upbeat at the moment." He held up his hand as she opened her lips to speak. "Look, I need to call Dominic right away and tell him you're safe and what's happening to Celine. He might not know that the village has been deserted, which probably means that Caldwell is concentrating on other areas that we should shore up for possible attack."

"You mean like that damn celebration Zakira is planning for Celine?" Eve asked bitterly.

"Possibly," Joe said. "Anyway, we need to know where there's movement. I'll tell you everything, but I want to get you and Michael to safer territory right away. We're heading out of the village and going north to join Caleb's strike team until we're ready to make a move on Caldwell."

Eve inhaled sharply. "And tell me that's going to be soon?"

Michael moved a step closer and smiled at her as he took her hand. "Of course it is, Mom. Dad and I are a great team. I told you that we'd come and get you and here we are. You've got to trust us."

"I do trust you." She leaned down and kissed his temple. "And I'm flattered you're letting me join your team. Now let's go and see if we can find any other bad guys who might be bothering Celine."

———

Dominic received a call from Seth Caleb hours later. "Are you busy? I have someone who wants to talk to you."

"It better be Celine," Dominic said. "I've been waiting since I heard that she was heading your way. Kontara said that Celine wasn't going to take a chance on her call being traced but would call when she decided it was safe. Is she okay?"

"She looks fine to me," Caleb said. "Though I don't know why she'd want to talk to you when you can't seem to keep track of her."

"Be quiet, Caleb." Celine was on the line. "I'm grateful that you took me in but I don't want Dominic to be any more annoyed than he has to be. But you can see that I didn't really have a choice, Dominic. Even Kontara realized that I'd be safer up here in the hills. Anywhere else near Shafira wouldn't have been safe." She paused. "Not for me or anyone I care about. I'm a target, and I'm not about to forget it. I'm not really safe here, either, but if I keep on the move, then I can risk an occasional contact."

"You could come to me," he said hoarsely. "You can trust me to keep you safe."

"But I can't trust you to keep yourself safe," she said gently. "I won't be bait for you, Dominic. We've already played that game. You have to keep on doing what's best to get rid of Caldwell and Zakira."

Dominic muttered a curse. "Then will you stay in Caleb's camp?"

"Until I don't think it's safe for him any longer. The same for Kontara. I've no intention of being caught again by those bastards." She paused and then had to clear her throat. "I hope I'll see you soon. I miss you." She hung up.

He called Caleb's phone back immediately.

Caleb answered. "Too late, Dominic. She's gone."

"I thought she probably would be. Keep an eye on her. Don't let anything happen to her."

"I'll do my best."

"I know you will."

"No threats? No intimidation? You must be in a very bad place."

"You have no idea."

"Oh, but I do," Caleb said. "It's good that we have a plan in place and a number of distractions looming on the horizon. I suggest we dive in and see what damage we can do…"

———

HELIPORT IN THE MOUNTAINS NEAR SHAFIRA
TWENTY-FOUR HOURS LATER

Kaboom!

"What the hell!" The night sky was suddenly lit with firecrackers and drones. The sound of explosions echoed in the darkness as Dominic ran toward his helicopter.

As if in answer to his exclamation, Dominic was receiving a call from Seth Caleb. "You appear to be having entirely too much fun over there in the heliport, Dominic. I think you'd be better served to come up to the mountains and let me and my team help a bit with the general cleanup. I assume you set off the fireworks?"

"Just as I told you I would," Dominic said. "But the explosives you set were a little more than I expected. I almost didn't get back to my helicopter in time." He looked back at the burning helicopters on the tarmac. "I don't believe Caldwell will be going anywhere anytime soon. Why are you calling? What's happening?" Then he answered his own question. "Don't tell me they've located Celine? You said you'd keep an eye out for her until I could finish setting up the attack agenda."

"And that's what I've done as far as possible, but it's getting increasingly difficult. We took one of Zakira's soldiers prisoner a couple hours ago, and he even gave us a description of the woman who's been targeted by Caldwell. He mentioned her violet eyes. Sound familiar?"

"You know it does. How close are they to her?"

"Not too far away. She's very good, and she's keeping ahead of them. But she was wounded, and I don't know how long she'll be able to do it. I've designated several of my men to try to keep her alive, and I'm going to be near the place where she was last seen myself soon. She seems to have a fondness for that waterfall, because she's been seen near there several times."

Dominic was remembering that day at Roxanne Falls and Celine's expression when she had first seen them. Her luminous smile and the way she'd looked under the mist..."She does like waterfalls."

"If you know that, maybe she's trying to reach out to you. I could go check out the area, but I thought you'd prefer to take care of the matter yourself." He paused. "I realize the situation is difficult for you."

Difficult? It was a hell of a lot more than that. "I'm already in my helicopter. Send me the directions." He was starting the rotors. "But I'm not selfish. Celine is going to live, and the rest of those assholes who are hunting her are going to die. I don't care how it happens. But you'll be my friend for life if you manage to point me in their direction."

"I believe I've already done it," Caleb said. "So come and join the party. I think it's time we got rid of Zakira and Caldwell. I know we agreed that the combined main attack would take place just after midnight. But do I have permission to remove them from the picture with a few well-placed sniper attacks? Or if you prefer, I still have all those explosives that I was keeping for a night just like tonight."

"Then we should definitely make use of them," Dominic said grimly. "Be patient, Caleb. All the plans are set, and we can wait a few more hours."

"I can, but I'm not sure about you," Caleb said. "Are you certain that you don't want to let me do a trial run? Aren't you tempted when you know Celine is somewhere down there near that jungle?"

"Of course I am." *Get thee behind me, Satan.* "But I'm trying to be selective and choose wisely." He was already following Caleb's flight plan and could see the waterfall ahead.

He could also see the men below in the jungle and hear the celebratory shots being fired from their rifles and heard their laughter and shouts as they hunted their prey. But the prey they were hunting was Celine, Dominic thought impatiently. Screw them. "I've changed my mind, we don't have to be too selective. We'll see about picking and choosing later. I'm going to land up there near the falls and hope you're right about her reaching out. I need to get her safely away before we blow those bastards to hell. Go on back to your camp and check everything out to make sure it's ready to go later. I'll call you if I need you at the falls."

He heard Caleb laughing as he began his descent.

There was no moon and it was pitch black in the woods when he landed, but he sat there a moment, his gaze searching the darkness.

Are you out there, Celine?

Be there, dammit.

I can't take much more of this. My so-called code is going straight to hell.

Then he saw her and jumped out of the helicopter and was running toward her. He grabbed her close and held her there for a moment before he pushed her away. "Why do you keep doing this? It wasn't bad enough that you managed to get yourself caught. You had to kill one of Caldwell's scumbags and give Zakira an excuse to make an example of you?"

"Shh." She put two fingers over his lips. "Be quiet. All I want to hear from you is that you've found a way to get rid of Caldwell and Zakira without getting yourself killed. They would have done all this ugliness anyway. We both know that it was in their plan." She moved closer to him. "Things just... happened. Was I supposed to let Jossland beat up on Eve? And it was our chance to escape. So I did it."

"You certainly did," Dominic said. "I nearly went crazy when Quinn told me about all the blood in that hut."

She frowned. "It was because it was the carotid artery. I had to make certain he'd bleed out fast."

"I don't need an explanation." He slipped his arm around her waist and pulled her toward the helicopter. "All I needed to know was that it wasn't your blood. Now, let me tell you how we're going to take down Caldwell and Zakira so that you won't be tempted to go after them yourself. Our team's heaviest wing is in the southeast hill acreage. Caleb has made sure that they're scattered and won't be found, because that's also near where Zakira is having his damn festival. All his thugs are there waiting eagerly. It was the perfect place to lay the trap. Thanks to that cell phone and radio equipment info you sent us, we're going to be able to wage an all-out attack against them here on the mountain in about another hour. We'll have separate strikes from the bridge path and the jungle maze route. I already have Caleb here in the hills, and Rashid will have his team guarding anything that's left of that heliport. I made sure it wasn't much."

"It sounds like mass destruction." Celine was frowning. "I know it's necessary, but what about the women captives that are probably there? I think Kontara would say they've already suffered enough."

Dominic was silent and then reluctantly nodded. "She would. We've been keeping an eye on the women's tent here in the hills. As far as Kontara can make out, our priest is keeping his soldiers and Caldwell's men busy preparing the ornate stands and sacrificial altar to make the festival ceremony something to remember."

She shivered. "You don't have to tell me anything more about those particular plans. I can imagine what they are."

"So could I," Dominic said grimly. "When I knew you were running all over these hills and could be caught at any moment, the only good thing was that I knew that I'd blow this mountain to smithereens before I'd ever let you or any of those other women end up in front of that ceremonial slaughterhouse."

Celine smiled. "Then that's truly a good thing, isn't it? You seem to have everything all planned."

"I've been a little irritated with the way they've treated you, so I thought I'd let them know it. Poof. Goodbye one and all. Join in at any point you like, Celine. As long as you don't move more than a few feet away from me."

"I think I could adjust to that." She gave a low whistle as

she thought about the scope of the plan. "Formidable. No wonder Catherine said she was glad you'd decided to take Caldwell down." She added ruefully, "I want Caldwell gone, but I can wait for a while. Jossland was enough for right now."

"Everything that's been going on was probably a little too much for you right now." He leaned forward and gently kissed her. "You're a damn good fighter, but you're basically a healer and not a killer. So if you don't mind, I'll take over getting rid of the terrible twins who have been plaguing us."

She shook her head. "That's not what I'd call watching your back. We should do it together."

"I was afraid that would be your reaction. But we're running out of time." He started pulling her toward the helicopter. "And now we've got to get you away from this damn mountain. Caleb told me that his men had sighted you several times in this area, and I don't want you falling into Zakira's hands before I get the chance to show you that it's okay to occasionally take turns."

"I like this mountain." She was getting into the helicopter. "It's beautiful, and it probably saved my life when I was on the run."

"Well, I'd prefer you rely on me to do that from now on. If you'll allow me the privilege. I promise that you can trust me more than those caves or that spectacular waterfall."

"I know I can," she said quietly. "Trust is important. And I hope you'll trust me, too. I realize sometimes I'm a little impulsive, but I'll always be there to watch your back." She paused. "And I want to be the one to do it."

He reached over and touched her cheek. "Then you've got

the job. And may heaven help you." He started the rotors. "Because I don't know anyone else who would want to—"

Splat!

A bullet shattered the window in front of them!

"Down!" Dominic shouted as he pushed her to the floor.

More bullets!

Celine heard shouts from the soldiers who were coming up the hill and firing at the helicopter.

"Out!" Dominic was already out of the helicopter himself and dragging her with him until she managed to get on her feet and was running with him toward the woods. "Keep low and head for the deep woods." He took her arm and half pulled her along the path. "I'm right beside you. I promise it's going to be okay. I was expecting this, so I set up a few surprises for them to protect you."

"No festival to make Zakira and Caldwell happy?" She tried to keep her voice from shaking. "How disappointing for them." She could hear the soldiers shouting in the jungle behind them, and her grasp instinctively tightened on Dominic's. "But it serves them right, doesn't it? I was getting a little tired of that nonsense."

"Just keep running. We have to make it past that line of trees for this to work."

"For what to work?

"We set up a perimeter to slow them down if they tried to launch an attack on our base camp."

"You have troops here?"

"Not exactly. Run faster."

More shots rang out behind them, and they could hear excited shouts from Caldwell's men.

"They've spotted us!" Celine said.

"Good."

A bullet whizzed by them. "Good?"

He led her around a small gully. "Yes. We need them to follow us for another few seconds."

As they ran past the tree line, Celine spotted a large black object just over six feet tall. Then another. Then another.

"What are those?" she asked.

"Keep moving. You'll see in a few seconds."

She heard more voices behind them, and the bullets were getting close to finding their mark.

"Get down!" Dominic pulled her into another small gully and pushed a button on his wristwatch.

"What did you just do?"

Celine heard a mechanized whirring, and she and Dominic peered over the gully just in time to see the black objects swing around and cut loose with a torrent of gunfire aimed back at their pursuers. The men's excited voices were replaced with screams of pain as the machine guns mowed them down with incredible precision.

Dominic ducked back down and checked his watch. "Each of those sentry guns is equipped with a two-thousand-round magazine. They're set up with motion sensors for their targeting."

The pursuers' anguished shouts continued as Celine ducked back down next to him. She might have been horrified by their death screams if they hadn't just been trying to kill her. "Cool gadgets."

"I thought you'd approve." He was dialing Caleb as he

spoke. When Caleb picked up, he said, "You know you said you wanted to escalate the action?"

"Yes, and you were being very boring about it."

"I hate to disappoint. Escalate." He paused. "All the way."

"Yes! I'll be right back with you." Caleb pressed DIS-CONNECT.

And Dominic grabbed Celine's elbow and pushed her into a run. "Let's keep going."

———

After he'd hung up with Dominic, Caleb crouched on a hillside with his binoculars, staring at the twisted spectacle of Zakira's army celebrating their dear leader with music, sparklers, and a feast that could have fed a group a hundred times its size. In the middle was a huge platform altar equipped with leg and arm restraints. The sight sickened him. Zakira was obviously prepared to serve up Celine's human sacrifice for his assembled guests.

To hell with that.

He reached for the knapsack Dominic had given him.

———

Celine and Dominic had traveled less than a mile from the site of the sentry guns when a familiar voice called out from the darkness.

"Celine Kelly!"

More than familiar to Celine. It had to be Caldwell.

"How naughty you were, Celine," he shouted again. "You're responsible for the death of almost twenty of my men. How does that feel? Not that I minded you ridding me of that fool Jossland. In fact, you chose a very convenient time. But it annoys me not to be in control of a situation. So I think I'll have to kill Dominic to teach you a lesson. Of course you're reserved for Zakira. But I'll enjoy watching your face as Dominic is torn apart."

Dominic was motioning her to stay silent, and there was no way she'd give Caldwell the satisfaction of even thinking she'd heard him. Evidently, she had discouraged him, because he didn't call out again.

"That wasn't pleasant," she murmured to Dominic. "I hope that surprise you arranged is right around the corner? I'm afraid I'm a trifle breathless."

"It is. Caleb reminded me that you're still wounded, so I made plans to accommodate." He had his arm around her waist again and was bearing most of her weight as they reached the edge of the forest. "There's a cave only a few yards away. Tuck yourself inside it, keep quiet, and prepare to watch the show." He was climbing a tall sycamore tree as he spoke and pulled out his automatic pistol and adjusted it on one of branches near the top of the tree. "Come on, Caleb," he whispered. "It's almost time. I promised her that surprise, and we don't want to disappoint her."

As if on cue, Caleb's voice came over his mobile phone. "I'm all set here. Zakira's soldiers are standing by for an attack at the parade grounds when they bring Celine down for the ceremony. Zakira has a particularly deadly-looking machete that he's brandishing while he's waiting for her."

"He'll never get a chance to use it," Dominic said coldly as he aimed at one of Caldwell's men who had appeared on the horizon. "Not if you did what I asked you to do."

"Of course I did," Caleb said. "There's nothing I like better than a carefully coordinated attack on a fine night like this. I told you how envious I was about you taking over the heliport action. I'm still available if you need any assistance."

"I'll let you know." Dominic took out the sniper, watching the man drop to the ground. He set up the next shot. "I'm well aware of your willingness to accommodate. Or perhaps I should use the term *eagerness* instead."

"Perhaps you should," Caleb said quietly. "It's definitely more appropriate. I consider Eve Duncan family, and those bastards have been putting her through hell. It's been a pleasure finding a way to work out the right payback."

"I believe we've found it," Dominic said. "Though I'm sure Caldwell will disagree. He was hurling threats at us when we were running through the forest and probably thinks he's got us cornered. But I was just about to phone and nag you for dragging your feet when you called me."

"I never permit nagging, Dominic. You should have realized that perfection always requires a little longer. But I'll forgive you since you've engineered such an entertaining evening for me." Then he added crisply, "I've just had Kontara forward Zakira's location coordinates to your phones."

"Perfect," Dominic said.

Caleb suddenly chuckled. "Well, it just got a little more perfect. Caldwell just showed up here with a couple of his men."

"Caldwell?" Dominic repeated. "He was just here."

"Evidently, he's impatient. He probably wants to borrow a detachment of Zakira's soldiers to hunt down you and Celine."

"Oh, my God," Dominic murmured. "We'll never have another chance like this."

"Tell me you're ready." Caleb was whispering. "Tell me you're going to let me be the one to do it."

"I'm not shutting you out. I thought I might send some of our best snipers to pick you up to help."

"Not necessary," Caleb said.

"You can't do this alone, Caleb."

"I'm not alone. I have Quinn, who has an entire team staked out on the next hill over. He's very eager to go after any stragglers who manage to survive our first attack. Not that I expect many of those. You'll recall he was very pissed off at Caldwell and Zakira after he found out the way Eve was treated in their less-than-tender care. Plus, I have a knapsack full of your puck explosives. We'll see if they're as impressive as you claim."

"It's still too risky," Dominic said. "Don't do it."

"It's already half done, Dominic. I think you just want to be here to see it for yourself. I'll tell you what: I'll link this phone to the pucks. In ninety seconds, you give the command."

"You're insane."

Caleb chuckled. "I've been called worse. Much worse. But I wouldn't disobey an order from you. Give the command and look to the west. You'll see a grand finale to end all grand finales." He was gone from the phone for a few seconds. Then he was back on the line. "That was Eve. She wants to talk to you before you give that order. Any objection?"

"What the hell?" Dominic asked in exasperation. "Why not? By all means. Next you'll want a group call."

"Nah, I'm too impatient to get on with the show," Caleb said. "But Eve would never ask anything like this without a reason." He paused. "You have eighty seconds now, Dominic."

Dominic ruefully shook his head, but he was already climbing down from the tree and running toward the cave where he'd left Celine. "Caleb wants to take on Zakira's entire army by himself. He's certifiable."

"It's obviously personal to him, too," Celine said. "He believes he's just getting the job done."

"Maybe." Dominic looked at his watch for another forty-five seconds, imagining Zakira, Caldwell, and their minions standing so proudly, waiting for what they thought would be their greatest triumph.

Screw them.

"But evidently Eve has something she wants to tell me." Dominic was quickly calling her number.

She picked up immediately.

"I only have a few seconds, Eve," he said. "Why do you want to talk to me?"

"It's not really you I want to speak to. I asked Caleb to connect your line to Zakira and Caldwell when you called me. I have something to say to them."

They could suddenly hear Caldwell muttering curses and then Zakira screaming orders at someone in the background. "I'm sorry to disturb your party, Caldwell," Eve called out to them. "But since Celine and I were to be your guests of honor and we're definitely not coming, it would have been ruined anyway. How about changing it to a surprise party with you as the primary guests? I think we did a good job of arranging for that theme."

"What's happening, Caldwell?" Zakira was shouting. "This is all your fault."

"Shut up," Caldwell roared. "Can't you see this has to be a trap? Isn't that right, Eve? And you're the one who always wants this stupid butchery, Zakira. I'm getting out of here!"

"Too late, Caldwell," Eve said. "I'm afraid Dominic is probably checking his watch now. Besides, you're the one who encouraged that butchery, remember? I have only one more thing to say. Soon there's going to be fire and explosions and intense pain. And while you're feeling it, I want you both to remember what you said to me that day you killed that poor innocent child for no reason at all. Listen very carefully," she said softly and deliberately. "It's happening because *we* chose it."

She pressed DISCONNECT, and her call vanished from Dominic's screen.

Dominic turned to Celine and said quietly, "I believe Eve said it all, didn't she?"

She nodded. "I'm glad she had the chance to do it. Some of the things they put her through were a torment, and she had to keep it all inside."

"She's not the only one." He glanced at his watch. "Eve's right. Time is up."

He held up his phone toward Celine. "You said you wanted to take turns when we saw a problem ahead. Well, this is one of those times, and it's both of our battle to fight. You give the command."

356

She took the phone and looked at it in bewilderment. "What command?"

He covered her hand on the phone with his own. "Initiate," he whispered.

She shrugged but then she suddenly smiled as she met his eyes and spoke into the telephone. "Initiate."

BOOM!

As Caleb promised, a huge explosion lit up the western sky. The ground shook, and the roar echoed off distant mountains.

———

FESTIVAL CEREMONIAL ALTAR

SHAFIRA MOUNTAINS

Caldwell sluggishly pulled himself to his feet and staggered forward. Fire and body parts were lying everywhere. What the hell had happened?

Dominic. Dominic had happened.

Caldwell was suddenly overcome by the odor of burning flesh. His own, he realized. His left leg was on fire, and every nerve ending was screaming in pain. He patted his leg to extinguish the blaze.

The blast's few survivors were lurching forward one step at a time, like extras in a zombie movie. They were dropping like flies all around him.

Caldwell reached for his hair, and he realized there was none. There wasn't even much of a scalp left.

He looked down. Zakira was lying half on, half off the sacrificial altar, twitching and vomiting. Most of his clothes had burned off, and he was desperately mouthing something.

Before Caldwell could understand what he was trying to say, Zakira was dead.

Good! Stupid bastard. Caldwell was glad to see the end of him. But a few moments later, his own pain overcame him, and he stumbled and fell, screaming as he fought desperately to get away from the agony attacking him.

In the next instant, he was dead as well.

———

Dominic put away his phone and took Celine into his arms. "Well done."

"Was it? I've never blown up anything before." She was gazing at the smoke darkening the sky. "What happens next?"

"Now we go and check out the helicopter and see if we can use it to take you to Caleb's encampment to make sure all is well with the people we care about. Then we make a number of decisions that I don't want you to have to think about yet. Will you trust me not to insist on blowing up anything else until we're certain it's needed?"

She nodded, her gaze still on the wisp of smoke on the horizon. "I believe that's not going to be a problem anytime soon." She turned and took his hand again. "Though I might even be willing to let you teach me exactly what I did with that one word you gave me to say..."

———

The first person Celine saw when they set the helicopter down in Seth Caleb's encampment fifteen minutes later was Kontara, who immediately strode over to Celine when she saw her get out of the aircraft. She grabbed her by the arms and gave her a shake as she stared into her face. "Are you all right?" She didn't wait for an answer. "You don't deserve to be. This wasn't supposed to happen. You promised you'd be careful."

"I tried to be." Celine shook her head. "Stop yelling at me. I did what I thought was best. I'm sorry you didn't think so, but you and Michael and Quinn got away and I'm not sorry about that." She added coaxingly, "And because you did, Eve was able to help me when they managed to catch me. And Dominic said that it was because of you getting Jossland's phone to Caleb that the two of them were able to get rid of Zakira and Caldwell. So it wasn't all bad, Kontara."

"I don't think you're convincing her," Dominic said as he shut the cockpit door. "Though I have to admit that I was probably more upset than she was at the time."

"No, you weren't," Kontara said curtly. "You should have taken better care of her. Eve told me her shoulder was injured. But it's clear that the bandage needs changing. Why didn't you do it?"

"We were a little busy," Dominic said. "I was about to do it the minute we landed."

"But you probably got busy talking to Caleb and Joe about the attack and put it off. Never mind. I'll take care of it."

"No, you won't," Celine said. "It's nearly healed. I'll do it myself." She turned back to Kontara. "Ever since you came here, you've been trying to watch out for me and practically trying to run the camp. And Dominic told me that you've also been trying to protect those women captives that were so mistreated. How are they?"

"Alive," Kontara said baldly. "Other than that...bewildered and grateful. It will take time for them to realize their lives have changed."

Celine nodded. "And you'll be there to help. It's clear that you've been a very important part in what went on here today, and other people probably need you more than I do." She reached over and gave her a hug. "But I could use a coffee or a cup of tea."

Kontara stared at her for a long moment. "So that's the way it is?"

Celine nodded. "Until it changes again. Because life is always changing. We both know that."

"Yes, we do." Kontara turned away. "I'll get your tea. But then you have to sit still while I bandage that wound."

"Compromises?" Dominic smiled. "If I can do anything for either one of you, let me know. I'll tell Rashid to keep an eye out for any problems." Then he gave a distinct grimace. "But it's important that we figure out how we're going to handle the diplomatic and financial nightmares that might face us after what happened tonight. Quinn is already talking about putting me in the center of it all." He was scowling. "But that's not going to happen if I can help it."

Celine shook her head. "By all means, pull all strings possible." She took the cup of tea Kontara was handing her. "Though both Kontara and I have learned to either adjust or handle those changes I mentioned...We'll get through this, Dominic."

"You're damn right we will." But he was no longer frowning, and she could see he was already planning exactly how he wanted those changes to proceed. He started to head across the grounds to where Quinn and Eve were talking to Caleb. "We'll talk about it later..." He glanced back over his shoulder. "Don't worry, you'll definitely get your turn, Celine."

"I don't have the slightest doubt of that." She smiled. "After I finish my tea, I'm going to take a short nap, and then I'll tell you how we're going to do it."

He chuckled. "I can hardly wait. Will you give me a hint?"

"It has to do with me going back to Boston to finish my internship and you staying here until you make sure that everything is going to be what you want it to be. That's necessary because we're both very demanding people. It also has to do with that lovely Gulfstream jet plane that you're going to use to come see me very frequently so that I can keep an eye on you when I sense there might be a need to watch your back." She smiled. "Does that sound like a good start?"

"An exceptional start," Dominic said. "But it's also going to take us an exceptionally difficult period to develop it in the way that will suit us best. I can think of all kinds of side trips and interesting byways that we'll have to explore." He smiled back. "So keep thinking and planning, because we have a long way to go!"

EPILOGUE

SHAFIRA PROVINCE, AFRICA
TWO WEEKS LATER

Hi, Mom." Michael ran into the workroom and gave her a quick hug. "Dad just called and told me to tell you that he'd finished up with that conference at Bon Jaka that Dominic had set up with all those governors and politicians who were trying to set up this village as some kind of glorified theme park."

"The people here have a strong sense of who they are. They won't let that happen, even if Folashade puts them on the map. We already have a twenty-four-city tour lined up for the sarcophagus and treasure. And now that the gold mine that Zakira stole has been recovered, the country is wealthier than it has ever been."

"Well, Dad says that this meeting was the last one, and now we can forget about them and think about packing up and going home."

"That sounds wonderful." Eve drew him a little closer. "I imagine you've been thinking about leaving here since the night you and your dad showed up and rescued me. You've gone through so much lately."

"No more than you did," he looked up at her and said. "It was okay because we were together. I think Dad had it worse than either of us, but he's been happier here now that he knows we're both safe and he could keep busy making sure that everything about this village is going in the right direction."

She chuckled. "You know your father very well. He can't stand chaos, and being busy is important to all of us." Her smile faded as her gaze went to the golden sarcophagus across the room. "And having a proper ending to a noble and worthwhile life is also important."

He was silent for a long moment. "You're not finished with Folashade," he finally said quietly. "Or perhaps she's not finished with you?"

How wise he was to be able to read her this well. "Maybe a little of both." She turned to look at him. "But I'll never be finished with you, Michael. So if you want me to leave right away and go back to the Lake Cottage, I'll do it. I'll arrange to take care of doing the final work on Folashade later."

"Later..." He moved across the room to stand beside the sarcophagus. "You know, the longer we worked on her, the more I got to like her." He paused. "But she's already had to wait a long time, Mom. That doesn't seem right. Couldn't it be that she was waiting for you? You told me how clever she was." He added, "Perhaps you were the only one she wanted. I'm certain I would have waited for you." He turned away from the sarcophagus. "So it would be wrong to leave now. I'll talk to Dad and make sure it's okay with him and we'll work it out so you can bring Folashade to her final home here after the tour. I'll work with you and maybe I can help Dad, too, if he'll let me learn how to make this village into the place Folashade wanted it to be." He was smiling as he walked back toward Eve. "Does that sound like a good plan?"

"It sounds like a wonderful plan." She could feel her eyes sting with tears as she looked at him. "I can hardly wait for it all to begin. Who knows? Maybe it was you our queen was waiting for!"

———

SHAFIRA
NINE MONTHS LATER
ONE DAY BEFORE THE GRAND OPENING OF THE
FOLASHADE TOUR IN ALEXANDRIA, EGYPT

"I just heard from Dominic," Joe said as he joined Eve on the veranda of the palace. "He should be landing the helicopter at the heliport in another fifteen minutes or so."

"Tell me about it," she said dryly. "Michael just told me the same thing and then ran down to the heliport to meet them. He's very excited." She frowned. "I've been wondering if we were right to keep him isolated all these months while we were finishing the exhibit? He seemed very happy but it was really a working vacation for him between helping me with the sculpture and you with overseeing the tour logistics. It was nothing like the holidays his friends in Scotland are having."

Joe chuckled. "Isolated? Are you joking? Michael would be bored to death if he couldn't learn at least one new thing every single day. Shafira gave him about a hundred more lessons than that, and he was always asking for more." He slipped his arm about her waist. "And we did pretty well striking a balance ourselves if I do say so."

"You mean you did." She laid her head on his shoulder. "You took over and cleared the decks for me to finish Folashade. Maybe I should ask you if I should have turned those tour details over to you when you were still busy coordinating the distribution of the silver bullet cure-all medication halfway across the world."

"Yes, you most certainly should have," he said firmly. "Do you think I'd let Michael get all the praise around here for his brilliance and ingenuity? I have to have proof when I tell everyone that he takes after his old man."

"He certainly does." She kissed him. "Now go and meet our guests and bring them here to the palace."

"You're not coming with me?"

She shook her head. "I want to straighten up the anteroom and get our queen prepared to receive her subjects. You have to admit that the reconstruction is unusual, and everyone might find it…unexpected."

"You're not nervous? It's magnificent and maybe the best thing you've ever done."

"No, I'm not nervous. I've created what I saw…and felt. That's all I could do. She wouldn't let me do anything else. I'm just eager to share it."

She turned and headed back into the palace.

———

Celine was the first person Eve saw ten minutes later. "Hi, Eve." She waved at her as she crested the hill and then hurried toward the veranda of the palace where Eve was waiting. "I thought I'd leave the guys to poke along behind me to talk construction and diplomacy and all those other things that men get so serious about. Joe was asking Dominic all kinds of technical questions about weapons and the guard unit he assigned here. I've seen more guards since we reached the heliport than I did when we took over the village from Caldwell and Zakira. And even Michael was busy playing with Cira and talking to Jane. He said he hadn't seen either of them since he'd been working here with you and Joe." She'd reached the veranda now and gave Eve a hug. "And besides, I wanted to get a few moments alone with you after Joe said something about you being a little nervous about the great unveiling."

"He shouldn't have mentioned that when I definitely told him I wasn't nervous." She smiled. "And you have no right to scoff about men being so serious about any given subjects when you weren't even sure that you'd be able to make it here today because you're so in demand as a surgeon that they're standing in line to get your services. How did you manage to rearrange your schedule?"

"Dominic," she said simply. "He knew it was important to me, and as usual he pulled strings and reached out to all the right people until he got what he wanted. Before I realized what had happened, we were on our way."

"Yes, that sounds like Dominic," Eve said. "I'm glad you were able to come. It was important that you be here."

Celine frowned. "I wouldn't have missed it. I would have found a way. But it was strange that Joe thought you might be upset. I was worried that it might have had something to do with the fact you'd gotten all that damn pressure to use my face on the mask."

Eve shook her head. "I can only tell you what I told Joe. I created what I saw and what I felt. I sincerely hope you like what I've done, Celine, but I somehow feel that Folashade would probably approve."

"Then that's good enough for me," Celine said gently. "Who am I to dispute the queen?"

"I hope no one," Eve said. "Since we've all gone to such trouble to make her happy." She saw Joe, Michael, Jane, and Dominic coming down the hill now and waved at them, but she was frowning as she turned to gaze searchingly down to the fountain at the center of the village. "I wonder where she—"

"I'm here." Kontara stepped out of the foyer of the palace. "I went in the back way and put some hors d'oeuvres in the fridge. Though I'd just as soon stay in the kitchen." She scowled. "I don't know why you invited me here for the big day, Eve. You know it's not my cup of tea."

"Dammit, because you're an important part of it." Celine was running across the veranda to hug her. "Now stop being so crabby and say you're glad to see me."

"Don't be pushy. You see that I talk to you on the phone every week," Kontara said. "I'm a busy woman. I don't have time to go to palaces for fancy social occasions."

"Just one occasion," Eve said patiently. "And you can spare the time from your busy schedule." She glanced at Celine. "The only way we could get her to stay here was to put her in charge of the five-star restaurant Joe is opening next week in the hotel area of the village."

"Wonderful," Celine said. "Control and artistry. Just your things, Kontara."

Eve chuckled. "Celine, take her inside to catch up and don't let her escape while I whisk everyone else into the anteroom and get this show on the road."

"As you command." Celine linked arms with Kontara and pulled her into the palace. "Come on, let's obey Eve. This is a big day for her, and we want everything to work out."

"I'm not arguing. Well, not much." Kontara wasn't looking at her. "It's a big day for me, too." She paused. "I've...missed you."

"Hey, me too," Celine said quietly. "And when we perceive a problem, we work on it. So that's what we'll have to do..."

———

"Thank you all for coming," Eve said quietly as she stepped in the front of the crowded anteroom filled mostly with family and friends.

She smiled as her gaze traveled around the room. "As you know, we're introducing Folashade to the world tomorrow and then sending her on tour so that she will be able to receive the admiration and understanding she never really received in all her years as queen and pharaoh. It's what we wanted, and she deserves it. But you're the only ones I really wanted to bring here to share Folashade's unveiling." She wrinkled her nose. "Practically everyone on the planet has heard about what they think happened in Shafira, thanks to the media. That's why they're so curious to come and see the mask and perhaps have a story to tell their relatives and neighbors. But you're the people who struggled and worked to help bring the queen out to the world, and eventually back to Shafira where she can lie in state. I was just the sculptor who listened and tried to understand what she was trying to say." She paused. "But my part wasn't easy, either. Because of all the lies Zakira and his ancestors were telling through the centuries, I had to filter and study to try to find out the truth about Folashade. I still don't know it all, but I'll keep trying." She chuckled ruefully. "But you're probably getting impatient. I brought you here to let you get a glimpse of the great queen, and here I keep talking and won't shut up." She was moving toward the silken sheet at the top of the reconstruction. "Though I should tell you one more thing. When I first asked Zakira why all his ancestors who were members in the council of priests of the court couldn't stand her when the reigning pharaoh insisted on making her his wife, one of the reasons he gave was that she was plain as a post, and no one understood why he didn't choose someone more presentable. Of course that was a criticism Zakira agreed with, but then he wasn't a very discerning individual. So I took the time and let Folashade tell me what she thought."

Michael was jumping to his feet and rushing forward to help her fold up the cover sheet. He was grinning at her as he murmured, "No ugly duckling?"

She smiled back at him. "Just a late bloomer." She let him take the folded sheet and stepped aside and gestured toward the golden mask of the sarcophagus and announced, "Folashade."

Dominic inhaled sharply as his gaze traveled over the beautifully carved features of the reconstruction. "My God. It's perfect." He took Celine's hand and squeezed it. "I didn't know what to expect, but this is spectacular." Folashade was sitting on a throne, and the mask was done in shimmering gold from the crown on her head, past her shoulders, and down to her waist, where the gold texture became draped and soft as it fell to her feet. Every detail of the body and face appeared alive and ready to step out of the sarcophagus at any moment. The face was totally riveting. The eyes were large, full deep-green emeralds, and slightly slanted at the corners. Her features were not perfect, but they reflected pride, kindness, intelligence, and humor. And yet there was also a touch of sternness and weariness that must have been the price of a life as full of tumult as hers had been.

"Power," Celine whispered. Her gaze flew to Eve. "That's what you saw in her. It's there in every line of her face. That's what Zakira and that council of priests couldn't understand."

Eve nodded. "Or maybe they did understand and were afraid of it. Zakira said that Hadabam, the pharaoh she married, had always been a bit sickly as a child. Folashade was a threat." She added, "And continued to be until the day she died. I'd bet that the council finally found a way to assassinate her, and when she realized she was dying she didn't want her son to also be a victim. So she arranged to send him to a place the council wouldn't be able to find him. Greece and Macedonia were mentioned, but the council never succeeded in locating him." She smiled at Dominic. "You've always liked challenges. Could I persuade you to try to find out what happened to him?"

"Tough proposition after four thousand years." He smiled back at her. "But very interesting."

"I thought you'd think so. Did he go and find an adventure

of his own? Or perhaps he'd had enough of fighting the people who had killed his mother and was looking for a different life. She had made it easy for him by arranging with her friends and supporters to make sure she disappeared from Shafira and was hidden away in the mountains, where she was given her final rites. No one was able to find her tomb for over four thousand years until Zakira managed to do it very recently with the help of a stolen gold mine and Ezra Caldwell, a criminal we were all happy to dispatch." She turned back to look at the sculpture and mask. "But our work isn't quite over. Now we have to protect what we've created and give Folashade what she lost. Alex Dominic has assigned one of his crack units to furnish the security for the palace and heliport for the people who want to visit her. That's not enough. We wanted to make it a welcoming place to celebrate her return. All the major tour companies have made Shafira a stop on their African tours. Fine restaurants, libraries, and the mazes and waterfalls that protected her will be available so that everyone can walk and enjoy the beauty and forget the nightmare. Kontara will be in charge of that portion of the exhibit." She grinned. "And heaven help anyone who gets in her way."

"Amen," Celine said. "It sounds like you and Joe have done a terrific job, Eve." She was still gazing at the gold mask in fascination. "That's a wonderful sculpture. I feel as if I actually know her."

"I'm glad you feel like that." Eve's eyes were twinkling. "Because I was feeling the same way when I was working on it. It wasn't quite…finished." She was quickly unfolding the bottom part of the silk sheet covering the sarcophagus as she spoke. "And neither was her story. I had no way to show the devotion of the people who had risked their lives to whisk her out of the palace and found her a place where the priests' council could no longer touch or steal from her." She looked at Celine and then at Kontara sitting next to her. "But she made sure her story continued, and I found a way to honor them." She whisked the silk sheet off the bottom of the sarcophagus to reveal the two figures seated on the floor beside the throne where Folashade reigned supreme. They were both in gold chest armor, and yet both were obviously women.

"Oh, my God." Celine's gaze was on the face of the sculpture of a dark-haired woman closer to her. "It's me?" Then her gaze flew to the other figure, whom she noticed had a long, thick red braid over one shoulder. "Kontara?"

"Say you didn't do that to me?" Kontara asked. "Please, can you change it, Eve?"

"Yes, but I won't do it," Eve said. "You were the one who brought Michael to Joe and saved them both. You're perfect for the sculpture." She winked as she added, "And you'll get used to people asking you if you posed for it. You were actually harder to do than Celine. I almost had her memorized by the time I started working on her face." She turned back to Celine. "I think you were still a little worried about me giving your face to the queen. But I realized that wouldn't be right. Zakira had it all wrong when he chose you to represent Folashade in his ghastly little scenario to make himself richer. You weren't a queen who was a trophy wife, you were a warrior. So is Kontara. That's what I made you. I created loyal guards to keep her safe. Because that's what you are, and that's the instinct that leads you into the darkest nights." She smiled at both of them. "Will you let her keep the guards that she knows will watch over her?"

"You told me you thought the queen approved," Celine said slowly. "How can we say no? I'm proud to be any part of your work, Eve."

Kontara nodded reluctantly. "Unless you find someone else you can substitute. I want it known I'm only a part-time guard." She smiled. "But I'm a full-time cook. So if you're finished with this presentation, I'll escape to the kitchen and put out the hors d'oeuvres I brought. You're not the only one who's an artist."

Everyone in the room was laughing as Eve nodded and made a shooing motion and the guests started drifting toward the dining area.

Eve lingered behind, her gaze on Folashade in her magnificent mask and the two guards in armor kneeling beside the throne looking up at her. Had she gotten all the expressions right? Had she caught the love and the loyalty and all the other more subtle emotions that had been present in the queen's expression? She'd thought so when she'd finished the work. But it was difficult to finish any of her sculptures. Perhaps because they were all still alive to her. However, she could see no flaws...for now.

She took a step closer to the sarcophagus. "I think it all went well today. They were all very impressed by you. We're doing the best we can. Just as you did all those many centuries ago. That's all we can ask of each other, isn't it?"

The overhead lights were glittering on the polished golden mask and catching in the tiny creases on those cheeks that Eve had so carefully formed and the fine delicate veins in the whites of her eyes she had spent weeks perfecting so that she'd appear absolutely alive and natural in every detail.

Eve said softly, "I really hope you enjoy your tour, Fola-shade. But I believe you might enjoy coming back here even more after all the excitement and glory are over and we can finally welcome you home. What do you think?"

Was it a trick of the light on that shimmering golden face? Because, for the briefest instant, it seemed as if Folashade might be smiling...

ABOUT THE AUTHOR

Iris Johansen is the #1 *New York Times* bestselling author of more than fifty consecutive bestsellers. Her series featuring forensic sculptor Eve Duncan has sold over twenty million copies and counting and was the subject of the acclaimed Lifetime movie *The Killing Game*. Along with her son, Roy, Iris has also co-authored the *New York Times* bestselling series featuring investigator Kendra Michaels. Johansen lives in Georgia and Florida.